Lives of Kings

Also by Lucy Leiderman in the
Seven Wanderers Trilogy

Lives of Magic
Lives of Kings
Lives of Seven (forthcoming)

✦ Seven Wanderers Trilogy ✦

Lucy Leiderman

Lives of Kings

DUNDURN
TORONTO

Editor: Allister Thompson　　　　　　Cover design by Courtney Horner
Design: Courtney Horner　　　　　　 Cover images © Ocean Photography
Printer: Webcom

Library and Archives Canada Cataloguing in Publication

Leiderman, Lucy, author
　　　Lives of kings / Lucy Leiderman.

Issued in print and electronic formats.
ISBN 978-1-4597-2355-9

　　　I. Title.

PS8623.E473L59 2014　　　　　jC813'.6　　　　C2014-902952-7
　　　　　　　　　　　　　　　　　　　　　　　　　C2014-902953-5

1　2　3　4　5　　　18　17　16　15　14

Conseil des Arts du Canada　Canada Council for the Arts　　ONTARIO ARTS COUNCIL
CONSEIL DES ARTS DE L'ONTARIO
an Ontario government agency
un organisme du gouvernement de l'Ontario

We acknowledge the support of the **Canada Council for the Arts** and the **Ontario Arts Council** for our publishing program. We also acknowledge the financial support of the **Government of Canada** through the **Canada Book Fund** and **Livres Canada Books**, and the **Government of Ontario** through the **Ontario Book Publishing Tax Credit** and the **Ontario Media Development Corporation**.

The author acknowledges the support of the Ontario Arts Council for this work, funded through the Writer's Reserve program.

Printed and bound in Canada.

Visit us at
Dundurn.com | @dundurnpress
Facebook.com/dundurnpress | Pinterest.com/dundurnpress

Dundurn
3 Church Street, Suite 500
Toronto, Ontario, Canada
M5E 1M2

✦ Seven Wanderers Trilogy ✦

Lucy Leiderman

Lives of Kings

DUNDURN
TORONTO

Editor: Allister Thompson   Cover design by Courtney Horner
Design: Courtney Horner   Cover images © Ocean Photography
Printer: Webcom

Library and Archives Canada Cataloguing in Publication

Leiderman, Lucy, author
      Lives of kings / Lucy Leiderman.

Issued in print and electronic formats.
ISBN 978-1-4597-2355-9

      I. Title.

PS8623.E473L59 2014   jC813'.6   C2014-902952-7
      C2014-902953-5

1   2   3   4   5   18   17   16   15   14

We acknowledge the support of the **Canada Council for the Arts** and the **Ontario Arts Council** for our publishing program. We also acknowledge the financial support of the **Government of Canada** through the **Canada Book Fund** and **Livres Canada Books**, and the **Government of Ontario** through the **Ontario Book Publishing Tax Credit** and the **Ontario Media Development Corporation**.

The author acknowledges the support of the Ontario Arts Council for this work, funded through the Writer's Reserve program.

Printed and bound in Canada.

VISIT US AT
Dundurn.com | @dundurnpress
Facebook.com/dundurnpress | Pinterest.com/dundurnpress

Dundurn
3 Church Street, Suite 500
Toronto, Ontario, Canada
M5E 1M2

To all the giants whose shoulders I stand on.

Chapter One

My legs itched and burned as I squirmed in my chair. I was sweating, and every breath I took warmed my throat. I didn't know how much longer I could survive here.

The laughter and pleasant conversation drifting all around didn't suit my dark mood. I swatted at something near my head for the hundredth time and gritted my teeth in annoyance.

"Relax," Garrison told me.

He sat across from me, holding a glass of white wine up to the light. A mosquito had flown into it and was floating at the top. He pursed his lips and put down the glass.

"I'm not really cut out for this place either, but you look a little crazy," he said.

Garrison's curly hair lay flat in the humidity, and sweat poured down his forehead. His height and thin frame made him look like a wet mop.

Since we lacked clothing for the weather, we had

bought outfits at the nearby tourist shop. Garrison's white shirt and shorts made him look like he was getting ready to play tennis. All I could find were coloured and patterned sheets that I had to wrap around myself to make a dress. Being unskilled in such things, I expected it to come loose any minute.

Tonight's selection was a black wrap with purple and yellow flowers. Many of the men on the island wore the same wraps as skirts, and I wondered if I was making a cultural faux pas. I looked down at my lap to make sure it hadn't come undone and spotted a large mosquito on my leg. I jumped up, shaking the table and spilling Garrison's wine.

"I told you they were biting me!" I hissed.

Standing, I could see my legs were covered with red splotches. The rest of me was faring only slightly better.

"You spilled my drink!" he complained.

"You're underage," I fired back.

"Here I'm not."

It was almost three weeks since we had stood at London Heathrow airport. We had been completely lost. More than anything, each of us wanted to go home. In those dark days after waking up to find I had nearly killed all my friends and myself, I missed my parents more than ever. They were my life before Kian, and a part of me wanted to feel like the old Gwen again.

I wasn't the only one. Garrison had been inserting references to home into every conversation, as if trying to brainwash me to go there. When had I become the leader of this little group? We were all just doing what had to be done — no one wanted to be here in hiding.

In England, after we were found and attacked, we were too scared to do anything other than what Kian had told the others while I slept — recover, leave, and put distance between them and us. "Them" being the magicians who had tried to enslave us and steal our magic after sending Kian to collect us and make sure we had magic in the first place. That plan didn't work out for them, but as long as we were alive and had the potential to become powerful, we were a threat.

It was strange not to have Kian around. After a week of healing and moping at the cottage — mostly moping — I let the others talk me into leaving our little hideaway and getting on with our lives. In truth, I was hopeful Kian would change his mind and come back. I felt like a sad puppy, sitting and staring out the window every day, waiting for him. But he didn't return.

My face and body had only just recovered from the snowstorm I used to battle the magicians when we left the cottage, knowing we had to get away. It always felt like they were right behind us.

Since seeing them in the flesh, I walked a little faster and listened a little bit more carefully. I was always on alert. They were so elusive that I felt I could expect anything. Even if I had shown the most power, I still needed Kian's help. Everything I had done since learning of my past life was with his help, and to be without him felt like I was missing something.

In London, we showed up at the airport without

a plan. The booth closest to us was a French airline. Seth, Moira, and I waited nearby while Garrison asked about the next flight we could catch.

"Flights within the next three hours with availability are …" The female attendant squinted at her screen as my stomach did cartwheels. Despite our need to get away and recover without the magicians on our trail, I was hoping for something close. Somewhere Kian could find us. Soon.

"We have four flights leaving to Paris," the attendant read. "One to Berlin, two to New York, one to Abu Dhabi, and one to Papeete."

We all looked at each other and my heart sank because I knew which one was going to win.

"Where's Papeete?" asked Seth.

"Tahiti," answered the attendant.

"And where exactly is that?" asked Garrison.

"French Polynesia," she replied.

She looked us all up and down. Our confused faces probably gave us away, because she decided to explain further.

"The islands are in the Pacific Ocean," she said, turning her screen to show us a dot in the middle of nowhere.

I had heard of Tahiti before but couldn't place it on a map. On her screen, it didn't even look as if it was land at all.

"However," she went on, turning her screen back, "each ticket is one thousand five hundred and thirty-four pounds."

Garrison nudged me and I reluctantly took out

the card that Kian had given them before leaving. He had set everything up for us, knowing using our magic might get us found all over again. I slid the gold card across the desk.

"Four tickets, please. One way."

The attendant's eyebrows raised in surprise. Her pointed nose and dark features gave her the look of a bird of prey, assessing us.

"Passports, please," she said in her prim British accent.

We had handed her our documents and soon were headed toward the farthest point we could find on Earth. Despite a sense of relief that we were putting distance between the magicians and us, I couldn't imagine how Kian would ever find us again.

The truth was that we had no idea how any of it worked. We didn't know if the magicians could find us or even if they were looking for us. I assumed they still needed our magic because they had been trying get it since before Kian found me in Oregon. But then where were they? Had we passed the threshold of weak-enough-to-capture into strong-enough-to-avoid? Without Kian, I felt blind. I had no idea what lay ahead of me, and that scared me.

I hated it here before we ever even landed. Now, weeks after first getting to the island that many considered paradise, my temper was on a short fuse. Everything bothered me.

A waiter dropped two dishes and the crash brought me back to the present. I sat down in my plastic chair and listened to a man play a song on a tiny guitar. The humidity was palpable. People chatted around us — carefree and on vacation. Our waitress brought me a glass of water that was mostly ice cubes.

"You know, in a hundred years this place might be gone," Garrison said. "The water is rising. Same with New York."

I sighed. Garrison wanted to go home. So did I. So did Seth and Moira. I knew what was coming next.

"When the wave hit New York last year," Garrison began, "I was just walking out of class."

He loved to tell the story, and I had heard it enough to memorize it. Though Garrison came from a wealthy suburb, he told it as if he were right there on the pier with Kian and me. I tuned out until he asked me a question.

"Did you ever see what happened to Brooklyn or New Jersey?" he said. "Houses were just out in the ocean. Just like that." He snapped his fingers.

At the time I had been too focused on myself to think too much about the faces of strangers who had been waiting in line to see the Statue of Liberty with us. The terrified looks and screams as the water rose in an instant still haunted me, and so much was just gone in the blink of an eye.

I had seen the true extent of the damage later on the news. They said it was an impromptu hurricane, but I knew better. I knew the magicians had a hand in a disaster that killed so many people. And they hadn't stopped since then.

The rising water levels we had heard so much about were affecting the way of life on the island. Just the other day we had tried going hiking, only to find a large portion of a preserved forest taped off. Apparently it was turning into a bog from underneath.

Any time I turned on the TV, a politician somewhere in the world was yelling about global warming. New York was still cleaning up. Big earthquakes happened daily everywhere from China to Indonesia and the Philippines. Everyone was on edge. The world was a disaster zone.

On the beaches in Tahiti, we watched workers fixing warning sirens to hold disaster drills for the first time since the war about seventy years ago. I knew a large portion of Australia had been under water for months, while another area was experiencing a drought.

Every day I tried to guess what the magicians were up to — what they were causing. What was their plan and what was just opportune timing?

"Hey!"

I snapped back to reality as Garrison waved a hand close to my face.

"What?"

"I was asking you what you missed most about home," he said.

I thought about it. I had only been in Oregon a few brief weeks when I ran away with Kian. I still considered San Francisco home.

"The noise," I said.

"I was going to say noise!" Garrison replied. "Not enough people curse here at total strangers."

I smiled and remembered walking home from school in San Francisco.

"No matter where you'd go, you could hear something else. A tram, a car, people talking on a patio," I said. "Here, on the beach, you can feel like you're the last person on Earth."

Or maybe that's just how I felt when I looked out into the nothingness and couldn't connect with my other half. I was torn between wanting to return to my old life and missing the presence of the old me. Since I had woken up in England, I just couldn't hear her anymore. I knew the others were having trouble too, but we didn't talk about it. It seemed like a personal battle.

"Where's Moira?" I asked.

Moira still looked shell-shocked when I sometimes caught her staring off blankly. She had joined our little group right when things were getting dangerous, and I worried she wasn't adapting to our life on the road. Since we got here she had retreated more into herself, and I kind of worried she'd just walk into the ocean one day.

"No idea," Garrison replied. "I invited her to come to dinner with us, but she didn't want to."

The dinners here began after dark, which happened much later in the evening, so we would end up having two or three pre-dinners. I felt like all I did was eat.

"And Seth?" I asked.

"Calling home."

Seth and Garrison had been in touch with their families regularly since leaving England. I hadn't called home yet. With Kian gone, I had no idea what my parents knew of me or where I was. Had the charm

he put on them to let me go worn off? I was too scared
to find out.

It might have been a coincidence that none of us
had brothers or sisters, or that all our parents were
older. I wondered if that somehow was intended so we
could leave them. The thought made me sad.

As if having heard her name, Moira came into the
little awning-covered area where we were sitting outside a restaurant. Torches lit the platform and the man
with the little guitar was still playing. While the rest
of us had gotten tanned in the island sun, Moira's skin
was pale as ever.

"There you are," Garrison said, smiling. "What
have you been up to?"

"Trying to rest," she replied, placing her elbows
on the table and briefly sinking her face into her hands.
She resurfaced, yawning.

Moira, unlike me, had refused to go islander and
adapt to the wraps. She had tied her long, dark hair
into a knot at the top of her head and wore a T-shirt
proclaiming something wonderful about the island.

"Tired?" I asked.

We shared a room and I knew she slept deeply
from night until morning, often staying in bed until
the early afternoon. Since I couldn't sleep, I became
very familiar with her habits. However, she had bags
under her eyes and always seemed exhausted.

Moira nodded as Garrison and I shared a concerned look.

"Are you ..." Garrison took a deep breath.
"Dreaming?"

Our magic and past lives often resurfaced in dreams. If Moira had gotten an inkling of her magic back, we could finally figure out what to do next. But she shook her head.

"No," she replied. "At least I can't remember anything in the morning."

I think everyone was a little traumatized. Our magic was suddenly stilted. The magicians had done their damage. Digging through our minds with sharp claws, searching for magic — I shuddered every time I remembered how close I had been to becoming enslaved by them.

I didn't want to close my eyes at night, despite how tired I was. Every time I did, I would see Kian there. My dreams would turn into nightmares in which he needed my help, but I was too far away.

I reached into my bag.

"Not more bug spray. Come on, Gwen, I can smell you from across the table."

I looked at Moira.

"I think you smell lovely," she said. "Like a lemon."

I sighed and slung my beaded canvas bag, another local purchase, over my shoulder.

"I'm going for a walk," I declared.

Before Garrison could argue, I was making my way out of the patio, where we had had a very fruity dinner.

We were staying in the biggest city on the island, which was still relatively small. The airport had a thatched roof and most of the low buildings looked exactly the same. Evenings and nights were becoming monotonous.

The patios, restaurants doubling as bars, and all other forms of communal meeting places were lit with torches that seemed to attract every insect around. We were all covered with bites and four times I had found various types of lizards in my luggage and clothing. Every time, I shrieked embarrassingly and couldn't seem to make my legs take me back into my room until someone went in and declared it reptile-free.

Soon after we first got here, Moira had seen a little snake in our kitchen area and nearly fainted, while Garrison had stepped on some kind of thorn on the beach and needed to see a doctor for emergency shots on day two of our stay. This island did not agree with us.

Still, no matter how long we'd been recovering, I felt the magic was gone. The memories were gone. I felt absolutely ordinary, like someone had put a cork in my magic. We all handled it differently, but it was isolating. Our magic was what had brought us together.

I regretted wishing for this during our adventures of the past few months, because in reality it now felt like everything that made me who I am was gone. I tried to sit, breathe, and focus like Kian taught me, but the only thing that accomplished was making me think of him.

I just wanted to go home — to see my family, the countless animals my veterinarian parents had undoubtedly collected, and to be normal again. But as always, I was torn. One half of me wanted to accept being normal. The other part refused.

Our hotel was right on the beach, and I walked through the dimly lit lobby to the back, where the wooden deck reached right onto the sand. No one had bothered to light the lanterns, but I could still see the deck chairs by moonlight. I carefully sat cross-legged. Just this morning Seth had gotten his foot stuck in one of these chairs and had fallen over loudly. Facing the ocean, I let the fresh salty breeze blow back my hair and flood my senses before closing my eyes.

Glimpses. Scenes flashed before my eyes of a vast landscape coloured every shade of blue and green. I felt the cool breeze replaced by a bitter wind for just a second, and then it was gone. The smell of salt water remained.

I worried magic was like a drug. I had never needed it before, but now that it was gone, I wanted it more than ever. I breathed steadily. Every time I looked inward, I would see the same thing — behind my eyelids, Kian looked back at me.

A hundred different memories met in one moment and then he would turn into the little boy I had known two thousand years ago. My feelings wanted to go in several different directions at once. I peeled away the Kian layer to look at what was beneath that and felt the same thing I had for the past weeks: a lock. My magic was bunched up behind some invisible force that I knew was my own creation. I retreated back to the Kian layer and found Seth there instead. His black hair and pale skin reminded me of Kian but almond-shaped hazel eyes stared back at me instead of round, blue ones.

"Can I interrupt?"

I jumped. He spoke the words in my mind at the same time as I heard them in my ears. I realized my eyes were still closed. When I looked up, he stood in front of me, dark but silhouetted in the moonlight.

"I'm not doing anything," I replied.

"I know exactly what you're doing," Seth said, sitting near my feet on the deck chair. "It's what we're all doing. There's no shame in trying to get it back."

Seth was the only person who seemed to be patiently waiting for whatever was next. He kept telling us any time we complained — and that happened often — that there was a reason for us being here.

We sat in silence for a few moments, listening to the waves. At first the noise had kept me up at night. Now I felt it make its way into my body, syncing with my breathing. I considered how much Seth had matured in the past few weeks. The role of older brother, now that we knew it to be the case, suited him.

"Let's go for a walk," he suggested, motioning toward the loungers. "These death traps have already gotten me once today."

I spotted his outstretched hand in the moonlight and took it, his cold, smooth palm gripping my fingers and pulling me up.

The sand on the beach was fine as powder and warm under my feet, even though the sun had set hours ago. We made our way along the water.

"Did Garrison tell you I was here?" I asked.

Seth shrugged in the moonlight. "He said you left in a huff."

"A huff?"

"I'm paraphrasing. He used words I'm not going to repeat."

In the past month we hadn't had much time alone together, and while I had been recovering in the cottage, everyone only approached me with kid gloves, as if I could snap at any moment.

"I'm ..." I gritted my teeth, knowing what my words would truly admit. "Sorry." I couldn't seem to raise my eyes from my feet.

"For what?" Seth asked innocently. I wasn't getting off the hook. He was going to make me say it.

"For ..." I waved my arms in exasperation. "Holding us back. For moping and pining and not really being myself."

I could feel him shrug again, his shoulders brushing up against mine. I hadn't realized he'd been walking so close.

"We need to help each other right now," Seth said. "My magic ..." it was his turn to gesture, looking for the right words. "I can feel your energy inside of you like knot. You're all ... tangled up. And I can't do much either. It's frustrating, I know."

His metaphor made me smile. It perfectly described how I felt. The hate flowing through me during the last time I had used magic felt raw, like it had grated through my insides to turn into the storm that nearly killed us all.

Inside of it, I could feel my real emotions. I was angry, but I was mostly scared. I feared the magicians and I feared for my friends. I had felt I needed to compensate for the fear, helplessness, and insecurity with magic. And it put us all in danger.

"I overdid it."

"You need to let it go."

"Stop reading me," I said half-heartedly and gently nudged him. When I looked back, he was smiling.

"I don't need to read you," he said. "I know you."

"Ouch!"

I stepped on a broken shell half-buried in the sand, sharp edge up toward me — of course. I sat heavily on the sand to examine my poor foot. My wrap-dress quickly filled with sand, and I sighed. I wasn't meant for beaches.

After I became fully convinced that the damage to my foot wouldn't lead to some deadly Pacific disease, I looked up to find Seth staring at me.

"What?" I asked.

He ran a hand through his hair.

"You look like silver," he said, smiling.

I looked down to find my hair falling over my shoulders, normally a mousy dark blond, was even paler in the moonlight. I suddenly felt like that broken shell, blending in with the sand, invisible until someone got hurt by me.

Seth knelt next to me. Suddenly the beach fell away. My stomach dropped into the sand and I felt rooted there. My vision went hazy and I could have sworn it was the grown Seth from the past who looked back at me. Something in my chest pulled to be closer to him. It scared me and I tried to pull back, but couldn't.

Uh-oh.

Magic gripped me and I felt like I was at the top of a rollercoaster, knowing I was about to experience a terrifying fall. I had no time to either celebrate or rue its return. Seth reached toward me and I took his hand.

✦

Suddenly he was much farther away. He drifted out of reach from my hand as an invisible force pushed me down to the floor, where I knelt. I wanted to cry out but I had no voice. My heart was racing, panic gripped my lungs, and I braced my hands on the dirty earthen floor to keep from shaking. The bitter cold seemed to rise from the ground and cling to my bones.

I dared look up to see Seth, as he once was, standing next to an old man covered in cloaks of different colours and patterns, his bearded jaw set in a grim line. The king. His father. Emotion flooded into me as I saw him. I wanted to grab him, hold him, protect him, but knew I couldn't. Somewhere my second life's mind forced me to focus. I tore my eyes away and took in my surroundings.

We were in a dark wooden room. Wooden pillars held up the tall ceiling and the thatched roof let slivers of sunlight shine through. There was a hole in the middle through which smoke escaped.

On the other side of the old man's perch stood Kian, a small and skinny child with a dirty mop of black hair and blue eyes wide with fear. He clutched his tan tunic and stared at his father, the king. Nearby, a woman with black hair and sad eyes stroked the head of another dark-haired woman, who sobbed quietly into her shoulder.

My hair hung loose around my face and fell away as I turned to look around me. I was kneeling with three people on my right, and two on my left. I spotted Moira and Garrison but didn't know the others. I forced my past self to stare into their faces, remembering every feature. Behind us stood five men in cloaks with different designs stitched into them.

"The fog has come over our land," the king said, and my eyes went back to him, "and has shrouded the truth between good and evil, right and wrong."

His voice struggled, and I couldn't decide if it was due to emotion or age.

"In any future, lives will be lost. Blood will be spilled. Pain will echo through our lands. We have been blessed by the gods with their kin." His arm swept out to us and rested on Seth's sleeve, gripping it tightly. He clutched it as if steadying himself, though he sat. "And they will help us decide our own fate, and turn the future for the good of the world."

The crying woman sobbed louder, and the dark woman holding her, who I knew to be the queen, let her tears fall silently to the floor. There was movement to my left. A man kneeling next to me, his chestnut hair flowing past his shoulders, sat back onto his heels looking stunned but determined.

I realized this was it. This was the moment the king had decided to have us killed. My stomach turned. In less than a day, I would die. The thought didn't frighten me as much as losing Seth. My past self was terrified of it.

The panic and grief she felt at being without him formed a lump in my throat that turned into a throbbing pain. My heart stopped when Seth turned and his eyes met mine. I knew then that I was ready to lose everything except him. I would betray my husband, my king, and my home. All I wanted was to reach out.

✦

I came back to my body with the force of falling onto the beach from above. Sucking in the night air, I coughed up sand that burned upon touching my skin. Seth instinctively came toward me to help, but I could feel the magic building. I had experienced this once before, but I had meant it to happen. Now it was beyond my control. My past self was still caught in the dream, and I couldn't stop it. The pain was too much.

The grief of losing him didn't subside with time. Every time she remembered life without him, how her husband had found her out and made her late, how Seth had gone without her to be sacrificed, how she wanted to die rather than to live without him, a new wave of anger and sadness would roll over me.

I did the one thing she would never do. When Seth reached for me, I used all my strength to push him away. It was for his own good. I added magic to my strength, and he was thrown backward into the sand, right before flames engulfed my vision and I felt the pure heat of my magic leave my body in a wave of fire.

Chapter Two

Kian kept low to the ground, making his way through the forest as quietly as possible. Though he already carried several dead rabbits in his bag, the deer would be welcome at home in the settlement. He was so focused on the hunt that he hadn't noticed how far into the forest he crept or how high the sun rose above him.

Finally, the deer stopped to drink from a pool and Kian lay on the hard ground, reaching to pull his bow from his back. An unwelcome but familiar vibration in the earth made him freeze.

The deer looked up, feeling it as well. Hooves carrying heavy loads were quickly coming his way. He looked back just in time to see the deer bolt. Kian sighed.

The Kaligan refused to accept their new surroundings. Coming from a land over the sea, they valued heavy armour and leather, even if it was high summer. They outfitted their horses with metal buckles and donned so many layers that they were practically roasting on horseback. The Romans had come far but refused to believe they were somewhere different.

The people of Kian's tribe had started calling them the Kaligan after the big boots they insisted on wearing. Calling them what they were, Romans, soldiers of the empire of all empires, made them strong and intimidating. Nicknames helped to make the threat less real.

It was a decade since the Kaligan came to Kian's homeland and gave it foreign names. Britannia. Caledonia. The land was really called Alapa, but it was now only said in hushed whispers.

Kaligan settlements were built and surrounded by tall walls of imported stones, while the tribes who had made peace with them were closely monitored. Men on horseback, weary to be so far from home, patrolled the forests around their villages. While the current general was a decent man, the legions were getting restless and the tribes knew war would come if anyone with a less firm hand succeeded him.

Kian's life had been a delicate balance between war and waiting for war. The Kaligan had come when he was just a child, but his father, the high king of Alapa and king of the Riada, had already been engaged in another battle.

The Godelan, a tribe to the north who captured slaves and stole magic, had committed a ritual forcing the Riada warriors to sacrifice themselves. Kian remembered little of the tribe whose name was no longer spoken, but to him the Godelan were more than just an extinct group — they were the reason he no longer had a brother, and the Riada had no king. While his father had believed slavery and corrupt magic were enough to make the Godelan the greater evil, the Kaligan had slaves in other countries, too, and Kian often wondered if his father had made the right decision.

The years after the Riada had lost their only magical warriors, descendants of the gods themselves, were difficult for the tribe. Always bowing to Kaligan demands, they had given up their homeland to move closer to Kaligan settlements so that the governors and generals could keep an eye on them. Other tribes, which had opted to fight, had either been killed off or moved north and died from cold during the winter. Kian's world had fallen apart. And though he hated himself for it, he had learned to speak the language of the Kaligan and adopted their ways.

Only a year after his older brother was sacrificed to put an end to the Godelan, his father died. His mother followed the year after that, though he suspected the cause was a broken heart.

With the Kaligan, Kian was king of nothing. Other men and women had stepped forward to organize the tribe, and he welcomed it. They were stronger and wiser. They had been kind to him, but the Kaligan had taken away his only home. He could not blame the Godelan magicians or hate them — he had never known them.

Kian placed his ear to the dirt to listen for the hooves. They were getting closer. Still low to the ground, he made his way to the small pond in the clearing. Silently, he left his bow and hunting bag under a large root, hidden from view, and slipped into the water. It was cold against his skin and he fought not to suck in breath from the shock. To keep still, he sank low until only the top of his head remained above water.

Kian breathed through his nose, taking long, steady breaths to calm himself. He had gone too far into their land without noticing. As soon as he thought it, he hated himself. It was his land, and if not his, then his brother's or the Riada's. Not theirs.

The sound of boots and hooves was closing in, and he slowly moved to stand with his back to the pond's edge. The mud sucked him in. With long grass hiding him, Kian observed the Kaligan coming into view.

The amount of dirt on the horses and leather suggested this group had been on the road for a while. The Kaligan took exceptional care of their shiny things, with some of the Riada going so far as to call them the Crow People for their love of metal.

Kian tried to find the faces under the deep helmets. It was a new type of helmet, and that was problematic. He still had his brother's stolen Kaligan uniform from when he used to spy on them from within their own ranks. If it was out of style, Kian could never hope to do the same, even if he did eventually grow into it; at only seventeen, he was smaller than his older brother.

He did not recognize any of the faces. They were new, come to relieve some of the other Kaligan living in the fort. More than anything he wished to know their plans. Women and families were slow to come.

Farms were erected as if made to be pulled down at a moment's notice. Would there be more war, or would the Kaligan leave them alone?

A leader, his chest and shoulders bearing the most metal Kian had seen on anyone, spoke quickly in their language. Kian understood it to mean they were setting up camp. Slow panic began to creep up his neck. How long could he stay in the freezing water? Not even summer in Alapa turned the water warm. For the millionth time, Kian wished to have been born like his brother, with some kind of magic that could have helped his tribe.

Several boys no older than him ran to start pitching tents and looking for firewood. The rest of the small unit began cutting down trees. It was late in the afternoon, but it would be hours until sunset. Kian knew he could not stay in the water that long. He was far too skinny not to feel the effects of the cold within minutes. Already, moving his muscles was becoming difficult.

He waited for the Kaligan to become busy, then, as stealthily as possible, he slid into the tall grasses behind him on the bank. Though he had not thought it possible, the cool breeze initially made him even colder. Covered in mud, he lay in the grass willing the sun to heat his back and bring some life back to his body. He could never escape in his current state.

As night fell, the Kaligan lit lanterns and torches. Kian averted his eyes as much as possible and stared into the night, preparing his eyesight for the dark forest beyond. He refused to grow accustomed to the light like the visitors in Alapa. The dark forest was part of his heritage and to navigate it ran in his blood. He fought to hold on to what he could of his Riada past.

Finally, with the moon to guide him, Kian waited for the Kaligan guards to walk past his hiding spot and ran to fetch his bag and bow, slipping into the forest. A minute later, he stopped to listen. No one had spotted him.

He was still damp and shivering, and the hours-long journey back to the new Riada village was gruelling. Running in the cold made his lungs ache. His side felt like a knife was stabbing into it and his body still shook. After a short while he abandoned all stealth and crashed through the forest, not noticing as branches cut into his skin. He felt his energy waning, but spending the night among the patrolling Kaligan or wild animals was not a good idea.

Kian finally ran into the small Riada village before dawn. Only a few structures had been built in the past years since heavy winters made it difficult to repair many buildings. A steep, sloping thatched roof marked where most of the village's adults slept. Smoke still rose from the fire pit.

The night had taken its toll and Kian could barely make it to the low building. He stumbled and fell.

"Kian!"

A man's voice called his name. Someone was on watch and had seen him approaching. Kian briefly considered it lucky he hadn't been shot at. The same man called someone else over.

"What happened to you, boy?"

It was a rhetorical question. The man who spoke it was in the process of turning Kian over and laying his bag and bow to the side. Kian came face to face with the last person he wanted to see.

Eched was his mother's younger brother. After his two older sisters died and there was no one to rule the Riada, he had taken on the role. Though he was kind to Kian, he was also stern. Now Eched stared at Kian in a mixture of anger and worry, black, bushy eyebrows knitted together over a long nose.

"Where have you been? I was near telling the watch to go out and look for you!"

So that was why they hadn't shot him. Kian was now feeling terrible in every way possible. His uncle made him feel guilty for losing track of the day. He tried to speak, but nothing came out.

"Look at you! Practically dead at the door. Bring him inside," Eched instructed.

Kian only vaguely protested as he was carried into the shelter. He had a small room to himself off the main room, and he was surprised to see someone had unskilfully started a fire. The room was filled with smoke.

Eched barked orders as they gently laid Kian on his low bed. Someone opened a window in the roof to let the smoke escape. Kian was left with a view of the night sky as his eyes shut. His uncle's voice was the last thing he heard before complete exhaustion won out.

✦

When he woke, Kian wasn't sure what had forced him into bed in the middle of the day. The gap in his roof was still open and the sun was directly above. He squinted until the sunshine felt like it sat atop his eyelashes.

From the throbbing pain in his head, his first guess was that someone had knocked him unconscious. Trying to remember the night before, he looked around the room and spotted his bow. The bag with the rabbits was gone, but the hunt had come back to him. He had spied the new Kaligan men and had gone too far. It was stupid and had proven his uncle right once again — he wasn't ready to lead the Riada. In fact, he wasn't even ready to contribute.

The fire crackled as someone fed it another log. Someone was in his room. Kian sat up with such a flourish that the pain in his head increased tenfold and he doubled over in pain.

"Are you all right?"

A long, dark braid descended into his vision. He followed it to a round face with big blue eyes staring shyly back at him.

"Eifa?"

Eifa was Eched's daughter. Kian's mother had always told him they would marry one day, and in recent years his uncle seemed determined to make the union happen. Kian had given every excuse imaginable for delaying the marriage, including the fact that he felt nothing for her. It didn't seem to matter.

"I'm taking care of you," Eifa said with a smile.

"Yes," Kian said, still holding his head. "I see that. How long have I been asleep?"

"Half a day," she replied.

Eifa struggled with a pot of water, spilling more than a third while trying to bring it to Kian's bedside. He watched helplessly, wincing at the mess. She was only fifteen, and Kian wondered how many of her actions were actually her father's wishes.

Finally resting the water near his bedside, Eifa wet a cloth and approached him. Kian recoiled at her sudden advances.

"What are you doing?" he blurted out. He had meant to be kinder, but he was still in a lot of pain.

"I am tending to your wounds," she said, sitting back.

"What wounds?"

Eifa pulled back the wool covers to reveal his blood-soaked legs. Vaguely, Kian remembered running through the woods, eager to get home before collapsing. He examined the long scrapes. Someone had already cleaned them once, but he still bled from the deep gashes. Just then he noticed his clothes were missing, and he covered himself.

"Did you undress me?" he asked indignantly.

Eifa looked away, colour flushing her cheeks. "Your clothes were nearly in tatters anyway," she said. "And as you are to be my husband ..."

"I am not —" Kian never got the opportunity to finish.

Eched came through his door without knocking, as usual. Eifa scurried to tend to the fire. Kian felt she had made some liberal interpretations of her father's wishes.

"Eat this."

Eched thrust jerky into Kian's hand, followed by cheese and fruit. Kian wanted to refuse. He wanted to keep what small amount of dignity he might possibly have left, but he was ravenous. He ate so quickly he did not even taste it. As soon as he was finished, he felt it coming violently back up.

Kian was sick over the side of his bed, the contents of his stomach burning his throat as they landed on the dirt floor. Eched stepped back, pursing his lips, while Kian wiped his mouth and looked up at his uncle. The older man had brows that never unfurled. Now they were knit as tight as ever.

"Let that be a lesson to you," he said, pointing at the mess. "You think you're invincible? You think you can go days without eating, chasing animals through the forest into Kaligan territory? Hiding in the cold with nothing but the shirt on your back?"

The words were angry but laced with concern. Kian knew his uncle meant well, but his anger seethed. He was not angry at the Kaligan, or the Riada, or Eched. He was angry at his own shortcomings. He was angry because he was not invincible — he was human and magicless.

"You," Eched stabbed a finger in Kian's direction, "need to be careful. You are the last heir of the high king. You have a duty to marry. Create heirs. Only then may the Riada have a champion again. The gods know we need one. That is your duty. Nothing more. You are not your brother."

Kian fought past the pain to stand. He was wise

enough to keep any retorts to himself and used the opportunity of putting on clothes to measure his words. He was so angry that he shook, but he knew his uncle was right.

A small part of him, one that he had tried to silence for years, still thought he possessed some magic. He and his brother were descended from the same gods, after all. He reasoned that he could have inherited some of the same gifts. Over the years he had told himself they were late in developing, that his magic would come. Every defeat was just another reminder that he was, in fact, merely human.

As he slid his tunic over his head, he took a deep breath. A large hand rested on his shoulder.

"I've known you your entire life, boy," his uncle said. Kian turned to face him. "You are your mother's son. She used to huff in the same way when she was angry with me."

Kian only stared. He did not trust himself to speak.

"Your mother wasn't very happy either, when she learned she would marry your father," Eched said. "She called him old. She locked herself away and cried for days. But my father knew her temperament. He knew that in time she would come to her senses, and she did."

Eched sat on Kian's bed, running a hand through the thick dark hair that was so similar to Kian's own.

"Your mother learned to love your father and do her duty to produce more powerful warriors for the Riada. We have been marrying in the family for generations to keep the lines pure," Eched said. He motioned for Eifa to come over and took her hand. "You are so like your mother. You will learn to love my daughter, and be kind to her, and in turn do your duty."

The girl made a clumsy attempt to step forward and take Kian's hand. It was too much for him. Despite his uncle's words being reasonable, Kian's legs were taking action. Before he could even realize what he was doing, he grabbed his bag, cloak, and bow, and was running from the main building, back into the forest.

The adrenaline came from needing to get away — to escape. A flight instinct had overcome him. He knew what was right, but he did not want to do any of it. He did not want to fulfil Eched's plans for him. He could not fathom that that was to be it for him, that he only existed to continue the line and not let his father and brother's deaths go to waste, or that he held no value apart from being born a part of his family.

Kian ran until his chest pained him and the stabbing sensation was back in his side. He needed to drink — he knew the pains of dehydration from spending long days in the forest. As soon as he slowed, weakness overtook him.

Kian stepped sideways onto a root that moved under his foot. Weak, he tumbled down a long ravine, with barely the strength to protect his head as he rolled, miraculously not spearing himself on any branches or broken trees.

Finally, he landed on soft ground. The earth was covered in leaves too green to have fallen naturally. Kian only thought about this for an instant since the sounds of a creek led him farther into the forest. His thoughts were on water, and he moved swiftly through the underbrush searching for it.

Kian pushed down all thoughts of panic. He was, once again, far from home with little idea on how to get back. He knelt and splashed his face several times, feeling energy slowly return. He was still exhausted, but his heart eased at having gotten away from the settlement and put distance between himself and Eched. He felt in his heart that what was left of the Riada was just a shadow of the truth — and a decades-long plan for more heirs wasn't going to help his people.

Kian examined his face in the water. New cuts bled along his arms and forehead. He picked leaves out of his hair. The blue in his eyes, also like his mother's, was another reminder of how he was unlike his brother or father. He had heard that when his brother was born, the king had seen the strange mix of green and brown and knew this was a child of the forest and the gods. Kian had no such story of his birth. His father had loved him, but two warriors in the family would have been better than one.

A shape appeared behind him and Kian turned swiftly, reaching for a dagger that was not at his waist. He cursed his foolishness. He was alone in the woods, with no weapon and no way home.

Without anything to defend himself with, Kian moved into a low fighting stance. The man in the brown cloak lifted up two dirty hands in surrender.

"Relax, young prince," he said. His voice was uncertain and cautious. He had a strange accent Kian had not heard before. Long, dirty brown locks hung from below his hood.

"How do you know who I am?" Kian asked. He hadn't been called that in nearly ten years.

The cloaked man shrugged.

"Remove your hood," Kian commanded, trying to sound like a prince. "Let me see your face."

The man shrugged again and pulled down the brown hood, revealing a long face with bright green eyes and long, dirty hair.

"Who are you?" Kian asked.

"Call me a relic," the man answered. "My tribe is gone, yet I remain."

The answer came to Kian before the man had even finished speaking.

"You're a Godel!" he accused. He remembered hearing of the long robes of the Godelan. Their slaves wore next to nothing. His father had been outraged when he heard the Godelan explain that to cover your body was a privilege, and only those with power should do so. Still, after so many years, the man still wore his robes.

"I am a man of no tribe," the man replied. "Just as you are a prince of no man."

"You're a magician. You are a slaver," Kian retorted.

"Just like the Romans, whom you and all the Riada bow down to," the magician replied simply. Kian was beginning to think this man had an answer for everything. More terrifying was the possibility that he was being bewitched into sympathizing.

"Tell me how to get home," Kian ordered. "I don't want to hear any more of your sorcery."

The man made an incredulous face, the first sign of any real emotion behind the calm mask. "Sorcery? It is the truth," he said.

"You're evil," Kian told him. "Our warriors were sacrificed because of your actions."

"If that were true," the magician said, "would I be here today?"

Kian considered this. He was hesitant to take anything the man said as true, but the magicians of the Godelan had been killed, as far as he could remember. Still, he had to shake his head to keep the man's words from entering his mind.

"Tell me how to get home," Kian repeated.

"Home to what?" the magician asked. "The settlement the Romans have forced you into? You are living like animals on a farm when you need to be in the wild."

Listening to magicians was dangerous. Kian had been taught that from birth. Again he tried to ignore the words that were so tempting to believe. A large part of him was now agreeing, getting angrier at the truth behind the magician's comments. Still he resisted.

"Tell me how to get home," Kian said again.

"I have a better idea," the magician said. "How about give you the magic you long for to save your tribe."

Kian stood silent, battling with his own will. He knew in his heart that this was wrong. This was not natural magic, and unnatural magic, forced from the earth for man's will, always had consequences.

"All right," the magician acquiesced when Kian continued to say nothing. "If magic is not enough for you, then I will offer you something better. Your brother."

Kian's breath caught in his throat. He had witnessed the deaths of his father, mother, and brother. What the Godel magician was proposing was impossible. But Kian knew their magic was once great.

"How can you do that?" Kian asked.

"I can do many incredible things," the Godel replied. "In these woods, I've had time to learn new things."

"What's in it for you?" Kian said. "Why would you do this? The warriors of the Riada destroyed your tribe."

"Simple," the magician said, shrugging again. "I can only offer you the chance to be reunited with your brother and the other warriors. You have to do something for me first."

"What?"

"Find them."

Chapter Three

Iwas blinded for a moment, my vision hazy with orange and yellow flames in the complete darkness of the beach. My mind, as if detached from my body, floated somewhere above me, worried about Seth. I couldn't do anything about it. I tried to force myself to return down to the beach, but a part of me knew I just had to wait.

I don't know how long I knelt on the sand, swaying with the breeze. Slowly, the sound of my heart hammering in my chest came to me and I knew I was settling back into myself. But just as I was getting a handle on things, I was knocked backward by a violent force. My back hit the sand and knocked what breath was left from my body. I coughed and sputtered for air.

"Gwen!"

I couldn't focus on anything.

"Gwen! Look at me."

I forced my eyes to co-operate. Seth was on top of me, patting awkwardly at my arms and legs.

"You're on fire!"

He was yelling into my face, but to be fair, it was like I was miles away. His words reached me as though through syrup.

Though I couldn't feel the flames, Seth was panicked enough that I knew he was telling the truth. I regained control of my limbs and rolled. We were uncoordinated in our efforts, but ultimately, managing to inhale only a minimal amount of sand, I was no longer smouldering.

Seth sat back, pulling me up with him.

"You know," he said, taking long moments to catch his breath, "I've been thinking about your fire thing."

"Yeah?"

"Yeah," he replied, running a hand through his dark hair, a nervous tic that reminded me of Kian. Or was it that Kian reminded me of Seth? I couldn't decide which brother was actually older. "It's not something you had ... back then," Seth said.

I nodded. Fire was never something I could control in my past life. It was a magic that had come to me later on. At least that's what I felt to be the truth from the memories I experienced.

The day the ritual took us forward in time, Seth and I had been ready to run away from everything, just to be together. It was the wrong thing to do. We both knew it, and I knew it now. I felt my past self's shame and guilt about it. But at the time, two thousand years ago, feelings seemed to win. Due to circumstances beyond our control, however, I was in fire when I died, and it somehow got carried forward.

"It's something that kind of changed when you
... became ... you. *This* you," Seth continued, spitting
out sand between words. "So whenever you do this fire
thing," he motioned to the smoking and charred trees
nearby, "it must be you."

I had never thought about it that way. Any time
anything magical happened I would quickly blame it
on my past self. Still, something about this nagged at
my mind.

Just then I felt people running toward us. The
vibrations of several bodies were easier to detect than
actual people approaching us in the night. A flashlight
shone on my face and I winced.

"What happened? What are you doing here?" the
person barked.

Two police officers were staring at us, waiting for
an explanation. The smell of burning hair made me
nervous — how obvious was it that the fire was my
fault? Luckily, whatever blast I sent out had disappeared into the sand and the ocean. A small patch of
trees was crackling as palm leaves burned. I tried to
keep the guilty look off of my face.

"Some kids were setting off fireworks," Seth said,
slipping an arm around my waist. I felt the hum of
magic coming off of him, though faint. "Over there."

He pointed to the burning trees.

The two security guards looked us over, not totally
convinced.

"You need to leave," they told us. "Go back to your
hotel."

With that they jogged toward the palm trees.

"Did you use magic on them?" I asked after they had left.

"I tried to," he said, frowning. "It's difficult. It's like there's a stopper or something." He got to his feet with a moan. "Let me know the next time you're going to throw me somewhere, okay?"

"Deal." I nodded. "What's that burning smell?"

Seth helped me up. My arms and legs appeared to be fine. I could feel my hair blowing against my back in the breeze, so at least I still had that. I took a few steps and felt cold.

"Uh, Gwen?" Seth was fighting laughter behind me. For all that I had nearly killed him, and myself, and anyone around us, he now stood smiling awkwardly.

"What?" I asked, dreading the answer.

"Your, uh, dress seems to have been, uh, caught between you and the sand ... got heated up."

I pieced it together. The back of my wrap was mostly in tatters. I made Seth look away as I rearranged the sarong, still thinking of his comment about my magic. Was he right? Was I doing this?

The thought made me nervous. If I was doing that to myself, what else was I doing? The way my mind, the logical modern-day Gwen mind, had retreated upon so much magic occupying my body worried me. It was the same thing that happened when I let the storm loose on the magicians and put all of my friends at risk, too. I couldn't risk letting my sense of reason just fly away into the night. Not to mention, what would be left then? Would I trade places with her? Would I become a passenger in my own body?

By the time we got back to the hotel, Moira and Garrison were already waiting for us in the lobby.

"What happened?" Garrison asked, rushing forward to check me for injuries.

"I'm fine." I brushed him off. "How did you know?"

"Seth's magic," Moira said, pointing at him. "I felt something was wrong. Did you hurt him?"

Huh. What else didn't I know about their connection? I looked from Seth to Moira as if I could see the threads that linked them. Her words made me feel even guiltier.

"Of course not," Seth answered for me. Though when he walked with a limp, the others looked at him skeptically. "I might have been knocked down," he conceded.

Moira led the way back to our hotel room, where I explained what had happened. They seconded Seth's comment about the fire being something of mine — not of my past life.

"Maybe that action," Garrison suggested, "something that happened between you and Seth, set off what's been blocking our magic since England. What were you doing when it happened?"

Seth and I looked awkwardly at each other.

"I don't know," I said finally, "but I need to get better at this."

"With more magic, you're more dangerous," Moira said thoughtfully.

"I know that."

Garrison slung an arm around my shoulders in the supportive way he always did, forgetting how crabby

I had been to him earlier that night. I appreciated that arm more than anything right then. I took a deep breath, readying myself for the barrage of questions that would follow my big reveal.

"I had another memory," I told my friends.

As expected, a wave of inquiries ensued. No one had remembered anything concrete from the past since we regained the moments that led up to our deaths and saw that seven of us were sent forward. At least when they realized I couldn't answer everything at once, they quieted down.

"I think it was when the king decided what we would do," I said, my eyes sliding to Seth. It was his father, and Kian's, who had opted to kill his first-born son in order to effectively destroy one of his enemies.

I told them about the others around me, confirming there were seven of us. I described the two crying women, so similar they could have been sisters. One was the queen, I was sure. Seth and Kian's mother. The other I didn't know.

I tried to remember the king's words exactly. The only part I left out was about Kian. I didn't know why, but I wasn't ready to talk about his place in my memories yet. He seemed too young and lost; I just didn't want to imagine him in the same circumstances now or think about where he was and what he was doing. Or worse, wonder if the magicians had found him.

As I found out in England after he poisoned me and brought me bound to the magicians, Kian had been kidnapped from the past by one of them. Only two had been reborn; one had found another way. Kian had always told me he didn't arrive here like we had, but I never questioned it until it was too late.

Countless times I replayed every conversation between us. I thought over his every word until I was basically torturing myself. I'd never thought to question him, letting him lie through silence. I just figured there was so much I didn't know that he couldn't explain all of it.

His vagueness, his mysterious actions, all of it had seemed normal because it was who he had always been to me. He had found me, he had rescued me countless times from both *them* and myself, and I hadn't seen past that.

I hadn't known he was just as scared as me, doing what they wanted him to so that he and his brother, Seth, could have a chance to go home. But he had been lied to. It was impossible to go back in time. Too much had happened. And I questioned every time I thought about him if his decision to help me escape came before or after he realized the magicians had lied to him and he could never go home. It made me angry, but I also missed him terribly.

When I finished telling the others what I had seen, the response wasn't what I was expecting. Garrison went to the desk in our small room and took out the travel magazine included with everyone's welcome package.

"Do you feel like you have your magic back?" he asked, leafing through it. I closed my eyes and looked inward. There was something — but it was still faint.

"A little bit," I admitted.

"I think it's a mental block," Garrison said. "The magicians, they just … well they almost killed us. They almost got us. They made us so scared that we just pushed everything down until the memories and magic only trickle in."

"That sounds about right," Seth agreed.

"And look at Moira," Garrison said, still without looking up from the magazine. "She looks like a zombie!"

"Hey!" Moira protested.

"Sorry," Garrison said, "but it's true. This whole thing has taken a toll on us. And Gwen, you've pretty much proved that there's nothing wrong with us. We've got the same magic we always had. It's us that are in the way. Kind of like how all that fire had to leave you just to unlock those memories."

I followed his train of thought. At this point I wanted to know more. I wanted to see more. And if there was a way to get back on track and not feel like we were just hiding out somewhere in the Pacific, I was willing to try it.

"So what do you suggest we do?" I asked.

"Well," Garrison said, holding up the magazine to his chest and away from us, "before you judge this idea, keep in mind that the only way we can hope to be stronger than they are is to regain all of our magic. And that means overcoming whatever is holding us back. Can we all agree on that?"

Everybody nodded. I knew Garrison well enough to know that he only ever prefaced his ideas or added disclaimers when they were particularly outrageous. It made me nervous.

"So," he said, laying the magazine on the bed.

"You're kidding," Seth said.

"No way." Moira backed away from it as if it would bite her.

I leaned in to see what the fuss was about.

In the travel magazine about the French Polynesian islands, there was an article about cultural heritage being preserved in the jungles in the form of witch doctors. A man or woman wearing so much straw and paint that it was impossible to tell what he or she really looked like was the main image in the article. I sighed.

"Think of it this way. They're kind of like the island psychologists," Garrison explained.

"Are they the ones that drilled holes in people's heads to get the demons out?" Seth asked.

"Probably not," Garrison said dismissively. "And if they did, I'm sure they don't do it anymore."

Silence.

I was skeptical. While Seth and Moira seemed to think a witch doctor would cause more harm than he or she was worth, I doubted any such person existed. It seemed to be a tourist attraction, if anything. But I was tired of feeling helpless, and the incident on the beach, as well as every other fire-related thing, was nerve-wracking. I had to make sure I wouldn't hurt anyone. My desperation not to be a danger probably led me to my next comment.

"Okay, let's do it."

As Seth and Moira began to protest, I hurried to explain.

"We can't sit here forever, waiting for the next

thing to either put us in danger or ruin some other part of the world. And we don't even know what they're up to! Maybe they're close to succeeding," I said. "And we have to face the fact that Kian isn't coming back."

That shut everyone up. They had all been thinking it, but it was no secret who his departure had affected most. When I said it out loud, it somehow became truth.

With reservations, Seth and Moira agreed to Garrison's witch doctor plan.

The next day, Garrison used his charm and friendly demeanour to somehow find a hotel employee who could point him to a tour guide who knew of a witch doctor nearby. I still felt ridiculous saying — or thinking, for that matter — the words "witch doctor," so I began to look forward to seeing the island psychologist.

Garrison was especially good at procurement. If something seemed hard to get or find, he was usually the best person to do it. He managed to convince a tour guide, who usually took tourists into the heart of the jungle, to take us to a man or woman — no one knew which — famous with the locals for offering what was called "alternative health care."

As Seth, Moira, and I sat sipping our hundredth fruity drink by the ocean, shaded by an oversized thatched umbrella, Garrison approached with a young local man in tow.

The man introduced himself as Ari and told us usually only the locals went to visit the priest, as he called him.

"We understand," I told him. "And we appreciate you helping us. We want to ..." I didn't know how to finish my sentence, not knowing what Garrison had told him. "Experience as much of the culture as we can."

Ari seemed to notice our ages for the first time. "Are you here with your parents?"

"Yes," Seth said.

Ari waited for more, but Seth had nothing.

"Okay," the man continued, still looking us over dubiously. "Just remember, no cameras. You must show respect. We leave at dawn tomorrow."

"Of course," Garrison assured him. "Like I said, we're curious about your culture. We want to know what ... the priest ... may say."

Ari left, still casting curious glances at us, no doubt trying to figure out what was so wrong with us that we would ask to see a witch doctor. Garrison, totally oblivious and always one for adventure, just gave us the thumbs-up with a wide grin.

He sat down next to me on my lounger, taking my drink from my hand.

"You guys could look a little bit more excited," he said. "Who gets the opportunity to do this kind of stuff?"

He was right, but it all came with a price. I had no idea what waited for me in my memories, and at the same time I was trying to keep my expectations in check since there could simply be nothing to find in the jungle.

"What if there are just more terrible things?"

I asked him. "It seems like painful memories are all there was."

Well, almost. My memories of Seth before losing him had initially given me hope and pushed me to look for him with Kian. The complications around whom I was meant to be with had turned those memories sour.

"Well, I for one feel like I've seen all the terrible things there could be," Garrison said, looking out to the ocean.

I suddenly felt like an idiot. I knew his past was by far the most painful, and I had been insensitive. Having only remembered his life as a soldier in a tribal garrison, he had asked his parents to call him that at a young age.

Garrison remembered his past life's family being killed by rival tribes and hadn't known anything else until we remembered our own battles as adults.

"I have to believe there must be something good back there," he said. "Don't you want to know what you made the sacrifice for? If there's anything on this planet that will help me remember and then make me strong enough to get those bastards once and for all, I'm up for it."

✦

We were all sweating more than I had ever believed anyone could sweat within only minutes of entering the jungle. The humidity was suffocating. Though I was still questioning Garrison's judgment in bringing us here, at least my belief that this was all a tourist attraction was fading with each step. Tourists would have to be crazy to do this.

The jungle rose and fell every few metres and made the hike exhausting. I watched my feet obsessively as vines, roots, and loose stones threatened to knock me off balance. There was more pure green here than I had ever seen in my life. The sounds of wildlife filled the air, and for the first little while, I was so focused on memorizing this crazy experience that I didn't notice all the bites I was getting from various sub-tropical insects.

There was a shuffle behind me and I turned to find Moira had slipped. A burly guide who didn't look happy at all to be trekking with us caught her with lightning-quick reflexes, grabbing her elbow in what seemed a painful grip.

"You okay?" Garrison called from ahead.

"Yes," Moira said, biting her lip. A thin line of blood trickled down her leg where her foot had slid in between two unstable rocks. "I'm okay," she emphasized, seeing me look. She waved me forward in a shooing motion.

I carefully avoided disaster myself when I nearly slipped on wet and mossy rocks and then almost rolled my ankle stepping on a vine. Seth did one faceplant during our journey, cutting his forearms, while Garrison happily kept up with the experienced guide, using his long legs to take bigger and more carefully thought-out steps.

After about two hours of hiking, we stopped for a break. We had been consistently making our way uphill, and everyone was panting. Ari took our water bottles and began to fill them with water that ran off some stones.

"This water pools at the top of the mountain and flows down to the villages," he explained. "The higher a village is, the more pure it is."

I didn't have time to worry about all the living things in my water. When he handed me my bottle, I drank.

Ari spoke in a different language to two other men. They motioned toward the clouds, looking as if they'd rather be anywhere else. The weather looked fine to me, but I understood now why we needed to leave in the early morning. It was important to get back before dark — making our way home after nightfall would be impossible. And in a place where even the fish and insects were carnivorous, I didn't want to find out what was lurking.

"They don't look too happy, do they?" Garrison said quietly. He had tied a sock around his forehead like a sweatband, and it looked ridiculous but effective. "You like the look?" he asked when he saw me looking.

"Love it," I replied. "Still think this is a good idea?" Garrison looked exhausted.

"Given that we're here already, that doesn't really matter," he said. Which meant no. Great.

When Ari returned, he also wore a worried look.

"What's the matter?" asked Seth.

The man, only slightly older than us, was wringing his hands. "The guides," he explained, gesturing,

"They don't want to go forward from here. They say the priest curses the healthy and heals the sick."

Garrison's eyebrows shot up. "As wonderful as that makes me feel about paying him a visit," he said, "we have an agreement."

Ari shifted from foot to foot.

"Haven't you ever brought anyone here?" I asked him. "I thought you were a tour guide, like from the hotel pamphlet."

I turned accusingly to Garrison. Where had he found this guy? Ari looked guilty while Garrison began to whistle in mock innocence. Guilt wasn't in his nature.

"I asked around," he told me. "There were only a few *real* witch doctors on the island, and this guy volunteered."

"We will wait for you here," Ari told us quickly. "The doctor is only another forty minutes hike directly north on this path."

There was no other way around it. If we wanted to do this today, we'd have to go on our own. Leaving the only three people who knew how to travel through the jungle behind us, we took our packs and headed up the mountain.

"This screams bad idea," Moira muttered.

For once we agreed on something. But at least we weren't wondering for long if we were going the right way. In half an hour, Seth screamed when he pulled back some branches and came face to face with a skull.

More skulls and skeletons beyond that first one didn't help to put us at ease. Moira was nearly in tears as all of the skulls and chalky symbols culminated in one sign at the end. It was in French. As the only one who could understand even a little French, she read it in a shaky voice.

"What does it mean?" Seth asked.

"I think it says something along the lines of, 'Leave your brothers behind,'" she said.

"Wonderful."

Despite everything telling us not to, and only Garrison urging us forward, we continued. After another few minutes, a rattling alerted us to someone else's presence. Humming followed the noise. We stopped and waited.

The man or woman under the costume seemed underwhelming. When he or she appeared, they were wearing a wig of straw and thick paint around his or her eyes. The small man or woman looked like leather — his or her skin was taut and darkened by the sun. I couldn't even begin to guess the age of the small person approaching me. It could have been anywhere from fifty to a hundred and twenty. The man or woman was compulsively shaking a rattle by their side.

The doctor carefully approached us. I noticed that the sounds of the jungle had died down. The trees were quiet. The birds had gone somewhere else. It was an eerie environment and we all stood rooted to the spot as the man or woman neared. He or she peered into each of our faces, pausing for an uncomfortably long time at Seth.

I felt myself buzzing with anticipation. I was ready to move if anything happened. As we stood together — four supposedly powerful people — I couldn't help but feel very vulnerable. After what seemed like ages we were invited through a series of gestures into a small grass hut we hadn't even noticed. At least I think we were invited. The witch doctor, priest, or whatever it was, waved for us to follow, and we did.

Inside, a strong smell of mint and vanilla hit me. It made its way into my head as if cutting straight through my skull. I suddenly felt more alive. I saw my friends' eyes widen as they followed me in.

"That'll wake you up," Garrison remarked.

When I inhaled, it was cold on my throat.

The hut wasn't tall enough for any of us to stand straight, and even the small man or woman, who was only about five feet tall, had to crouch. We awkwardly bumped along until we sat on a natural ridge — probably a fallen trunk or something.

The loose items lying around looked old and worn. Utensils, hats, and buckets littered the floor. Smoke rose from a small fire and escaped out through a hole in the ceiling. The hut was woven together with leaves from the trees around. It was intricate and skilful work.

The witch doctor took a seat across from us and stared into our faces. I sat between Seth and Garrison and took the opportunity to squeeze Garrison's knee quite hard, reminding him this was his idea.

When the small person opened its mouth, a more familiar language came out than I was expecting. He or she spoke French, and we all turned to Moira, but within seconds she was shaking her head, completely lost.

"*Lentement*," she asked pleadingly. I knew the word for slowly. It was the same in Spanish. I had tried to learn in school, but if Moira's French was on par with my Spanish, we were in trouble.

The witch doctor went on, breaking words with what seemed like clucking. The voice was too high to be a man, so I decided it was a woman.

"Something about ... butter," Moira said after a few moments.

"Butter?" Seth asked skeptically.

"No, wait." Moira squinted at the woman as if that would help her language skills. "Fear."

I couldn't imagine how the two would go together. Suddenly the very small and leathery woman stood and stuck out a pointed finger at Moira. We all sat back in surprise.

"Ow," Moira complained as the woman stabbed a finger into her chest. "Stop that!"

She swatted lightly so as not to break the frail witch doctor's arm. Still, the woman vigorously stabbed on as if accusing her of something. Then she turned and said something to the rest of us, which we of course didn't understand. I was starting to think this whole trip was a little useless.

She went to a brewing pot, where something the colour of sickly mucus was steaming. Immediately, I didn't like where this was going. I knew this was meant to be ingested, and my stomach turned at the thought.

I think my friends had the same idea since we all exchanged worried glances.

Sure enough, the woman hobbled around, hunched

over, took out empty shells, and used them as cups to dip into the liquid. It ran over her hands, still steaming, but she didn't seem to notice. She thrust the makeshift cups into our hesitant hands and sat on a low wooden stool, waiting.

Everyone turned to Garrison. I wanted to see him take the first sip. He smelled the liquid and recoiled, but then shrugged, plugged his noise, and drank everything from the little shell.

I thought briefly about how we had come so far and escaped so much danger just to be poisoned by a little old woman in the jungle.

Garrison seemed to be okay, so Seth and Moira followed, with me being the last to drink out of my small cup. Though I had plugged my nose, the disgusting taste stayed in my mouth. It was like a mixture of earth, grime, and some kind of oil. My heart sped up, waiting for something magical to happen. The woman made herself busy, weaving a basket together from her low stool, humming to herself as if forgetting we were there.

A few minutes passed. We all sat around waiting, nervous and expectant. I slowly began to feel very silly for actually thinking any of this would work. A witch doctor surrounded by predictable paraphernalia in a jungle filled with tourists could not help us with our magic. And who knew what she thought we were there for? We hadn't even said anything about it. Maybe she thought we were lost. Or had a case of traveller's diarrhea. Communication was a problem.

I stood. "This isn't working."

The witch doctor didn't even look up at me. Her humming was starting to annoy me. It seemed louder than before. The humidity was itchy, and being so hot was making me cranky.

I looked to my friends. It had been ten minutes since the woman was yelling at Moira and stabbing her in the chest. Now Moira didn't look so great. She was still sitting, waiting for something to happen, but her long, dark hair was soaked with sweat and she looked considerably paler. In fact, so did Seth and Garrison.

I needed air.

Though the hut was small, by the time I reached the doorway the woman's humming was all I could hear. An impulse I couldn't identify pushed me to get out, urged me to move even if my limbs were getting heavier. I took two steps out from the hut when I heard my name.

"Gwen, wait." Seth was coming after me, but he was struggling. The same thing was happening to him. He reached out for my hand and managed to take it, just as we both fell backward and everything went dark — but only for an instant.

✦

A bright light burned through my eyelashes. Daylight and a bright blue sky made me squint. We weren't in a jungle anymore. I lay on cool grass with Seth resting his head on my stomach. He looked up at me just as I stared at him — this wasn't like any other time I had seen a memory. Though

I knew this was a different place, I still felt like myself. I listened for my past life, but she remained dormant.

We were younger than in any of our other memories, closer to teenagers. Dressed in many stiff layers, I knew the body was not my own, but still, I felt more in control than I had ever been. Garrison and Moira were nowhere in sight.

I tried to ask where the others were, but no words escaped my mouth. I could only stare. I couldn't tell if Seth was having the same problem. He slowly stood and I followed. We huddled together as we surveyed the small clearing where two horses grazed under cover of the trees. He wrapped an arm around me and I felt more at peace than I had in months. Unfortunately, that only lasted for an instant.

I noticed I held something in the hand that wasn't entwined with Seth's and opened my fingers to find an intricate wooden carving of an eagle biting into my palm. Seth turned to me. It was the first time I had seen him so young in the past. While I was still modern Gwen, I began to feel my past life in my chest. She loved him, and all of the negativity, fear, and insecurity that would come later didn't exist yet.

He gripped my hand tighter.

"Through all of it," he said, "we stay together."

I nodded. The world around us melted away. I had to plant my feet and grip Seth's hand just to keep from falling over. It was like the sped-up movie Kian had pulled out of my head when he first kidnapped me, but now I was at the centre of it. Through past Gwen's eyes I saw my life from young girl to grown woman, and for the first time I could see how Seth was an integral part of it.

I saw us playing as children and showing the first signs of magic. I witnessed us getting in trouble for using magic and scaring the elders. We pushed our limits and were always together. I saw the old man I knew to be Seth's father. His crown was silver. I met the others in our tribe with magic. The two dark-haired women I had seen holding each other and crying now sat together, brushing the hair of the little girls. I saw the lives of Garrison and Moira. Others — a stout boy, thin girl, and boy with a long braid, were inter- twined with our lives.

In instants, or what could have been years, we grew. There was a reason Seth was to marry Moira, but I didn't know what it was. The two women appeared again, happy with the union, and I realized they were sisters. People came and paid tribute to the king, leaving gifts.

The magicians came, and I nearly lost my balance in shock. The same men who had hunted us in this world laid gifts at the king's feet. Kian was a baby, and they each placed a kiss on his forehead. They bowed to Seth.

The king made a marriage for me, but I wasn't happy. The sight of my past husband still made my heart beat faster. I hadn't forgotten that my memory of him became too real and attacked me. I had killed him, or at least tried to. In these memories, though, he was kinder, trying to win my attention. I wasn't interested. I could never give up the bond I had with Seth — not for anyone.

Years passed. Life turned hard. Kian grew. The others had their own lives to lead, and we didn't see each other as much. The only time I felt happiness was when I was with Seth. The Romans came. The king made hard choices and Seth wore their uniform. People began to disappear. Everyone was nervous. Bodies worked to death would appear. War was on the horizon, but not with the army to the south.

Then familiar memories floated passed us, as if our lives had been rivers, and we stood as stones. Battles, war. The seven of us who had magic were reunited, though tensions grew between Seth and Moira. She was angry and bitter, just like my own husband. Still, I felt pride in fighting alongside my own kind and using my magic.

We moved the earth — we were more powerful than any enemy. But the magicians had more bodies, more slaves, and caused more death than we could imagine. We called them by another name. Godelan. It stuck in my throat as if my past hated it as much as my present. I saw the battle where we were too late, then the king's decision for us to follow the Godelan, and then the fire and ritual that ended our lives.

Chapter Four

As Kian walked farther into the woods after the strange Godel, he tried to hush all of his protesting instincts. His heart wasn't settled about the deal he had made with the man from the enemy tribe. Still, Kian had to admit he had a point. The Godelan who caused his tribe's warriors to sacrifice themselves were dead. And the Romans had slaves, too.

If this man could lead him to his brother and the other warriors, then he had to try. The Riada needed their champions back.

"Where are we going?" Kian asked after an hour of walking. "My uncle will be looking for me soon."

"Yes," the man replied. "But he will not find you."

Kian stopped suddenly. He had agreed to go with the Godel, not leave with him forever. The man turned around, eyes wide as if surprised at Kian's reaction.

"You have enchanted these woods!" Kian accused. "I cannot run away. My tribe will think I am dead. Or worse, a coward." He nearly stomped his foot in frustration, berating himself.

"Relax," the man told him, hiking up his robe to walk through the underbrush. "When you return with your brother, the hero, everyone will thank you."

The Godel waited for a few moments and then continued walking. Kian had only seconds to decide. Huffing, he continued to follow.

"You have yet to tell me how that is done," he noted.

"You're right, I do," the Godel replied.

Kian waited, but it became obvious he wasn't going to get his answer.

"What shall I call you?" he asked the man in front of him. "What is your name?"

The man clicked his tongue from up ahead. "So much power in a name," he replied. "Why don't you call me what I am?"

"A Godel?"

Again, he clicked his tongue. "You say it with such distaste. That won't do. What else am I?"

"A magician," Kian replied.

The man let out a sharp laugh. "You talk of magic with nearly the same disdain as you do your enemies."

"It has taken away everyone and everything that I have loved," Kian said.

"No." The man stopped and turned to confront him. "That's where you are wrong. Be careful of your opinions of magic. It can take away, and it can also grant. People, however, — the Romans, your father — it was their decisions that led you and me to this moment."

Kian couldn't tell if he was being bewitched or

not. Magician was making sense. He knew he shouldn't trust a man who had been living in the woods and who had practically abducted him, but he had to push forward and learn. If it meant getting his family back, getting the tribe's champions back, he would have to try.

They walked for several hours until the sun was low. Kian had lost all track of where he was. The fall had disoriented him, and he was still in pain. Also, hunger and the chill of the evening had set in.

"Why don't you tell me your real name?" he asked Magician.

The man answered without turning around. "If you hold a man's name, and you are the right man, you can control him," he replied simply. "Didn't they teach you anything?"

"I don't have magic," Kian replied. "How do you control him?"

"That is not for you to know," Magician said sharply.

"Why then?" Kian asked, trying again. "Why can you control someone with their name?"

"Because we come from the earth," Magician replied. "From Goram and Eila, the gods who created the first humans."

"I don't understand," Kian said honestly, but Magician had lost his talkative mood.

By the time they got to Magician's cabin, all Kian wanted was food and shelter. Answers could wait.

The cottage was by a small lake, where frogs croaked loudly in the evening light. The forest began to thin as they approached the cottage, and by the time they got there, all the trees had bare branches. No greenery grew around Magician's house.

Magician hadn't said a word in a long while. The desolate cottage made Kian take pause, yet again, about his decision. At the door, Magician turned around.

"Reluctant, Prince Kian?" he asked, knowing the answer.

Kian felt if he left now, and Magician didn't kill him, he'd die in the woods anyway. "What kind of a man lives in solitude like this?" he asked.

Magician looked around, as if surprised by the lack of company. "A busy man," he replied finally. "You will learn to love it."

As if to prove his point, Magician led the way into the small cottage, and with a flick of the wrist, a roaring fire was lit. The smoke rose neatly out of a hole in the thatched roof.

The rest of the place was bare — a few rugs, cooking pots, some logs on which to sit, and two small beds on opposite ends of the room. Hundreds of small items and objects littered wooden shelves, while the most prominent feature of the room was a large desk and bench. Kian eyed the sleeping arrangement.

"Were you expecting someone?"

"Of course," Magician replied. "I have always had an offer for you. The question was when you would be ready to accept it."

✦

Weeks went by and the summer passed into winter. In the north, fall lasted only a week or so, and Kian guessed Magician lived even farther north than where the Riada had moved since the leaves barely had a chance to change colour before they were frozen in frost. Despite the seasons, Magician's cottage looked the same, barren.

Magician was expert at dodging Kian's questions. Since coming to live with him, Kian had not seen anyone else in the forest at all. The man had chosen his location well.

Kian was still suspicious of his motives, but the man had magic. Kian knew magic could do wondrous things, and more than anything he wanted to bring back to the Riada what his tribe needed most: a king.

Despite apparently having waited for him for years, Magician was mostly indifferent to Kian's presence. He did request that Kian cut his long black hair and get rid of his cloak. When Kian asked why, Magician only danced away from the question.

"These are the terms of my offer," Magician said.

Kian doubted it was the truth, but he couldn't see the harm in cutting his hair or getting a new cloak, so he agreed.

Kian served as an apprentice, working at a narrow bench and helping Magician with various magical tasks. Still, the man had given no inclination Kian could ever work magic himself — a fact that wasn't lost on him.

"Where does your magic come from?" he asked.

Magician did not stop his work, scratching flakes off of a scaly purple rock with a chisel and collecting them in a satchel. "All magic comes from the earth. Everybody knows that."

Kian considered. "But you were not born with it," he said. "You are not descended from the gods like the Riada."

"No," Magician said, "I suppose I am not. Some people are not born with power. They take it. And that's what I did."

The bitterness in his voice was unmistakable.

Kian smiled behind Magician's back. He had hoped to get some kind of emotional reaction from him — anything that would push Magician into revealing the truth about who he was and how we was going to get the warriors back.

"By sacrificing people without magic?" Kian said. "Would that not make it dark magic? Evil power?"

The Magician didn't skip a beat. "You speak of evil as if you know it. The strong take power. Those who do not must not be strong." Magician looked up at Kian for the first time. "And do not forget, your beloved Romans have slaves in every corner of this world and sacrifice more than you can imagine for every one of their gods."

"The Riada do not love the Kaligan," Kian insisted, getting angry.

Magician went back to his rock. "Well, they certainly do all that is asked of them," he said. "You either love your master, or fear him. Which is it?"

Kian stood so quickly, he nearly knocked over the table. His fists were clenched and anger throbbed in his head. "The Kaligan do not master the Riada!" he hissed through clenched teeth.

Magician failed to show any kind of surprise at this outburst. Only when Kian had stormed outside, slamming the small wooden door behind him, did he realize that Magician had turned his own plan against him.

Kian crouched with his head in his hands by the pond. If only there was a sign that he was doing the right thing. Anything could be happening with the Riada right now, and he was not there to help. He reminded himself that his ability to help was limited, but not knowing was worst of all. And what if his tribe thought him a coward? How long would they wait before they gave up on him?

Footsteps roused him from his thoughts. He bolted upright to find Magician standing behind him. The smaller man wore his old, dirty cloak as if it were a royal cape.

"I want to send a letter home," Kian said without turning around.

"Fine," Magician said.

That night, Kian scrawled the few symbols of their language that he had learned as a child. His pictures of the animals that created the world and became the written language of the people looked as if a small child had drawn them. Still, he managed to communicate that he was safe and that he would return soon.

During winter, Kian spent most his time just trying to stay alive. Bitter cold enveloped the cabin, and when he was not searching for food, he was bringing in firewood. He missed his home, though in reality it was the people he longed for. The Riada had only lived in the new village for a few years after the Kaligan forced them to move. Still, Kian missed his uncle Eched and the rest of the tribe he had known his entire life, and who had taken care of him after the death of his brother, father, and mother.

Kian soon realized Magician had no intention of actually teaching him magic. And that was fine with him, as long as he could perform the task Magician wanted him to and find his brother.

"Why don't you use your magic to keep us warm?" he asked one night, his hands cracked and bleeding from the frozen branches in his arms.

"Magic is fading from this world," Magician said, lost in his work at the bench. "I must conserve as much as I can to accomplish our goals."

Kian took a deep breath. Every time he asked the most important question, he only got a tiny piece of the puzzle. Now, enough time had passed that he could ask again.

"How will you bring the Riada warriors back?"

"I already told you," Magician said. "You will."

"But how will I find them?" Kian pressed.

"I am figuring that out," Magician replied.

"And when?"

"That is for me to know," Magician said.

It was all Kian could do to not punch a wall, or Magician. He knew both would probably end badly for him.

Two months into the winter, Magician finally gathered enough of whatever he had been extracting from the rocks to clean up the workbench. When Kian came in one morning to see everything gone, he thought for an instant that Magician had left without him. When the man came in from outside, snow turned into icicles in his wild hair, Kian actually breathed a sigh of relief.

"We're leaving," Magician barked.

"To where?" Kian asked.

"To where it all started, of course," Magician said. "Pack your bag for a journey."

Kian rushed to obey. He didn't know what Magician meant or what he was talking about, but he just wanted to complete his part of the task and go home. Magician walked around the room as if he was retracing his steps, picking up odd items and placing them gently into a large canvas bag.

"Where exactly are we going?" Kian asked.

"To the hilltop where your tribe performed the ritual to send their souls after my people," Magician said.

Kian paused. Magician's frankness was odd, but worry swept over him.

"Are we doing the same?" Kian asked, trying to keep the fear from his voice. He did not see how dying would allow him to come back to his tribe.

"No," Magician said, eyeing another trinket before putting it down and placing something else in the bag. "Every five years the opportunity to follow the magic that left appears, and we can join your kind in their time."

"Why didn't you go five years ago?" Kian asked.

"I didn't have you," Magician said simply. "Time moves differently, especially the way we shall use it. I cannot know at what stage of life the Riada warriors are."

"So you need someone who would recognize them," Kian finished. "Like me."

Magician dug under a wooden bench to pull out some pieces of silver and pocket them. "Exactly. I need you to find your kind."

"Why don't we go after your people first?" Kian asked.

"What an excellent question," Magician said, turning to face him. His eyes lit up with malice and Kian could sense the sarcasm in his tone. "I cannot follow my people because your father decided to burn down our village after our defeat. The whole thing — poof." Magician snapped his fingers to emphasize his point. "The magic that took them is gone. Only your hilltop remains. We cannot know the Godelan and the Riada even live in the same time."

Kian had forgotten. He was young then. Between the death of the magicians and the warriors' sacrifice, his father had destroyed all that was left of the Godelan. Though to be fair, they had done much of the damage themselves, and anyone who could have fled did.

"My father was your king," Kian reminded Magician. "You disobeyed him."

"Yes," Magician said, spinning a round piece of brass between his fingers before tossing it back onto a pile of items that weren't fit for the bag. "King of kings. Our high king. That title was meant for your brother, wasn't it? Then you. But here you are, helping the enemy."

Kian was taken aback. "Are you the enemy? I am only doing this to help my people."

"Of course," Magician said. "And I want the same thing you do."

"Why?"

It was a question Kian had asked many times, and many times Magician somehow got out of answering it. He had told Kian a variety of stories, but Kian didn't believe a single one. He just hoped that when he did find out, it wouldn't be too late to save himself and the others and return home.

"There is no place for me in this world," Magician said tragically. Kian had heard this one before. "Maybe when you are king you will remember how I helped your kind. We are, after all, united in our enemy."

Kian couldn't bring himself to believe in Magician's noble intentions and hopes of redemption. He did, however, know that as much as Magician hated the other tribes, he hated the Romans more.

Yet a man who still wore the robes that identified him as better than his peers, even though they were all dead, was clinging to every ounce of power he had left. Kian couldn't imagine him giving it away and pledging himself to the Riada.

They left that same day, travelling during the night to keep warm and sleeping during the day in what brief sunlight occurred during the darkest winter months. Hungry and cold, Kian missed his old home and what was left of his family more than ever. But finally so close to being reunited with his brother, he could not regret his decision.

Three days' travel to the southwest would bring them to the Riada lands. On the coast, the tribe had their backs to the water. The Romans didn't like that and had forced them to move in order to be encircled by their legions. Kian hadn't been back in years.

On the second day of travelling, Kian felt the familiar vibration in the earth as he slept at midday. He sat up in a panic.

"We need to move," he said, waking Magician.

The man stood, brushing the leaves off his cloak but leaving a variety of twigs and foliage in his long matted hair.

Kian grabbed his bow and his small bag of belongings and was gone into the bushes before he realized that Magician hadn't followed him. He turned.

"What are you doing? Let's go, the Kaligan are coming."

Magician shook his head. "No," he said calmly. "I will not run from them. These are my lands, not theirs."

His low tone was dangerous, but Kian doubted he had ever seen a real legion. And by the sound of feet and hooves, one was approaching through the pass just near them. Scouts would spot them instantly. The procession was moving slowly, but they were close.

"They'll kill us, there's hundreds of them," Kian told him.

"I know," replied Magician. "They have passed through these woods every winter at this time for the past three winters."

Kian didn't understand. The hand that gripped his bow was nearly frozen. "You set this up?"

"I did," said Magician. "I've been working with the

earth for years trying to get it the way it needs to be for us to step through to where your kind will be. We need to walk through earth in transformation, in order to be transformed."

"I don't understand," Kian said. "How can earth be transformed into something else?"

"Well, earth can become air." Magician waved his arms. "But that is difficult. It is easier to make the earth become liquid. We take the strongest parts of the earth, turn it to liquid, and we'll have enough magic to carry both of us through."

"So why do you need the Kaligan?" Kian asked. The sound of boots was getting closer. He was nearly hopping from foot to foot in agitation.

"What kind of earth can become liquid?" Magician asked Kian. "Molten? We have silver in this land, but not much. The Romans have gold."

Kian nearly laughed out loud. "Your plan is to get captured by the Romans in order to *rob* them?" he asked in disbelief, hoping he had misunderstood. "And then what? Escape from a camp of a thousand men?"

"Yes," Magician said simply.

Kian breathed deeply, trying to steady his nerves. Before he could say anything else, shouts sounded from beyond the trees. The Kaligan were yelling at them in their language, telling them not to move. Kian took another deep breath.

This had happened to him once before. He had been travelling with his uncle when the Kaligan came, yelling these were their woods and any travellers needed to have good reason to be there. They demanded their party stand before the Roman leader, who sat atop his horse like a statue in leather and buckles.

Kian was young and hadn't known if he would live or die. Some men and women of the Riada or other tribes simply vanished in the woods, and it was often said the Kaligan were responsible. All depended on who led the legion, and Kian had never felt like taking his chances.

Men in uniforms ran onto the small pathway where Kian and Magician had slept. They were older than many of the new recruits he had seen and wore uniforms that were less polished, still the style his brother had worn a decade ago. In a glance, he knew this was a neglected legion.

Magician only smiled at the panic on Kian's face. "Don't worry, prince," he said. "The Romans will provide many things for us tonight. I guarantee you."

Kian didn't have time to think about the promise. Two men grabbed him and forced him to his knees. Two others did the same to Magician.

A stately man dismounted from his horse and came over. His helmet had the tallest adornments and his buckles were made of fine gold, even though they were quite worn. Small brown eyes that darted between Kian and Magician topped his long nose. Any hair he once had was gone, though a grey beard nearly hid his grim line of a mouth.

Kian could see this was a hard man, and he also knew this was the legion's commander. They were in trouble. Behind him, several men kept their distance but followed carefully.

For all that he was being held down, Magician seemed unimpressed.

"Do you speak the language?" the commander said to both of them.

Kian nearly rolled his eyes. The Kaligan liked to think their language was the only true tongue, and everything else was just the growls of barbarians.

Kian glanced at Magician, who nodded to him before answering.

"Yes," he replied in the Kaligan tongue.

"What are you called?" the commander asked.

Kian had to think for only a moment. "Master," he said. "And Apprentice." To his surprise, a small curve appeared in commander's thin mouth. He was actually smiling.

"Then I am to be called M-A," said the commander, "and these are my men. We were given orders to kill any natives we come across. Give me a reason why we should not kill you."

It seemed like an honest question. As far as Kian could tell, M-A was being earnest. Perhaps he didn't truly want to kill them. But Kian knew he was a Kaligan, and as a Kaligan he would do what he was told. Kian was lost for words, so M-A prompted him.

"Ask your master then, why we should spare your lives."

Kian turned to Magician and began to translate, but Magician cut him off halfway.

"I know what he said," Magician spat, eyeing the men surrounding them. "Tell him we wish to speak to his general."

"What?" Kian sputtered. "That's completely out of our way! Why would we want that?"

"Do it," Magician said in a low tone.

Kian sighed, clenching his fists, and relayed the message. M-A's response was expected.

"And why would the general like to speak to you?"

Kian turned to Magician, beginning to translate again before being cut off just as abruptly.

"Tell him we have information on a rebellion by one of the southern tribes," Magician said.

Again Kian was about to protest, but Magician's eyes flashed with fury. Kian doubted Magician could possess any real information, considering the solitude he lived in, but he relayed the words to the Kaligan commander.

M-A considered, rubbing his grey beard. "Fine," he said finally. "You are our prisoners tonight. Death can wait until tomorrow."

Chapter Five

It felt like a thousand different hands were shaking me. I was getting pulled from my memories, pulled from Seth, and I was fighting it. Sharp nails dug into my shoulders and tried to yank me back to reality, but I resisted. Finally, the squawking voice calling me grew louder and louder. I opened my eyes.

I still lay on the ground outside the tent. The back of my head pounded with sharp pain. Seth lay near me, unconscious. The strange woman stood over me, her face even more leathery and weathered up close. The sight was suddenly frightening, and I scrambled back.

"What did you do to us?" I accused. "What happened? What was that drink?"

As I sat up, I tried to wake Seth. I shook his shoulder, but nothing happened. The panic grew in my stomach and threatened to bubble up. I thought I was going to be sick, but maybe that was just from the ingredients of the drink.

Despite my scrambling, she managed to put her

small index and middle finger to my forehead, right between my eyes. I froze.

"What are you doing?"

As she opened her mouth, I understood the words coming out, though I was positive she wasn't speaking English. She pressed her fingers harder to my forehead with each word, and somehow I could understand.

"The drink was a sleeping brew," she said in a thin, raspy voice. "It allowed you to let go of this world and fall deeper into your past. You have seen all there is to see, and though you may not have understood the threads woven into your destiny, you now have access to them."

"That's it?" I was on my knees, staring in shock. "Is this as powerful as I will ever be?"

The tears in my eyes told me more about myself than about my past. I couldn't bear the fact that I would be without magic or with little magic forever. Everyone had had such high hopes for me.

"No," she said.

From my position on the ground, she seemed to grow an extra three feet. Suddenly she was no longer a small, hunched-over woman, but almost a giant, with a youthful, lean build. I still stared into the same eyes, however — they were ancient beyond understanding.

"You have access to the Earth's magic, though not much remains since your enemies take what they can," she said. "To be truly powerful, you must embrace your past. Become one with the magic."

She had grown into something completely differ-ent now. A very tall woman with long black hair and red paint around her eyes stared at me, her fingers still pressing right between my eyes.

"What are you?" I asked, breathless.

"Your gods had their children, and I had mine," she answered.

The raspy voice now sounded more like an echo, spoken by a hundred people at once. It rang in my ears in a thunderous chorus.

I couldn't think of anything to say. I just stared and thought over her words. I was terrified of letting go of this world. What if I never got me back?

"Go." The goddess, or whatever she was, urged me to get up.

I scrambled clumsily to my feet, careful not to break contact with her.

"Wake your friends. A challenge approaches. Remember my words."

I nodded and was about to do as she said when I stopped with one last question.

"What did you say to Moira?"

"It is not for me to reveal," she replied. "But you will know soon enough."

"How?" I asked. "She didn't understand you."

"Yes, she did."

Seth made a noise as he stirred. When I glanced back up, she was gone — both the little old woman and her other self. My hands shook from everything that had just happened. Adrenaline, fear, or the island sleeping concoction had put me on edge, and I could barely speak.

Seth was moving uneasily and moaning in his

sleep. His head darted from side to side. I tried to hold it steady so he wouldn't hurt himself. He suddenly gasped and sat up, trying to fight me.

"Hey!" I yelled. "It's me! Relax!"

"Gwen?"

Something in his eyes readjusted and I could tell that he only saw me for the first time.

"Yes, it's me. Come on, we have to go."

As I sat up, Seth grabbed my sleeve.

"They know. We have to leave."

"What? Who?" I immediately felt stupid for even asking. As soon as the words were out of my mouth, I knew exactly whom he meant. The magicians. Or as I now knew they were called, the Godelan — all that was left of them.

"After you got pulled out," Seth explained, sweat running down his face, "I saw them. Now. I somehow saw them in what I think must be this moment. They felt us remember and they know we can access the magic now."

When I continued to look at him confusedly, Seth went on.

"It was night wherever they were. I just saw a glimpse, but I know they know. Something changed just now, and they felt it, too."

"The woman said we'll only get all of our magic when we stop holding back the other half," I told him. "We need to become like we were."

We both looked around for her again, but she was gone.

"The magicians and us, we must share some kind

of bond through the ritual," I said. It was the only thing that made sense. They could always know what we were doing, how powerful we were, and which of us were the most useful to them. "If they felt what we did, then we have to move quickly."

As if on cue, the earth shook gently beneath our feet.

"Earthquake?" I asked Seth, knowing the answer.

"Something tells me this might not be a natural disaster," he replied.

We ran to get Garrison and Moira. They were both slouched over in the deserted hut. I was only mildly surprised to find it empty.

"Where'd she go?" Seth asked as he shook Garrison.

I shrugged. There was no time to think about it.

Garrison and Moira had the same lost look in their eyes when we managed to wake them. It was as though they were looking into something else as I sat directly in front of them. It took several minutes for the life to come back into their eyes, but at least the earth didn't shake any more.

"How do you feel?" Seth asked Garrison.

The humidity in the tent was making it hard to breathe.

"Like I got my life back," Garrison replied.

Moira nodded.

"I remember more than just our dying moments," Garrison said, rubbing his curls as if surprised to find them there. "I actually feel like I was that person now."

Garrison had always been the bravest among us,

and I knew that. He took this new knowledge as an opportunity and didn't fear it at all. I, however, was apprehensive.

"We have to go," Seth told them. "The Godelan know where we are. They felt ... whatever this was."

We miraculously managed to find the same path we had come down. As we huffed and puffed through the jungle, hoping we were going the right way, Seth recounted most of what he had seen of his past life. It was still shocking that it was mostly the same as my experience. We had shared so much of our lives.

Then he told us about the glimpse of whatever place the Godelan were in.

"How did you do that?" Garrison asked.

"It's almost like they're the flip side of the coin," Seth explained, gasping for breath as we rushed through the tall grasses. "If I go too far into the past and stay there too long, I end up with them. Gwen got pulled out, and on my own it was like I went deeper. When I went deep enough, I saw them on the other side."

Now we just had to figure out what to do when we learned their location.

"Gwen has a theory that since we share the same ritual for being here, we're tied to each other some-how, and I guess we have the past in common," Seth explained.

"That's genius!" Garrison declared. Again he was the only one who seemed fit enough to take on the jun-gle. Moira had already slipped twice. "But did you say Gwen got pulled out?"

My turn to explain.

I was still trying to make sense of it in my own mind, but the others deserved to know. I told them what had happened with the woman-goddess when I woke up, and what she said.

"We already knew that," Garrison said when I was done. "Kian always told us we'd have to remember the past to get our magic back."

"Yeah, that's the safe part," I said. "But becoming more powerful than the magicians means becoming our past lives and somehow not losing ourselves."

"Well then, that's what we'll have to do," Moira said between gasps. It was the first time she had spoken in a while.

The only part I had left out of my story was what the woman had said about Moira. I would keep that information to myself for now.

"I don't know," I said. "I feel like the magic will have consequences. How can we be sure nothing will happen to us?"

"What's the worst that can happen?" Seth asked. I felt the question was directed at me. "I was happy with you."

Awkward silence floated between us. His blatant disregard of Moira's feelings was probably what had made her so angry in the past. He just didn't realize what he was doing.

"Well, we weren't all happy with each other," I reminded him, trying to be as subtle as possible.

"If you're referring to me," Moira said from behind us, "I'm over it."

"Really?" I asked skeptically. "Because I remember you telling me that you wanted to kill me."

"What?" Garrison and Seth said together.

I had never told them that.

"It was a long time ago, when I was confused about who I was. And I didn't have a reason, I told you that. I just knew I wanted to," Moira explained, brushing it off as if the comment had been nothing. I wanted to believe her, but having relived the past so recently, the anger in her past self was more relevant to me than ever.

"And now?" I asked.

"Now," she huffed, pushing branches and leaves out of the way, "I know who I am."

Just then the ground shook again. I had almost forgotten about the earthquakes.

"What are they doing?" Garrison asked no one in particular.

"They know where we are," Seth said.

"So they're trying to shake us to death?" Moira said. "I don't think that'll work."

I could see figures ahead. True to his word, Ari and the two guides had waited for us, even though they had to brace themselves against the small quakes.

"Why would they cause an earthquake?" Moira continued. "There's hardly any earth."

As soon she said it, I saw fear come over her face. We all realized the true plan at the same time.

"No," I said, "there isn't a lot of earth. But there's a lot of water."

I was just getting a grip on magic. The storm I

caused in England had drained all of my strength after moving small pieces of earth and conjuring up some wind. To take on a tsunami was unthinkable, and it would drown this whole island.

Even in the best-case scenario, we might only be able to save ourselves. A familiar dread crept up on me.

"They must have decided we're not worth the trouble," Garrison said. "They'll go after the ones we haven't found yet for power. Killing us is easier."

We were all pale, sweating, and looked sufficiently terrified for the guides and Ari to think the worst when they saw us.

"What happened?" Ari said, rushing forward. "Did you meet her?"

"She wasn't home," Seth said quickly before anyone else could answer.

I gave him a look, but he gently shook his head. Maybe he had a point. After all, how could we explain what was going on?

"Are these tremors normal?" Garrison asked Ari hopefully.

"Once in a long while, we have a mild shake," Ari said. "But like this, one after another, no, I have never felt this in my life. We need to get back right away."

I got the feeling that the guides, based on how quickly they took off without a backwards glance, had had the same thought for a while. We probably should thank Ari that they hadn't fled and that we weren't stuck in the jungle.

We ploughed through the trees in silence for what could have been hours. Everyone was lost in thought, though a lot of my own thoughts revolved around how I never wanted to set foot in a jungle again. Maybe it was distraction or exhaustion, but the trip back seemed to be a lot faster. The guides ignored us, and as we broke through the jungle they ran for the town.

Garrison grabbed my arm just as I was about to follow them.

"Wait," he mouthed.

Ari turned back, confused, when he saw the four of us weren't following.

"What are you doing? You need to find shelter," he said.

"We're okay," Garrison told him. There was an authority in his voice I hadn't heard before. "You can go. Thank you for your help."

Ari appeared to consider this for a moment, then nodded and left. Garrison led us back into the jungle a little until we were hidden. I almost groaned.

"How do you feel?" he asked Seth. We all knew he was truly asking about Seth's magic. Was it strong enough?

Seth and Moira's magic, as Kian had explained to us, focused more on the mind, while Garrison and I were more connected to the earth. He had once compared it to different talents in the same sport. Those kinds of talents, however, would be of little use against a disaster.

"Got anything else?" Garrison asked him. "Gwen?"

It was time to shove all of my insecurities and fears about becoming *her* aside. If the Godelan got their way, I would never see my family or Kian again.

I planted my feet in the ground and pushed. It shifted beneath me.

"Whoa!" Garrison cautioned, grabbing for a branch. "More earthquakes are what we're trying to avoid here."

I reached down and grabbed fistfuls of soil, channelling some kind of intuition I realized I had been ignoring. Then I lifted my arms and the earth moved to create a wall. Everyone was impressed, but I was still worried.

"We're going to need something bigger," I said, looking over the earthen wall my own height. Not only was it small, but it was also weak.

Garrison clicked his fingers a few times. Nothing happened, though after a minute, a small tornado appeared between his hands.

"What can we do to stop it?" he asked, opening his arms and expanding the cyclone. "Can we blow it back?"

"A wave?" Moira said. "No way. You'll probably just make it worse. And you'd need a lot of wind."

"Can we build something?" Seth asked.

I shook my head. "The earth here is too weak and flimsy. The sand will never hold."

We stood silent for a minute, thinking. Garrison played with the wind between his hands, lost in thought, while I absent-mindedly scorched a leaf between my fingers. I only realized it when the ash fell from my hand.

"There may be something," Seth said finally. "About magic. I remember that magic like this is created. It's built just like anything else from the ingredients that make it work. The power that the magicians have is cobbled together from a bunch of little things — it's why they needed us. Maybe Moira and I can unravel it somehow and quiet it down?"

The rules of magic and power were a foreign language to modern Gwen, and yet as I stood and used even small bits of magic, I knew the past Gwen was coming forward. She understood Seth's words. Maybe he was letting his past self through too, and perhaps sacrificing our identity was just the price we had to pay.

"That's as good a plan as any," Garrison said. He took a few steps back toward the town and then suddenly stopped. On the fringes of the jungle, Ari was cowering from us, his eyes wide with fear.

"What are you?" he yelled.

His tone implied a calm conversation was out of the question.

"We can explain," Moira started, trying to defuse the situation.

"No, we can't," Garrison said. "Not now. Maybe later, but not now." He stomped his foot. The earth grew around Ari's feet and held him in place. The poor man nearly wailed with fright. I felt bad for him, but we couldn't get wrapped up in this. We had bigger problems.

"Ari," Garrison said. "Where do most earthquakes happen?"

"Please don't hurt me," he replied.

Now I really felt bad for him. Garrison didn't have

the softest look in his eyes. I could see how the situation might seem dangerous. I began to step forward, but Seth stopped me.

"Let him do this," he whispered.

"He's acting weird," I replied.

"Only doing what you said," Seth said, raising his eyebrows. Understanding dawned on me. Garrison was letting his memories rule. "Exactly," Seth added.

Garrison looked out into the ocean. "Please," he said, his tone firm, "tell me where the earthquakes come from."

"The ocean," Ari replied. He still looked at us like we were demons. When Garrison didn't move, he added, "To the southeast. Usually."

"Great, thanks," Garrison said, and headed toward town at a jog. Moira and Seth followed, though I still hesitated. I didn't know why I felt so bad. I never wanted anything about me to cause someone fear.

"You're leaving me here?" the man yelled.

"Don't worry," I told him. "It's for your own good."

"What if there's a tsunami?"

I considered. "Well, then we're all in trouble, so it doesn't matter."

It wasn't a very consoling thought, but I didn't have any of those. I ran to catch up to the others. By the time we got into town, several hours had passed since we were in the hut with the witch doctor.

The sun was getting low. It shot red evening light across the island. Seeing people milling around, cleaning up objects that had fallen during the smaller shakes, made me nervous. Did they suspect this was just the beginning? Did they have any plans?

"Why here?" I asked Garrison.

"It's like in battle," he replied. "If you're weak and outnumbered, you hit the weakest defence. They don't have much magic. They'll target any faults that already exist in the land."

"Everything looks fine here," Seth said, looking out onto the ocean.

Then, just as my heart was beginning to slow and exhaustion was setting in, the ground rolled beneath me. It happened so fast I could only take in the screams from all around. I heard a building crumble and car horns going off. I could barely stay on my feet, and Seth fell on all fours.

"I can feel the magic in this," he yelled above the noise. "It's thick, like a knot."

I wasn't really listening. Since we were on high ground, I caught sight of the beach simply falling way. Water sloshed back-and-forth, burying anyone who was out there in strong waves.

I froze. It reminded me of New York when the ocean had surged to engulf the pier. Kian and I had run then, because I wasn't strong enough to do anything about it. Resolve now began to overtake fear, and I did as Kian had taught me — tuned everything out and looked deep inside myself for the past and for my magic.

I planted my feet and let it flow over me. Every tremble I traced back to its origin. Ari was right — it was somewhere to the southeast. Finally, it stopped. The car horns remained. Screams were amplified.

"I don't know earthquakes," Moira said, "but that felt big."

"It was," I told her. "We used to get them a lot in San Francisco. They were really bad in the last few years."

I didn't mention it was because of the Godelan and their big plans for the world.

"It was full of magic," Seth said. "I could see it all tangled in there."

Moira nodded.

"Well, can you untangle it?" Garrison asked.

Seth and Moira looked at each other uncertainly.

"Well?" Garrison pressed. "Can you?"

"We could try," Moira said, looking at Seth for confirmation. "But we'd need time. If it's something like a wave, we would have to stop it for a while."

It was my turn to look uncertain. "That's a pretty big ask."

"Do we have a choice?" Seth asked.

Sirens sounded across the island and were followed by more screams and scrambling. The noise sounded old, like something from a black-and-white movie, and echoed throughout the town.

"What's that?" Moira asked.

"Tsunami warning," Garrison answered.

He led the way down the hill to the beach, where we faced the direction the earthquake was coming from. The water was already much higher than I remembered it. A lot of the sand seemed to have broken away. Tourists who hadn't noticed were still suntanning and walking along the beach. That changed as the water began to recede.

I couldn't believe my eyes. The water left the beach as if it was being sucked away by the ocean. Some searched for people who had been in the water when the quake struck and were swept terrifyingly away as the water raced back toward the ocean.

"It's happening," Seth whispered.

I was horrified. Screaming people surrounded us, running. The sirens were still blaring and yet the little island was defenceless against the vastness of the sea. All I could think was that I was not ready.

Within minutes, only the four of us remained on the beach. We stood side by side as I tried to imagine what drowning was like and if I would get another life after this one if this killed me.

In hindsight, I was a mess of fear, panic, resolve, and several other emotions I can't even pinpoint. I was sorry that we would probably die, and I was angry at Kian for not being there to help us. At the same time, I was happy he wasn't and hoped he was safe somewhere far away.

The wind was rising and my hair whipped my face. Sand blew into our eyes and I breathed it in. I felt Seth take my hand.

"Gwen," he yelled above the storm, "you have to reconnect!"

It was like trying to push a boulder up a hill. I strained with every ounce of my being to find power.

"I'm trying!" I yelled back.

Garrison took my other hand. "We need to give Seth and Moira time," he shouted. "Just put everything you have into holding it!"

Easier said than done. I was digging through my mind to try to find the old Gwen. I went through every memory and every dream that had scared me. Magic started to hum in my heart. Then I saw the wave.

From far away, it looked like some kind of science experiment where the water flows in a way that just doesn't make sense. The waves were breaking on each other at the same time as they were gathering speed and size. A few boats that had the misfortune of being in their path disappeared in an instant.

Fear choked down magic.

"Gwen?" Seth yelled.

Either I had blanched or he felt a change in me, but he knew something was off. I felt like I was grasping at straws as I tried to hold my past life close while terrified.

"I'm scared," I mouthed to keep from shouting in the storm.

Seth looked to either side of us. Moira had gone completely still. Her eyes closed, she looked serene and at peace. Garrison, however, stared at the ocean with an air of fierce determination. I could feel the magic pouring off him in waves.

"You have to find something stronger than fear," Seth yelled. My eyes filled with tears. I had never tried so hard in my life. "You have the whole story now. Use it!"

Still nothing. The wind made it hard to catch a breath.

"I can't!" I screamed.

He squeezed my hand and a glimmer of magic reappeared in my mind's eye. I chased it, realizing the memory of him had been stronger than anything else in my past, including hatred for the Godelan.

The earth shook, but this time with a steady rumble. The wave was getting close.

"Stop it as far out as possible," Garrison yelled. "That way if we're not strong enough, we have enough time to at least push it back."

I turned back to Seth. Panic was mounting. I knew he had made the connection with his past, because it was as if someone else looked back at me through his eyes. Someone who knew me better than I knew myself, and who would do anything for me. There was only one thing I could think to do to coax out the old Gwen.

I closed my eyes and tried to shut out my environment. The wind died away, the sand stopped stinging my face. The earth beneath my feet calmed and the sound of rushing water disappeared. I took a deep breath.

Fine. You win, I told past Gwen. *You can have him.* And shoving Kian to the very back of my mind, I leaned in to kiss Seth.

As soon as our lips met, the rush of memories overcame me. I felt absolute happiness flood my heart, and the magic in my body increased tenfold. Just like the suit of magic I had conjured in New York, it fit me perfectly. As long as I let her be with him, she was close to the surface, and I had her magic.

Fear was replaced by determination and love for my friends, Seth, and everyone else I would save. I had never before felt such a sense of responsibility, but old Gwen had been raised with it. She had the last bits of power in a world free of magic, and it was her responsibility to protect others, especially from the Godelan. I felt how she despised them. Her emotions fuelled me.

I broke our kiss and let the world back in. We were running out of time. Seth smiled at me, and I couldn't ·tell which man I was looking at.

I held my breath as the wave approached, counting down for it to be within reach. Magic bubbled underneath the water. I braced my feet and closed my eyes, feeling the magic hurdle through the ocean toward the beach.

It was messy, like Seth had said, completely knotted. No one took care with this; it had been pulled together as quickly as possible. But I knew, from somewhere deep inside my memories, that messy magic was also weak magic.

Now!

I heard Seth's voice in my head rather than in my ears. At his call, I put everything I had into stopping the magic in its tracks.

The power Garrison and I had intermingled until we were acting like a wall, but the weight of the Godelans' power was too strong. It pushed back against our defences, and my feet slid backwards in the sand. The wave came closer.

After a few moments, the weight lessened. I could feel the knots unravelling, discarded into the ocean. Seth and Moira were actually doing it.

Still, Garrison and I struggled under the weight and it became hard to breathe. I could feel him beginning to fade next to me. He was slipping into the sand, choking on the power crushing our chests. But we had to hold it, so I pushed harder. Another few moments and the weight weakened again.

A little bit longer, Seth's voice said in my mind.

My head was buzzing. Breathing was hard. All I could do was force everything I had into the magic, placing it like obstacles in the way of their magic. Though the force was getting weaker, holding it off was getting harder.

We were absolutely exhausted, mentally and physically. The day had been taxing. We'd been poisoned, hiked through the jungle for hours, and lived an entire life in memories.

When I was sure I couldn't take it anymore, I heard Moira in my head.

Let go!

She didn't have to ask twice.

I opened my eyes to see the wave collapse in on itself from very high above us. As the water fell just a short distance from where we stood, I summoned my last ounce of magic to blow us back enough not to be swept out. The water rushed over us and I let it, absolutely exhausted.

I could only relax for a few seconds. Scrambling to all fours, soaked, I stood nearly at the road. Some of the island would flood, but it wasn't that bad.

"I told you to warn me next time you do that," Seth said. He tried rubbing his eyes with his sleeves, but everything was covered in sand. We found Moira and Garrison nearby. Garrison was so exhausted he could barely walk.

"Kian was right," he said weakly. "You are the most powerful."

I scoffed. "Seth and Moira took that thing apart. I could never do that."

The sight of the beach was surreal. It was like the entire island was a raft set directly in the water.

Darkness was beginning to set in, but the town was coming to life. Sirens blared, people came darting out, and everyone seemed to have something to do. I had only one thing in mind.

"We need to get back to the hotel," I said, "and get ready to leave."

"After a nap," Garrison said firmly.

✦

What was meant to be a nap turned into a marathon sleep. We were all so tired that I woke up fourteen hours later, fully dressed, on top of the covers, with Garrison at my feet. He was curled up at the end of the bed like a puppy. Seth slept in a chair, while Moira was asleep in her own bed.

I shook Garrison awake just as rays of sunlight broke through our window and roused the others.

"Wake up, it's morning."

The first few instants of peace, before I remembered the previous day, were quickly replaced by panic. We had given the Godelan a big head start. I tried to console myself by knowing no flights could take off from the airport, which was probably still flooded, but having slept for so long, I knew the world outside could have changed in that time. Garrison read my expression.

"Don't worry," he said sleepily. "It'll be a while before they can gather that amount of magic again."

"That's not what we should be worried about," Seth said flatly.

He had turned on the television. Set to the local channels and news by default, the image featured a giant wave breaking close to the beach, and four people standing right at the brink of it.

"Uh-oh."

Moira scooted closer to the TV. "There's no way they can tell who that is," she said. "It could be trees, or anything."

As if in reaction to her words, the image zoomed in on our faces, blurry, but very much us. Seth flipped the channel to Australian news, and they were playing the same video. New Zealand as well. A caption proclaimed that the video of the mystery daredevils had become an online sensation. *Great.*

Just as we were all calculating the improbability of us being able to leave the island together without being recognized, the phone rang. We exchanged nervous glances until Garrison got up to get it. He lifted the receiver and just listened.

A voice on the other end talked for a good minute. I couldn't hear the words, but I could tell that it was angry. Had someone tracked us down?

I anticipated the police busting through the door at any moment. No matter how many faces or mouthed questions we could direct at Garrison, he just stared ahead, listening. Finally, he put down the receiver.

"Kian wants us to meet him," he said. "He's found a way to destroy the Godelan."

Chapter Six

Kian shifted on the hard earth, trying not to panic. His hands were tied behind his back and he sat tethered to a pole in one of the Kaligan supply tents. Magician sat opposite him, apparently napping.

The tent was nearly pitch black. The only light came from the flaps that blew open with the wind. Soldiers were having a meal at many communal fires, and the prisoners had been put where they could not bother anyone.

M-A had humoured Magician and Kian. He had even fed them, which Kian welcomed, for all that he knew he ought to hate the Kaligan. The wars had always somehow seemed far removed from him. Now that he was in the midst of one, he was terrified.

His initial observation had been correct — these men had been on the road for a long time, and their patience was wearing thin, especially with natives of Alapa. Attacked, their supplies raided, and constantly on the lookout, the men were suspicious of Magician's intentions.

And they were right to be. Shortly after being secured and left alone, Magician had explained to Kian exactly how they would rob the Kaligan of the metals they needed for the ritual.

Admittedly, gold was everywhere. Perhaps to the Kaligan they seemed like small amounts, but to Kian, who rarely saw any metal at all, the army sported more gold than in all of the kingdoms in the north. Even the army's banners were golden bulls on scarlet fields.

Kian guessed Alapa wasn't the best place in the Kaligan Empire to be sent to. In fact, judging by what he heard while being transported by the Kaligan, their emperor punished people by sending them to the north.

Magician had told Kian to sleep. They would have a long night ahead of them walking to the ritual spot. Kian considered how awfully optimistic that was of him. He tried to have faith in Magician and closed his eyes, but sleep wouldn't come.

Just when Kian heard the Kaligan shifting and moving around outside, obviously done their meal, the biggest bonfire went out. Magician's eyes opened in the darkness and something flashed within them.

Dozens of men cursed. Some minutes passed before they lit the fire again, and soon it was roaring to life, as bright as the one that had gone out. Magician's face was stony. Kian thought he saw him huff in the darkness, then the fire went out again. This time the cursing was louder, and more men joined in.

"What are you doing?" Kian whispered into the darkness. "Is this your big distraction?"

"What are you sitting next to, Prince?" Magician asked.

Kian looked around at the supplies for the first time. "Firewood," he said finally. This confused him. "Why would they travel with firewood?"

"Think," Magician told him, annoyed. "They travel in the winter, when dry wood is hard to find. They would have to go farther into the woods to collect it. A Roman alone is an easy Roman to kill. They travel with wood to protect themselves from us. They fear us. And we will show them why."

Kian briefly considered that he would make a bad soldier. And a bad leader.

More time passed now between when the fire went out and when a new one was lit. And as soon as it was lit, it promptly went out again. Angry footsteps vibrated the frozen ground beneath Kian. They approached quickly, tearing open the flap and letting even more of winter in. Kian shivered in the chill.

"Move, native."

Kian had to tuck his legs in quickly because three men surrounded him to pick up the dry wood. M-A came in behind them, exclaiming that the northern winter built character.

Just as the men were almost out of the tent with the new wood, Magician motioned to Kian.

"Tell him I know why their fire won't start," Magician said.

Kian hesitated. Magician's plan could go wrong, and there was no coming back from it if it did.

"Tell them," Magician pressed angrily.

"M-A!" Kian called in their language.

The man turned around, curious. "What is it, boy?"

Kian took a deep breath. "My master knows why your fire won't start."

"Tell him they are cursed and will have no warmth in all of their future journeys," Magician prompted.

Kian repeated this to M-A.

The commander seemed unimpressed, his grey eyebrows rising to nearly where a hairline would have been had he still possessed any hair. He shook his head, coming slowly back into the tent.

"I will never understand your superstitions," he told Kian, though he looked toward Magician. "In case my general lets you live tomorrow and I am not the last Roman you meet, take this word of warning, boy: don't try to push your ways on the men of the south. The only thing they may care to take from the north is your women."

Kian's nails bit into his skin. His fists were clenched behind his back, but he kept his temper even. "Don't you have your own gods?" he asked as innocently as he could.

"Yes," M-A replied. "And they unfortunately didn't seem to follow us to this land. They truly wield great power, and I cannot wait to get back into their sight."

"Tell him I will work magic," Magician said. "Just like his gods. And I will bring back their fire."

Kian bit the inside of his cheek in frustration until it bled into his mouth, but still he relayed the message to M-A.

For a second it looked like M-A was going to laugh

and walk out of the tent. A big part of Kian hoped that would happen. But then the man seemed to reconsider.

M-A called a few of his pages to come in and untie Magician. When they got him to his feet, his legs were unable to hold him up. He stumbled, and the two pages struggled to hold him up.

"An old man's body cannot live a young prisoner's life," Magician said in a pained voice Kian knew to be fake. He translated the words for M-A but knew the real Magician would rather die than show any weakness. It was all an act.

As they passed Kian, M-A leading the way back to the dark camp, Magician stumbled again. Something fell out of his pocket close to Kian's hands. He waited until everyone was out of the tent to investigate.

Feeling around blindly, Kian found a jagged piece of metal. Hoping Magician would give him enough time, he diligently began to hack away at the thick rope.

"We have entertainment," M-A shouted just outside the tent. "This man claims he can work magic like the gods and bring back our fire!"

The men jeered. Kian felt their boots on the ground, coming toward the fire pit to view this native and the mysteriously extinguished fire. Magician's plan was working. He was enough of a distraction to attract everyone and allow Kian to roam around unfettered.

The Kaligan rope, while thick, was very dry. The fibres snapped and tore, and while much of his skin came away with the rope, Kian was able to free himself before Magician had even begun his show.

Sneaking to the entrance of the tent, he listened

until he was sure everyone was busy. Then, staying low under cover of night, he snuck toward the tents that contained the gifts. Kian and Magician had spied the riches this legion was bringing their general and their emperor. Kian had never seen Magician look so smug.

The gold was right in the middle of the procession, behind the supplies tent but before all of the important commanders' tents. For all that the Kaligan carried large quantities of gold, they had grown used to being alone in a wild landscape, only attacked in the forests where Kian's people had the advantage. Camping out in the open with scouts on the perimeter, the Kaligan had nothing to fear. Their treasure was left largely unattended, and now Kian would take advantage of that.

He found the tent with gifts of food and thick liquids in barrels. Some smelled absolutely foul and were stained with bright colours. Others smelled richly of some kind of fruit Kian had never tasted before. The gold was in a box.

In the short time Magician had whispered the plan from across the supply tent, Kian had been panicking too much to think of the finer details.

Now his heart raced wildly as he looked for an object small enough to carry but large enough that Magician would say it was enough. Kian couldn't imagine how many provisions the treasure he looked through could buy for his tribe, but he did know he could not buy his way out of this situation. What the Riada needed was their hope back. And magic.

Finally, he spotted a bulky object wrapped in canvas. He unwrapped it to reveal a golden eagle. It was perfect. He tucked it under his arm and was almost out of the tent when the familiar sound of heavy footsteps forced him to hide next to the entrance.

Kian breathed a quiet sigh of relief when he saw that only one soldier entered, lazily looking around on casual patrol. Kian quickly considered his options. If he waited, the man might not leave quickly enough for him to meet Magician where they had agreed. If he didn't wait, the soldier could raise an alarm and Kian would be caught.

His choice was made for him when he shifted the golden eagle in his arms and it rustled against his cloak. The Kaligan soldier turned around quickly, grabbing for the short sword at his waist. Kian raised the eagle and hit the man hard on the head before he could even think about what he was doing.

A piece of the eagle's wing clattered to the floor as the man collapsed with a significant dent in his helmet. Had he not been wearing a helmet, the blow would have killed him.

Kian's hands shook as he stepped over the prone form and ran from the camp into the woods, doing his best to stay hidden. His legs carried him quickly.

Though the bare branches of winter didn't provide a lot of cover, the moonless night meant darkness for Kian. Distant fires, now burning brightly, reflected off the eagle tucked under his arm. Its weight was beginning to hurt him, and Kian set it down in the snow as he watched the camp from above, waiting for a sign that Magician had managed to escape.

Kian felt like he hid and held his breath for ages. Several times he considered if he was hiding in the right spot. He glanced at the stars to confirm he was in the northeast corner of the camp, but the longer he waited, the more he doubted himself. He couldn't remember a time when he wasn't cold and hungry. He wished, not for the last time, he'd never begun this journey in the first place. Still, he convinced himself nothing would compare with the joy of having his people's warriors back.

Eventually, shouts from below startled him into crouching lower. He ducked and covered himself with his cloak, hoping to blend in. Shapes rushed around the camp. Were they looking for him or for Magician?

Just as he finally decided that he would freeze to death out in the cold, a dark shape hurried toward him in the dark. At first Kian moved back into the shadows, keeping the eagle close in case he had to use it as a weapon again. Then he noticed the familiar movements of Magician.

The man wore a frown skewed in disgust.

"What happened?" Kian asked.

"Did you get it?" Magician countered.

Kian nodded and took the eagle from under his cloak. He waited for approval, but Magician seemed neither pleased nor disappointed.

"What happened?" Kian asked again.

Magician began walking away toward the woods. As Kian was getting ready to ask again, Magician finally responded.

"I put on their show. I started their fires. I should have let them burn." Magician's hatred for the Kaligan was not a surprise.

"Why didn't you?"

"Because," answered Magician, "I cursed them with a worse fate. As they laughed and mocked the magic of this land, I cursed them to wander, doomed, until one day they would be exterminated. And their fate would be lost to time and memory, just like that of our tribes."

Again, Kian felt disconnected from the conflicts that caused such hatred in everyone he knew. The hate Magician held for the Kaligan was matched only by the hate Kian's uncle Eched had for the Godelan.

Kian wondered if Eched could ever forgive his working with a Godel to win back the warriors. Surely it wouldn't matter if the Kaligan were gone and the tribe would have its king and magic back.

"They let you get away?"

"They didn't let me do anything," Magician fired back. "I wanted to leave, so I did. They thought they tied me up and ran off looking for you. The idiots were convinced I conjured the flames yet thought rope would hold me."

Kian held in his emotions, reining in his hope that he would see his brother again. All the weeks and months with Magician were just bottled hope for him. And after running away from his tribe, there had been no returning without a solution — something better than just producing children in hopes of creating more warriors. By the time that happened, the Riada might vanish completely.

Magician was quite spry for an older man. Kian struggled to keep up throughout the night, fighting cold, exhaustion, and hunger as he carried the heavy golden eagle through the forest.

Snow covered the ground and he worried his feet might be beyond saving after this adventure. His hand felt frozen to the statue, and a sharp ache stabbed his lungs when he pulled in deep gulps of frigid air. Finally, to keep from falling asleep as he marched, Kian addressed Magician.

"How did you know he'd agree? M-A? How did you know?"

"He is a commander," Magician said. "At one time he had a commander. That man probably made a fool out of him. And now he cannot resist making a fool out of those who are beneath him. A cycle of power well wasted."

As they walked, Kian had been thinking of M-A. The commander seemed very logical and scoffed at the ways of the tribes. He hadn't believed Magician and probably wouldn't ever believe magic was involved in their escape. But he hadn't wanted to give his name. M-A's reasoning was similar to what Magician had said about names — how a name was a powerful thing to learn about someone. But surely M-A wouldn't believe that?

"Did M-A not want to give us his name because he was afraid?"

Magician actually let out a harsh bark of laughter. "The Roman is not lost to the ways of magic, for all that he claims he does not believe."

"You told me names matter because the gods made people from earth," Kian said. "How is that?"

Magician turned to glance back at him. "You are full of questions tonight," he replied. "Goram and Eila talked life into people from the earth. They called the first men and women, and they came. Your name is the first thing you are given. It separates you from what you were before your birth and what you become after your death: earth. To hold your name is to hold life."

"And that's why you won't tell me your name," Kian said.

"Correct."

"But you know my name."

"Correct."

"Can you control me?"

Magician turned with an annoyed look. "If you suddenly find yourself remembering everything I ever told you, you will also remember that I said only the right person may control you by your name."

Kian thought. "So you're not the right person?"

No answer.

"Am I the right person?"

"You could be."

Magician took to mumbling something to himself. Kian couldn't tell if it was to deter more conversation or if he was actually angry.

Another hour passed. Dawn was on the horizon when Kian finally glimpsed the hill where the ritual was to take place. Though he was nearly frozen and dreadfully tired, something flared into life in his chest.

He hadn't known the pain that existed there, dormant. Yet as he looked upon the space where his own father had said the words that had ultimately killed his brother and everyone else capable of saving the Riada, he was shocked to a halt. He had not been to the place since he was a child.

Magician noticed he had stopped. "What are you doing?"

Kian shook the images of the flames from his mind. The woman who had intrigued him so much as a child had been swallowed by them. Soon he would have them all back. He would bring them home.

They reached the place as the first rays of sunlight spread across the landscape, and Kian wondered if it was his perspective that had changed, or the actual countryside. When he was a child, this hill had seemed like a mountain. And after the ritual, it was a monument to the misery of his people. Now it was just a small bump in the earth.

Magician began to drop the items from his bag into the centre of the ring of stones, charred from the fire so many years ago.

"I never thought I would return here with my enemy," Kian thought out loud.

"I am not your enemy," Magician said, still busy. "The Romans are your true enemy. They are the ones who force their language and customs on our land, erasing our history."

Magician took the golden eagle Kian had stolen and threw it into the middle of the fire pit with pieces of silver and brass.

"Why didn't you speak to them yourself the whole time? You know their language," Kian said angrily as Magician came to stand next to him, observing his work.

"There is always an element of mystery and fear," Magician explained, "when one does not understand. That is something you will know about me. I like to be feared."

Suddenly he raised the dagger well over his head and pulled at Kian's arm until his cloak fell back and his bare skin was exposed. Kian realized too late what was happening and fought in vain.

"What are you doing?"

"One last ingredient," Magician explained. "Blood."

Kian struggled as Magician held him in a deadly grip. His strength was impressive and unexpected.

"Kian?"

Both Kian and Magician were caught off guard. The voice had called from the other side of the hill. They looked at each other. The brief look of confusion on Magician's face was replaced by something more sinister.

"Prince Kian?" the voice called. "Is that you?"

Magician let Kian's arm go and retreated a few paces as the man climbed the hill to meet them.

A familiar face crested the hill. Kian's heart did somersaults as he took in the first person from his own tribe he'd seen in months. He braced himself for anger; after all, it would appear that he had deserted and left them. But instead, the man, who was only slightly older than him, broke into a wide smile.

Kian had known Adar since they were children. The man with chestnut hair had been friendly to him, even though most people didn't know how to act in case he became king one day. Adar was one of the hunters, and even so far from home he carried a bow and a quiver at his side.

Kian had often wished for the life of a hunter. Adar had married a Riada girl he chose himself, and his only task was to provide food for the tribe.

"Is it really you?" Adar asked again. There were tears in his eyes. Kian was happy for the sentiment, but this was an unexpected reaction. Panic touched his heart and made it race.

Adar grabbed Kian's shoulders, smiled widely again, and embraced him. The look on his face was one of sadness and happy surprise all at once.

"What's the matter?" Kian asked. "Why have you come so far? What's happened to the Riada? Is it my uncle? Is he alive?"

To his relief, Adar gave out a laugh. "Relax, Kian," he said. "Everybody's fine. The same as before you disappeared. I only come this way to hunt because supplies are running short. The Kaligan are taking everything. And I still know this land better than anyone."

Kian could tell there was something he wasn't telling. "Then what is it? I can tell something is wrong."

Adar gripped his shoulders again, as if making sure he was real. "It's you," the man said, surprise still overtaking his emotions. "We thought you were dead."

"Dead?" Kian asked. "Why dead?"

No. This wasn't how it was supposed to go at all. He hadn't wanted anyone to suffer or lose hope. He hadn't wanted anyone to look for him. He was going to save them.

"Shortly after you left," Adar said, "We ..." He shook his head in wonder. "We found your body. We thought a bear had mauled you. Eaten before the winter. We thought it was surely you, with your hair and your cloak ..."

Kian began to understand. His mind raced as he fit together the pieces. Magician had tricked him. He had wanted Kian's tribe to think he was dead, so that Kian would truly stay for as long as he was needed. His heart ached for his uncle and anyone of the Riada who had mourned for him and had lost hope. He was the last connection to the gods, and without him, there would be no more warriors.

"Adar." Kian grabbed the man's arm. "Go home, tell them it was just a misunderstanding. Tell them I'm alive and that I'm bringing back the warriors. I'll bring home everyone who's ever had magic, and we'll take back our lands!"

Adar looked at him sympathetically but didn't move. Kian nearly screamed in frustration. This is exactly why he hadn't gone home to tell everyone. No one would believe him.

"Kian," Adar said, using the calm tone one typically uses with someone who has lost his mind, "our champions are dead. We stand on their graves. You cannot bring them back."

"But I can!" Kian nearly shouted. "I can. I know a magician who can do it."

"A magician?" Adar asked. "Kian, there is no more gods' magic left. Magicians are gone. You know that."

"But this Godel can do it," Kian insisted.

"Godel?"

Something flashed in Adar's eyes. Hate. Another reason Kian hadn't tried to go home and explain his plan.

"Kian," Adar's tone was low, and held anger, "whatever deal he promised you, only evil can come from it. He cannot bring our seven back."

Kian was about to open his mouth to disagree, but Magician's voice rang out from behind the standing stones. He had been hiding.

"The hunter is right," he announced. "There will be no bringing the seven back."

Kian's anger mounted, and he turned to Magician, but just then, Magician grabbed for Adar's throat. He squeezed with his hand, and as he did, Adar struggled for breath.

"Stop it!" Kian yelled. "Stop!"

He stood, conflicted between Adar and Magician. If he helped Adar, he might never see his brother again. But Magician had just told him the only thing he wanted was actually impossible.

"You told me you could bring them back!" Kian screamed.

"I told you that you could have your brother back, Prince," Magician corrected him, his eyes never leaving Adar. "And to do so, you would have to find the others."

"What?"

Adar collapsed to his knees.

Kian didn't know what to do.

"Magic is in short supply here," Magician said, as if it was obvious. "In the future, where my brothers and your kind have gone, I imagine it is nearly gone. Bring me the others, we'll take their magic, and you can have your brother and go home. That is our deal."

"No!" Kian yelled. "I won't do that."

He tried to get in Magician's line of sight, to step between him and Adar, but Magician pushed him backward with incredible strength. Kian realized too late that he had been hiding his power the whole time.

Adar fought against Magician's magic but was losing.

Helpless tears streamed down Kian's face as Magician rooted him the spot while he took Adar's last breath. The instant the man died, Kian was free of Magician's grip. He collapsed to his knees.

"You didn't have to do that!" Kian screamed. "He was going to go home. He wasn't going to stop us."

"But then the Riada would know this ritual is possible," Magician told him. "They would know it had been possible the whole time. They'd know they could have spared the lives of their children and saviours and simply sent them forward instead of killing them. Think of how disappointed they would be."

"You don't care about the Riada," Kian said through gritted teeth.

"No," Magician agreed. "I don't. But I do care about preserving my methods, and I've worked ten years on this. My own kind didn't know it was possible. I knew I could do it, and that's why I stayed. And now I have."

Puzzle pieces continued to click together.

"You were one of the Godelan who stole the souls and magic out of your own people," Kian accused. "But you were too much of a coward to die."

Magician smirked.

Kian tried to go after him but found himself frozen again. His anger overflowed into sadness, regret, and disappointment, and he buried his face in his hands. He knew he had made a grave mistake. Even if he got his brother back, how could he face his tribe?

"You speak of cowards, Prince?" Magician asked. "You ran from your people and sought the company of your enemy, all so that you could have your brother back and have him lead your people instead of you."

Kian screamed, still unable to move. The anger was too much to bear. Magician approached him and lifted his arm once more. Kian didn't even protest. The man ran the dagger swiftly along his forearm until the blade was covered in blood, and then tossed it into the fire.

"Now," Magician said, "you will come with me. You will find the others, you will surrender them to my brothers and me, and then you can have your own brother back. Just like I promised."

"No." Kian shook his head. "I won't." Magician ignored him, lighting a fire in the pit that roared to life in seconds. Kian refused to look up.

"The spell is underway," Magician said. "I will go to the future, find others of my kind, and, eventually, find yours. I will make sure that each of them is killed, and you can go home to tell the Riada what you've done. Or you can help me find them, and spare your brother."

He finally allowed Kian to stand. Magician released him, but misery descended like a shroud. More than anything he wanted to fall into the fire and die, but he knew he couldn't. At least one shred of goodness had to come from this mistake, and he would do anything to make that happen.

He stared into the flames, trying to block out the sight of Adar's body and the knowledge that his uncle and the tribe thought he was dead. He could only look for the good he was committed to doing one day. He would save his brother, no matter what. He would bring him back and let the Riada have their king, even if he died in the process.

"What is going to happen to this land?" Kian asked hoarsely.

"I cannot know the future," Magician replied.

"When will we reappear?"

"When the first of your kind experiences magic," Magician said.

The tears were drying on Kian's face, leaving cold streaks. He stepped close to the fire until it hurt his face and body.

Magician said some words in a language Kian didn't know. They reverberated until they became a constant hum. The humming turned to shouts, whispers, and screams.

Magician smiled at the sounds of agony but Kian couldn't stand them and had to cover his ears, only to find the noises were inside his mind. A black space started to grow in the fire as a sliver, and with it a chill hit Kian's face even as the flames threatened to burn him.

He wanted it to end. The noise was unbearable. As Magician took a step forward, Kian did as well — straight into the fire.

A moment of sheer agony passed through him as the flames met his skin and engulfed him. He held his breath and forced himself to keep going.

Two steps, and he stumbled on the rocks lining the pit, falling hard on all fours. The blackness turned out to be a glimpse into the night. It was just as cold here now as it was when they left. For a moment Kian thought nothing had happened.

Magician walked around, observing the stars as if he could read them. He seemed just as lost as Kian.

"Get up, Prince," Magician said.

"Where are we?" Kian's voice came out as a rasp. The contrast between heat and cold was causing him to shake uncontrollably, and his teeth chattered. He slowly got to his feet.

There was no fire in this pit, no golden statues or silver coins nearby. Adar's body was gone.

"I don't know," Magician admitted. "We are in the same place, at the time when the first Riada warrior experiences magic."

"So," Kian reasoned, "they could be old men?"

"Or children," Magician said.

"And your people?" Kian asked.

"We'll have to find them," Magician said. "Not to worry, I can find magic. We are all connected."

Kian laughed hoarsely. "They will not be angry at you for failing to fulfil the ritual? You left them to die."

Magician's eyes flashed with anger. "My fate has been worse than theirs. Time moves differently in this world, but I have no doubt they have fared well. And I know they will forgive me when they see the wonderful gift I have brought them."

"And what's that?" Kian asked.

"You."

Chapter Seven

"What did he say?" I asked Garrison for the hundredth time. "Exactly?"

He sighed and buried his face in a magazine. We sat in an airport in Singapore, waiting for a connecting flight to London.

Kian had tracked us down after seeing us on the news. Garrison said he hadn't been angry when he called — just worried. Kian, it turned out, hadn't gone that far. I don't know where he was, but he was waiting for us to arrive in Ireland. Unfortunately, getting off a tiny island after a natural disaster shuts down all air traffic is difficult.

The witch doctor's sleeping draught had side effects, and I found myself dreaming of the past more vividly than ever. We were at a loss for magic after using it on the tsunami, but at least now we knew who the magicians really were. It felt better to call them by their real name: Godelan.

I still couldn't find any information about their tribe; it seemed to be as lost as ours, but I had seen them pledge themselves to our king. It had to mean something.

Since they now knew where we were, we abandoned all care with magic. Getting off the island was still difficult, though, and we tried to avoid being seen together as much as possible, travelling in pairs as siblings.

Two days after the earthquake, Seth and Moira were on a plane to Sydney, Australia. It made me uneasy. The witch doctor's words about Moira spun in my head, and I watched her while still on the island, waiting for something to happen. She remained her normal self, though — quiet and reserved.

Garrison and I followed the next day on a flight to Melbourne. From there we flew to Singapore to meet the others. Then we would fly to London and then together to Ireland.

I was growing to hate airports. Airports, airplanes, and everything that had to do with travelling, including eating the terrible food that you can only find in airports. After two straight days of stressing about what to do when we saw Kian again, as well as what Seth was up to, Garrison had had just about enough of me.

I was nervous in a very human way. Modern Gwen felt anxiety. Seth and I had never discussed what happened between us when we saved the island, and Kian had disappeared after kidnapping me. Then rescuing me. Then leaving me while I was basically comatose.

Sometimes I'd be angry, other times I worried about him. I began to bite my nails and nearly fought with Garrison when he knocked my hand out of my mouth for the tenth time on the flight to Australia. The stewardess told us to shush.

"Come on." I shook Garrison's shoulder. "Tell me again."

He sighed. "Fine. Again, he said that free from the magicians, I mean the Godelan — whatever — he realized the key to defeating them was in their past."

"But what does that *mean?*"

We had gone through this routine a dozen times. Back in the hotel, hypotheses had flown around until Garrison had ventured that maybe it was just a trick and the Godelan had Kian captive again. I wouldn't even entertain that thought. I was certain the answer had something to do with the fact that they had come to see the king. He *was* their king, once. That was all I knew.

Obviously, disobeying that king wasn't a problem, since a full-on war broke out shortly after the scene I witnessed in my memories.

Passengers walked quickly by us. Everyone was rushing. I couldn't tell if they were coming or going. Sitting was difficult; the Godelan must be doing something right now. Kian was doing something right now. Life was happening, and I was just sitting here.

Garrison slapped my hand. I hadn't even noticed I was biting my nails again.

"Stop that!"

"No," he said simply. "You've been a tightly wound ball of nerves ever since we left our tropical paradise. Tell me why."

I feigned deep thought for a second. "Maybe it has

something to do with battling a giant tsunami?" I said sarcastically.

Garrison gave me a look. "Or could it be because you're nervous about seeing the person who brought you into all of this and then left you?"

I opened and closed my mouth like a fish out of water. Somewhere, a woman announced that a flight to Seoul was boarding. I turned to the monitors to distract myself.

The news showed images of Australia. The south was practically on fire from all the bushfires during a drought, while much of the north was flooded. Another screen mentioned the earthquake and tsunami in the Pacific.

"Don't worry." Garrison tapped my knee. "There are worse things."

Garrison had been very young, only seven, when he got his memories back. For the last ten years he hadn't had Kian to show him the way — and meeting Seth was a chance encounter.

Kian had said the magic would arise for each of us at different times, though he certainly did his part in helping me along. He found me first because I had used magic during an earthquake in San Francisco, before I even knew what I was capable of. I might have been more powerful, but Garrison had been the first, and he had been living with painful memories for a decade.

In our past, he was a true warrior. It was all he had ever known. Seth told me once that Garrison remembered having a family that was killed during all the fighting between tribes, but the memories we had gotten back in England focused only on our last days. I hadn't even thought about the fact that reliving his entire past life from the sleeping potion might not have been a happy experience.

"Did more memories make things worse?" I felt guilty for not asking before.

"No," Garrison replied simply. "The life I lived wasn't awesome before, you know that. But seeing the whole picture and piecing some things together is helpful. I got some good to go with the bad."

Another few hours passed before we saw that Seth and Moira's flight had arrived. Moving through the airport like well-travelled experts, we found the arrival gate. I almost laughed when I saw their faces. I had never seen a better illustration of the word "surly."

Seth came to envelop both Garrison and me in a hug. We got one arm each. Moira's smile was strained.

"How long before our next flight?" she asked. She rarely offered any small talk.

"Four hours," Garrison replied. "Why?"

"Let's get to our gate," she said simply, leading the way.

Garrison followed her, though he managed to throw a confused look back toward Seth and me.

Seth sighed. "I'm hungry."

He headed directly for the first shop.

"So your flight was fun?" I asked mockingly.

"She's been like that since we left," he said. It only took him an instant to pick out some snacks, and we got in line behind an elderly couple. "I don't remember her being so ... cocky."

"Cocky?" I asked.

"She's using magic on everyone and everything," Seth explained. "It's unnecessary."

"Well, do something about it," I suggested.

"Why me?"

I shrugged. "She was your wife," I tried.

Seth gave me a look to suggest my argument was ridiculous. "Yeah, I don't think that matters very much anymore."

The couple in front of us turned slightly at his words. I guessed they spoke English and were confused by our conversation.

The cashier was taking forever to explain to a man why he couldn't use his own country's currency. I was too familiar with this situation. Too accustomed to how airports work. It seemed like a lifetime ago that I was excited and terrified to take my first trip with Kian.

"You know," I mused, "you and Moira could pass for brother and sister."

"Remember those two women we saw?" Seth asked. "One of them was my mother, and I think her sister was Moira's."

"Really?"

"Pretty sure."

"But," I put the pieces together, "that would make you and Moira first cousins."

Now the couple in front of us really did turn around to give us an even more disapproving look. Luckily, it was their turn just then. They paid for their magazines and left, eyeing us the whole way.

Seth and I laughed as we stepped up to the cashier. These moments where we got to enjoy our special circumstances and have fun like regular teenagers were rare. I stared at his smiling face as he paid. He happened to turn while I was still looking.

"Gwen?"

To keep him from seeing the blush spreading over my face, I turned and led the way back into the terminal.

Was it my past life enjoying his company so much, or were my feelings for him actually growing? It was a tough call. I used the silence while he ate to try to figure it out, but I couldn't find any trace of the old memories, just the new sight of Seth smiling. It made my heart beat a little faster. *Huh.*

"So you married your cousin?" I said aloud as we strolled back to Garrison and Moira.

Seth looked at me knowingly. "I think we both know it wasn't by choice."

"But why would your father want you to marry into your own family?" I asked.

Seth brought his hand to his chin in a mock pondering gesture. "Maybe to keep magic in the family?" he guessed with a smirk.

"Then why didn't you marry me?" The question caught him off guard.

Seth stopped, staring straight ahead for several moments, until I was beginning to wonder if I should remind him I was still there. While we had our memories back, some of the finer details of choices in our past were lost to time. We might never know.

"I'm not sure why I didn't marry you," Seth said

finally. Unexpectedly, he took my hands in his. "But I'm sure I would have. Maybe it was tradition, or some kind of exchange. It doesn't matter. I know that it's you I always wanted to be with. You bring out the magic in me. You were my first memory."

"And you were mine," I found myself saying. Who was that girl swooning in the middle of the airport? Was that me? Falling for what my past life had wanted the whole time? I checked myself, casually trying to pull my hands out of his grasp.

The fact that I was doing exactly what the past me wanted made me nervous and suspicious. *Or,* the sensible side said in my head, *maybe Kian left you and you're actually going for someone you know you can trust and love.* Right. Or that.

Either way, I was beginning to see why Moira had been so angry in her past and why those emotions had carried over. Seth could speak with such certainty that his wife would no doubt mind. Seeing us together now would have brought up those feelings all over again. Renewed guilt started to bubble up inside me. Even if Seth didn't feel it, I still did.

We got back to the gate to find Garrison sitting alone, long legs stretched out in front of him, arms crossed across his chest and his head thrown back. I was always amazed at how he could sleep anywhere.

Seth sat down next to him and slapped him across the face with a chocolate bar. He woke up with a start.

"Why did you do that?"

"Because lunch," Seth said, holding up the snack. "Peace offering?"

Garrison took it as I looked around.

"Where's Moira?" I asked.

"Restroom."

I made my way over to the restroom. It was surprisingly deserted. The long row of grey stalls was empty, and Moira stood illuminated by the harsh white lights in front of the mirrors. Her long, dark hair was now a bright blond. It looked awful with her dark features.

"What are you doing?" I asked.

"We'll be harder to find if we're disguised," Moira said. "Here, look."

She grabbed my arm in a grip that was a little too rough to be friendly and pulled me over to the mirror. My hair slowly turned black, as if ink were being poured onto it from the crown of my head.

I stepped back. Perhaps it was seeing someone else work magic on me that made me so nervous, or doing it in public, but either way, Moira had completely lost her sense of discretion.

"Change it back," I said.

"Fine." Her tone implied I was overreacting. "But look."

She picked up the ends of my hair. The hair that met her fist was black, but on the other side the ends were my normal ashy blond.

"It's just an illusion," she said. "You think it's black. I can't actually make it black. Only you can actually change things." There was a hint of disappointment in her voice.

As colour drifted up my hair from her fist and turned it back to normal, I couldn't help but stare at Moira in wonder. The girl who was so scared in England now seemed gone. Maybe she'd had reason to be scared. I wasn't a big fan of this new reckless Moira.

Her own hair flowed back to its normal colour just as a woman walked in, towing her luggage. She stopped in shock when she saw the change happening.

I turned, opening my mouth to explain, but I wasn't fast enough. The woman turned and tried to backtrack out of the restroom faster than I could say anything.

"Wait!" I yelled, panic creeping up my spine.

It wouldn't take long for airport security to find us, and we had nowhere to go. She was almost at the door when Moira reached out to her and she crumpled like the life had been drained from her, much like the colour in my hair.

"What did you do?" I turned to Moira. I was trying to keep my voice low. At least the arrogance was gone from Moira's eyes. She didn't seem to have known she possessed the power to do that. She ran to the woman, turning her over carefully.

"I don't know," she said. There was a tremor in her voice. She was scared. "I just wanted her to stop."

The woman was middle-aged, and in her smart suit she looked like a business traveller. Her compact, efficient suitcase supported my theory.

"Wake her up," I told Moira sternly, though I already knew what her response would be.

"I don't know how," Moira said, tears coming to her eyes.

"What were you thinking?"

As soon as the words were out of my mouth, I realized I sounded like Kian. I knew I wasn't being constructive.

Luckily, just as we were both about to fly into a full panic, knowing someone could come in at any moment, the woman began to stir.

"Pull out her memory of you," I said to Moira.

She sat back, eyes wide. "I don't know how!" she scream-whispered.

"Try."

Moira bit her lip, leaning over the woman and shrouding her in her long, dark hair. She put her fingers to the woman's temples. As she concentrated, I considered that I had never noticed the similarities between her and Seth. They even bit their bottom lips in the same way when they were nervous or thinking.

Why hadn't Kian ever mentioned it? I supposed it wasn't in his best interest to have us making connections, seeing as his plan was to use us to get Seth back to the past. Something we knew to be impossible. After Kian left, I'd swung from angry to sympathetic and back again every hour like a pendulum.

The woman began to wake up. I looked to Moira.

"I got them," Moira said, still looking confused at her own abilities. "It's like they were just sitting at the top of her mind, so it was easy."

When the woman opened her eyes, at least she looked bewildered rather than terrified.

"What happened?" she asked.

It had only been about a minute since Moira

knocked her out, but she didn't need to know that.

"We found you unconscious here," I lied. "Are you okay?"

We helped her to stand and gather her belongings. Apart from being disoriented, she seemed fine. We helped her to her gate and left. I hoped there would not be any side effects.

Walking in silence, I could feel Moira casting nervous glances at me. Finally, she stepped in front of me as we made our way back to the others.

"Please don't tell them what happened."

I wanted to be mean to her. I wanted to tell her that it would serve her right for her arrogance and that I wouldn't keep any secrets for her. But I recognized the fear on her face.

Her past was winning. Just as I hadn't noticed how similar she was to Seth, I hadn't noticed her changing for the worse. No one had. Even Kian hadn't had time to teach her like he had us. Maybe Moira's situation was our fault.

"Why?" I asked, not wanting to show that I had already made my decision.

"I'm trying to be good, like you," Moira said. "I'm really trying."

I didn't understand why she had to try so hard and told her so.

"Well," Moira waved her arms to take in the people around us, lowering her voice, "I can do so much, and they can't. We could do anything. We're more powerful than all of their rules and … limitations. It's hard to keep myself down."

My mind raced. "You can't think like that," I told her. How far gone was she? "We're not keeping ourselves down — we're keeping ourselves human. That's the difference between us and the Godelan."

"I know," Moira said. She obviously wanted to end the conversation, but I wasn't done.

"The Godelan wanted to enslave anyone without magic," I said. "We know that now. We saw it. That's why we went to war and why we're here in the first place. Tell me you understand."

Moira paused for only a moment. "I understand. Please don't tell them."

My heart was conflicted. Unable to decide if I was making a mistake, I agreed. But as we made our way back to Seth and Garrison and pretended like nothing happened, I watched her, waiting for a sign that the Moira I had met was gone.

We finally boarded a flight to London, and the end of our journey was in sight. Just a short flight after that, and we'd have a new mess of problems to consider.

✦

I had lost a lot of my things while we travelled, and getting something warm was at the top of my list as soon as we stepped out of the airport and crammed into a little taxi in Dublin. Christmas had passed while I was still comatose somewhere in northern England, so now everyone was bracing for the end of winter and the last snow.

Even inside the car, I could see my breath. We all

huddled together. Seth and Garrison were still wearing shorts. None of us had jackets.

"Where are you coming from?" asked the taxi driver.

I barely understood him. The accents here were like English on fast-forward.

"Vacation," I replied, not wanting to get into it.

"And where are we going?" asked the driver, pulling onto the highway.

We all looked at each other. None of us had cellphones. We weren't able to look something up in the car like the rest of the world. Kian had said we could be tracked that way, but I was beginning to doubt that. The Godelan tracked our magic, not GPS. It was probably more accurate that he had wanted us to lose touch with the world at home and immerse ourselves in the past.

It seemed like at least one of us had done more of that than was ideal. I glanced at Moira. She was different, and I was worried that no amount of attention now could make up for how much of herself she'd already given over to her past, stronger self.

"Ladies? Gents?" the driver prompted.

"Can you take us to a hotel in the centre of town?" Garrison asked. He flipped through a little guidebook he had bought at the airport. "Somewhere near the universities?"

The driver agreed, and we were off.

I tapped Garrison's shoulder.

"Why universities?" I whispered.

"I think he's been looking for clues in some old

book," Garrison said. He turned back to the taxi driver. "Can you turn the heat up, please?"

The grey winter sky and cold weather weren't doing anything for my mood. After three days of travelling, all I wanted was to sleep in a real bed.

Dublin was unlike any city I had been in before. It seemed like old was mashed in with new everywhere. Glittering new glass malls stood next to old row homes where young people sat outside their windows and smoked, even in the chill air.

The city felt nicer than New York, where there were so many things going on and so much noise that it was hard to focus on anything. It was definitely a change from the south Pacific.

The taxi driver dropped us off in front of a building I'd never even know was a hotel.

We walked in, pulling torn luggage behind us and stumbling along like we were the weary undead. I didn't blame the hostess for the look she gave us, but I did nearly cry when she told us she didn't have two double rooms — only one double room and one family suite with four bedrooms.

Seth didn't check with us before going for the suite. He was just as anxious to finally be able to relax. I didn't remember the climb up to the room that morning, dumping my stuff in the main living area and promptly falling asleep on my perfectly made bed.

I only woke up with a start in the evening. The room was pitch black and I suddenly panicked that I was alone. I hadn't been alone in months. For all that

Moira and I hadn't exactly bonded on our journey, I was still missing the company.

I bolted out into the living room, where Moira sat watching TV.

"Couldn't sleep," she replied before I even said anything.

Seth and Garrison eventually emerged from their own rooms, each sleepily rubbing their eyes and yawning. My head was starting to ache and my stomach told me food would fix it.

"What's for dinner?" Seth asked.

I pulled out a tray from one of the cupboards. "Instant coffee," I replied, "or various types of sugars." Taking a look at our options, I made up my mind. "I'll go get something from outside. I need some fresh air."

My headache was growing from bad to extremely uncomfortable.

"It's freezing out," Seth told me as I put on a sweater over another sweater.

"I'll be back in a bit."

As soon as I walked out of the lobby doors, the brisk air hit me like a brick and actually made the ache worse for a few seconds. I stood and braced myself against the glass doors, but it dissipated slowly.

Taking deep breaths, the cold bit into my lungs. It would take some getting used to. It reminded me of all the things I'd like to forget, including being kidnapped and stripped down as a sacrifice for some ritual. And Kian had been the one who put me there. Had his guidance and his actions saved me or put my life in danger?

Lost in thought, I didn't notice where I was going. I

passed one street and then turned down another looking for a good food option. For a city centre, it had shockingly few fast food places. I was starting to get cold when I spied pizza down the street. It'd be cold when I got back, but it was still better than instant coffee.

Suddenly, someone reached out from the alleyway and grabbed me, pulling me off my feet. A mix of old and new Gwen fought as a hand was placed over my mouth. I kicked. My foot met something and my captor doubled over in pain.

I tried to claw my way free, but lo and behold, biting my nails turned out to not to have been such a good idea. After a few seconds of terrifying struggle, a pair of blue eyes looked out at me from the darkness. I stilled.

When Kian was sure I recognized him, he let go. I couldn't move. My back against the cold brick wall, I was at a loss for words.

"I deserved that," Kian said hoarsely. He limped to the side, and the light illuminated his face. He looked the same. I didn't know if I was surprised or not. After all, it had only been about two months since I saw him. His hair was a mess and he was underdressed for the weather, as usual. I guess I was too.

"What are you doing?" I asked.

"I wanted to catch you alone," he replied. I hadn't realized until that moment how much I missed his voice. "I didn't know if anyone was with you. I feel you deserve some … answers … before I meet everyone else."

"I feel that way too," I said.

Chapter Eight

The night was cold. Kian reluctantly followed Magician to a cottage just at the bottom of the hill, but it was abandoned. They rummaged inside for something that might give them a clue as to what year they had returned to the hill, but didn't find anything.

Too miserable to speak, Kian forced his legs to move forward after the man he hated, each step bringing him further into circumstances he now knew to be a mistake.

They walked until the early dawn, eventually reaching a road made of stone. Carts that moved faster than horses flew by, their lights illuminating the land around them and blinding both Kian and Magician.

"What is this place?" Kian finally asked.

"It's the same place," Magician said. "Different time."

Kian lost track of how far they walked. At one point in the night, one of the carts stopped in front of them. It made a loud noise.

"Do you want a ride or not?" a man asked them impatiently.

Both Kian and Magician jumped back, surprised to find a man inside. They ran into the woods before stopping to think about it.

"Horseless," Magician remarked. "Horses must no longer exist."

They made it to a large cabin illuminated by bright lights. It appeared to be some kind of dining hall, with many carts stopped outside. Dozens of people sat at small tables inside. Kian observed them through the windows while Magician examined each light closely, remarking how there appeared to be no fire.

"This won't do," Magician said more to himself than to Kian. "I am completely lost in this world. People seem to move faster. We will never succeed if we move at the pace of our past."

Kian's heart sank even further when, instead of entering through the front door of the cabin and indulging in some of the food Kian had spied on plates, Magician walked around to the back. There, a sour smell and huge dirty buckets littered the back wall of the cabin.

A man emptied the garbage into a larger bin. He wore an apron and thin gloves. Magician moved toward him.

"What are you doing?" Kian asked.

"Getting an advantage," Magician replied.

As light from the cabin fell onto the man's face, Kian realized he was young, probably younger than him. He appeared to have something inside his ears;

two long wires ran down from either side of his head and into his pocket. He didn't hear Magician approach quickly from behind.

Magician seized the man's temples, and he froze. Kian knew enough to realize Magician was taking his memories of this world. A minute passed, then two. Magician still gripped the man's head until his eyes began to flutter.

This time Kian couldn't stand by. He rushed forward and pulled at Magician's arms.

"Get off him," he yelled. "You're killing him."

"So?"

"You have what you need," Kian said. "Let go."

Magician was weaker in this world. His magic didn't allow him to both get rid of Kian and someone else at the same time, as he had in the past. Kian felt him falter, and he released the man, who toppled to the ground, unconscious.

Kian bent down to make sure he was breathing. He was alive, but he would be missing much of his past. Magician recovered quickly.

"Fine," he said. "Let's go."

Magician first took Kian to a house in the nearby village. When he was sure no one was home, he used his magic on the door and they walked inside. Kian couldn't make sense of the furnishings and all of the items he couldn't even begin to name. There were even carpets on the floors, and plenty of chairs throughout the two-storey home.

"Do kings live here?" he asked Magician.

The man laughed. "You have much to learn,"

he said, as if he had always known the ways of this world. He took Kian to a closet in a room with a very comfortable-looking bed. Kian longed to lie down on it and sleep away his anguish.

Kian was outfitted with a new set of clothes that felt completely foreign to him. They were much more comfortable, and the softness felt luxurious under his fingertips, but everything was so thin and light. It would take him a while to get used to it. Downstairs, Magician took two coats from another closet.

"Aren't you going to change?" Kian asked, motioning to Magician's robes. The man simply put on the coat overtop.

"I will always wear the robes of my people," he said. "One day they will be as feared and respected here as they were in our time."

He lifted his sleeve and took out a sharp knife he had gotten from the kitchen. Turning his hand palm up, he cut until blood ran from his wrist down to his forearm. And as it did, veins, nerves, and the blood mixed to form a map.

"What's happening?" Kian asked.

"I'm being shown the magic," Magician said, obsessively following each new scrawl on his forearm.

He looked like he was reading every single line, then nodded with his mouth open, as if he understood it all. Finally, when it faded and only the blood remained, he lowered his sleeve and looked to Kian.

"We're going to cross the ocean," he said.

"And find my kind?" Kian asked hopefully.

"Eventually," Magician replied. "Someone is just

beginning to collect their magic. But it is weak. We will need to wait for something stronger to link us to the Riada warriors."

"Well, how long will that take?" Kian asked.

Magician's menacing look implied what Kian could have guessed: he didn't know.

"What do we do now?" Kian asked.

"We find my brothers," Magician said. "We are in luck. Since your kind is just waking up, it appears mine are already powerful."

✦

Kian didn't question Magician throughout much of their journey. The world of the future was incredibly frightening. Magician had been right. Things moved faster, and people travelled farther. Kian received so many scares that his heart felt tired and ached, though he wasn't sure if it was his regret that caused the pain or the stress of being in this strange new world.

He tried at first to take in as much as he could so that one day he might escape Magician and warn the Riada. But no matter what he did, he seemed to do it wrong.

The future's food did help to restore some of his energy, however. It was rich and plentiful. Though it made no sense to him, he found himself able to read the symbols and speak the language of the people living in this land. When he first saw the date on the boxes with moving images, he grew concerned.

"This can't be right," he said to Magician. "The

number of the year. It is too big. There are four numbers."

Magician had many of the answers, but not all of them. He observed the date on the box for a while but shrugged it off.

"We have no idea how they count time," he said. "The only way to know for sure how long has passed is to find when our time occurred."

Everywhere they travelled, people gave them strange looks. Magician refused to alter his appearance or change his clothes. And after a while of seemingly getting everything wrong, Kian began to shut down and just stop trying. It was all just too hard.

Magician used his magic only when he had to, but those times were frequent. They didn't have any money or identities in this world, but with magic they managed to cross the ocean in a large machine made of metal that moved faster than Kian could make sense of. Even with Magician's new memories and knowledge, he too seemed to have a hard time accepting it, calling the airplane a metal tomb. Kian spent the journey bracing himself against the plane slamming into the edge of the world, but it never happened.

Eventually, after seeing so many things that frightened and confused him, Kian set foot in a new country.

The name of the country, the United States of America, made him think. He couldn't figure out if it was a name or a declaration. Either way, no one smiled at the airport and people generally seemed to be stern.

He and Magician lined up to wait for a man in one of the carts that would take them where they needed to go. Kian took a deep breath as they climbed in and the man behind the wheel took them down another stone road at a terrifying speed.

"What happens," Magician asked from the front seat, "if you are travelling this quickly and hit another *car*?"

The driver looked at him as if he had grown horns. "You die."

Kian grabbed the back seat. It seemed like a big risk just to get somewhere faster.

As though giving a cue for Magician not to ask any more questions, the driver turned a knob near his wheel and a voice filled the car, talking quickly about a storm that was approaching the area called District of Columbia. Kian looked out the window to find the report accurate. Dark clouds approached.

He was more than glad to finally climb out of the car. The street they found themselves on was strewn with dead leaves and lined with bare trees, more cars, and brick houses.

Even to Kian the houses appeared wealthy. A few people walked down the stone walkway lining the street. They were tethered to dogs, and it looked as if the dogs were leading them somewhere. Kian was trying to figure this out when Magician pointed to a particularly large house.

"It is that one," he said.

If he was nervous, he didn't show it.

Kian had known Magician long enough to know he would always feign confidence. Still, he had figured out what truly happened. The evil man who had tricked him into coming to the future with him, all so that he could steal the magic from the champions of the Riada, had abandoned his fellow Godelan so that he could live.

Magician tapped three times on the door. Some time passed. Just as he was about to tap again, the door opened and they stood face to face with a man dressed all in grey. His black hair had flecks of grey and his eyes were like molten silver. The expression on his face went from curious to murderous in an instant.

Before Magician could speak, the man extended a hand and Magician grabbed for his throat, choking and gasping for air, much like he had done to Adar. Kian stood, frozen, unsure what to do. If this man killed Magician, perhaps he could find the others on his own.

"Wait," Magician croaked.

The man didn't relent. He tilted his head to the side as veins throbbed in his neck with the power he used.

"So you found us, coward," he said in a low, dangerous tone.

"They're here," Magician managed.

Uncertainly flashed in the eyes of the man at the door. "Who?"

Magician motioned to his throat. He couldn't speak. The man opened his fist just a little bit, and Magician sucked in deep breaths.

"Who?" he repeated.

"The Riada seven," gasped Magician. "They followed you. Used the same ritual. Were ... reborn."

The man narrowed his eyes. Kian could see him

considering Magician's words. Being untrustworthy was obviously not a quality he had developed recently.

"Where are they?" the man asked.

Magician rubbed his throat, taking breaths that looked painful. "I don't know," he said, "but he can find them."

Magician pointed to Kian, whose heart sank. This was it. The last shackles of his terrible mistake were fastened. Magician had revealed his secret to the Godelan, whom the seven had died to get rid of. Now he had no choice. He had to go along with it if he ever hoped to find his brother, and maybe somehow he would find a way to warn them.

The man at the door looked at Kian as if seeing him for the first time. His thin mouth curved into a smile, but it only made him look even more dangerous. He turned his gaze back to Magician, where it lingered between distaste and contempt.

"Come in."

Kian and Magician were led inside the home, where large chandeliers floated above the stairs, and this man, the former Godel, appeared to live in luxury. He motioned to a plush couch where they sat while he spoke into a small box, telling someone else to come to his house. He then poured brown liquid from a decanter into a clear cup.

Kian observed the craftsmanship of the glass. He had never seen such careful and fine work. So much of the modern world's innovations had simply flown by him too quickly for him to notice. He stopped when he saw the man looking.

"You are new, aren't you?" he asked Kian. It was a rhetorical question. He didn't wait to hear the answer. "So the coward is telling the truth. You can recognize them. What is your name?"

"Kian."

The man's eyes widened, and he turned to Magician.

"Prince Kian!" he told Magician, as if the other man didn't know it already. "Well, congratulations. Whatever scam you thought up to get him here must have been good." He turned back to Kian. "You may call me Stone," the man said. "My name in this world is Frederick Stone."

Kian wondered if he had chosen that name for his apparent love of grey.

"How did you get here?" Stone asked Magician.

Kian quickly began to realize that as confident as Magician appeared, he had been the least powerful of the three Godels who worked magic. Stone spoke to him with such contempt that it was becoming clear why Magician had refused to take off the robe that identified him as powerful.

Kian listened, staring into his cup of strong liquid and biting the inside of his cheek until it bled. Magician explained everything that had happened, repeating some parts twice. He told Stone about how he had found Kian in the forest and what kind of deal they had struck.

Stone glanced at Kian but didn't say anything about the Riada.

Kian began to realize this man was not like

Magician. He was less predictable and harder to read, which made him even more dangerous. As Magician spoke, there came another knock on the door. Stone disappeared to answer it and came back with another man. This one rushed in and stared at Magician and Kian almost greedily.

"So it is true!" he exclaimed. He was slightly taller than Stone, though still shorter than Magician. His hair was beginning to thin, but he wore the same type of clothing as Stone, a jacket and pants of the same shiny grey over a white shirt.

"Donald," Stone said, "this is Kian. You remember the youngest son of the high king, all grown up?"

The man named Donald gave a slight bow. Kian couldn't tell if it was sarcastic.

"Hello," he said formally. "I'm Donald Leigh. I think you have a story I should hear."

Kian was about to reply that he didn't, but Stone pressed Magician to begin the story anew. And so Kian had his failures retold all over again. When Magician was done for the second time, he huffed.

"Now will someone please tell me how much time has passed?" he asked.

Stone and Donald looked at each other.

"About two thousand years," Stone said finally.

Both Magician and Kian sat back in awe. The ritual had been a lot more powerful than either of them had suspected.

"What is left of our people?" asked Magician.

"Nothing," Donald replied, anger rising in his voice. Stone flashed him a warning glance.

"There is nothing of the Godelan?" asked Magician, as if to make sure he understood correctly.

"Worse," Stone replied. "There is nothing of any of the tribes. Not the Godelan, not the Riada, and not anyone else."

"What happened?"

"Two thousand years," replied Stone as if it was obvious.

"No," Donald cut in. "It was the Romans. They conquered all civilizations in the Western world, erased them, and became the world of today. At least the wealthy world."

Kian was anxious to cut in and ask how big the world truly was, but the man named Donald seemed erratic and spoke angrily. Kian decided he would tread lightly around this one, and bide his time. While he was sure that Stone was dangerous, Donald went from calm to raging in a breath. If anyone would kill first and ask questions later, it would be him.

"For years," Donald continued, "we wondered how the Romans had defeated the Riada and their warriors. But if what you say is true, if they followed us into death rather than defend our people, the seven are to blame. They are not only responsible for our deaths, but for the Roman victory."

Kian hated himself for remaining quiet. He listened to the three men discuss their past, nursing his drink and feeling as if he was falling further and further away from his goal. He was treading deep in the hate and evil that the Godelan caused.

These three men had once been loyal to his father

but wanted power. He could only listen in horror as they spoke about gaining magic from people's souls and their failed experiments with raising the dead. It was a while before they remembered him again.

"So, Kian," Stone said, "how will you help us find the seven warriors?"

He said it while resting on the arm of the sofa as if he was asking about the weather. Kian was stunned into silence. He had no answer. Luckily, Magician answered for him.

"We don't know what form they are in," he said. "Or where they are. All we know is that he can recognize them. When the time will come for any one of them to use enough magic to trace, I can use the spell I used to find you and send Kian to fetch them."

"Why don't we go ourselves and destroy them?" Donald asked.

As Stone sighed his disappointment with Donald's foolishness, Kian realized just how dangerous he was.

"Because," Magician said, "they may recognize us and use magic against us. If they have their full memories, they'll be stronger than us."

"Stronger than you, maybe," Donald retorted. "We've been harnessing the magic of the earth for as long as we've been here, pulling up every magical root we can find."

Magician seemed confused. "Why?"

"Our revenge." Donald waved his hands as if revenge was an item sitting in the living room with them. "The Romans destroyed one thousand years of our people. We will destroy two thousand of theirs. We can use the earth magic to create enough chaos to gain control — and with the magic of the seven, the destruction will be swift and complete. In that chaos, all the other truths of this world will fall away until only magic will be powerful. And we will be the only ones with it."

"You want to rule the world?" Magician asked. His brows were furrowed. Kian supposed Magician had wanted something similar, but the Earth was much bigger now than it was in their time.

Magician was having trouble imagining it.

"Why not?" asked Donald. "When everything they count on has been destroyed, we can have our own time again."

"That's insane," Kian said. The words tumbled out of his mouth of their own accord. All three men, including Stone, who had been silent, turned to him.

"No," Stone said. "It is unfinished business. But Donald is being a little dramatic. We won't destroy the world and send it back into pre-history. We also won't need to kill your kind."

"You won't?" Kian asked. He looked skeptically at Magician, who was still trying to play catch-up as best he could.

"No," said Stone. "I, unlike my brethren, think in the long term. And in the long term, by the time we're able to find any of the seven, they will be starting to gain magic. Our old friend is right — they will be stronger than us if they get everything back. But if the process takes time, we can nurture them, provoke them to ignite the magic, and when they are strong again, we will take it."

Kian knew he would regret asking, but he had to know. "How?"

"The same way we once did it," Stone said.

Kian didn't know what this was but didn't want to ask either. When Stone saw uncertainty playing across his face, he shrugged. "It's either take their magic or kill them. Which would you rather us do?"

Kian squeezed his fist together until the nails were biting into his palm. "And then I can have my brother?"

"Yes," Magician said.

"And we can go home?"

"Yes," Magician repeated.

The other two exchanged a glance, and for a moment Kian was worried they would interject and change the agreement. He was hardly in a position to bargain. But they nodded.

As the magicians talked late into the night, Kian was excused to wander the house and make his way to the guest bedroom. Despite the relative freedom, he reminded himself he was a prisoner. This was not the deal he had agreed to.

The room was warm and the bed was the most comfortable thing he had ever lain on. He was exhausted, both physically and mentally, and he longed for sleep as an escape from his constant misery. He had joined the enemy and betrayed his tribe.

Kian lay on his back, eyes wide open. He could only stare at the ceiling and replay all of his mistakes over and over.

Finally, he couldn't stand it. He opened the window until the room became freezing cold and lay on the floor next to the bed. He would not allow himself to sink into the luxury they offered him. It came at a terrible price.

Kian lay on the hardwood and repeated to himself, over and over again, that he was a prisoner, that his people were in grave danger, and that he would always try to help them in any way he could. No matter how long it took.

After another few hours of shivering on the floor, sleep still eluded him. He decided to wander the house again. Perhaps he would find something to offer him a way out of this mess.

The house was old and every stair creaked. Kian tiptoed as much as he could, but he knew nothing about being quiet in a modern house. He paced and stopped to listen, just as he had while he hunted in the forest.

The first room he came to was where Stone must have written letters since there were paper and books everywhere. A wide table with only one chair behind it held more information than Kian could take in. A window showed the city below. Taking in the expanse, Kian couldn't imagine how many people occupied the thousands of lights he could see in the distance.

Next, he found the kitchen. He walked to the end of the long room, where several metal boxes hummed and showed the time. He briefly wondered why people here needed so many reminders about the time. Probably because they were busy; that was why they moved so quickly.

Kian had just decided there was nothing here for

him when he passed a metal bar hanging on the wall. The bar had several large knives stuck to it as if by magic. The knives ranged from long to wide, but they all looked deadly sharp.

Kian tried to see how firmly affixed they were to the bar and was surprised when one came off with ease. He felt the weight. It was heavy. He ran his thumb along the end and a thin line of blood appeared. He ignored the searing pain. His mind didn't have time for pain. Kian considered his options.

He could find all three men and stab them in the heart. He would have lost his tribe but at least rid the world of the Godelan once and for all and spared the seven. But Kian realized there was no way he would have the time to kill all of them before one would overpower him with magic. So he could try to kill one — but then he'd be dead and the other two would still be after the seven. They'd probably be even crueller to them, especially his brother, in revenge for Kian's actions.

Another option occurred to him: he could kill himself. He would be free from his misery, and it would be a start in attempting to atone for leaving his tribe and the death of Adar. He would also then never help the Godelan find any of his people, which would give them a chance to develop their memories and full magic before being found.

Kian brought the blade up to his neck and felt the pinch as it met skin. A hundred different scenarios ran through his head as he tried to reason that the seven, including his brother, would be better off if he wasn't in their way. However, a small voice of reason told him otherwise.

His conscience told him that to live and search for them would be better atonement than death for his betrayal of the Riada. It also told him that alive he could try to help the seven and prepare them, even if it had to be under the watchful eye of the Godelan. Without him, they could be caught unaware, and then nothing would protect them.

Slowly, he put the knife back onto the metal bar and let out a deep breath, continuing his search of the house.

Voices came from a room at the back, closed off from the hall by a set of double doors. Kian crept to it, listening. The Godelan reminiscing of their pasts and horrible deeds hadn't interested Kian in the least; in fact, it had made him feel even worse. Now, however, they spoke of the seven.

The three Godels spoke of their vulnerability, and Kian heard Stone thank Magician for the warning. Their voices were too muffled for Kian to hear more. He snuck closer and pushed lightly on one of the double doors, hoping it would not make a sound.

He was lucky. It swung open just enough for him to hear and peek through. His heart raced.

The three men ignored the fire burning in the hearth and instead had emptied a bin and lit another fire in it. Each one held a small wooden box open in front of him. Kian recognized the three boxes as some of the trinkets Magician had brought with him. He wondered how many other valuable things Magician had played off as worthless artifacts during Kian's time with him.

"We have to get rid of them," Stone said. "Now that we know the seven are here, we cannot risk keeping them." He turned to Magician. "Should we be worried about the boy?"

"He is powerless," Magician replied. "He can do nothing."

Kian's mind backtracked through everything he had heard that night, but he couldn't imagine what the three were trying to hide. He resolved to find out what was inside those boxes.

"Once we do this," Magician warned, "there is no going back."

Donald let out a short, mirthless laugh. "I think we've already made those commitments," he said. "Let's get this done."

As if on cue, all three dumped the contents of their boxes into the fire. But even as the boxes were turned upside down, nothing fell out of them. Some specks of dirt went into the fire, but otherwise they were empty.

Still, the fire roared to life and the house began to shake. Kian tumbled to the side, losing his footing, but the noise of the old house settling was enough to keep him hidden. Suddenly a sound like all the air being sucked out of the room forced him closer to the door but also froze him in place.

The Godelan were immobilized. Kian scolded himself for leaving the knife in the kitchen. If he had kept it, he could have killed them all now. Instead he was glued to the gap between the doors, watching. Would the spell kill them?

It gripped them for over a minute before Kian saw the first signs of anything taking place. Slowly, painfully, shadows seemed to be torn away from the men and sucked into the little wooden box each of them carried. As the last of the shadow was encased, the lids snapped shut. The fire immediately sank back to normal and the three emerged from their strange state, gasping for air and gripping their chests.

"That was more painful than I thought it would be," Donald admitted. "I feel strange."

"Of course you do," Stone told him, gripping his own box with both hands close to his heart. "There's a part of you missing."

"What shall we do with them?" Magician asked.

"Hide them," Stone said.

He turned toward the door and Kian had no choice but to bolt into another room, around the kitchen, and up the stairs to the bedroom. He ran as quickly and quietly as he could, all the while feeling the Godelan were going to catch him at any moment.

Kian closed the door to his bedroom just as one of them came up the stairs. He lay on the cold floor again, shivering and listening intently but pretending to be asleep.

A Godel walked up to his door.

Kian thought his heart would break free from his ribcage as it pounded in his chest. Then the Godel walked away, sufficiently convinced that Kian was asleep. He let out a deep breath.

Kian knew that everything from this moment on would be difficult. He was in the company of evil men, and they would probably lie to him. They might be kind to him, making him comfortable, but only to fool him. They would try to win him over, or they might be cruel. But it was all for the sake of their own twisted plans.

He knew what he had seen tonight was only a small example of what they were capable of, and lacking magic, he could do nothing about it. But in this world, there were seven people who could. And no matter what deal he had made with Magician, he would do his best to find these people and prepare them to win.

Chapter Nine

We shivered in the alleyway in silence until Kian limped to some crates stacked outside a door. He sat heavily, nursing his knee.

I took a few hesitant steps forward, afraid to get too close but not wanting to seem distant. Despite all the confusion over the last few months, I was very happy to see him. I just couldn't let myself show it. I couldn't let him think he was off the hook for what he had done. I had forgiven him in the heat of the moment, but the consequences of his actions still followed us.

I had spent weeks wondering what my life would have been like without him. Would I be graduating this year? Or would the seven of us have found each other already? Or would I be long dead, soul and magic enslaved to the Godelan?

I crossed my arms over my body as I shivered in the cold.

"Why aren't you wearing a jacket?" Kian asked.

The concern in his voice nearly made me smile. Nearly.

"I think you owe me an explanation," I said. I could tell he was stalling.

He nodded, staring at the ground and running a hand through his hair. I knew his fidgets. I knew he was searching for the right words, so I just waited quietly in the cold.

"I was so young," Kian said finally, "and so stupid when all of this happened."

I wanted to comfort him but kept my distance. Even after I'd forgiven him, he had left.

"I was seven years old when my brother died," Kian started. "Eight years old when my father died. Nine years old when my mother died. And ten years old when the Romans made our tribe leave our home. I lived for years knowing that if I could only have been born like him, I could have saved everyone. But I wasn't."

He was being earnest, and I was seeing the most honest side of him. Tears came to my eyes as I imagined what the life we left behind must have been like for everyone else. When we died, we took hope with us.

"I've had a lot of time to myself recently," Kian continued, "to think about what I did and why I did it. It was wrong. And I told myself it was right for a very long time. I told myself it was right even when I had to give you up. And you made me realize I had been lying to myself."

I tried to cut in, to ask him what he was talking about, but he went on.

"After you showed me more kindness than I had ever shown you," he said, "after you managed somehow to forgive me and then save my life when they came, I couldn't face you without offering what I had initially promised — my help."

There was a lump in my throat that I tried to will away.

"Why didn't you wait until I woke up?" I asked.

Kian shrugged, smiling slightly. "I figured that when you came to your senses, after all the trouble I had caused you, you wouldn't want to talk to me. I wanted to do something to at least start to make up for things. And I think I found something. I think I can actually help to end what I started."

I had too many questions for the conversation to move forward.

"You need to start from the beginning," I told him. "What is it that you did?"

"It's a long story," Kian replied. "And it's cold. Can I tell you about it somewhere more comfortable?"

I reluctantly agreed. My emotions were still a mess, but I was freezing, so I helped him to limp to a nearby coffee shop. I had kicked Kian in the knee, and though I knew he was trying to put on a brave face, it must have been painful. I apologized, but he only brushed it away.

"Like I said, I deserve it," he said, smiling.

"You're happy about this?"

"It's nice to be near you," he replied.

I didn't know what to do with that so I just ignored it completely.

"Why didn't you just say hi? Why did you have to grab me like that?" I asked.

Kian actually laughed. "I figured if you saw me and had time to think about it, you might have blasted me with magic or something."

That brought to mind another important issue.

"You're completely magicless now," I said.

He nodded. "Completely. Luckily, I've been stealing from the magicians for years. Saving for a situation such as this one and hiding the money in various accounts."

So he had known that one day he would betray them.

"We know who they are now," I said. "We know they're Godels."

Kian's eyebrows shot up. I could tell he wanted to ask me how we knew that and pose a hundred different questions, but as soon as he opened his mouth, he appeared to remember his promise. "After my story," he said, "I'd like to hear yours."

"Agreed."

The coffee shop was warm, cozy, and luckily nearly empty. I paid for a hot chocolate to warm up and we found the table farthest away from everyone else.

"Remember," Kian said, "I told you it's a long story."

I didn't know how much time passed as he finally told me the truth — all of it. And he certainly didn't spare himself. He told me about how helpless he had felt, how his uncle had wanted him to marry and produce more warriors, how the Romans were gaining power and the situation was on the brink of war all the time.

He told me how he first met the man I had called Third Magician, and how he had used Kian to get to this world.

As Kian talked, tears shone in his eyes and his voice quavered. I couldn't imagine the life he had lived, and for the first time I understood what had driven him to do what he did. His actions during the entire time I had known him took on a new light. I began to appreciate how I must have confused him and frustrated his plans. When he finished, I took his hand again.

"Ten years?" I asked. "You've been with the Godelan for ten years?"

He nodded. "On and off. Fruitless searches led me away, but I would always return like to a tether. Or like a dog on a leash."

"Don't say that," I told him. "You were trapped for so long."

"And now I'm not," he said. "Thanks to you. And I've had time to finally discover what happened to my people, and to the Romans."

"And?"

Kian shrugged. "Time did what no man's army could do. Erased all of it. It's all gone."

I thought back to ten years ago. I was seven years old. Nearly eight. I was living in San Francisco with my parents, whom I was now really starting to miss.

"Hey!" I suddenly realized something. "You said you came here ten years ago?"

"Yes."

"It must have been Garrison that brought you here. He started getting his memories at seven." I thought about it some more. "If it wasn't for him, you might not have shown up until we were all grown up. Until I had to stop that earthquake at home."

"I guess so," Kian said thoughtfully. Then he looked up from the table as if he was bracing himself for bad news. "So what do you think, now that you know what happened?"

It would be premature to decide anything, though I was doing my best to put my own biased feelings aside and see things from his perspective. He might have drastically changed my life, but I had changed his as well.

"I think the truth helps," I said. "It's a start."

Kian nodded. "So will you tell me your story?"

Committing to my promise, I delved into what we had done upon leaving England, leaving out all the parts about my moodiness over his departure. I told him how we got to the islands just to hide, and how fear had blocked off our magic.

We had stifled ourselves to the point of regressing to the people we were before Kian found us, but with the knowledge that we could be so much more.

I told him about the witch doctor and the sleeping potion. Kian gripped my hand harder and interrupted several times during this part of my story, turning into his old protective self. His questions seemed to involve repeating exactly what I had just said, as if he had misheard.

"You went into the jungle with strangers leading you somewhere?" he asked, his voice rising.

"Yes," I told him, and went on with my story.

"You drank a sleeping potion?" he asked a few minutes later, voice getting even louder.

"Yes," I said again.

"Those have terrible consequences, Gwen! Have you had any lasting effects?"

I stopped missing the overprotective Kian as soon as I realized he was back.

"A few headaches, but I'm fine. We're all fine," I reassured him, leaving out the vivid dreams of the past.

At least he quieted while I tried to recount as much of my past life as I could remember living through. And when he heard the sleeping potion had worked and worn off quickly, he relaxed a bit — until I told him about the goddess woman who appeared in the jungle.

"You spoke with one of their gods?" Kian asked loudly.

"Hush," I told him, looking around at the few other customers in the shop. "Yes."

When I got to the part about the earthquakes and tsunami, he kept interjecting that he should have been there. My first reaction was to remind him he had no magic and he therefore couldn't have helped, but I changed my mind and simply told him it had worked out fine. I didn't mention anything about how I had become strong enough nor about my connecting to Seth.

"I saw you on the news," Kian said, showing me the first smile since I started my story. "They called you daredevils. Said you were the luckiest people on Earth."

Eventually, we knew we had to go and meet the

others. Kian had made things as right with me as he could, given the circumstances, but I knew why he was procrastinating.

"Relax," I told him. "The others will understand. Seth will understand."

Kian nodded, and I slowly helped him limp back to the hotel.

Though it was a cold winter night, supporting his weight on my shoulders all the way back to the hotel left me breathless. I seriously regretted kicking him, and not just because of the pain he was in.

The lobby was deserted, so at least I was spared having to explain whom I was bringing up. We stepped into the tiny elevator and made it up to our floor, where strange noises made us both stop and listen. My stomach dropped to my feet. It sounded like a fight.

From behind the double doors to our suite, something scratched across the floor. A glass item shattered and a thud sounded like someone was pushed into something. Only one explanation came to mind — the Godels must have found them.

My heart beat so quickly that it ached for my friends as we rushed to the door.

"Wait here," I told Kian, trying to lean him against a wall.

"No way."

I didn't have time to argue. I threw open the doors and rushed in. But when we saw the intruders, we both tried to backpedal so quickly, I nearly toppled to the floor with Kian in tow. I struggled to make sense of what I was seeing.

Our hotel room was completely trashed. Chairs and the table were smashed into kindling, cushions had been stabbed, and the stuffing littered the floor. One sofa was turned over. The remains of broken plates littered the floor and random cutlery was thrown around the room. Seth, Garrison, and Moira were backed against a wall, their hands up in surrender.

Seth saw us. "Run!" he yelled.

Too late.

Three large men turned to face us. Dressed in plain brown tunics that resembled something from our past lives, they had trodded mud all over the floor from their big boots. Their faces and heads showed deep gashes, as did their arms. In fact, the wounds smelled putrid and looked torn, as if animals had been picking at them.

Still, the most shocking thing was the random assortment of improvised weapons sticking out of them at all angles. Forks, knives, scissors, and other random sharp things stuck out everywhere. My friends had put up a fight. I spotted heavy candlesticks and picture frames on the ground, blood around the edges.

The men advanced. I hopped across the overturned couch, but Kian couldn't move. One of the men clumsily stumbled toward him as I dodged another, took a mirror off the wall and doubled back to smash it across the head of the man reaching for Kian's throat. The glass shattered and cut my hands. Garrison leapt at the third man and pinned him to the ground.

"Ugh, he stinks!"

For a second, I thought it had worked. The man

who had reached for Kian stumbled forward and collapsed across him. Kian was pinned to the floor, his bad leg rendering him helpless. At least the body on top of him went still. But after a moment, the zombie-like man woke up again and turned to me, angrier than ever.

"What are these things?" I yelled to no one in particular.

In the melee, Seth had grabbed the arms of one of the men and pinned them while Moira tried in vain to stab him with some scissors. It would have been quite gruesome if the man had been hurt. Defying all reason, he didn't even bleed.

"Zombies!" Seth yelled.

"Not zombies," Kian corrected. He was trying to keep one off him by kicking with his good leg. "Ghosts. Gwen, I told you that sleeping potion would have side effects!"

I really didn't think this was time for I-told-you-so. Garrison danced around me, leading one of them on a chase while he thought of what to do next.

"Ghosts?" he asked nervously, continuing to run.

They did have the eerie quality similar to the time I had seen my former husband. Was one of my friends bringing them back from the past? No matter what we did, we couldn't kill them.

"Trust me," Kian grunted, stabbing a fork into the eye of his attacker. The man, or whatever he was, didn't even flinch. "They're magical. Whoever is conjuring them has to will them away."

All three of my friends paused. It was clear from

their faces that they had no idea who was doing it, just as I wouldn't have recognized my own husband if I hadn't seen him in my memories.

Having the ghosts walking around and trying to hurt us didn't leave a lot of time to think. I took a cushion and felt the fire, always burning inside of me when I had magic at my disposal, extend through my fingers and creep into the material. It was engulfed in flames in seconds.

I had meant to distract the ghosts, holding on to the cushion so as not to bring the whole hotel down. My own hands seemed immune to the flames. But my magic had the opposite effect. The ghosts didn't seem to notice, while my friends panicked even more and started to scream at me.

Something strange happened. As soon as everyone was distracted enough to think that I was going to kill them all in a fiery inferno, the ghosts simply vanished. Utensils, scissors, and other knick-knacks clattered to the floor.

I stomped on the fire I had created, and it disappeared. We all sat around in shock, gasping for breath. Moira put a hand to her chest.

"I nearly had a heart attack!" she exclaimed.

"Are you trying to burn this place to the ground?" Garrison yelled.

"Well, it worked, didn't it?" I yelled back.

"Whose memory was that?" Moira demanded.

"Yeah, who got attacked in the past by zombies?" Garrison added.

Everyone quieted as I remembered my own

encounter with the past. We each held stories inside of us, some of which we might never know. There had been important people to us in the past — some who had benefitted from our magic, and some who had been our victims.

"They weren't zombies," I said. "When I saw my past life's husband, he had a little statue sticking out of his neck — because I put it there. That was a memory that I felt guilty for. If those were ghosts, then whoever was remembering them killed them."

"I know who it was," Kian said.

He was confined to the floor but trying to clamber up. I went over to help him.

"What happened to you?" Garrison asked him.

"It's nice to see you, too." Kian gave a strained smile. "Gwen kicked me."

"Wow, Gwen," Garrison replied without skipping a beat. "I didn't know you were still so mad."

"I wasn't!" I began. I had to keep myself from launching into an argument. Instead I turned to Kian. "So who was that?"

I helped him onto the couch as he winced.

Kian turned to Seth. "Gwen told me you took a sleeping draught from a woman in order to remember your past life and gain magic."

"It was Garrison's idea," Seth said immediately.

"Of course it was," Kian replied, pursing his lips.

He was still unhappy about it, and I could tell he fought the instinct to start chastising us.

"Going so deep into your magic often has consequences," Kian said. "Just as when Gwen kept losing control and ghosts from her past that still haunt her memories began to appear. Those were yours."

"I don't remember fighting them," Seth said immediately.

"Maybe," Kian agreed, "but you did kill them."

"I don't remember that," Seth said immediately. "Why would I kill them?"

"Because they're Romans," Kian replied calmly, as if killing a Roman was a daily occurrence. "But that's how I know it was you. You spied among them. And though you've remembered a lot about your lives by now, you'll probably never remember everything."

Kian spoke as if Seth and his brother were two different people. Perhaps in his mind they were. He would have never remembered the old Seth being this age. His brother was always a man to him.

"So that was me?" Seth asked, stunned. "But I had no idea. I had no control over them."

"Neither did I when it happened to me," I told him. I was trying to be reassuring, but the memory gave me chills. "The only thing you can do is take power away from it by pushing it to the back of your mind, getting distracted, and not letting your ghosts take over. I tried to do it with magic and nearly ended up killing myself."

While everyone calmed down enough to welcome Kian back and demand his story, I began to clean. I considered whether or not to put the utensils in the dishwasher. They were clean but had technically stabbed several corpses. In the end I opted for the heavy wash.

Seth helped to bandage my hands and Moira's head. She had hit it against a picture frame when one of the ghosts threw her into it. While Kian spoke, we managed to at least pile the ruined, broken things together and sweep up the mess. The ghosts had luckily taken the mud with them when they disappeared.

The others had plenty of questions for Kian, and to his credit he answered them all as honestly as he could. When we got to the part where he grabbed me in the alley, he glossed it over and I told the others we had bumped into each other.

"What a coincidence," Moira remarked sarcastically.

I ignored her.

Having forgotten to bring food home, we ordered room service and ate on the couch, reminding me of our time in England before things got complicated.

"So the big answer," Garrison said. "What is it? How do we defeat them?"

Kian put away his plate and limped from the kitchenette to the couch. He smiled. "That can wait until tomorrow," he said. "It's late."

"Where are we going tomorrow?" Moira asked.

"The university," he replied.

"I called it!" Garrison clapped his hands. "I knew you were around there. How did you find us anyway? Do you have some kind of magic tracking us?"

Kian raised his eyebrows. "You're using my credit cards."

"Right. That."

We sat in silence for a few moments, exhaustion setting in. My palms pounded in sync with my heartbeat. The deep slices wouldn't heal quickly. I tried to send my magic through to the pain, but it only dulled somewhat.

As Moira and Garrison eventually left for bed, I was left alone with Kian and Seth.

Seth made eyes at me, wordlessly asking me to leave. I understood. He wanted some time alone with his brother, with whom he had been living but hadn't recognized. Having recently relived our past, I could only image that Seth's connection to Kian had gotten stronger. It was a strange dynamic, their roles reversed as older and younger brothers, but as I made my own way to bed, I found falling asleep was a lot easier now that we were all together again.

✦

Kian briefly showed us around Dublin in the morning and then took us to the university residence where he had been staying. My palms felt as if weeks had passed when I awoke the next morning, the cuts having turned into angry red welts. Kian still limped, but at least no more ghosts had come to bother us.

The school looked ancient and imposing. Tall stone columns were built into the façade, and dozens of windows hinted at immeasurable numbers of books.

Kian first led us to smaller houses on the grounds to pick up his things. I noticed he was travelling with a little new suitcase, except this one was bright green, unlike his old silver one.

"What?" he asked.

"Nothing." I smiled. The green was exactly like

my suitcase, which he had made fun of when we first met.

We made our way into a grand hall where open staircases led to the upper floors, each decorated with its own emblem on the bannister. Polished wood lined the walls, covered the floors, and made up the decadent frames of the oil paintings of important people.

The windows I had seen from outside allowed light to flood in and reflect off stained glass, bathing everything in a variety of colours. Still, the wood somehow seemed stifling.

Down a hall and around a corner, we finally came to a set of double doors. We weren't the only ones coming for an early morning visit. Entering the large library, we stared at the huge amount of books the university had collected. They sat atop the wooden shelves as if patiently waiting for someone to come and pick them up.

A few other people had come in with us but turned left and walked into a curtained room next to the main entrance.

"What's in there?" I asked Kian in a hushed tone. He was about to lead us in the opposite direction.

"A very famous old book," Kian replied. "It is also from our land, but compared to what we need, it's practically futuristic."

I didn't have time to wonder. Kian led us into the library, and I had to tear myself away from eyeing every single spine. I was a terrible person to bring into a library or bookstore. Not only did I have to read every single title, but I also loved to touch the books.

All the different textures, not to mention age and dust and jackets, made it an adventure. Even now I ran my hand along the shelves we walked past.

Kian came to a small section comprised of only a few books, titled *Early Celtic Mythology, Pre-Christian*. He pulled down a few books and brought them to an old table that was pushed up against a back wall. No one was in sight.

We huddled around as Kian opened the book to a page where a sketch depicted a woman lying next to a man. He pointed to it.

"Goram and Eila," he said. "Do those names sound familiar?"

We thought about it. They did. Vaguely.

"They were our gods," Kian explained. "The ones from whom you get your magic. They created the first men and women. And I found the answer to beating the Godelan in the same story I had heard since I was a child. I just hadn't made the connection."

Garrison sat. "All right," he said. "Tell us the story."

I was skeptical, but a hunch was better than nothing, and I felt us approaching another standstill in our progress in defeating the Godelan. Kian took a deep breath as if he was about to share a secret.

"Goram and Eila lived in the Otherworld with all the other gods. They were a tribe, much like our people," he began, "but they were not allowed to be together because they were both promised to someone else. So they found a new world to run away to. It became the world of mortals."

He was right. I had heard this story a hundred

times. We all had. Still, we listened intently, drawing as much of our past memories from it as possible.

"When Eila's father found their secret world," Kian continued, "he suspected why his daughter had escaped there and he began to watch it, waiting for her and Goram to appear. But Eila was much more clever than her father and knew about his plan. When she would want to be with Goram, they would disguise themselves and change into various animal forms so that they could enjoy the world they created."

Here, Kian flipped to another page with strange animal symbols that also looked vaguely familiar.

"That's why our language was often written in the shapes of animals. Each curve had a meaning to honour them," he said. "Eila's father grew more and more suspicious. One day, as she and Goram flew over their land, her father struck him down. When Goram fell to earth, he was broken into a million pieces, and that became our land. Eila's father then banished her to our world and never let her return home. Which was just as well, since she was so grief-stricken, she could never leave Goram. She stayed by his side and gave birth to the first people."

"I remember the story," I told him, "but what does that have to do with how we defeat the Godelan?"

Kian smiled. He'd been waiting for this question. This was his big reveal. "The man you call Third Magician, the man I called Magician, once told me that in fact we are all made from earth," Kian said. "We are earth before we are born and we are earth after we die. What binds us to our human selves during life is our human name."

Seth sat up quickly, as if having realized something. "Their names," he said. "We need to find out their names."

Kian broke into an even wider grin. "Exactly. Magician told me that the right person could control someone by his or her name. I figured out the right person is the High King. As their ruler, the king of kings and of our people, you can find a way to make them obedient to you as our father once did."

"They disobeyed our father," Seth reminded him.

"Because being king isn't all-binding," Kian said. "Magician once hinted that I may have power with the names, but without magic, I cannot bind them. Our father didn't have magic either. But you are the rightful High King now, and you could do it."

The magic was familiar, and somehow, though it would sound crazy to anyone else, it made perfect sense to me.

"I can't believe I didn't think of it before," Kian said. "Though you do need magic to truly wield that power. Father couldn't keep them obedient, and neither can I."

"One problem," I said. "How do we find out their names?"

"I haven't thought of that," Kian admitted. "But this is their weakness. If you find the names, you can undo them."

Chapter Ten

We stayed in Dublin for another few days researching what the libraries had to offer and cleaning up our hotel room as best we could. I dreaded finding out how much they would charge us for the damage.

Two days into our search for information on name magic, a librarian told us a library in Oxford had another text that could be useful. She warned us, however, that no one had succeeded in reading it. The strange animal symbols didn't mean anything to anyone. Hopeful that perhaps being near it or touching it would give us something, anything, to go on, we decided to give it a shot.

While Garrison was enjoying what he called time off, and Moira disappeared for hours, Seth and Kian finally got to spend time together. They were becoming brothers again, and I liked watching them becoming more reconciled with whatever mistakes had torn them apart in the past.

The downside of this was that I had a lot of alone time in huge libraries with their dusty books, reading gory myths and wondering what the Godelan had in store for us if they did happen to find us first. After all, they had tried to kill us by wiping a whole island off the map.

We weren't getting any closer to finding the other three people of our kind, and the fruitless search for the Godels' real names soon became frustrating.

I got back to the hotel after midnight the night before we were setting off for London. Our flight was the next afternoon, and I just wanted to bury my head under a pillow until we were due to leave. Finding no information about the Godelan or our own tribe, the Riada, felt like I was moving backward every day.

My head ached from straining to read old, confusing books, and my eyes were so heavy I could feel my eyelids. My feet hurt from walking down dozens of aisles of shelves and sifting through hundreds of books. I knew it was my own fault — I had thrown myself into the work. No one forced me. But I craved doing something, even if that something was, apparently, redundant.

I dropped my coat and bag on a chair in the dark and headed to my room.

"Hey!"

As my foot hit something solid, I flew forward onto my knees, nearly missing smacking my head on the coffee table. I scuffled with the thing on the floor for a few seconds until Kian turned on the light. He winced, holding his side.

"What were you doing on the floor?" I whispered angrily.

Really, I was mad at myself. I felt like my hurting him accidentally could eventually be misconstrued as bottled-up anger. Which, I was nearly sure, it wasn't.

Kian had been lying on the floor between the couch, chair, and coffee table. He had actually chosen the only part of the living room that wasn't even carpeted. The floor must have been cold and hard.

"It's more comfortable," he said quietly, still rubbing his ribs. I knew he was lying.

Things had changed since we were together the previous year. I felt more grown up — like we were equals. Now that I knew how clueless he was as a teenager brought to this world, his mystique was gone, dissolved into a kid who had been saddled with too much responsibility and tragedy and had made a mistake.

"I don't believe you," I said. "I've seen you sleep in a lot of soft beds. Why are you on the floor?"

"It reminds me of home," he said. But he phrased it more like a question.

"Nope," I said. "Try again."

Kian sighed. "I like this sometimes. I started sleeping on the floor when Magician brought me here."

"Why?" I asked, though I already knew the answer.

Kian shook his head. "I don't know."

"Yes, you do," I told him. "You're punishing yourself."

"Because I failed," he admitted. "I got too comfortable with this life — with you. I forgot how much I hated them, and I did exactly as they asked. The situation is being repaired slowly. But I can't let myself forget again."

Maybe it was because it was late and I was exhausted, or because my fruitless searches had brought up nothing and my sadness mixed with his was too much to bear, but I stepped forward until I stood directly in front of him.

It was all I could bring myself to do. I stood and waited. Slowly, hesitantly, Kian wrapped his arms around me and rested his head on top of mine. I breathed in, trying to take in this moment and make it a part of me.

"You're not going to do it again," I said into his neck. "You'll never forget who you are, and you won't give up on us. After all, we need you."

I felt him take a deep breath and nod.

"How long have you been sleeping on the ground?"

Kian, still hugging me, shrugged. "Since I left you," he whispered.

"Come on," I said, pulling away.

I took his hand and headed to my room. In hindsight, exhaustion made me braver than I ever could be during a reasonable hour.

I was surprised he didn't ask questions, protest, or do anything to stop me. We seemed to understand each other. Having lost his shell-like exterior that he'd worn on and off since I met him, Kian was human and vulnerable.

He followed me into the room. I was too tired to do anything but kick off my shoes and climb under the covers. Kian stood over the bed for a moment.

"What?" I asked him sleepily.

"This is more than I deserve," he said.

"You don't know what you deserve. Everyone's done bad things in the past, myself and your brother included." Seth had only told him the full story a few days ago. "Dishonourable things. Cowardly things. But you move on and try not to repeat them. That's what separates us from the Godelan."

In the darkness I could only see his shape, considering. Finally, he climbed under the covers and lay next to me, staring up at the ceiling.

"How is it?" I asked. "Being in bed?"

He turned to me and I saw a small smile. "I like the company," he said. "Reminds me of New York, when I could reach out and hold your hand while you slept."

That caught me off guard. "Did you?"

"Sometimes," he admitted. "You'd be turning in your sleep. Mumbling. Sometimes you'd cry. Your nightmares woke me up, and I held your hand."

I propped myself up on one elbow to look at him. "Why didn't you ever tell me that?"

I felt Kian shrug. "I guess there's never been the right moment."

I lay back down but got closer and rested my head on his chest. While this was a bolder move than I had ever taken, tiredness and comfort pushed all other thoughts away. Kian's silence and warmth lulled me to sleep almost immediately.

✦

Wind whipped by me, but I didn't mind. This was summer wind, and I rejoiced in it. I felt light and free — like magic itself. I was not past Gwen. I was not anyone. I was a wisp in time and I let my soul soar, looking out to a vast sea that was the richest shade of dark blue I had ever seen. My heart felt freer and more hopeful than I had ever experienced in any of my memories.

I surveyed the horizon. Suddenly, something was wrong. The dream went from being pleasant to terrifying as a deep-rooted fear took over. A row of ships sailed toward me. These ships were new to me, the kind that could bring many men over large bodies of water. But now they approached. Something glinted in the sunlight. A reflection. They had metal. They had weapons.

I ran to the village. As I struggled for breath but urged myself forward, my vision blurred. Life sped until I had used all of my energy, and it was still not enough. The Riada dressed for battle. I tried to scream at them to stop, to wait, to learn whom they were dealing with, but they couldn't hear me. The ships landed. We went to meet them, ready for war.

Suddenly, I stood in front of only the burned-out shells of ships. The invading people were gone. They had set their own ships on fire and trespassed on our land. How would we know them now from our own?

✦

I awoke with a gasp.

The movement of the train had seemed unnatural at first, as if my whole world was moving. I was still tired from the delay at the Dublin airport and had fallen asleep on our way from London to Oxford. Kian sat next to me and took my hand reassuringly. He smiled, but there was worry in his eyes. He put a hand to my forehead.

"You're sweating in January," he told me with a frown. "Are you okay? Did you have that dream again?"

I nodded.

The dream had visited me in my sleep last night, forcing me to get up early in the morning, leaving Kian in my bed. When my friends awoke and found me in the kitchen while he still slept, I avoided answering any questions by making myself busy packing my things. The others had so far not commented on the new sleeping arrangements, though I watched Seth carefully for any sign that he minded. So far, nothing.

I found the dream exhausting. This time I had known what was going to happen, but still I felt confused, scared, and desperate, just like I had the first time. It wasn't a memory, like my other strange dreams — this was something more, and I felt blind for missing the meaning in it.

Rain hammered the window of the carriage. The delay of our flight had been due to extremely bad weather. While it seemed typical of England, even locals shook their heads at how much rain had fallen.

At the same time as people ditched their soaked and turned-out umbrellas in the aisles, a screen in front of me played terrifying images of a drought in Africa. Apparently it was the worst in years, and a ring of experts argued about who was responsible for global warming. I could have told them. The Godelan wanted the world — their own version of it.

"I'm going to go find Seth and Garrison," Kian said, getting up. They had left to get lunch.

I nodded, but as soon as he was gone, I met Moira's cold gaze.

"What?" I asked, taken aback.

"I know what you're doing," she said.

There was anger behind her look that I hadn't seen before. She hadn't been herself in the last week, but when I thought more about it, I realized that I didn't know what "herself" actually was anymore. If the Moira we met in England was gone, who was left?

"I don't know what you're talking about."

"Yes you do," she fired back.

I thought about how I could possibly have offended her.

"I didn't tell anyone about what happened at the airport," I said defensively.

I was mad at myself for being so apologetic when I had done nothing wrong, but I was tired, the weather was miserable, and I didn't feel like a confrontation.

"I know you didn't," she said. "You don't need to get rid of me by turning the others against me; you already have."

I was at a loss for words. "What?" I fumbled for something to say. "I haven't turned anyone against you!"

Moira's gaze softened. Her mouth opened slightly in surprise, as if she hadn't expected her own behaviour. "It's not your fault, Gwen. I know that," she said earnestly, the animosity gone.

I was confused and worried. Her behaviour was catapulting between angry and whatever the alternative was. I never got to ask her what she meant because Kian came back with Seth and Garrison in tow, and Moira shone a smile in their direction then went directly back to reading her magazine.

"What's the matter?" Kian asked me, sitting down. "You look stunned."

I continued to stare at Moira but she wouldn't meet my gaze.

"Nothing," I said, not wanting to drag anyone else into this.

She had had problems with me from the start, and considering our histories, I didn't blame her. What worried me was if she had her magic back, she was powerful and wanted revenge. She was obviously of two minds. I just had to watch out for which one would win.

Oxford was probably a lovely city. Certainly, judging by the postcards, I would have loved to look around. But we didn't get to see any of that. As the train pulled into the station, we piled into an old-fashioned taxi and went directly to the student residences. Since the new winter semester had just begun, it was our only option.

We pulled up to the building after taking so many twists and turns down narrow, cobblestoned streets that I lost track. The college we were staying at was named after some saint, or something else religious that I forgot as soon as it was told to me. It certainly looked old and Gothic, with tall spires and impressive panel windows.

The taxi driver practically threw our bags at us,

wanting to get out of the terrible weather as quickly as possible. After an elderly man showed us to our room — all the while sticking his nose up as if it was beneath him to help us — I was beginning to regret coming here.

The room itself was nothing fancy, with three bunk beds and some night tables. There was a common living room area that made me feel like I was in some movie about college kids or a reality TV show.

Surprisingly, no one was around.

"Where is everyone?" I asked the man.

He looked down his nose at me for the hundredth time, as if I was bothering him.

"Supper," he said loudly. "If you follow the hall and go down the stairs, you'll come to the main hall. The dining hall is beyond that." He enunciated every word as if we didn't speak English.

As soon as he left, Garrison burst out laughing. "I think your American offended him."

I rolled my eyes, deciding everywhere that looked this fancy came with a price. And a rag-tag group of teenagers with one misfit adult really stood out.

Hungry, since all Seth and Garrison had managed to get on the train were chocolate bars and potato chips, we followed his directions.

The college was bigger than it appeared from the outside, with intricate carvings everywhere and stained-glass windows. Through a large set of heavy wooden double doors, we followed voices into the dining hall.

Just like in a movie, everyone sat along long benches in dark robes at tables that ran the length of the room. Portraits of fancy-looking men hung all over the walls. A few people turned their heads when we entered, but the looks that lasted were mostly girls eyeing my friends. Garrison smiled stupidly while Seth and Kian simultaneously took a step back as if each gaze was a shove.

Finding some seats in the middle of one of the tables by ourselves, we were served our meals by unhappy-looking students. They moved around the room practically invisible to the others. When I thanked one for bringing me water, she didn't even reply.

"This place is weird," Seth said, digging into a mixture of mashed potatoes and French onion soup.

"Everyone in robes," Kian shook his head. "It makes me nervous."

"And they all talk and look down at you as if they have big boats," Garrison added.

Moira rolled her eyes at them. "That's what Oxford is," she said as if it was obvious. "Everyone knows. You grow up with an awe of the place, as if it's a fortress."

"It looks like one," Garrison agreed.

"There's a place here that's about a thousand years old," Moira said.

"Kian's still a thousand years older than that," Garrison reminded her. He was right. I sat next to a relic.

"It's not a competition," I told him.

"But if it was," Garrison said, "Kian would win."

All of a sudden the sound of rain hitting the windows changed. The difference wasn't obvious at first, but the entire room quieted as many voices stopped to listen. Then the noise got louder until it sounded like rocks were smashing against the windows, and the glass broke.

Screams filled the room, half drowned out by the rattle of ice falling from the sky. Broken glass showered down. The scratching of the long benches as everyone scrambled for cover at once was barely audible, even in the big room.

The five of us ducked under the table. Using magic hadn't even occurred to me — I was too surprised. As we put our arms over our heads, I couldn't help but feel a little useless. One of the things that had smashed the windows rolled near the table.

I couldn't believe my eyes. I had to touch it to see it was real. I crawled toward it without even looking where I was going.

"Gwen!" Seth called.

"Gwen, come back!" Kian yelled.

I got distracted and looked back at them. My hand landed directly on a piece of broken glass, and I hissed in pain. Still, I managed to retrieve the thing that had fallen through the window and retreat back under the table.

The cold soothed my hand. Seth helped me get the piece of glass out of my palm while I handed the ice ball to Kian.

"What is it?" I asked.

"It looks like freakishly large hail," Seth said.

Kian passed the piece around to the others. It was eerily round, as if someone had formed and solidified a snowball and then sent it crashing down to earth.

"Oh no!" Moira pointed out to the aisle.

There hadn't been enough space under the tables for everyone. Some students who had gotten stuck and lost in the dining hall during the chaos tried to shield themselves as best as possible. But the hail kept pummelling the room as it broke through the windows, and I counted at least two people unconscious.

"Is it them?" I asked no one in particular. "Are they trying to kill us? Do they know we're here?"

Seth shook his head. "I can sense magic in this, but it's like it's an echo of something," he yelled over the noise. "A chain reaction."

Moira nodded.

"Garrison." I grabbed him by the sleeve and pulled him close to me. "See those paintings? We're going to use them to cover the windows while the others get everyone out. Okay?"

Garrison briefly stuck his head out from under the table to look around at the paintings. "You mean the very expensive, historic-looking ones?"

"Yes!" I yelled.

I tried to block out the noise and reached for my magic. To my surprise, it was right at the edge of my senses, like something in my peripheral vision. I still couldn't direct it without gestures, though, so I swept my arms out from under the table as if I were gathering a pile of cushions, dragging the paintings from their long-held places on the wall. Garrison did the same as our friends watched nervously for the instant the chaos died down.

With hail the size of my fist raining down on

people's heads, the chaos kept us from notice. The canvases provided surprisingly strong resistance against the assault from outside, though, and it wouldn't take long for people to notice the strange behaviour of the paintings and look for its source.

When the noise dissipated somewhat and people began to come out from under tables, albeit hesitantly, Kian, Seth, and Moira led the way out of the dining hall. It didn't take a lot of convincing. Garrison and I went last, letting the paintings fall to the ground behind us as the hail chased us out.

In the end, our first day in Oxford wasn't ideal. My hands throbbed again where my old wounds had barely healed. The weather kept us in our room the whole time, because even though the common area windows had been smashed in and it was freezing and destroyed, our own room's windows faced the other direction and were fine.

We lay on our bunks, staring at the ceiling, waiting for the strange weather to cease. There wasn't much else we could do since we couldn't take on the whole sky. Whatever the Godelan were doing was having effects around the whole world, upsetting nature and putting everyone at risk. And all we could do was wait it out.

My strange dream circled over and over in my head. The scenario of the burned-out ships hadn't come up in any text I read about the tribes in ancient Scotland, England, or Wales. I was just as clueless as I had been in my dream.

I looked across the room to see that only Kian

wore a smile as he lay on the bottom bunk with his arms folded behind his head. I climbed down and went over.

The events of the day were so unexpected that our adrenaline rush had been followed by a total crash. Seth and Garrison were passed out, while Moira had fallen asleep while reading. It was barely evening. The sound of sirens passed by our building every few minutes.

"What are you so happy about?" I asked.

"I finally feel like I helped," Kian replied. "You were great today. You have your magic. You have your memories. And you're not in the hands of the Godelan. That's the best-case scenario — it's all I could hope for."

I couldn't help but smile in return. "Don't get too excited," I told him. "You never know what's going to happen tomorrow."

"That's tomorrow," Kian said seriously. "Not today."

I was hesitant to return to my bunk but forced myself to walk away. Sleeping with him next to me the previous night made my dreams and panic not seem so bad. He was right — it was all about the company.

✦

In the morning we found the fanciest library I had ever seen. Surrounded by a courtyard, its windows had been shuttered to keep the light off the precious old books inside. Because of this, it was also spared from the hail.

At least nothing was falling from the sky today — it was overcast, but I'd take cloudy dryness over baseball-sized hail any day.

A narrow set of steps led us to a desk, where an elderly woman sat typing slowly into a computer that looked as old as I was. I was beginning to think that everyone hired at the university had not changed jobs in about fifty years. She politely asked us what we wanted. We told her. She said no.

"I'm sorry," Garrison said, turning on the charm. "We travelled a long way to see this specific item."

"I'm sorry, too," the woman said primly. "There is no one to show you in today, and there are far too many of you anyway."

Just then a man came in behind us. Dressed in a tweed coat and shiny round glasses, he was a walking library stereotype.

"It's all right, Margaret," he told the woman from the door. "I don't mind visitors today."

They exchanged brief pleasantries, making us feel invisible, though we stood awkwardly between them. I found out his name was Roger and he wasn't supposed to be in, but he had come to check on the books. He put a hand to his chest in exaggerated relief when he found out that nothing was broken. Apparently half the campus was smashed to pieces.

"Hello," Roger said, turning back to us. "I am one of the curators here; how may I help you?"

"We're looking for a text," Kian said. "It would have been something from Scotland, about two thousand years ago."

Rogers gave out a short laugh. When he saw we weren't joking, his expression turned to pity. "I'm afraid there's no such thing," he told us. "Written language did not exist in that area until Christian times, and even then we're looking at twelve hundred years in the past. Maximum."

Kian frowned. "We were told it would be here."

"But they did warn us it would be unreadable," I added, trying to be helpful.

Roger stared at us for moment. I could practically see the wheels turning in his mind. "Come with me," he said finally.

Before we could agree, he led the way through a narrow door and up some stairs to a floor where manuscripts lined shelves in the thousands. We hurried to keep up with him until he came to a long desk with glass on top like a sneeze guard and handed us gloves.

"Please put these on," he told us. "And do not touch anything."

"What's this screen for?" Garrison asked.

"To preserve the manuscripts," Roger answered.

"Reminds me of a sneeze-proof window at a salad bar," Seth murmured quietly enough for Roger not to hear.

The man disappeared for over ten minutes while we sat awkwardly in stiff white gloves, afraid to touch anything for fear that it would just turn to dust if we breathed on it. At least that was the impression given to us by the way the library protected its manuscripts.

Finally, Roger reappeared. But to our surprise, he carried fairly modern-looking white pages with some scribbles on them.

"I only have one item like what you describe," he

said. "And it's not quite a text. It's a slab of rock in our basement. There are only hieroglyphs on it. Completely unreadable."

Roger laid the white printer pages in front of us. They looked like an art project I had done in school many times as a child. You lay a page over something with texture and then run a pencil over it until an imprint of the image begins to come up. Except now, instead of the leaves and pennies I had used, these images were far more intricate. Animals and decorative spirals were lined up and repeated in an order that was too neat to be meaningless.

"Where did this slab come from?" Garrison asked.

As Roger arranged the pages in front of us under the sneeze screen, even though they were new, I was watching Kian. Surely he would be the best person to be able to read this. But he only squinted at the drawings as if trying to remember something that had escaped him.

"It was an old discovery," Roger said. "From the eighteenth century, when the north was quite in fashion. There was a lot of funding invested in learning about the culture there, and they found this just shy of the border between England and Scotland, on the west coast."

I think it happened at the same time for all of us. Moira gripped the desk in shock as Seth and Garrison leaned forward. I could only stare. The animals began to take on shape and meaning in my mind. I could practically feel my brain expanding to learn this new language. My eyes felt out of focus and then were taking in the information across the pages like I was reading a book.

My heart skipped a beat.

"What is it?" Kian asked. "What do you see?"

"Can't you read it?" asked Garrison.

Kian's face was a mixture of anger and disappointment. "No," he said. "All I see are pictures."

"Do you know what this is?" Roger asked, confused. To his credit, we were probably the strangest visitors he had ever had. He looked at our faces, realizing there was comprehension there.

Garrison began to open his mouth. I knew he would tell Kian what was written on the pages, but I hit his elbow and motioned to Roger. The man was looking at all of us, his mouth ajar in anticipation. Seth stood and gripped his arm.

"Sorry," Seth said to Roger. I sensed a light touch of magic travel through the room. "This wasn't what we were looking for."

For a moment we all watched nervously to see what the curator would do. Then he seemed to notice we were there for the first time.

"Oh, hello," he said cheerfully. "Did I get a little spacey there? I'm sorry this wasn't what you were looking for. Let me know if I can be of any more assistance."

"We will," I told him. "Thank you."

We gave him back his gloves and piled out of the library, waiting until we were outside to speak.

"What did you do to him?" Garrison asked.

"Just took the last memories," Seth said. I glanced

at Moira, remembering the woman in the airport bathroom, but she didn't meet my gaze and only stared at the ground. "It's easy when they're fresh. They're just sitting top of the mind."

"Would you be able to get old memories back?" Kian asked. We all turned to him. "I can't remember anything of our old language. It's like knowledge of this one replaced it. I feel so disconnected."

Seth frowned at his younger brother, who towered over him. "I can try."

Kian wanted to know what the stone said, but we decided to wait until we were back in our room.

Passing the main hall of the college, I glanced into the dining room. There were no students in today, and cleaners swept up the broken glass. There were patches of blood in places where people hadn't been able to duck for cover quickly enough. Torn and broken paintings lay all over the floors by the walls.

When I spotted a cleaner by the entrance, I couldn't resist.

"What happened?" I asked him. "This looks like an awful disaster."

The man shook his head, resting his broom against the wall. "Could have been worse," he said gravely. "Hailstorm did a world of damage, but the drafts in these old buildings might have saved some lives."

"Drafts?"

"Pulled the coverings right to the windows," he explained.

"Oh."

It clicked. They thought air currents had somehow

sucked the paintings clear off the walls and covered the windows with them. Any reasonable person could have seen that made no sense, but what was the other explanation? Magic?

I nodded politely. At least there was no video of us, as there had been with the tsunami. As we piled back into out little room, Seth closed the door.

"Right," he said, with an air of command. "We need to break into that museum and destroy that rock."

As we nodded our consent, Kian just looked confused.

"Why? What does it say?" he asked for the tenth time.

"How to kill us," Seth told him.

Chapter Eleven

"Kill you?" he asked. "But I thought you couldn't be killed without coming back again?"

"So did I," I said. "Once we're in the ritual. We never figured out how to get out, apart from having our souls and magic enslaved to others." Which wasn't a very appealing option. "This describes how to stop that ritual, but there's a pretty big catch."

We needed to destroy that rock as quickly as possible without anyone finding out about it. The thought that the Godelan could have beaten us to it and already seen it made me itch to just run out and smash the thing.

"What did it say?" Kian asked again.

"The whole thing sounded like it was written for us," Seth said. "As if the Riada realized that even when we found the Godelan, we might not know what to do with them. It said there are many deaths. The sacrifice of magic, that thing they tried to do to Gwen, was one of them."

Kian glanced at me, another apology in his eyes.

"Or we could die like anyone else," Seth said. "But then we would still continue somewhere in the future. The ritual starts the pattern and it's hard to break. Then there was something written about the ring of fire that trapped our souls."

Yeah, I remembered that ring of fire.

"But," Seth continued, "it said that we can only be set free, I take that to mean made officially dead, by the same ritual and the same blood that trapped us in the first place."

This seemed to mean something serious to the others, but I was clueless. I hadn't thought this last part actually held meaning for them until I saw their grim faces and suddenly felt left out.

"What?" I asked. "What does that mean? What blood trapped us?"

"There's blood used in the ritual," Seth explained. "Just a little bit. You were ... late. You didn't see."

In our past lives, Seth and I had been due to run away together. We were going to abandon our tribe and live out the rest of our lives in exile just to be together. It hadn't been my finest moment as a champion.

That day went horribly wrong, however, or right — depending on how you looked at it. After my husband began to suspect what I was about to do, he tried to stop me. I had to kill him. Maybe. Either way, I had fought him off and ended up stabbing him with a gift from Seth.

I was late to meet Seth; he had thought I couldn't go through with it, and I realized too late that he had

gone back to our tribe to die. Not being able to stand
the thought of living without him, I dove into the ritual through the circle of fire at the very last moment,
inheriting fire as a new magic.

"Our father," Kian told me, "provided his own blood
to perform the ritual."

"Well, we're two thousand years away from your
father," Moira said. "How can he kill us?"

"That can't be what it means," I reasoned. "The
stone was written for the future. It must mean something other than blood."

"Kin," Seth said suddenly. "It means Kian's blood,
or my blood, can be used in a ritual to kill us. Kill us
dead, I mean. No coming back."

"The ritual can only be done once every five years,
though," Garrison added. "Something about a cycle."

"Magician once told me that," Kian said. "It's how
we got here. The magic only works every five years."

"Well, how long has it been since you got here?"
Seth asked him.

Kian considered for a moment. "Ten years, last
December."

"Great," Moira muttered. "So they can kill us for
the next eight months?"

"Or we kill them," Garrison said.

"You forgot the big catch," I reminded them.

"What is it?" Kian asked.

"It says that we cannot kill or be killed by anyone
born of the same land as us," I told them. "How do you
suppose we get around that?"

"It must mean tribe," Seth argued.

I shook my head. "Tribe was used as another word. This says *land*. They can't kill us and we can't kill them."

Everyone went quiet, thinking of alternate meanings for the word.

"Then what's the point of the stone?" Seth asked. "We have to be able to get around that somehow."

We continued arguing until hunger forced us to seek out food in what seemed like a storm-ravaged town. Most places were damaged in some way, but a few tucked-away pubs had been spared the wrath of hail. We took our food to go in order to observe the library and find a way to get into it after it was closed.

"The Godelan all want different things," Kian said while simultaneously trying to eat a sandwich and sneak around the back of the library.

"Like what?" asked Garrison.

I was behind Kian and saw him shrug. Garrison led the way as if well versed in sneaking.

"Stone, the silver-haired one, wants power. Now. He likes how much of it he would have if he could be the most powerful person in this world," Kian said. "Donald, that's the one who isn't Magician, he holds a grudge against the Romans and our tribe for letting them win. He wants the world back to the way it was."

"And Magician?" asked Garrison. "The man you came with?"

I saw his pace faltered. The man I had called Third Magician, the one who looked out of place in the modern world, had caused him all of this heartache. When Kian had rescued me from them, he broke free from their hold on him. Still, talking about the man who had tricked him away from his family was hard.

"I don't know what he wants," Kian said. "He doesn't know much of this world, but he's obsessed with status. He'll side with whoever will win. I'm not surprised they tried to kill you instead of going after you again — they probably couldn't agree on what to do with you."

"But killing us can mean we'll be back again," I reminded him. "That's not ideal."

"No," Kian replied, "but they really can't agree on anything."

"You mean you think the other two will fight with each other?" Seth asked.

"There is no way they can both have what they want," Kian reasoned.

"But they needed our magic," I said quietly. "What will they do without it?"

"My guess," Kian said, finishing his lunch, "is that they've used a considerable amount of their power setting the destruction of the Earth in motion and, probably, hiding their names. They must be low on magic — that's why they don't want to face you anymore. Or," he paused, "it could be the other thing, but I don't want to think about that."

I caught his arm, forcing him to stop and face me.

"What other thing?" I asked urgently.

"Don't worry, Gwen," he told me reassuringly. "I spent a while watching them, and I don't think it's the case."

When I continued to stare at him, silently demanding answers, he relented.

"They could have captured one of your kind and used their magic," he said.

Damn. The thought hadn't even occurred to me.

"But we would know. They'd be much more powerful. Your magic is pure."

I don't know how much more powerful they could get. Every time I saw a TV, it played images from some disaster around the world. They had caused the tsunami, seemingly effortlessly. What would they do if they had even more power? The droughts in Africa had caused death tolls that I couldn't even fathom.

Continents were slowly being submerged under water. Staving off a tsunami had taken almost everything I had, and it included surrendering to my old self. I was starting to feel anything short of giving up on modern Gwen would not be enough to save anyone.

Kian's eyes read my face as if he could see every thought that ran through my mind. He brushed the hair away from my face, and I tried to push all of my worries down, focusing on that sensation. I hadn't even thought of the Godelan capturing someone we hadn't reached yet. It created a whole new anxiety inside me.

"Hey, are you coming?"

Kian and I both jumped. Seth had rounded the corner.

"Garrison found a way up through the roof," Seth said, and then disappeared around the corner.

I sighed. I could only handle one problem at a time. I made a mental note to speak with Seth tonight before our little adventure into the world of breaking and entering.

On the rainy weekday, I realized we didn't really need to sneak around. Any students left on the campus after the storm had classes far way. Still, Garrison's way into the library was spy-worthy.

He stood in an impossibly narrow alleyway filled with pebbles that were nearly washed away by rain. Piles of garbage, and I was sure a few carcasses, were trapped in the alley as well. The other wall belonged to a college. He squinted into the sky as he observed the climb.

"Easy," Garrison said. "The walls are close enough for us to —" He climbed instead of finishing his sentence. With his back pressed against the library and his feet climbing up the wall of the college next door, he went up a few feet. There was only about eighty feet to go until the roof.

"Why don't we just blow in a window or something?" Moira asked, crossing her arms over her chest, annoyed.

Seth and Garrison both ignored her.

"We don't want to create more trouble," I told her. "If it looks like someone broke in, they'll probably check to see what's gone or broken and will find what we did faster. It would be better if we are gone by the time they figure it out."

Moira made a sound between acquiescence and further annoyance. Kian shot me a glance of confusion.

He hadn't witnessed her transformation quite like we had — especially how I had, for that matter.

"That'll do it," Garrison said, jumping down to where he started.

He walked back to our dorm with a limp, and I hoped it wasn't a testament to how hard the wall was to climb.

The afternoon quickly passed into evening while I worried about Seth, Kian, my future friends I hadn't even met yet, and anyone else falling into the hands of the Godelan. I needed air and to be alone with my thoughts, so I put on my jacket and went out. Everybody was thinking too loudly in there.

I didn't get far, though. The dark and abandoned hall was like a warning about the outside world. Leaving alone seemed unwise. An hour later, I stood in the abandoned kitchen of our student housing building, where rain had soaked into the wooden floors. No one had even bothered to put plastic over the big hole in the wall where a window used to be before it was smashed by ice pellets.

"You okay?"

Seth came in to get a soda from the fridge. I took a breath.

"Thinking of home," I said. "I'll be fine."

He nodded.

"Do you miss home?" I asked.

"Of course," Seth replied. "But we have to do this right now. When we win, we can go back, have lives, and not look over our shoulders."

"Use magic?" I asked him.

"Don't know," he admitted. "Maybe."

A few moments of silence passed while I worked up my courage.

"I appreciate your understanding," I told him finally. "Really."

"About?" Seth asked.

I felt a blush coming on. It was hard for me to speak about my feelings. He was the one person I felt strongly enough about to take this giant risk for. All I could do was nod in the direction of our room.

"You know," I said.

Despite myself, my eyes focused solely on my feet.

"Kian?" Seth asked.

There was a silence that made me nervous. I looked up to find Seth deep in thought, staring out the would-be window as if he could see anything in the early evening darkness.

"You are okay, aren't you?" I asked.

To my relief, he broke out in a smile. "Yeah," he said. "I feel like for the first time my past isn't yearning for something. Don't get me wrong — I love you more than I even understand. It's just a part of who I am. It's something I was born with. You're woven into everything. But having Kian here ..." Seth shook his head, looking for words. "You don't know how happy I am. I've always wanted a little brother in this life." He laughed to himself. "I didn't think he'd come in that ... form ... but what'll you do?"

"What happened on the island ..."

We had still never spoken about it.

"We had to let ourselves go," Seth said. Had he

always been so much wiser than me? Probably. "And I don't regret anything. I'd do anything to protect you."

I smiled and took his arm, leaning in to hug him. Suddenly his words gripped me, and pieces of our history clicked together in my mind as if pieces of a puzzle. I stepped back, stunned.

"What?" Seth asked in the half-light.

I could only stand and stare at him, waiting for my mind to find something wrong with my logic. But I couldn't.

"Gwen?" Seth stepped toward me, concerned. "Are you okay?"

A dull ache was rising in my heart, but it wasn't mine. It was past Gwen, having realized her mistake.

"You would do anything to protect me," I repeated.

Seth nodded. "Anything."

I let a few moments pass as the words bubbled up in my throat.

"I was wrong," I asked quietly. "Wasn't I?"

"About what?" he asked, lost. It somehow surprised me that he couldn't see my thoughts like Kian could. Maybe he didn't know me as well as he thought.

"The way things happened on the day we died," I told him. "I was wrong."

Seth looked about to argue, then sighed. Confirmation made the dull ache grow.

"You were never going to meet me," I said. "You were never going to run away with me. This isn't the first time you're letting me go."

My words held no emotion. Past Gwen was too stunned, and I was just trying to keep up with the revelations that would ultimately unlock my magic and free me from the past.

I waited for Seth to speak. It took a minute of silence before he offered an explanation.

"Like I said," he told me, taking my hand. "I love you more than I understand."

"You were going to leave me alone," I accused.

"But at least you would be alive," Seth told me. "I couldn't leave. I couldn't abandon my people. They were *my* people, Gwen. If I abandoned the Riada, I would be disobeying my father and leaving my family. I just couldn't do that. But knowing you'd live was consolation for me."

I took a deep breath. "How long have you known?"

"Since we got our memories back on the hill," Seth replied. "It made sense. When I first saw you in New York I was so happy, but also surprised. It didn't make sense to me until later. And then you remembered your version of things, and I just didn't see the need to take that away from you."

I processed the information, embedding this new version of events into my memory.

"You okay?" Seth asked again.

He looked into my eyes with absolutely no hint of ill intent. It was the only reason I let him get so close. My instincts told me to be defensive, to take out my anger for being so wrong on him and not let him know just how strange it all felt. But he meant what he said, and I made a point of showing the feelings washing over me. He didn't know me like Kian, though. He couldn't tell what I was thinking.

"Gwen," he asked again. "You okay?"

"Yeah," I told him. "I'll be fine."

I was surprised to find a tear running down my cheek. I hastily wiped it away.

Kian and Garrison emerged from our room down the hall. It was time for our heist, or rather, vandalism.

"Gwen, are you okay?" Kian asked when he saw my face.

I did my best to force a smile, though my mind still felt like putty.

"Why does everyone keep asking me that? Yes, I'm fine." I looked down the hall, but the dorm door was closed behind them. "Isn't Moira coming?"

Garrison and Kian exchanged looks.

"She said she trusted us to handle it," Garrison said shortly. He ended the conversation by walking out the door before I could ask any more questions. We had to follow him, though I had time for one quick glance back at our room. I could see Moira's shadow move under the door.

Climbing that stupid wall was one of the least pleasant things I have ever done. My back felt raw by the time I got up there. It was still wet and slippery. My feet kept threatening to give way underneath me, and the uneven bricks made everything hurt.

My legs were trembling by the time I reached the top and Seth pulled me up. Kian came up shortly after me, and I couldn't help but feel he had waited patiently while I struggled.

We slipped into the library with surprising ease, Garrison undoing an inside latch through the glass.

"I amaze myself," he said as the small knob flew to the other end of the window, seemingly of its own accord.

Seth scoffed at him. "You held off a tsunami, but this is amazing?"

"Smashing the glass would have been a lot easier than flicking a switch with magic," Garrison said as if it were obvious.

I looked at Kian. He had taught me to target my magic in the early days of our travels. I was always learning new ways he had helped me.

We wandered through the library, sneaking though there were no cameras and no alarm system.

"It's weird how they keep all of these priceless books in here and don't guard the place," I remarked.

"Who'd want to destroy this old stuff, though?" Garrison asked. There was no hint of sarcasm in his voice.

"Well," I said. "Us, for one."

We soon found that the truly expensive books, first editions and other valuables, were held in locked cases that were in fact guarded with alarms. Garrison was right — no one had a reason to come in here and destroy old books and artifacts. Except us.

We had torn up the paper the librarian gave us right after we left the library, but the rock still existed. And as long as it did, anyone could figure out how to kill us.

It took an hour to find it, even after we retraced Roger's steps exactly as we remembered them. At last, leaned against a wall next to a series of paintings, we found the two thousand-year-old rock standing unceremoniously.

Garrison, Seth, and Kian looked to me, and I suddenly realized we hadn't brought mallets.

"We're not going to smash this, are we?" I asked.

The others shook their heads. They wanted me to destroy it.

Now that I stood in front of this relic — the only thing left of my former home — it was hard to think of destroying it. Thoughts of hiding it began to float through my head.

"Gwen," Kian said, putting a gentle hand on my shoulder. "It was created to deliver a message to us by our people. It's done its job. Let it go."

He was right. Still, with Seth's confession about what had really happened in the past, I felt like I was losing too much tonight.

I took a deep breath, and with a heavy heart, I put my hand on the cold rock. Feeling the words inscribed on it as if they spoke into my hand, I felt for magic inside. It was very faint, but still there. Wanting to keep something of it, I drew it into myself and then felt magic trickle through my fingers back into the stone.

When I opened my eyes and looked, it had crumbled underneath my fingers, and nothing remained but a pile of dust. It made me inexplicably sad to see it like that. Perhaps I was comparing it to my own past.

Kian draped an arm over my shoulders and placed a kiss on the top of my head. "You did the right thing," he said.

I sighed. "I know. But I'm not convinced it was all that harmful. Even if someone else figured out how to kill us, they couldn't do it without you. And you would never do that."

"No," Kian agreed. "I wouldn't. But because I would be against it doesn't mean they couldn't get my blood, or Seth's blood, some other way."

When I thought about it that way, I pushed my sadness about the stone to the back of my mind. If it kept Seth and Kian safe in the case of someone trying to kill us, then it was worth it to get rid of it.

"Our other problem," Garrison said in the darkness, "is that we are still no closer to finding out the Godels' names."

"I think I can actually help with that," Kian said.

I looked up at him.

"I remembered something that I hadn't really thought of in a long time. The first night all of them where together again, I saw them do some magic that removed something from them. I think it must have been their names."

"Would they actually do that?" Seth asked. "Would they take their own knowledge and names just because they found out we're here, in this time?"

Kian nodded gravely. "To keep power, they would do anything."

"Well, where do we start?" I asked. I motioned to the pile of dust that used to be the stone. "We've looked for clues to our history, but I'm thinking it might take a long time to find."

"This isn't something books can tell us," Garrison

said. "We have to think about who they are as people and what they would do with such a big secret."

Coming back to our little dormitory was easier than getting into the library. Knowing that no one watched or guarded the place, we took our time, examining all the books that were hidden away in sections closed to visitors. I felt rebellious as I dragged my finger along their spines, knowing I would never be allowed to touch them otherwise.

We eventually had to make the climb down the narrow passage between buildings (I mostly fell rather than climbed) and limped back to our accommodations shortly before midnight.

Moira looked to be asleep, her back turned to the room, though a small light was still on.

The college felt like a war zone in some ways. The windows, blown out in winter, made everything cold. I climbed into bed fully clothed, wishing, inappropriately, for some company.

"We're leaving tomorrow, right?" I asked no one in particular. Now that we had gotten as much as we could from Oxford, it was time to move on. They had a lot of cleaning up to do, and I was perfectly happy to leave them to it.

"Yes," Garrison replied. "London, right?"

"Right," Kian replied.

"Why London?" I asked.

There was silence.

"Would you rather stay here?" Garrison asked.

"No."

"Then London it is," he said.

My teeth chattered. I wasn't against a warm place to sleep and streets that weren't so eerily deserted.

"And we start training again tomorrow," Garrison said.

I could hear excitement in his voice. When Kian had forced us to do the archaic drills of sword and archery fighting, only Garrison had remotely enjoyed them.

As Seth turned off the light and the room went dark, my mind drifted to how much had happened today. I had destroyed one of the last pieces of my people's history. I found out that Seth had never meant to spend the rest of his life with me. I hadn't changed the future. He had. The knowledge was still stirring in my mind as if my past self processed it and decided what this meant.

Suddenly I felt a presence in my thoughts. It was unsettling, and I lay in the dark trying to feel it move through my mind. Was I imagining this? Kian touching my cheek suddenly was brought to the front of my mind, but I hadn't called up the memory.

My time with Kian began to flip past my memories like an open book, and I wasn't doing any of it. There was definitely a presence there. Beginning to panic, I fought back. I caught a brief glimpse of someone else's memories, but it was dark and hazy. I couldn't make anything out.

It felt similar to when Seth had gone too far when trying to locate the Godelan with his magic, and I tried to find him through his mind to bring it back. But this was not a nice presence, and it wasn't welcome. Too confused to move, I pushed the presence out of my mind and eventually felt nothing but my own thoughts again. I surfed through my memories, making sure everything was still there.

Though I knew I was alone in my own head now, I held my guard up as long as I could, worried that whatever had just helped itself to my innermost thoughts would come back. Eventually, though, the night got a hold of me.

✦

I hovered above a fire. My initial thoughts were worry that I would burn myself, but I soon realized I was the wind again. This was a dream. I smelled smoke. I knew that through the trees the ships of the strangers still burned.

Unable to do much but hover, I listened to the stories being told around the fire. People guessed about the origin of the people from the ships, what they wanted, and why they refused to go back to where they had come from.

There were stories about men who had found islands of immortality, men who had lost their crews to sirens and were now doomed to sail alone, and other stories all involving grand adventures at sea. I had no opinion. All I knew was that there were foreigners in my land, and I could feel their every footstep as if someone walked over my heart.

Suddenly I was sucked out of the dream and into darkness. I panicked and tried to scream. I could feel something pulling me. I was moving so quickly that I anticipated hitting something, and at this speed it would surely kill me. My fear made me forget that I was in a dream.

Despite feeling only like a presence, not a human being with a body, I just tried to breathe while being dragged through what felt like hot wind and freezing water at the same time. What surrounded me was unlike anything I had ever experienced, and though I was not in pain, I could not bear it any longer. I tried to scream again, but it stifled me. When I was nearing complete and utter terror, it finally came to an end.

I was resting at the top of a red, sandy cliff. The sun beat down over the. landscape. Below me a prickly forest fanned out as far as the eye could see. Similar cliffs to the one I sat on dotted the landscape. I was perched next to some metal rings embedded in the earth. Each ring held a rope, though one of them had been dug in too close to the edge. As the ropes moved, the tension forced it to create more space around the stake, shaking away the earth. It would soon loosen.

Still in my ethereal dream state, I peered over the edge. At the end of all those ropes, a young man dangled. It took me a moment to realize he was climbing, which suggested he had put himself into this situation. All I could see was the top of his helmet as he struggled across the side of the cliff.

As if from far away, I began to understand that he would soon have to let go. There was nowhere for him to go, and he was struggling. And when he let go, he would fall the hundred metres back into the forest. The stake would give out.

I could do nothing but watch as he looked in vain for something to hold on to, but when he tried to reach too far, his feet slipped from their perch and he was left dangling in the air again. For a second, he floated. Then, as if feeling his mistake, he looked up. Our eyes met.

I saw understanding in his grey eyes. For a split second I could have sworn he knew me and that he was one of us — one of the seven. And then he fell.

Being my dreamy self, I swooped down over the cliff and flew after him, suddenly full of panic once more. I dropped straight through the air and into the tree canopy. A deadly thing for anyone else was nothing for me; in my dream I was nothing but ether. I passed it all without even shaking a leaf.

Then I saw him. Barely two feet above the forest floor, he floated much like I had when I had fallen into the ocean. He looked scared and worried. I wished I could help him. Talk to him. Explain it to him. But this was only a dream.

He gasped for breath, arms and legs bleeding from the many cuts he had received while falling. He would have cracked his head open on a branch if it weren't for his helmet. Still, he floated until he looked over his shoulder, realized what had happened, and then fell to the ground with a thud.

✦

I smelled smoke before I opened my eyes. Seth was shaking me awake. I brushed him off, wanting to make sure I hadn't set the whole room on fire.

As I jumped up, I hit my head on the ceiling above the top bunk. Hard.

I sank back into bed, holding my head and groaning.

"Gwen?" Seth asked. I could tell he was trying not to laugh.

Good. If he had time to laugh at me for making a fool out of myself, I had probably not burned someone.

I told him I was fine and rolled over to check the damage. Luckily, only the sheets were a bit scorched. Seth blew on the hand he had used to wake me up. Behind him, Garrison and Kian looked at me expectantly.

"What?" I asked.

"You were yelling in your sleep," Garrison said. "Screaming."

They were looking at me for an answer, so I gave them the only one I could think of.

"I saw him — the next one like us. I think I know where he is."

Chapter Twelve

"That doesn't make sense," Kian said.

It was about the seventh time he had repeated it. He shook his head like clues would fall out of it.

"To be there, you'd have to have some kind of connection with him. Who was it?"

We were waiting for the bus to London. Without any direction, it seemed like as good a place as any to wait for a memory, as frustrating as that was.

The station was pretty empty, seeing as how so many people left after the storm when classes were cancelled. We stood apart from the other few people waiting to go to London.

Every time I set foot outside, it reminded me of why I hated winter. The cold, blustery weather made every task harder than it should be. My teeth chattered.

"Maybe we're related," I guessed. "You said everyone with magic came from the same source, right? Maybe he's kind of reaching out to me."

It was my turn to shake my head. I had recognized

his eyes, so similar to mine, and there was something familiar about him, but I had no other ideas.

Kian sank deep into thought. I wasn't expecting an answer when he huffed. "I can't remember if you had anyone close to you," he said. "I was so young."

I patted his arm to show him it was okay.

"I don't remember the others, either," Seth said. He and Garrison had been playing memory games to try to figure out who I had dreamed about. The only person who seemed to have nothing to say was Moira. I kept eyeing her, wondering if I should say something. She seemed like a ticking time bomb, and I had made a resolution to eventually propose she go home.

Apart from Moira, who looked to have her own stuff going on, I felt like I was the only one not going crazy about who I saw in my dream. It looked like he was using magic and was fine for now, and I somehow was confident I would see him again. I wasn't even concerned about my dream with the burning ships. I had bigger problems.

I hadn't told anyone about feeling something in my mind. I didn't want to worry them in case it was the Godelan, who might have discovered a new trick to get into my head. Or maybe I was going crazy. I tried to tell myself it was okay to crack under this pressure. Still, having memories I didn't summon pop up in my mind was scary.

Over the next few days, I lived in my own mind most of the time. I was on constant alert for intrusions into my memories, which happened sporadically. Each time things I hadn't thought about would be pulled up like pictures being dug out of the album that was my brain. It was random and unpredictable, and I felt like I was going insane.

Having my magic always close at hand to defend myself was exhausting, which led to numerous naps. That meant I was right back to either finding burning ships or being pulled away to the life of some guy I didn't know but who looked familiar. The stranger reappeared in my dreams in various situations as he discovered magic and experimented with it. Life began to feel like an endless routine of things that unsettled me.

It didn't help that London is a bustling city, and we quickly figured out that to gather our thoughts and do any kind of training whatsoever, we'd have to stay indoors. Plus, March weather had brought a new onslaught of snow and ice unseasonable for England, so the whole country basically shut down.

My friends had to pull me out of bed on the grey days, while Kian had left some paper and a pen next to my bed. Every night when I woke up sweating and disoriented I had to write down everything I had seen in order for us to find the person I was dreaming about.

After four nights I had pages of scribbles about office buildings, highways, deserts, dogs, and a lot of spiky-looking plants. Since it was winter in the northern hemisphere and quite hot wherever he was, we were guessing he was somewhere far away.

A week passed. The little jabs into my mind were getting stronger, hesitant at first but now gaining confidence. I was beginning to think of it as an entity of its own, like something resurfacing. Sometimes I considered that maybe it was all in my head, and my fond memories of Kian were popping up because I needed them. But then less than happy memories came up, too — images of how he had kidnapped me flashed through my mind, and how I had been tied up and left to the Godelan. All the rage and disappointment bubbled to the surface of my mind like a geyser, and I had to fight not to be angry all over again. I was so busy controlling my thoughts that everything around me started to float by unseen.

We rented a house close to the city centre. It was a little eerie because while everything was pristine, much of the furniture had sheets draped over it. We had to walk around the sizeable brick townhouse uncovering sofas and beds as if they were artifacts.

We each had our own room, and as much as I enjoyed the privacy, sometimes when I woke in the middle of the night I would come downstairs and sit on the couch, reminding myself that Seth, Garrison, and Kian slept in the rooms that surrounded the living room.

I eventually found the courage to tell Kian about what Seth said to me, and how I had been wrong all the time. I wasn't sure how to feel about the fact that it seemed to make Kian happy. He reined in his emotions and sympathetically patted me on the head, rubbing my arm and telling me it was better to know the truth. Still, I knew he was happy that his brother hadn't betrayed the tribe — he really was the hero Kian had always imagined him to be.

When it wasn't hurting my pride, it seemed kind

of funny that no matter how we had plotted or planned, we had both ended up here in the end.

The daily intrusions of that force into my mind made me keep my distance from Kian. I'd sit on the couch in the middle of the night, staring at his door, worried that at any moment I'd feel that presence again and it would bring up old feelings that would make me furious. I was so angry, I worried about what I could do to him with my magic. I couldn't allow myself to let him in while something I didn't understand was riffling around my mind.

Kian made us train in the living room. This time we had actually moved all the furniture in hopes of keeping our deposit, and the rest of the house became our entire world while snowed in. One of our first purchases was a computer. Seth and Garrison spent hours chatting with their families, to whom Kian hadn't had to lie.

I heard them tell their families plenty of tall tales about school trips, but the lies came easily and I could hear two sets of proud parents exclaiming in awe about all the places we had been. I was too nervous about being face to face with my own parents again. Would they remember the lie? Would they remember me? Would they be angry?

✦

I couldn't catch my breath. It took me longer this time to realize I was in a dream. I panicked as deep greens and browns sped past my face. Huge men surrounded me. There was no feeling as the branches whipped my face or the ground rolled underneath me. I couldn't feel the thick fist holding my collar and pulling me forward. This wasn't my life — either of them. This was something else.

Then the smell reached me, and I knew I was about to round the corner and see the burning ships again. The dream was back. Resigning myself to it, I looked for any details that might be new. But the dream was always the same — various bits and pieces about finding burning ships.

The forest gave way to a rocky shore at the foot of the grey ocean. It could have been a lake for all I knew, but it was immense. I couldn't see land on the other side, but then again, fog blanketed the horizon. For the tenth time, I noticed how everything seemed so big — the people, the trees, the ships.

As I watched the thick smoke shade the fog drifting nearby, the ships, four that I could see, began to give way to the flames. The crackling was like an oversized hearth fire, and suddenly beams began to fall apart and snap.

People ran to stop the fire from spreading to the forest, but the ships hadn't run aground very far. I couldn't even figure out how they came on land, but being up close made it look like giants had picked them up like toys and placed them there.

The clips became repetitive, as if time sped up. I braced myself. I knew this routine. Suddenly I was sucked up and away as if something was pulling me from the inside out. When I could tell up from down and left from right again, and the world had stopped tumbling around me, I knew I was with him — the stranger who kept pulling me out of my dream.

Like Kian had taught me, I began to look around. It was

a hot, sunny day as I drifted nearby. He was my age — I knew it must be the case, though he looked older than any of us. A short blond beard obscured the lower part of his face and his brown hair was held back with a sweatband. With his broad shoulders and determined, bear-like scowl, he could have passed as older than Kian.

As my consciousness hovered, he climbed a bike in a quiet parking lot. I stayed with him while he rode down a winding path with parks on one side and trees on the other. I could tell he was deep in thought. Something was bothering him, and I bet it had something to do with magic.

Then, as he rounded a corner and the bushes opened onto a broad harbour, I had my answer. Across the water, near a golden bridge that reminded me so much of my home in San Francisco, a white landmark stood out like one of the pointy plants I had seen. I knew immediately that it was an opera house. I had seen it in books and postcards since I was young. He was in Sydney.

✦

I woke up halfway out of my bed. The clock read four in the morning, but I didn't care. As I raced to the stairs, I paused outside Moira's room. She had been growing more reserved, and it made me uneasy being around her. Still, she was as much a part of this as any of us.

Hesitantly, hoping she wouldn't want to come out, I knocked on her door. Then I sped downstairs, knocking on Seth's, Garrison's, and Kian's doors and waiting impatiently, hopping from foot to foot in the living room until they came out.

As sleepy people began to shuffle in, including Moira from upstairs, I could barely keep it in.

"He's in Sydney," I told them before they had even joined me in the living room.

No one needed an explanation. Garrison's face lit up immediately.

"We're going to Australia!" he announced. "Good job, Gwen." He gave me a pat on the back. "Just two more to go."

"How'd you do it?" Seth asked.

I was about to answer when I noticed Kian hadn't come out. I ran to knock on his door again, but Garrison pulled my hand back.

"He's not here," he said.

I could feel the panic growing on my face before Garrison rushed to explain.

"Don't worry!" he said, gripping me by the shoulders and holding me steady as if I was about to run screaming into the street. "He'll be back in the morning. He went last night up to the cottage we stayed at to pick something up."

I hated to admit that I had, in fact, been about to run screaming into the street. Kian wasn't like us. He had no magic, and he had made our enemies his enemies by taking our side. Having him disappear in the middle of the night was panic-worthy.

"Why didn't he tell me?"

The question was directed to Seth. Since they had become as close as brothers again, I didn't believe Kian would go without letting Seth know exactly what he was doing.

"Because he had to do this alone," Seth said.

I opened my mouth to ask another question, but he silenced me with a pleading look.

"He'll be back in the morning, Gwen," Seth said. "Wait to speak to him."

I took the hint and shut up, letting Seth and Garrison discuss the things they could do in Australia while looking for our fifth. Moira only mentioned that she would look forward to nicer weather and then went back to sleep.

I must have fallen asleep while they talked because I woke up to Kian's face. He was staring at me as I slept and didn't stop even after I frowned at him.

"What are you doing?" I asked hoarsely.

My mouth was dry.

"Watching you drool," he said, laughing. "Does the great warrior have a stuffy nose?"

I sat up. Sure enough, there was drool all over the couch pillow. Wiping my face and feeling more than a little embarrassed, I tried to give him my best groggy look of disapproval.

"You're in a good mood," I remarked. "Why didn't you tell me you were leaving?"

"Because you would have wanted to go with me," he said.

"And that's a bad thing?"

"Obviously," Kian replied. "If you had gone with me, you would not have found out where your fifth is, and we'd still have no direction."

A very pragmatic Gwen, somewhere in the back of my mind, let me know I was being clingy and annoying. Which was not very warrior-like at all. I vowed to course correct, so I let the subject drop.

I didn't have to wait long for answers, however. Kian came to the breakfast table with a very dingy pillowcase, holding it up as if it was a trophy.

"What is that?" Garrison asked.

Instead of answering, Kian pushed our plates to the edges of the table and dumped out the bag.

At first I didn't think there was anything in it except for dirt. Then a few items fell out, including some round metal pieces that looked strangely textured, a wooden carving that was quite dirty, and some pointy metal things that looked like they could be arrowheads.

One flat, round piece was bigger than the rest and quite beautiful, with intricate carvings, and though filthy, it looked to be pure silver. It had a sharp needle on the back that was as long as my palm.

Kian picked up this piece, by far the nicest thing in the small collection, and presented it to Seth with a wide smile. We all turned to Seth as well, who looked totally lost.

"Take it," Kian urged.

Reluctantly, Seth took the item and turned it around in his hands, examining it. After a while, when he was clearly not gleaning any kind of meaning from it, Kian's smile turned to a frown.

"It was yours," Kian told him. Seth just continued to look confused. "When Magician and I came to this place, I had a few things with me. It wasn't much. Actually, this is it."

The measly pile made me quite sad for Kian and reminded me of how he came to be here. I needed to remember him whenever I started feeling sorry for myself.

"The cottage at the bottom of the hill, where I took you, that was the first place we found when we got here," Kian continued. "While we looked for something to give us a clue as to the year, I took the chance to hide these items there."

"Why didn't you tell us when we were there?" I asked.

Kian shrugged. I could practically see shame weigh down his shoulders as he slouched. "I guess I wasn't ready to tell you everything yet," he said. "Or to lie more. I did not really want to explain how I had come to be there, or who I had come with." He turned back to Seth. "But don't you remember?"

Seth turned it around in his hands once more, but finally shrugged and put it down on the table. "Sorry, I have no idea what it is."

As soon as the artifact was on the table, Moira snatched it up. She did it so abruptly that I sat up in surprise.

"Because it's mine," she said.

Her tone implied we were trying to keep something from her. It was the first real emotion she had exhibited in a while, apart from her standard apathetic discontent. However, I didn't like that it had gone further into the territory of madness.

Before any of us could speak, she stormed from the table. We heard her door slam upstairs.

Kian looked absolutely lost. He turned to Seth, and I was shocked to see tears in his eyes. It made me want to cry. Or run away to avoid the feelings. Or both.

"After you were gone," he said quietly, "I thought I took something of yours, to remember you. But it wasn't even yours at all."

Of all the terrifying, painful, and traumatic things that had happened since I saw Kian for the first time, one of the most heartbreaking was seeing Seth stand to give an awkward hug to his big little brother.

"All this time I had a vague memory of you — just an idea of who you were," Kian said. "But I had no clue. I didn't even believe you were him — you — until you had your memories back."

Seth gave a half-laugh. "Why not?" he asked jokingly. "Am I not heroic enough for you?"

"With everything I learned," Kian motioned to me with his head and I felt a blush creep up my face for my past life's transgressions, "I wasn't sure who you were. I just hoped I was right. That all of this wasn't for nothing."

"It wasn't," Seth told him. "Besides, you did have something of mine."

"What?" Kian asked.

Seth smiled knowingly at me. I guess not a lot of people remembered his wood-carving habit. I might not have either had I not planted one of his carvings deep into the jugular vein of my past husband.

He took the dirty wooden carving from the pile. When he turned it in his fingers, I began to see that it was a sea lion. .

"I made this for you when you were born," Seth said.

It still amazed me how he could transition so well between the past and the future. A stubborn voice told me it was because he was at peace with his past and his decisions. I hushed that part of my brain because it meant I'd have to start thinking about my own choices.

"It's a very rounded sea lion," Seth continued. "Because you were a baby, and our mother feared you'd cut off your fat little arm or something if I made it sharp. If you didn't know it was from me, why did you keep it?"

Kian looked at the little figurine as if in a whole new light. "I thought our mother had given it to me." He exhaled deeply. "I always carried it with me. I feel like I know nothing."

"We need to learn together," Seth said.

For the first time, I could see it. Without my emotions running amuck or guesses and visions about the past, I could see how Seth could be king. I could imagine how people would look up to him and he could lead. I could also understand why I would love him as much as I had, and why I would do anything for him. But he was better than me. He was honourable and loyal and meant to be king. That was why he left me, and that was why he could make peace with that decision.

That thinking led me down a path I wasn't ready to take. I didn't know how to look back and take on my past's decisions as if they were my own. Instead, I let Kian finish explaining about the rest of the items and we talked about going to Australia, casting hesitant glances in the direction of Moira's upstairs bedroom.

Luckily, her funk didn't last long. By the time we were practising our sparring in the living room, she was apparently feeling better and came down to join us. She even participated, which was rare.

Kian raised his eyebrows questioningly at me as she walked past him, as if nothing had happened. I just shrugged. Maybe it was residual guilt for not including her more, but I didn't question her behaviour. Though she still preferred to listen instead of talk, and her sullen demeanour didn't allow me to guess at what she was thinking, at least she was being part of the group.

We had moved the furniture to the corners, but Garrison had become so skilled at the drills that Kian let him lead us through the steps. Moira joined in as Kian lounged on one of the couches, watching us go through the same movements over and over again. There was a spark of some recognition, but I definitely didn't take to it like Garrison had. No wonder he had been a soldier. Or maybe it was the other way around. I couldn't tell anymore.

I glanced up to find Kian watching me with a smile. His expression was a mixture of pride and amusement. I tried to return the smile, but somewhere between the happiness going from my brain to my face, the memory of him placing a cloth over my mouth until I couldn't breathe resurfaced. I felt the brush of the presence in my mind again. The anger rose so quickly, my heart skipped a beat. I missed the next step.

"Gwen?" Kian asked, standing.

I waved him off, trying not to look at him to avoid the emotions that came with it. What was happening to me?

"I'm fine," I said.

I rushed to keep up with Seth, Garrison, and Moira, who hadn't even noticed.

I thought about the presence in my mind all morning. Trying not to panic about the possibility that someone else might be trying to get in there, I consoled myself thinking that I just couldn't decide how I really felt. Though as soon as the feeling passed and I looked back to Kian, I knew I forgave him. And I knew I would protect him, even if I protected him from me.

✦

When we were finally able to explore London, I relished the distraction. I was thankful that the first flight we could find to Australia gave us a few more days to relax, though I also found plenty of time to second-guess myself. We were in a neighbourhood with winding roads and lots of shops. The cobblestone streets were so uneven, narrow, and full of pedestrians that cars knew better than to try to drive here. Despite the cold and snow, vendors in booths sold random things. I saw everything from candlesticks to patchwork handbags and leather notebooks.

Garrison bought a giant feather quill, and we all laughed at him and asked what exactly he was planning on doing with it. He just said he liked it. While Moira looked at scarves and the others admired some very shiny swords and daggers behind a glass display, I found a man in a small booth whittling. Rows of small wooden animals lined the wall. He was truly talented, and the animals looked very lifelike.

After what I learned that morning, I wanted to get one for Kian. I hadn't realized how transient his lifestyle was and how little he had collected in his decade here. My eyes glossed over the animals until one caught my eye and I felt it was the perfect fit. I hesitated for only a moment, thinking it might be too feminine. Still, it reminded me of him, so I paid for it and had the man wrap it in newspaper.

As I braced myself against the wind and walked toward the shop with all the weapons on display, I stopped by the booth where Moira had just purchased a scarf.

"What did you get?"

She showed me a green scarf before tucking it in her bag and quickly walking away. I turned to follow when I saw the woman putting a blank scrap of paper into the register. She smiled at me pleasantly when she saw me looking.

"Can I help you, dear?" she asked.

The woman had no idea she had just been robbed. I didn't know what to say. How could I tell her that Moira had used magic on her? And what would happen to her, or me, if I did say something? Instead I forced a smile to my face.

"No, thank you," I said, and left.

Moira waited by the others in front of the armour shop. The anger built to boiling point as I walked the few dozen metres over to them.

"Why did you do that?" I asked Moira, trying to keep my voice low. "You have money, why didn't you just pay that woman?"

"What does it matter?" Moira shot back. "We got away with it all the time before."

"When we were running!" I said through clenched teeth. "When we had to. When it was a necessity."

"What happened?" Seth asked. He turned to Moira. "What did you do?"

"She robbed that woman by using magic on her," I answered.

The others made various noises of disapproval. It was true that Kian had gotten away with a few brain-washes, but the magic was not his, and we were racing against time for our survival. We got away with fooling companies for plane tickets — not random women in small markets.

"Don't you feel any sense of responsibility?" I demanded. "For all the sacrifices that were made to have you be here, in this moment, you don't feel you owe something more to your magic than stealing?" Hm. I was beginning to sound a lot like Kian. "Why did you do that?"

Moira pursed her lips and something flashed behind her eyes. The new energy I had seen in her became an icy exterior shell.

"Because I can," she said defiantly. Her tone changed and my heart skipped a beat. Only later would

I realize the feeling was dread. "I have magic and I am more powerful than all of these humans."

She was a little bit too loud for my liking. The rest of us exchanged nervous glances and Seth took her gently by the arm, leading her into a street nearby that was so narrow it could have been an alleyway. No windows lined the walls here, just a narrow gap where two buildings did not come together. The daylight became shadow.

I expected her to pull away from him — to do anything as defiant as she sounded, but she let herself be led with her head held high as if we were truly accusing her of something ludicrous.

"You *are* human," Seth reminded her. He spoke quietly and firmly into her ear as we escaped the prying eyes and ears of the shoppers on the main road. "Having magic does not change that."

Moira pulled her elbow out of his reach. "I'm more than that," she said. Again, her head was held high and it bothered me. It was as if she was lording it over us.

"Maybe more, but still human," Seth told her.

"You're wrong," she replied, lips pursed.

"Why can't you just be one of us?" Seth asked, exasperated, trying to keep his voice down. He was beginning to lose his temper. I wondered if there was anything from the past underlying his frustration with her, or if the past months were enough. It was certainly enough for me.

"Why?" Moira's voice was disbelieving. She was practically yelling, and I could see tears springing to her eyes. "*Why?*"

Suddenly my mind was flooded. I nearly lost my balance as my vision went hazy with all of the memories that suddenly popped up, unbidden. It was as if the hand that had gently leafed through my brain in the previous weeks suddenly lost all patience and dug right in, raking through everything — both pleasant and not so pleasant.

Kian, Garrison, Seth — people I knew and didn't know flipped through my mind like a scrolling marquee I couldn't control. As if they were the pages of a book, I didn't even have time to fully grasp each one before it turned into something else. My parents, strangers, the boy in Australia — it was all a fast-moving blur.

I sucked in a breath as I began to fall backwards. Garrison, who had been standing next to me, caught me. My vision focused on Kian's face staring worriedly into mine. I tried to wave him off. The thoughts finally stopped on the one that had begun my adventure. Seth.

When Kian had told me everything about our history, I of course hadn't believed him. Plus, at the time I was convinced he was holding me hostage. I wasn't going to come with him, and I'm not sure if he would've forced me, but after he initiated something in my memories, images of Seth and the intense emotions I felt for him pushed me to agree to go with Kian.

It was a memory that had made me blush then, and had the same effect now — a midday frolic in a tiny, frigid waterfall that opened into a pond. Two thousand years ago we hadn't had bathing suits. My feelings for Seth were intense, and as confused as I was, I couldn't help but feel proud of myself that I could now distinguish my past emotions from my present. At least I knew I was getting better at this. At the time, when I first saw it, I had been racked with fear and manifestations of my power.

What seemed like ages to me was really only seconds to everyone else. Kian took my hand and helped me stand up straight again. I couldn't get the red out of my face as that unwelcome prying hand in my mind was still holding on to the image of Seth from the past.

"*She's* why!" Moira yelled.

"Gwen hasn't done anything to you," Seth said angrily.

"You will *always* defend her," she snapped. "Like you always have."

More random memories that I hadn't even known I possessed flashed before my eyes — Seth smiling at me, Moira in the background.

"It was you," I said. My voice was weaker than I thought it would be. "You've been going into my mind for weeks!" Kian's hold on me quickly turned from supportive to holding me back as I scrambled to face her. "Why?"

"You used magic on her?" Seth asked Moira.

She ignored him. "Maybe," she said to me snidely, "I just wanted to see what all the fuss was about. How you could have turned my own husband against me. How you managed to make a *child*," she gestured at Kian, "who barely even remembered you fall in love with you and give up everything for you!"

I didn't even have a chance to respond. Seth jumped in, and maybe it was for the better. The anger was pounding in my heart, and as Kian and Garrison stood with their mouths open, shocked at all the revelations, Seth and Moira could finally settle their marital dispute that had begun two thousand years ago.

"Are you crazy?" Seth asked. "Gwen never turned me against you! I never wanted to marry you! You knew that perfectly well! I always respected you, anyway. You were never mistreated."

"Oh, really?" Moira nearly shrieked.

She reached for me suddenly, and my head flared in pain. I began to sink into a place where all I saw was silver. It was similar to how Kian had shown me the past when I had woken up after using magic for the first time. Except now Moira pulled at only the memories she wanted.

Various scenes from the lives Seth and I shared together in secret were broadcast to all my friends. Behind the pain, somewhere I was aching for it to stop out of sheer embarrassment. The waterfalls, our meetings on the rocks overlooking the watchtowers — all shown for everyone to see.

"Stop."

It wasn't a yell, yet Seth's voice echoed in a commanding, booming way that forced Moira into retreat mode. She immediately backed up. The images disappeared and I was left to wrap my arms around myself. I felt totally violated. And angry.

Stepping away from Kian, I advanced.

Moira tried to move back from me, but she soon hit the brick wall behind her. Maybe it was Seth's tone or what I could only assume was the wrathful expression on my face, but fear played across her features. As she looked side to side, seeking escape, her hair fell away from the sweater under her coat and I could see the silver brooch pinned to her lapel.

I understood. Moira was gone. A twinge of sadness for the girl I had met in England not long ago — a brief mourning — touched my heart before I was back to the problem at hand. I should have realized. I'd have plenty of time to blame myself later, but for now I had to deal with the fact that this person was the embodiment of the past, and it looked like we couldn't coexist.

It took a great deal of effort to control my anger and not just smash her with the bricks from the wall. Instead I pulled forward the ones around her, trapping her in a silhouette of brick.

The fear in her eyes brought me satisfaction for only a second — and then I hated myself. I felt someone take my hand. I turned and was surprised to find it was Garrison, not Kian.

He gave me a look of understanding, and I remembered his own story. His family was murdered. He had lived a life of war and death. And though he relished the training, I knew in an instant from his face that he would never choose that life for anyone else. I had to let the anger go.

I heard the bricks fall to the ground behind me before I turned back to Moira. She was still pressed to the wall, though my trap was gone.

"You're not going to stop her?" she asked Seth breathlessly.

He shrugged, his face coldly indifferent. "She's

right to be angry. You may think that you're the most powerful here because you've managed to escape the past and destroy the innocent girl who has given you a second life, but I am your king. And you still answer to me."

There was hate in Moira's face. Again the grief touched my heart. Could I have saved the girl?

"So you don't deny any of it," Moira accused.

"It's none of your business," Seth said.

"I am your wife!" she exclaimed.

"You *were* my wife," Seth agreed. "And my cousin. From an arranged marriage. Despite the fact that I loved someone else."

"And you would have married her."

It was another accusation, as if there was something fundamentally wrong with that.

Seth briefly glanced at me. How different would our lives have been had we been allowed to be together? Would we even be here? If an alternate past flashed before his eyes as it did mine, he didn't show it. Instead, he glanced over my shoulder at Kian, and then turned back to Moira.

"Why does that matter?" he asked. "This is the world now, but I haven't forgotten our world before — or our laws. You know the punishment for using magic against one of your tribe."

"You're banishing me?" Moira said indignantly. "From what? This isn't your land. You aren't king here."

"We are the last of the Riada," Seth said. His voice was like stone — cold and firm. "Where we go, our tribe is, and I will be the king I was meant to be. You are banished from us. Leave."

As we all stood and watched, my heart still beating wildly and hands shaking, Seth stood his ground. Moira, still casting looks of hatred at each of us, but especially me, walked away. It had taken two thousand years to get Seth to finally stand up to her.

It was a heavy, surreal moment, and I was in shock at everything that had happened. I hated how blind I had been, how I didn't have time to notice anyone else's problems, and now we were all paying the price.

Moira rounded the corner into the market and blended into a group of pedestrians. I lost sight of her in seconds.

Chapter Thirteen

"You really weren't going to stop me, were you?" I asked Seth breathlessly.

"I didn't have to, did I?"

I guess he didn't.

None of us had moved in a while. I wanted to make sense of things, and frankly, I wasn't sure how seriously Moira had taken Seth's banishment. Sure, he was king and it looked like she had listened to him, but would she be waiting for us around the corner? Would she try to get into my mind again?

I couldn't stand the fact that I was actually frightened, but the mind magic was something I didn't have on my own. I could only tap into someone else's, as I had when I pulled Seth back from the Godelan trap in Central Park. That feeling of claws digging through my memories and knowing more about me than I did myself was terrifying. It felt like my mind had gone through a blender and was now oozing out of my ears.

As my heart rate eventually slowed and the cold

began to sneak into my limbs, the physical pain of what she had done to me made me wince. I leaned on Kian again and realized Garrison had let go of me. When I looked at him, he was nursing his hand.

"Did I hurt you?"

Garrison gave me a tense smile. "Nothing I can't handle," he said, showing me a very pink hand. I thought I saw some magic weaving its way over it, helping it to heal.

I must have been burning up when Moira was either digging through my mind or when I was angry. I hadn't even noticed.

"It's okay," Garrison said. "It's like your defence mechanism. You're like a skunk. But with fire instead of smell."

His remarks elicited a few smiles, but I wasn't sure if I liked the comparison. I would take smelling over nearly charring my friends any day.

Eventually, we just couldn't take the cold anymore and Seth led us back into the market. I was watchful and hypersensitive for anyone who had noticed the commotion, but no one looked our way.

By the time we got back to our rented house, Moira was gone and so were her things. Seth made us wait while he scouted around the house to see if she had left any magic behind — magic that could become potentially dangerous. It was another cold reminder of our new reality.

"She wouldn't really do that, would she?" Garrison asked. "I mean, she's pissed at your love triangle or whatever, but she wouldn't hurt us?"

In hindsight, I can't believe I didn't just drown in embarrassment that day. It was like someone digging through all your dirty laundry and insecurities and waving them in front of the people who matter most to you.

"I don't know," Seth said, ignoring the second part of his comment. "We can't assume anything anymore. Did you see her eyes? It was like a different person. And I knew that person."

Their interaction had seemed familiar. Certainly the disdain between them felt more natural than any attraction between Seth and myself. I wondered about that, trying not to get myself too down. Had the past Seth disliked her more than he had loved me?

"She brought out something in me I don't like," Seth said. He shook his head as if he could get the memory out. "It was like I had my mind totally made up. I felt so closed to everything else."

It certainly had looked that way.

As he went inside to check the house, Garrison, Kian, and I stood in silence outside. I could tell Garrison was uncomfortable with what he had seen, but we would just have to put it behind us. And Kian? I could only imagine what was running through his mind. Moira's words about him being a child stuck with me, each one stabbing me in the heart.

I looked at the man who had been left to deal with the consequences of our decisions, who had made his own mistakes, and who had come so far just to help us. I didn't know how to answer Moira's question. With Seth, our relationship had spanned a lifetime. With Kian, I felt responsible for him. Just as I knew he felt responsible for me. We were tied to each other in a way I couldn't figure out.

Seth didn't find anything, and for a day we unofficially pretended we didn't notice Moira's absence. That night, as Kian and Seth pored over the best ways to get to Australia — there weren't many since it was really far — Garrison came to sling an arm around me while I stared blankly at a fake fire on the television.

"You okay?"

"Well ..." I thought about the day. "Considering I had all my deepest, darkest secrets and personal moments pulled out in front of the people I'd least like to see them in some kind of brain torture, which resulted in the loss of one of the seven people in this world who is like me and whom I need in order to fulfil our ultimate destiny, I'm only somewhat okay."

"Yeah." Garrison nodded sympathetically. "I figured that would be the case."

"Thanks, though."

"For what?"

"Reminding me what's important." I rested my head on his shoulder. "It felt horrible not being able to defend myself, or even to be able to do the same to her. It made me want to ..." I looked for the best word. "*Win.* Do something worse to her. Just to end it."

I was ashamed just saying it. It was as if I had been attacked with a sword, but I didn't have one, so I was on the verge of being okay with picking up a boulder and squashing my enemy.

"That's the warrior in you talking," Garrison told me quietly.

"You know?" I was surprised.

"I know," he replied. "The feeling of always having to just *end* things. Knowing that if something hurts you, it will hurt you again and again until you *win*. Feeling like nothing's enough until you are the only one standing … I know all of those feelings."

I looked at him disbelievingly.

"Oh yeah," he confirmed. "I was a pretty aggressive seven-year-old. No magic, but a lot of heart." He smiled.

"What happened?"

"I got beat up a lot," he replied casually. "I was a pretty small kid, always antagonizing the bigger guys. My parents may have home-schooled me for a reason. But I know how hard it is to rein those feelings in. We're strong. Very strong. And you may be the strongest. But if you start to become entitled and take advantage of that — well, you become like the Godelan. Or Moira."

"Don't say that," I said.

The guilt was still fresh.

"Okay, not Moira," Garrison said. "But her past life. You become a tyrant. And then the villain. Your story becomes just waiting for a hero to take on the quest of bringing you down. And no one remembers that you were once the hero yourself."

"I'm worried I can understand her," I said. "At least how she feels about everyone else, and our own strength. When I couldn't fight back … when she was in my mind, I was ready to do anything to stop her."

"Don't be worried," Seth said, coming with Kian to sit across from us. "You're better."

He had our printed tickets and handed them out. "We leave in the morning, and I'm going to teach you how to keep someone like Moira out."

After shaking off the encounter with Moira, Seth was back to his normal self.

We awkwardly discussed what had happened with her, and I finally told them about the airport. I was expecting anger for not telling them sooner, but everyone seemed to understand that I had made a promise. I was just trying to help her deal with the past.

At least that's what I told myself. My guilty conscience pushed me into thinking it was just my own aversion to realizing something bad was happening in front of me, because I didn't know how to deal with it.

"How do you know how to stop it from happening again?" I asked Seth.

"I don't," he replied. "But you can't succeed until you try."

I'd rather have Seth riffling around my mind than Moira. I didn't think there was anything about me he didn't know. Except my feelings for Kian. Or did he? Crap. Well, that was one good incentive to learn how to keep him out.

"What will happen to her?" Kian asked. He still glanced worriedly at me as if Moira hid inside my mind.

"Don't worry, little brother," Seth told him. "I'm ready to be king now. If it happens, I'll handle it."

✦

The flight was long. Somehow going to Tahiti had seemed blissfully far, as if the more miles we put between ourselves and what happened with the Godelan, the safer we'd be. Now Australia seemed like a trek that wouldn't end.

By the time we got to our stopover in China, I had drool all over my face and my entire body felt as dry as a raisin. I was groggy and tired, dragging my carry-on into the terminal and planting myself in the first chair I could find at our gate. My friends didn't fare much better.

In addition to the uncomfortable plane, I was still having the dreams with the burning ships. I tightly clutched the little notebook Kian had given me, writing down every street and shop sign I came across when I dreamt about our fifth so that we could find him faster.

The airport was loud and busy. I had thought of China as being much more unique than the typical shiny, uncomfortable chairs, fancy stores, and glass windows showing all the airplanes parked beyond. But it looked just like the rest of the world. The news was set to BBC, though it must have been a Chinese version because they spoke about floods and landslides in places I couldn't pronounce, with death tolls in the thousands. I closed my eyes.

The desire to believe none of this was my fault, or my responsibility, was immense. There were a million reasons for any of these disasters to be happening — reasons that were discussed and hypothesized about by people far smarter than me. I wanted to believe them, but all I saw when I closed my eyes were the Godelan.

I imagined them standing around a globe, seeing where they had to turn magic against itself to shift things into chaos. They wouldn't stop at anything, but now they knew we were strong enough to fight. I had always thought they underestimated us, but I guess drawing their own names away and hiding them somewhere as soon as they knew we were here was not the act of someone who is underestimating the situation.

My eyes flew open.

"Hey," I said to Garrison. He sat next to me while Kian and Seth had gone to find food. "If you were a Godel, where would you hide your name?"

Garrison looked at me as if I were stupid. "If I knew that, I'd have mentioned it earlier."

"No, I mean what *type* of place."

"Somewhere we wouldn't go?"

"What if we'd go anywhere?"

Garrison huffed. "I feel like you're driving at something here," he told me. "Do you maybe want to tell me?"

"I think they must have hidden their names somewhere vulnerable," I said. "On the planet. Somewhere where even if we went we'd be too scared of changing anything in order to extract the names."

"What makes you say that?"

I thought about our earlier conversation about winning. Beating the enemy. Destroying them.

"We're not villains," I said. "We're the heroes. We won't hurt people. They see that as our weakness."

When I told the others, I was surprised at how readily everyone accepted my hypothesis, even though

Kian warned me to keep an open mind. He said that the man he called Stone, which I found fitting for the silver-haired magician, thought like a snake — all winding, roundabout schemes.

"He's like the pin laced with poison," Kian told me as we boarded our flight to Sydney. "An invisible evil that you may not even suspect. Donald, the other one, is more like the battering ram at the gates. That makes him easier to predict, though just as dangerous."

We were in the middle of a huge plane. I'd never been on one so big. Just the row in the middle between two aisles that held more people on either side was ten people wide. The four of us, with Seth at the aisle, sat next to a family of loud British vacationers.

"And Magician? The one who brought you here?"

I hadn't ever really asked much more than this, because I could tell Kian's decisions still haunted him.

"I suppose he is a little bit like I was," Kian said, sliding into the seat next to me. "Holding on to a fantasy."

✦

Late March in Australia was actually fall for them, but as soon as we walked out of the air-conditioned airport and into the street, I felt like I was going to melt. Was it just because we were coming from winter? No. Our taxi driver confirmed the entire south was experiencing abnormal heat and a drought.

Overall, I found Sydney like any nice American downtown. A little like San Francisco, even, though without all the hills. The wide boardwalk we could see in the distance allowed people to walk along the water, enjoying the fresh breeze coming from the ocean. This helped deal with the smoggy weather.

Our hotel, luckily, was down the road from a shopping mall, so one of the first things we did was to go buy summer clothes. We got back just in time for check-in and found someone had already brought our bags up to our rooms.

The three rooms were linked by a middle room, in which my ugly green bag was placed neatly next to the desk.

"Is this in case I set myself on fire while I'm asleep again?" I joked, waving to the adjoining doors that would allow them to rescue me if necessary. Enough time had passed for me to joke about it.

"Pure coincidence," Seth promised.

That evening we pored over the information I had collected. We looked up the restaurants, street signs, and any other markers I could identify in my dreams. I didn't have much except for the fact that this guy was incredibly active.

"Gwen," Seth said, trying hard not to get angry, "a bunch of trees is not a point on a map."

"I was talking about a bunch of rocks, this time," I told him.

He gave a terse huff.

Our best bet was a rock-climbing place I had seen numerous times. It took me a while to figure out what it was since I had never set foot in one myself. When I first saw the strange walls, hanging ropes everywhere and a clientele that was mostly men, I thought it was some kind of military facility. When I caught sight of the logo, I woke up, reaching for my little notebook.

As far as I could tell, he went there several times a week. All we had to do was wait.

Our first night in Australia was difficult. I was tired but couldn't sleep. The time difference — and a number of other unsolved issues — weighed on my mind.

A few days passed as we visited all of his favourite places. Perhaps they weren't his favourites at all and he barely went there, but we didn't have much else to go on. I was on full alert for that feeling of connectedness, like when I had found Seth and Garrison, or when we had found Moira, but nothing happened.

Four days after arriving in Australia, we were back at the rock-climbing place, sitting in a rental car like creepy detectives. Seth decided he was going to look inside, but we argued with him. If this person saw us, he might get scared and leave, or go into hiding, and we'd never find him. But we were all restless, so we agreed to sneak around back and peek through the windows.

The building was a tall one-storey warehouse, not too far from the centre but not quite in a bustling neighbourhood. A thin metal fence cordoned off the industrial perimeter, but Kian simply reached over it and unlatched the gate to get inside. There was a dirty pool behind the place, as if there was a better season than summer to swim, and it was just closed for the time being. The murky waters had become opaque.

"Not exactly high security," Garrison muttered.

"What would someone steal?" I asked. "The walls?"

It still boggled my mind that someone would actually pay to climb things — or that places existed with walls to climb.

Feeling more like creeps than detectives now, we peered through the dusty windows. With their helmets and harnesses, it was difficult to make out the faces of the clientele. We spent an hour like that when suddenly I felt something pull at my insides.

It was a twitch, not directionally like what had brought me to Seth and Garrison, but it was more than we had gotten in the last few days.

"Did you feel that?" Seth asked.

"No," Kian replied.

We all turned to him awkwardly.

"Oh," he said.

Kian, never having gone through any ritual binding himself to any of us, didn't have the same draw to the others.

"He must be close!"

Seth stuck his head closer to the window, as if that would help him see well through the grime on the glass. It didn't.

"What does he look like again?" Garrison asked.

I pulled up the memory.

"Tall," I said uncertainly. I had spent my time looking around, not trying to catch glimpses of him.

"Anything else?" Garrison asked, sarcasm lacing his voice.

"Brown hair," I said. "Maybe not brown. A little lighter than brown."

I heard Kian chuckle behind me at their frustration. I was really bad at this.

"Longer. Shoulder length. Maybe a bit shorter. Grey eyes."

We all squinted through the dirty window. More than half of the room could have fit that description. Still, the feeling was getting stronger. It was as if my insides were being sucked toward some kind of magnet outside of my body. My heart raced.

"Enough of this," Garrison declared. "I'm going inside."

"Good idea," Seth said.

Before Kian or I could say anything, they were bounding to the other side of the building. Just as they were about to round the corner, a big fist came out of nowhere and hit Garrison so hard in the face that he fell straight to the ground. Seth tried to stop so quickly that he fell over Garrison and went flying forward. It would have been comical had the fist connecting to Garrison's face not made such a definitive sound.

Kian and I ran. I didn't even need to see who the fist was attached to as the person rounded the corner. I threw up my arms and intended for the lawn to rise up and envelop the large man, but he anticipated it. He stepped on the earth as it rose into a mound and pushed it back down.

I paused, shocked.

"Gwen!"

Kian pushed me down as the eavestrough from the building swung down and nearly whacked me in the head. I got up as fast as I could, only to find the dirty pool behind me was rising in a sheet and coming my way. I reached inside in a panic for my magic. I had nothing in the outside world to fight with that couldn't be turned against me.

Fire slipped through my fingers and met the wall of water.

Everything slowed. I stood face to face with our attacker. The eyes that looked back at me were so familiar, yet escaped me, like an answer on the tip of your tongue. He was the one we had been waiting for. Just as I had seen him in my dreams, he stood before me, looking just as shocked as I was, but also scared and angry. And for the first time there was a solid note of recollection.

As we faced each other, the magic I was holding strained my muscles. I let out a shallow breath, trying not to gasp from exertion.

Though only seventeen, he was probably done growing. He was a huge, hulking man, though through my memories I knew his eyes were usually kind, and I had never fought him before.

Suddenly it clicked. I recognized him from the vision of when the king had handed down his decision, ultimately our death sentence — this man had been right next to me.

The water hit the fire and we were enveloped in a dense steam. I choked in the haze and could only make out the stranger in front of me by his shape. I didn't dare move — Garrison was somewhere around my feet. The shape in front of me crumpled and fell to the ground. Garrison yelled.

I had to sit, blind and lightheaded, until the mist cleared and we could actually see. It turned out that Seth had snuck up behind our new friend and put him to sleep while I distracted him. I could see Seth felt guilty about using his magic on us by the way he refused to leave the larger man's side.

When the steam cleared, we assessed the damage. Kian announced Garrison's nose was most definitely broken. When we pried him out from underneath our new friend, who had fallen on him, his face and shirt were covered in blood. He took his hands away from his face, and it didn't even look like a nose anymore. I tried not to wince.

"'Ow 'ad id it?" Garrison asked.

"Not that bad," I lied.

Kian helped him up while Seth and I looked at the prone figure on the ground. At least it didn't look like anyone had noticed us behind the warehouse. This would have been much more awkward and difficult to contain had he come upon us in the parking lot.

"What do we do with him?" I asked.

His gym bag lay beside him. He hadn't even gone in yet. He must have sensed us before he got close to the doors.

Seth walked around the body a few times, as if examining it from different angles. I knew he was trying to find a good way to move this guy, but from any side, he was still big. He was taller than Kian by about half a foot, and more muscular than anyone I had seen before up close.

Garrison couldn't bend over with his bloody nose, so after securing him in the car, Kian ran back to Seth and me.

I still don't know how we did it, though magic was definitely a factor. I tried to roll the body on the ground along the turf, but I couldn't do this into the parking lot or someone would notice. We had to lift him. Seth and Kian hoisted him up, each one under an arm, as I hopped around them trying to be helpful, even though I really wasn't.

It was a sprint to the car, since anyone could have stopped us at any moment to ask why we were carrying this unconscious man and stuffing him into a vehicle, and I had no answers prepared.

I briefly considered how easy Kian had it when he had tossed me over his shoulder. I was wondering if he was thinking the same thing as he and Seth nearly toppled under the weight, sweat beading on their foreheads just from the short walk to the car.

Getting him into the car was another challenge. I was struck with paranoia, as if we had just killed him.

While I kept lookout, Kian and Seth managed to push him in, which ended up with him in a weird position resting on Garrison's lap. Garrison, who still had his head tilted backwards, could do nothing but squeeze himself as far toward the door as possible. When Kian and Seth got back into the car, finally ready to go, we realized there was no room for me. I stood in the parking lot.

Improvising, I had to climb into the trunk of the hatchback, hugging my legs with only my head popping up over the seats. This was probably the most awkward thing I had ever done in my life. I really did feel like we had just killed somebody and kept watching out for the police on our tail.

When I wasn't doing that, I was asking Seth to feel the guy's pulse to make sure he was still alive. Which was a little annoying, I admit.

We hadn't been able to predict any of what would happen. Finding our newest friend could have gone as smoothly as when Kian and I had found Seth and Garrison, or as complicated as when we had found Moira. If this experience taught me anything, it was that we were all different — and finding numbers six and seven was a question still very much up in the air.

Upon pulling up to the hotel, we realized a further flaw in our plan — we had no way to get him up to our room without anyone noticing. And Garrison was still bleeding all over the car and himself. It looked like someone had been shot.

Seth ran in to find out where the service elevator was, and after a lot of shuffling feet and hoisting limbs, our broken little group managed to get him into my room without anyone seeing.

While Seth and Kian laid him carefully out on the floor, reminding me of how I had woken up with Kian in my own backyard, I gently moved Garrison's hands away from his face. His nose looked even worse than before and had swollen to the size of a pomegranate.

"Ba?" Garrison asked, more nasal than ever.

"It's okay, I can try to fix it," I told him, trying to sound reassuring.

"Dry?"

"Well, I've never really done anything so … delicate."

I looked at his broken nose from a dozen different angles, trying to figure out what went where. He didn't seem convinced by my abilities, but I wasn't either. I didn't actually know how to heal, so the plan had been to move his bones back into place. Now that I looked at it, though, I had no idea what that place was.

"You're going to make him look like a Picasso," Seth joked. "Or maybe Michael already did."

Garrison shot him a sideways glare. He couldn't really move his head.

"Michael?" I asked.

"I found his ID," Seth said. "Michael Davis."

I turned back to Garrison. The dried blood everywhere made my stomach churn. I had no idea where things went, so I tried for the healing. It was hard, and I don't know how long I stood over his chair as he leaned his head back and tried breathing.

I felt very little connection with my magic inside the hotel. There were no natural things to move or shift. After failing to find the connection with a more concentrated magic that could heal him, I focused on the sunshine falling on my hands from the window and warming them. I drank in the feeling of rays against my face and pulled on the threads that laced over my hair and the back of my neck, bringing everything into me. Finally, it flowed throw my fingers.

Satisfying cracks and pops, along with Garrison's shrieks of pain — which Seth quickly muffled — told me something was working. It wasn't until I had drained my own magic and felt faint that I finally stopped and looked.

Garrison's nose looked pretty much right. His face was a mess, with blood caked everywhere and tears running down his face, but it was otherwise fine. As soon as I tried to move, however, I sat heavily on the ground.

I shook my head to clear it and got up to reassure my friends.

"Just overdid it, I think."

"Thanks," Garrison said, standing and feeling his nose. "Try not to make it hurt so much next time."

"Try not to get punched in the face next time," I retorted.

Garrison looked at me, deadpan. "You know that will be harder than what I asked you," he said.

"I guess that's true," I admitted.

At that moment, Michael groaned.

We hurried over to where he lay on the carpet, all of us peering over him as if he was some kind of feature attraction. Garrison stood with his hands protectively covering his new nose, just in case.

Michael's eyes fluttered, then opened. For an instant, he looked at all of us with nothing but sheer curiosity. Then he must have realized his situation. He sat up suddenly. When his eyes focused on me, he nearly jumped out of his own skin.

"You!" he screamed, backing away from me. He was

still sitting, and when his back hit the bed and he had nowhere else to go, true panic set in. His eyes darted wildly for an escape. It was strange to have someone so big scared of me. "Get away from me! You and — and all of you!"

We certainly weren't expecting co-operation after what happened earlier, but this was something else. Before any of us could open our mouths to ask him why he was so frightened, he began yelling again.

"Get away! Leave! Go!"

I was really curious about where he expected me to go.

"Vanish, ghost!"

Chapter Fourteen

The bed behind Michael began to shake. I could feel him drawing magic as if the air was gravitating around him. He was about to use it again, and I was too spent to defend myself.

"Wait!" Kian said, anticipating the same thing. "We're here to help you."

Michael was still staring at me, barely listening to Kian.

"Everybody get out!" Kian yelled. There was such urgency in his voice that no one protested.

Seth, Garrison, and I sprinted out of the room, closing the door behind us and just waiting to hear something smash. I could feel the vibrations from the bed as it bounced on the floor. Only after we left did I realize how stupid it was to leave the only person without magic with Michael.

Surprisingly, though, we could hear nothing breaking, and even the vibrations slowed until they stopped altogether. It seemed everything was calm. Frankly, I was happy for the break. My vision was still hazy, and I felt weak.

It was well over an hour before Kian came out looking tired and worn, like a surgeon exiting the operating room. We all jumped upon seeing him, asking questions about Michael.

"He's adjusting," Kian said. "I told him the story. Everything this time, along with who I am," he added. "It seems that he's felt something was off for a while. Since last year, in fact."

Kian turned to me and gave me a shrewd look. "He thought, probably still thinks, that you're a ghost," he said. "As much as you've been seeing him, apparently he's been seeing vague reflections of you."

"How does that even work?" I asked. It was unnerving to think so much in my dreams was reality.

Kian shrugged. "There must be some kind of connection. Or a memory. I just don't know what it is. But you can come in and talk to him now."

We entered slowly, as if the large teen were a deer that could bolt at any moment. He still sat exactly where we left him, back to the bed, arms hugging his knees. His eyes were wide with shock.

"Did you do that thing to him with the memories?" I quietly asked Kian, meaning the silver screen effect of seeing your hidden life flash before your eyes. He shook his head.

"No magic, remember?"

I kept forgetting.

Seth and Garrison sat slowly in front of Michael, as if he'd run away if they moved too fast. Kian and I joined them, forming a semi-circle in front of him. I doubt this made him feel more at ease, but him bolting from the room was a real concern.

"So," Michael said finally. "You're like me?"

We nodded. He turned to me.

"And you and I are …?"

I didn't know how to answer that, so a response full of guesses would have to do.

"I think we have some kind of past," I told him. "I thought I was just dreaming. I had no idea you could actually see me. But when we're … similar … we feel drawn to each other, because we're meant to find one another." At least that's how I thought it worked.

"When Kian first found me," I told him, "and I started remembering, it may have triggered you, too. Garrison has known for a while, so has Seth. But Moira only began to experience things when we found her."

I nearly bit my tongue. The others exchanged awkward glances as we tried to telepathically communicate a response to Michael's obvious next question.

"Who's she? Where is she?" he asked. There was nervousness in his voice that implied to be like us meant to drop like flies from the face of the earth.

"She's like us," Seth told him. "But she went home."

"And you're all saving the world?" he asked. If he hadn't said it with such an ominous look on his face, I would have thought he was joking.

"We're trying to," I said.

I didn't know how much Kian had told him. The hour he spent in here was probably used to keep repeating the same information over and over again, since it was just so hard to believe. But Michael had used magic. He had shown more control than I ever had when Kian first found me.

"Where did you learn to use your magic?" I asked, making sure to keep my voice gentle.

"I … nowhere," Michael said. "It's just there when I need it. Somehow, things work out."

Lucky.

"Like when you fell from the cliff?" I asked.

His eyes widened. "You were there, too?" he asked. "Yeah, that was the first time. I was stupid. Should have tied my lines better, but I got lazy. I fell, and things just worked out."

He was obviously gifted and strong. Now, how to tell him that without freaking him out? We could certainly use his help.

Michael took a deep breath. "What happens now?"

We all exchanged glances.

"Now, if you'd like to join us, you'll go home and make something up," Seth said. "Tell your family you'll be back, that you'll be okay, and I can come with you to make it more convincing."

"How will you make it more convincing?" Michael asked. When Seth only smiled, his brows furrowed. "Oh, right."

After fielding several more questions about the logistics of our travels, Michael slowly got up and we followed him. We had agreed to take him to his small house outside the city centre, where he and Seth would talk his parents into letting him leave.

It wasn't easy. With every step Michael made, I

could sense he wasn't sure whether to move forward or turn around. But as with all of us, learning the truth about himself pushed him to join us.

When we drove to his neighbourhood and parked in front of a blue bungalow, Michael didn't even reach for the door handle. He just sat, hunched over, packed into a car full of strangers. I didn't blame him for being unsure. It didn't even sound like a good deal to me anymore, especially after what happened with Moira.

Eventually, at Seth's prompt, he opened the door and walked to the house. I thought I would calm down when they entered, but instead losing sight of them just made me worry even more.

"Calm down," Kian told me, placing a hand on my shoulder. I felt the tension ease under his touch.

"Can you believe you were haunting this guy?" Garrison chuckled.

The tension came back in an instant.

"I obviously didn't mean to," I retorted.

"But you're sure you've never seen him before in the past?"

I thought about it. "I have seen him. I remember him from our memories of invading the Godelan, from being in front of the king, and things like that. Where we all were," I said. As a man, he had been as hulking and imposing a figure as he was now. "He was always near, and I guess I remember seeing his face more often than others I didn't recognize." It could have been only perspective, though. I didn't remember anything specific about him.

The amount I still didn't know about the past

bothered me and made me think that I would never know the whole story. Perhaps it was for the best. Maybe I wasn't meant to live with two full lives in my head. Or maybe I'd never be as powerful since I chose to keep this life. Unlike Moira. Was she more powerful than us now?

Kian took my hand as I thought. I often wondered if he heard my thoughts, since he seemed to anticipate my need for moral support. His timing was impeccable.

"You know what I'm thinking?" I asked quietly.

He smiled at me. "I know your worried face."

We sat for another half hour in silence. Finally, Seth and Michael came out of the house. Michael wore a huge, stuffed backpack that loomed over his head. I'd never seen a pack so big, and yet he carried it on his shoulders as if it weighed nothing. He struggled to get it into the trunk and then climbed in, folding over so that he'd fit in the tiny car.

"If I'm going to be travelling with you guys," he said as he finally managed to shut the door, "can I request more size-appropriate transportation in the future?"

"You got it," Garrison replied immediately. He was glued to the door on the other size and didn't look very comfortable himself.

"How did it go?" I asked.

Michael tried to shrug in the small space. "I was going to move out anyway this fall to go to school," he said. "This is a little different. But if the problem's as bad as the guy up front said it was, I'd rather use my ... ability ... for some good."

He had forgotten Kian's name. I wondered how much had stuck, given the amount of information and shock he had absorbed in the last few hours.

"To be honest," Michael continued, chattier now as the situation washed over him, "ever since that fall I took while climbing, I was expecting aliens or something to come get me. You guys are a relief. Sorry about your nose, mate," he said to Garrison. "I felt something around the corner that just made my guts want to fly away."

"It's okay," Garrison said, feeling his nose.

After the original panic subsided, Michael seemed determined. It was both good and bad. Good, because he needed that determination. A lot had happened since I myself was panicked upon seeing Kian in the rain. It was also bad because the rest of us were all exhausted. We only made it back to the hotel as the sun was setting, and Michael wouldn't stop talking.

Questions would often punctuate his stories of his childhood and tales of all of his extracurricular activities. After missing a second question in a row directed at me, I finally had to interrupt him and tell him I was too tired after healing Garrison. Which led to a series of other questions. Michael eventually caught on that our attention was waning when we sat in the hotel room he'd share with Kian and kept eyeing the doors.

"I'm talking too much, aren't I?"

We all rushed to say no. Even though the answer was yes.

"I've just always felt a bit different," Michael

confessed. "It's nice to have people that are in the same situation. Feeling the same way."

"Of course," Seth said. "We'll feel even more the same way, though, after we've had a little sleep."

That night, I didn't even bother finding pajamas as I got under the covers of my bed. Sleep wouldn't last long, however. I woke up only an hour later to snores that seemed like they were shaking the hotel.

I couldn't believe how loud Michael was. I was left staring at the hotel room ceiling, vowing to buy ear-plugs the next day, though I knew they could not stand up to his volume.

After a half hour or so, I heard a small knock on the door connecting my room to Kian and Michael's. I opened it to find Kian, dishevelled and clutching a pillow.

"Can I sleep here tonight?" he said.

✦

Training with Michael was far more exhausting than with Kian. Every day, we drove out in the cramped car to a section of a large park that turned into a forest. Michael led us on an hour-long hike to a place where he had never seen another soul, and we practised our magic. Archery. Grappling. Sword-fighting. It was all a blur.

Of course, none of these defences could ever be used against the Godelan, but it kept us on our toes, and Kian was right — the repetition that linked us so strongly to the activities of our past lives did bring up random memories, and thus increased our magic.

At least it was cooler in the forest than in the

scorching sun everywhere else. We had been in Australia for over two weeks and I had barely seen a cloud. While that would usually be a good thing, signs of drought were everywhere.

As I immersed myself in the exhausting activities of my past, I received for the first time glimpses into my younger years. My parents. Horses. I even began to see Garrison, Seth, Moira, and the others as teenagers, much like we were now. Michael was ever-present in my earlier memories, and my theory of us being related somehow was reinforced by the fact that it appeared I had known him a long time.

Michael was very strong, and his magic leaned in the direction of Garrison's and mine, versus the more mind-oriented like Seth and Moira's. Even Garrison had to take timeouts from the training, struggling and out of breath. Michael relished the idea of moving trees and boulders, as if he had craved this power his whole life and simply hadn't known.

During our exercises, between dodging Garrison and Michael's physical magic, Seth also took time to teach me how to protect myself against a mental attack like Moira's. He emphasized over and over that he had no idea what he was doing — but he would explain to me how he got into my mind and ways that I could force him out.

The forest was full of distractions. Upon Seth's first attempts to get into my head, he was so delicate and careful that I could barely feel anything. He increased the magic he was forcing on me incrementally, until I began to feel like I had with Moira. He commented on how much power he needed just to replicate what she had done on a daily basis for weeks.

"That must really be a strong suit of hers," he commented.

"Great."

I had so far been wholly unable to push him out.

Nearby, an old trunk crashed to the ground as Michael turned to us, his eyes lit up as if he couldn't believe what he had done. His expression was quite goofy and childlike, especially on such a large man. I smiled in return. At least he was having fun with it.

Kian had told him about the disasters worldwide and how the Godelan were trying to revive the past by destroying the present. I think he understood, but he had never stood face to face with a tsunami. He had never heard screams as people were swallowed up by waves. He had never had the enemy tell him it was entirely his fault.

"Gwen?" Seth called. "Come on back, Gwen. I can hear you thinking."

"I don't feel anything," I told him.

"I'm not doing anything," Seth replied. "But I can see it on your face. Come on — don't give up. Let's go again."

At least having Seth dig through my brain wasn't as invasive as having Moira do it. Any romantic connection we might have had was fading, but I still trusted him completely. We had lived a whole life together, and now we were on our second. And having him in my mind felt more like someone leafing through a book versus Moira's raking with claws.

After another afternoon of being unable to push him out even a little bit, I declared it impossible. "I can't find you," I complained. "It's like you're every-where. And you go through memories too quickly."

"Wow," Seth laughed. "What is it with all this whining?"

"I'm serious!"

"Okay."

He moved the hair out of his eyes, exactly like Kian. Or was it vice versa?

"How about instead of forcing me out, you try to trap me? It's better than nothing, right?"

"What do you mean?"

"If you feel me in a memory," Seth said. "Try to keep me there. When I see something from your mind, it's just a surface impression. Like words or a picture on a page. But there's so much more to it; I just choose to move on to the next thing. Why don't you try to trap me in that memory?"

I hesitantly agreed, and immediately felt him pulling up things I wasn't thinking about. Memories flashed by just as they had the previous dozen times we had done this exercise. I couldn't grasp any single one because I couldn't tell what Seth would pull up next. It was as if he had dived into the treasure chest of my mind and was throwing things out at random.

Just when I was about to be overwhelmed, I found some kind of pattern. Seth was going through my time in Oregon, chronologically from when I'd arrived with my parents. The images struck a nerve. I had been missing them more than ever because of the new memories of my past, when I had parents who were significantly less understanding and loving than my current ones. I felt guilty for not appreciating them when I had the chance.

As I began to think deeper about Oregon, I sank into the memory. And without realizing it, dragged Seth along with me. My parents' faces beaming at me. The smell of the ocean, the grey sky, then tall trees as far as the eye could see. I remembered thinking that what I was looking at hadn't changed in a thousand years, and being overwhelmed by the lasting power of it all.

I was their only child, and I had left. In the past few months I hadn't let myself think about them, telling myself I was doing this for everyone's good, but was I just being selfish? Was I putting myself first? I stayed in that moment, remembering their faces as they looked from the ocean to me, for several seconds.

Seth's voice snapped me out of it.

"Whoa!"

He was sitting cross-legged in front of me and swayed as if a strong wind had nearly knocked him over.

"That was weird. But you did it!"

He smiled and clapped me on the shoulder. I doubted my success, though. I hadn't felt his presence at all.

"Were you really there with me?" I asked.

"Of course," Seth said. "And I couldn't leave. It was like a rollercoaster ride. I just kind of hovered in the air like I didn't exist. Good job, Gwen."

My eyes widened with realization. I was an idiot. I put a hand over my eyes to block out the distractions, thinking my theory through before I voiced it aloud.

"Gwen?" Seth asked. "What's up?"

"The burning ships," I said.

I took the hand away from my face. He still looked confused.

"The burning ships I've been dreaming about every night until we met Michael aren't a dream. They're a memory. It must be his memory. That's how I managed to connect with him. It felt exactly like how you just described."

We both turned to watch Garrison try to wrestle with Michael. His efforts were futile. Though tall, Garrison was lanky and Michael was nearly twice as wide. Kian sat nearby on a tree stump and laughed at them.

"Remind me to ask him about that," I said.

✦

Getting back to our hotel was always an awkward experience. Kian would put his things in his room and come directly to mine, where everyone would gather to order dinner. We'd been too exhausted and busy to talk about the fact that he escaped Michael's snores every night in here, and if the others noticed, they kept it to themselves.

That night as we ate, I asked Michael about the ships.

"I know, it's weird, huh?" he asked between

mouthfuls of chicken and fries. He ate more than all of us put together.

"Do you know what it means?" I asked.

He shook his head. "At this point, really, it's hard to tell if I actually remember some things or if you guys just described it to me and so now I think I remember," he said. "I know something I can actually picture, like battles and stuff. But I think the ships are different. I've been having that dream forever."

"In the dream," I prompted him, "I felt like everything was really big, or that I was small. Young, maybe?"

He nodded. "That sounds about right. But what you describe is everything I know. We're sitting around a fire. Big bang. Everyone goes running. Find the ships washed ashore and they're on fire. Everyone's talking about how those Godelan are invading."

"Wait, what?"

I think we all spoke at the same time.

"Yeah," Michael said nonchalantly. "I never knew the name for them, but once you said it I knew it was right. The Godelan who we've been fighting for … well, forever, they're not even from our lands. They came on those ships to get away from their own land. Set them on fire to avoid being sent back. I think they were under attack themselves."

It was hard not to sigh. Michael had assumed we knew too much. This piece of information was important.

"That sounds right," Garrison suddenly added. His eyes were staring into the distance as if looking at something else. While we were all the same age now, I often forgot we hadn't been in the past. "I think Michael and I were older. I remember this vaguely, from when I was young. Stories about how the Godelan came to our land for magic. They didn't have enough of it where they were from ... or they were sent away for using it ... something like that."

Michael looked at us, most likely confused about our knowing grins. "What?"

Seth explained about the stone we found with information on how to leave the ritual without coming back, and how we had destroyed it.

"It makes sense," he said. "It said we couldn't use the knowledge against anyone from our own land. The Godelan don't come from our land. Problem solved."

While knowing how we could get rid of them was a bit of a comfort, the Godelan were not likely to go easily. They had all still sworn loyalty the king. Our immediate mission was the same. We had to learn their names in order to call in that loyalty.

As we parted ways for the night, Kian headed directly into my room. I felt guilty for enjoying his company so much, especially since it was so much better than having sullen Moira around. But after several weeks I was beginning to think we weren't actually too busy to talk. We were both just avoiding it.

Despite the grins Garrison tended to throw my way over breakfast, we just slept at night, though during the day every touch seemed meaningful. We just were never alone.

As I riffled around for a clean shirt in my luggage, I came upon what I had bought Kian in the market in

London, right before our fallout with Moira. His lack of belongings in this time made me want to give him something.

I stuffed it in my bag to give to him tomorrow since our daily routine of not speaking about the situation had begun. Kian brushed his teeth and turned out the light as soon as I got into bed. Before long, I could hear Michael's room-shaking snores. We all wore earplugs by this point, and I was surprised no one at the hotel had complained yet.

The next day I practiced blocking mind attacks with Seth for less than an hour. After getting it right once, it seemed to come naturally, and he offered Garrison some training, too.

Garrison, usually unwilling to miss a second of fake fighting, happily joined him. Michael had raised the bar for all of us when it came to feats of strength. Despite Kian's agility and skill, without magic Michael had him on the ground, wincing in pain, even faster than Garrison. Despite this, I didn't hate the drills, though Kian hovered like a mother hen. It made me smile when I remembered the gift I had for him.

Around noon we took a break and I seized the first moment the other three were busy with something else. I pulled the bundle out of my bag and unwrapped the newspaper around it.

"Here you go," I said.

Kian looked from the wooden figurine to me, puzzled.

"I got you this," I explained. "As a gift."

He took it and turned it over in his hands. I couldn't

tell if he thought the idea was stupid or sentimental. I waited.

"Why a bird?" he said finally.

"It's a heron," I told him. "It reminded me of you. The way you hover."

Finally, he smiled. The others were returning, so he tucked it into his jacket and wrapped an arm around me, giving me a tight squeeze.

"Thank you," he whispered into my ear.

The gesture made me feel a blush creeping up until Garrison informed me it was still my turn to work with Michael. We walked to an open area he had cleared of trees while Kian climbed up into a branch. I wondered if he was playing with my bird comment, or if I was actually more right about it than I had known.

I dreaded fighting with Michael and told him so. What I thought were muscle aches really turned out to be bruised bones, and I couldn't fight his strength.

"Brute strength isn't everything," Kian called from his tree when he heard me complaining. "It could never have fixed Garrison's nose. He would have a hole in his head right now."

"And delicate pressure can't have done this," I told him, waving my arms at the trunk graveyard around me. We had probably broken several dozen bylaws with our creative rearrangement of the forest.

"Hey, can I ask you something?" Michael said as we reached the centre of the cleared area.

"Sure."

Anything to delay my inevitable defeat.

"If you say you barely had any magic when you found out who you were, how did you get it?"

I thought about it. The story was a little ironic. "Actually, the Godelan," I told him. "They wanted to siphon our magic right when it was strongest but before we knew how to defend ourselves. Before we had our memories back, they tested us. They made us think we were in danger, threatening anything that would get us to fight or be scared. They thought that would get our magic back faster. They faked bullets and gunfights just to reach our magic. And it almost worked."

"How did they find you?"

I glanced at Kian without meaning to.

"Kian was sent to find us," I reminded Michael. "The Godelan have no connection to us, so they don't feel that pull you felt. All they know is where magic is being used, so they would send Kian, and then he needed me to recognize the others."

I noticed Michael looking around, paranoid, and guessed his next question.

"So why don't they come now, to take our magic if they still need it?"

"Now we're too strong," I said. I hoped it was true. "They still need our power, but at this point, with our memories it would take more magic just to take ours from us. Think of them like sharks — they reserve their energy because they never know when they're going to get more."

Michael seemed unconvinced. "But they can still destroy the world? Even without our magic?"

I sighed. It was a lot of questions for one afternoon. I didn't know if I was telling the truth, but I tried to give him some peace of mind nonetheless.

"Probably not. Or they'll have to do it much slower than with our power," I said. "But the Earth is a moving, living thing. They've done so much already that the effects will be felt for a long time."

He was nodding when Kian yelled at us to begin.

Michael was strong, but after spending the morning with him I had figured out his patterns. He always stepped out with his right foot first, meaning that something was going to hit me from the right. Then he pushed with the left.

This time, instead of stepping back instinctively, I stepped forward and got so close to him that the mound he had called up scraped by behind me.

From this distance, he was clumsy. Being smaller, I had a lot more space to deal with. The instant he took a step back, I caught his foot in midair with a strong gust of wind and used my magic to rush myself forward, actually knocking him over.

In my peripheral vision, I noticed Seth and Garrison had come to watch. Someone cheered. It was probably Garrison.

While Michael was down I reached for something sinewy to restrain him but couldn't find anything. Not being prepared cost me time, and he was back on his feet in an instant. He reached and my feet left the ground. I hadn't thought of actually lifting or moving people before.

Air rushed by me, keeping me afloat, and I tried

to redirect it at him. It worked, and as a blast sent him flying, I also careened backwards, straight into a tree.

As much as Michael would apologize to me, I knew it was my fault. It was like pushing somebody while standing on ice. My own magic forced me backwards, and as my back hit the tall, rough tree, my head snapped back. The last thing I remembered was a crack in my ears and then everything went black.

✦

I was rushing forward with my eyes closed.

Why?

I panicked, thinking I would trip over something, but it turned out my own arm was wiping at my eyes. I was crying, rushing from one dark, damp room to another. Someone's footsteps sounded behind me as I turned and paced back and forth. I didn't care. I was angry. Upset. Frustrated. Disappointed.

A big part of me wanted to pick up the entire structure and toss it into the ocean beyond the walls, with me in it. My emotions were spinning and I felt different than in most of my memories. I was spryer. I was more powerful. I guessed I was younger. This was confirmed when I finally turned and saw who had been following me. Michael.

He was younger as well, his beard short and blonder than I remember from later memories. He was also leaner and more muscular than in the memories I had of us before our deaths. How long would it be until we'd go together into battle against the Godelan?

For now, he just looked at me helplessly. I knew he didn't know what to say.

"You need to calm down," he told me.

"No," I shot back. "I refuse."

He went to the door and poked his head out, as if listening for something.

"They will be dismissed soon, and they will come, and you know he will need your blessing," he said.

I knew the "he" in question was Seth.

"Why does he need anything from me anymore? He goes by his father's wishes," I said bitterly.

He looked at me as if he was going to slap me. "You need to pull yourself together. You're going to disgrace yourself and our entire family." It was a warning. "Your father will find you another match."

I wanted to scream and kick, but I somehow forced my voice down.

"I don't want another match," I said through gritted teeth. There were more tears in my eyes. My throat felt constricted.

I turned around, wanting to make my suffering just a tiny bit more private, but a thick hand rested on my shoulder.

"I'm sorry. I truly am. But this is how we live here."

"Then I don't want to live here," I blurted out.

He sighed. "Think about it. This is a marriage of convenience. You know the king does not expect love from either side."

I turned in disbelief. "This is supposed to make me feel better?"

He sighed, raising his eyebrows as if hinting at something beyond his words. "All I am saying is that you cannot rule out your chances of being together at all. He does not love her. You just won't be together in the eyes of the king. Or the tribe."

I stood back. Shocked. Absorbing his words. "That's not right."

"It may be argued," he fired back, "that being forced to marry the person of your father's choosing is not right either."

I wiped away my tears, considering his words. Could it work?

"But," he said, placing both hands on my shoulders and looking very seriously into my eyes, "I mean when I say that you will not be together in the eyes of the king. Or the tribe. Do you understand me?"

I understood the meaning of his words. No one could ever know.

Shouts came down the hall. Still sniffing and wiping at my eyes, I was forced against the back wall of the small room. There was no furniture. Just two shelves by the door, and we leaned against them, hidden from view.

"Why are we hiding?" I whispered.

"Do you want to answer questions in your state right now?"

I shook my head.

"Be careful of how you present your feelings," he told me. "Give yourself away and you won't even receive the chance of discretion."

Again, I understood the subtext. Michael was suggesting an affair was the only way I would not have to lose Seth completely.

I gulped down my last few sniffles and fell silent as footsteps approached. Modern Gwen couldn't recognize the voice, but the old me knew who it was.

My chest flooded with anguish. The voice belonged to past-Moira. The woman who would have the only thing I had ever wanted, despite never even asking for it.

I hated her and then immediately regretted my feelings. Judging by her tone, she wanted this marriage as much as I did. She was being forced into a situation. I couldn't hold it against her. I vowed to try to make the best of this.

"Mother," she yelled. "Mother, let go of me!"

It sounded like she was being corralled through the hallway.

"Shameful!" a woman's voice cried. "Shameful behaviour in front of the king. So disgraceful."

"I don't want to marry him," past-Moira replied. It was practically a growl.

"Foolish child," he mother chided. "How can you be so surprised? You have been told that you would be queen since birth. I have groomed you for this your entire life. Do you not want it anymore?"

I could feel the guilt layered on even from a room away. Past-Moira's voice softened.

"Of course I want to be queen," she said. "The king can't control any of the neighbouring tribes and kingdoms. He's weak. I'd be queen now if I could."

Her mother shushed her but didn't discourage the treasonous talk.

Someone sighed.

"Is there no other way?" past-Moira asked.

"No," her mother replied.

I heard footsteps as they walked farther away, though we stood still behind the shelves for minutes after the muffled voices had faded.

I opened my mouth, about to tell past-Michael that I was going to see the king. I would expose past-Moira for how she had spoken about him, and maybe he would call off the marriage. But before I could move, past-Michael extended an arm across me, barring my way.

"Don't you even think about it," he said.

"Why not?" I demanded. "You heard what she said."

"She's not wrong," he replied. "Besides, you go to the king and then what? You think he will call off the marriage because of some gossip?"

I opened and closed my mouth uselessly.

"No," he told me. "You're going to live your life and accept our ways. You're also going to remember this, and in the case that she ever raises a word against you for your future actions, you will have this weapon to hold against her. Understood?"

I nodded, feeling lower than ever. This wasn't how it was supposed to go. This wasn't how I wanted to live my life. But I was trapped.

✦

I opened my eyes to the worst headache of my life. I winced and tried to roll over, thinking I would throw up. There was something wet on the back of my neck that trickled down as I moved.

As much as I didn't want to know, I reached and felt with my fingers. The area behind my ear was tender. When my fingers came away, they were covered in blood. I lay back again.

Everyone was hovering over me. Michael was

apologizing, Seth and Garrison were staring helplessly, Kian was trying to ask me something. I couldn't think straight.

The grass I lay on was soft. The sky was still bright blue, as if only seconds had passed. Everything seemed to lull me to sleep, though as soon as my eyes began to close, Kian would shake me awake again.

My mind wandered to the memory. Why did that come back to me? Had Michael brought up instances where he had profoundly affected my life with his advice or instruction? Had Moira always been so self-serving that her actions now weren't really my fault?

Eventually, Kian's voice cut through the ringing in my ears and his shaking me got annoying enough for me to wriggle out of his grasp. I sat up, very, very slowly. Everyone was staring at me as if they expected me to burst into flames.

The memory had made me upset. Residual emotions from the past still affected me, though less now than before. The feeling of being trapped and abiding by someone else's rules hadn't gone away. I knew it wouldn't. My life now was as limited as my life then, and yet I proceeded with both for what I thought was the common good.

"I want to go home," I said.

Chapter Fifteen

"**G**wen, eat your oatmeal."

I waited until my mother turned around then slid it across the table to Michael, taking his empty bowl and placing it in front of me. While I didn't want to treat him like a garbage disposal, the food was terrible, and he seemed ready to eat anything.

My parents sat on stools eating their own awful oatmeal behind the kitchen bar. They were on another diet, and so all of the food in the house seemed thicker, browner, and more tasteless than it had to be.

Our kitchen table had only ever been made to accommodate three, maybe four people, so every meal was like a game of musical chairs as Seth, Garrison, Michael, Kian, and I tried to find somewhere to perch.

I couldn't complain. We had arrived unannounced, and for the all that they hadn't seen or heard from me in months, and then I showed up with four other strangers, my parents were being very accommodating. The house only had three bedrooms, one of which was an office, so my four friends were camping in the living room.

It appeared as though Kian's intricate though completely spontaneous lies about my whereabouts had worn off when he lost his magic in December. When he first showed up around the house in September, we had together made up some story about why I had to go with him. I couldn't even remember the details myself.

It was strange to think of myself as I was then — curious, terrified, and adventurous. What was I now? The only thing that came to mind was travel weariness.

With no magical cover story, my parents hadn't known exactly where I was or what I was doing for months, but at least they were still under some kind of magic telling them it was okay that I was gone, and that I would be back. Which was a good thing, or else I would have come home to hysterics.

As it was, walking up the vaguely familiar driveway was nerve-wracking. I had no idea how they would react. But luckily it turned out I had worried for nothing. My parents were happy to see me, and I was happier than I could have imagined being back in Oregon, even though it didn't truly feel like home.

The difference between my parents and me was obvious, though we had always gotten along peacefully. Still, even my friends' eyes widened when they saw my mom and dad.

Both veterinarians who preferred to work from a clinic they had built in the house so that they would never have to leave, they were quite stout. Large, in fact. And their personalities matched their physiques. Loud and happy, they bounced around the old house, the creaky wooden floorboards protesting with each step.

I let it all sink in. Though my hands shook as I knocked on the door to what was technically my own house, I happily received several bone-crushing hugs and made quick introductions, dodging all the questions about where I had been.

I mumbled something about school and hoped the magic placed on them earlier was still strong enough to have them drop it. They did. Though my dad gave Kian the same look he had given him the first time they met, what seemed like forever ago. It was a raised eyebrow with a scowl, which stood out since he was the happiest person I knew. Aside from my mother.

Falling into our quiet life was easier than I thought it would be, even if we had four guests. My parents made them feel welcome, didn't delve too deep into my travels, and were otherwise quite busy with the clinic.

Howls and barks rang out at all hours of the day and night, and it was funny to see that my own home in Oregon, in what was not an extraordinary life, was harder for my friends to get used to than some of the exotic places we had been.

Back in Australia, the decision to come had been made fairly quickly. We were all tired of being on the road. And without knowing when our next clue to a direction would appear, all we could do was wait. It only made sense to hide out somewhere familiar and comfortable. Not that Oregon was either of these things to me. I had lived there for only a few short weeks before Kian came into my life.

For the next few days after hitting my head in the woods, I had to sit still and be woken up by Kian every few hours just in case. The result was grogginess and general unhappiness. I couldn't wait to leave, though I hadn't been able to bring myself to face my parents, talk to them, phone them, or lie even more about what I was doing.

The result was that I missed them. I felt burned out and needed the break.

Shortly after the first memory of Michael, I began having others at random points in the day. Moving made me dizzy, so I attributed it to boredom mixed with daydreaming. Phrases, small actions, or even just the birds outside my window would trigger scenes I hadn't thought of before. A full moon brought back glimpses of hunts, scouting in the woods with friends from a former life.

As if the knock to the head had broken open some kind of floodgate, the memories were coming to me now mostly as knowledge, not entire scenes I would relive.

Michael, it seemed, had dubbed himself my chaperone in our past life. After Seth's marriage to Moira, it was Michael who offered to be a lookout for our meetings. He hadn't trusted me not to be seen. This, mixed with everyday ancient life, filled my dreams and thoughts during the days when I couldn't move much at all.

A few days after getting to Oregon, we tried to find a quiet spot in the woods for using magic. I was still sore everywhere, so I sat out with Kian while Garrison, Seth, and Michael ran through a series of routines.

By this time, Michael had remembered our last days of his own accord. Kian's strategy of endless training worked. Michael was also stronger, but it was still brute force. The art of delicacy wasn't something that came easily to him.

"Do you remember when we met here?" Kian asked me suddenly.

"Of course," I replied.

How could I forget? I fell off a cliff, landed on the ocean as if hitting the pavement, fainted, and got kidnapped by him. It was a big day for me.

"You looked so scared," Kian laughed.

I turned to him, surprised. "Why are you laughing? Is it funny how scared I was?"

He shook his head, unable to put on a straight face. "It's just strange to think of you then," he said. "It was raining. You had put stuff all over your face and it was getting wet, making you look like an inkblot. You were tripping over your own feet."

Despite the warning signs of my crossed arms, raised eyebrows, and creased forehead, he didn't stop laughing.

"That was makeup, thanks," I told him, embarrassed and bitter. "I was tripping over my feet because a past life inside of me was pumping magic through my system, and I was a little scared because there was a creepy drifter following me through the woods. Is that unreasonable?"

Kian shook his head, still smiling.

"Oh, as if you were well-travelled and all-knowing back then?" I snapped. "With your old-style talking and your robotic movements and your cryptic every-thing?"

He threw up his hands in surrender. "You are right," he said. "You've changed me. I was broken when we met."

I wasn't expecting that. I immediately felt bad for bringing up his strange traits, most of which he seemed to have abandoned during our journey together.

"How do you mean?" I asked.

"You were my first real contact with this new world," Kian replied, as if it was obvious. "Looking for you was the first thing I had ever done that wasn't under the watchful eye of the Godelan, or of Magi-cian. I'm ashamed to admit it, but I was kept on a short leash for a long time. And I let myself be, because of what I was promised. Maybe I didn't even believe it, but I had no choice. If I had admitted to myself that I was being used, what was I supposed to do with my life? You gave me a reason."

The conversation had shifted from light to heavy very quickly. Always being surrounded by the others, Kian and I rarely had a chance to speak alone. Even though we shared a room in Australia, it had been purely functional — first for Michael's snoring and then for my possible concussion. And if it wasn't as utilitarian as we were both making it out to be, well, neither of us had the time or the right words to talk about it.

"Come walk with me," Kian said.

Still lost in thought, I didn't move as he got up and reached out to help me up from the fallen trunk. I took it. Every moment we had found together in the last while had always been intruded upon.

Now, while Seth, Garrison, and Michael were busy and had even wandered off slightly, we finally had a chance to be alone. Not that I knew what to do with that chance. My stomach turned as he took my hand and didn't let go, even as we walked side by side. Some people call that butterflies. I lean more toward nausea.

"What did it feel like when you ... changed? Started feeling your past?" he asked.

We walked along the same road on which I had tried to catch the school bus. Soon, my last year of high school would be over without my ever having set foot in a classroom. Sudden panic overwhelmed me when I thought about the worldly things I was abandoning, including a diploma. I let the thought linger as I considered my life after our mission.

"It felt like I was drunk," I said. "Heightened senses and awareness, but at the same time the paranoia that I could be imagining all of it."

He smiled.

"Are we meant to die?" I asked.

Perhaps I said it so calmly because I already knew the answer.

"I don't know," Kian replied, squeezing my hand tighter.

"What other purpose would we have in this world other than to defeat the Godelan?" I asked rhetorically.

"There's nothing to do for us here after that. No place in this world. We must have been intended to die in the process."

"The same could be said for me," he said. "Certainly I don't have a place in this world either, but I intend to try my best to live. Besides, you're talking about your past life. After the Godelan are done, she has nothing else to accomplish. You can have a life."

I remembered how it felt not to possess magic anymore. It was lonely, like a hole in your heart, or missing something that you know won't be back. I didn't know how I'd feel about that.

We came to a stop in the middle of the road.

"What?" I asked Kian. He was smiling knowingly.

"Recognize this spot?"

I looked around.

I didn't, but I knew what it could be. This was probably where I had tripped over my feet, fallen down a slope, got a million bruises, and ended up in the ocean. It was the first, but not the last, clumsy fall Kian would see me take.

I walked to the edge and glanced over. It didn't look like anyone had been crashing through it. Funny how nature could pummel me, but I hadn't even left a mark on it.

"It seems like a long way down," I said.

"It was," he agreed.

"You know, when I fell, I remember how nervous you looked," I said. "You tried to grab for me. I think I knew in that split second that you probably weren't trying to kill me."

Kian laughed. "Nervous? I was terrified. I finally find you, and then you tumble over the edge of a cliff. I had no idea your magic would save you." He joined me by the edge, looking down. "I was running after you, getting ready to jump in the water."

He had seemed so steely and distant, it was strange hearing about his perspective. I was thinking about what would have happened had I not been the first one found when he took my hand again and pulled me back to the road.

"I don't have magic anymore," he told me.

"So you won't go running in after me if I fall again?" I asked, batting my eyelashes and playing the perfect damsel in distress.

He turned and gave me a look that caught me off guard. I knew the next words out of his mouth were going to be sincere.

"Of course I would," he said. "But I don't have magic anymore, so it probably wouldn't end very well for me."

My stomach did an extra flip as he came closer. I suddenly felt my mouth go dry.

"You know I would do anything for you, right?" he said, taking another step toward me.

I could only nod. To any other two people, the words might have sounded romanticized or exaggerated. After what Kian had put himself through to save me, I knew it was the truth.

Slowly, he leaned until his face blocked the wind, and I was enveloped in warmth. Our lips met and I could do nothing but enjoy the moment as the cold

April day faded and I only lived in the space between us.

This was different than any other time in the last months when Kian and I had actually found some time to be alone. There was no confusion or vexation. For the first time, there was only honesty and complete understanding. As he wrapped his arms around me, I was ready to sink into this feeling forever.

A loud boom sounded from nearby like thunder, shaking the earth beneath our feet. We jumped apart. Instantly my heart was pounding.

My first reaction was to look up at the sky, thinking lightning had struck the woods just on the other side of the road. It was a grey day, but I dreaded that the noise wasn't a natural occurrence. Seconds later, my fears were confirmed as I heard Seth yelling my name, and then Kian's.

We ran at full speed back to where the others had been using magic and going through the drills Kian had taught us. I nearly tripped on a root but managed not to fall. Pain like fire raced up my ankle and into my leg, but I kept going anyway.

Kian, whose long legs had given him an advantage when running in the forest, got to the clearing first. He stopped suddenly and I nearly bulldozed him by careening straight into his back. He was looking around, resembling a bird more than ever as his brow furrowed and he cocked his head to the side, listening. I saw why quickly enough — the clearing was empty.

"Kian! Gwen!"

Seth was yelling again. This time we followed the

voices to a hollow. Long and narrow, but deep and filled with dirt and leaves, it looked like a trench separating one part of the forest from the other. Close to where a boulder ended the grotto, Seth and Michael huddled over an unconscious Garrison.

"What did he do?" I asked.

Michael helped me climb in since the walls on either side were nearly six feet tall and I didn't want to risk collapsing the earth even further.

"Stupid," Garrison suddenly muttered.

I sighed in relief. At least he was alive.

The four of us huddling over him formed a bit of a dark cave, so we had to back up, despite my desire to both take care of him and smack him for worrying me. I guess I couldn't really be angry. If there was one person who made magical mistakes resulting in injuries, it was me.

"We were trying to build up this path," Michael explained, waving to the far side of the trench. "It looks like something formed by ice, and we wanted to see if we could move it."

"Why?" Kian asked.

Michael looked at Garrison and Seth, obviously lacking a good answer. "To see if we could," he said.

Kian nearly groaned. If he were anyone else, he would have waved his arms in exasperation.

"When it comes time to fight the Godelan," Michael rushed to explain, "we'll be ready. Our magic will be stronger."

"That's not how it works!" Kian was close to yelling, but he worked to get his temper under control. I could see the strained effort in his tense movements. "You can't make yourself stronger by pushing yourself to extremes. Magic is not like muscles. Your magic is tied to your past life. You need inner growth. Understanding. Compassion. Balance."

Michael was quiet for a long moment. He looked a bit like a child caught doing something bad. "I didn't know that," he said softly.

Kian sighed. "Of course you didn't, because I didn't tell you. But in the future, before you make any assumptions, just ask me, okay?"

The others nodded.

With Michael's brawn, we managed to carry Garrison back to the house. Well, it was mostly Michael, but we all fluttered around him. Garrison looked a bit like a wooden puppet, all rigid arms and legs flailing around as he was carried, using his last energy to emphasize how embarrassed he was to be carried around like a princess by a knight.

Luckily, my parents were busy with the cats and dogs (they even had a horse tied up in the backyard) so we were able to put Garrison into my bed without drawing any attention. Seth stayed with him while the rest of us went back into the woods to see what could have caused him to use so much magic.

By this time, my paranoia had kicked in and I was watching over my shoulder constantly for any sign of the Godelan. If they were behind this, then we weren't safe here anymore and my visit home would have to be cut short. I couldn't involve my parents in my problems.

Kian jumped into the trench and turned to help me. The ground smelled damp and fresh. I could tell it had been covered just a short while ago. It wasn't soggy and rotten like the rest of the forest, still thawing in the unusually warm weather for April.

"We moved this rock a part of the way," Michael explained, pointing to the rock face that was cracked clean in two. That must have been the boom we had heard. Michael showed us how they had moved it at least ten feet. "But then it wouldn't budge."

Kian ran his fingers over the split in the rock. The edges looked fresh and razor sharp.

"It's warm," he observed. "There's still magic here."

There was something unusual about the stone. If I tried to sense its shape and how I could use it, I couldn't see its definition.

"Hey, Michael, you climbed the rocks and cliffs because you always had a feeling about what to grab a hold of, because you knew its shape, right?" I said, guessing.

He had proven himself exceptionally skilled at moving the earth. Unless any of us had found ways to trick him or use his own size against him, we could never win any of the drills.

"Yeah," he said. "I guess so."

"Well, tell me the shape of this rock," I said, stepping aside.

He approached carefully, bouncing a little on his feet as if to get a feel for the ground he walked on. He eyed the rock before placing his hands on it and bouncing some more.

"I can't feel it," he admitted. "I don't see where it ends."

"Probably because it doesn't," I told him. "You were trying to move a part of the continent. You could have sent us all right into the ocean if Garrison wasn't trying to do it all by himself."

Again, I realized I sounded a lot like Kian, but it was true. They hadn't really used a lot of thought when overdrawing on their magic. I couldn't believe my friends had nearly just collapsed part of Oregon. Michael's chastised child expression lasted for only a few minutes as we walked back to the house. Moments later, he was already imagining all the possibilities.

"So do you think if Seth and I were helping, the three of us could have moved the whole cliff?" he asked.

Both Kian and I ignored his question.

Garrison eventually recovered his energy, but having all the information before throwing his magic into something was a lesson that was engrained in him and all of us. His magic came back as slowly as mine had when I had caused a snowstorm that let us escape the Godelan in the winter. He pined for activities while he was restricted to my bed, so many days found us playing board games around a little breakfast-in-bed table in my room.

I was happy enough to camp in the living room with everyone else, telling my parents Garrison had fallen outside on the path. Which was true enough. Kian and I managed to steal a few more moments alone together, but between my parents and running up and down the stairs to talk to Garrison because, as he said, he was dying of boredom, I had little time to spare.

A few weeks passed quietly enough, and May came around. Seth and Kian would often get into deep discussions about how much time we had left to kill the Godelan once and for all, and how much time they had to do the same for us.

Ultimately, we were as vulnerable as they were for another seven months. But before we could ever get close enough to act on a ritual that would take them out of the initial ritual they had performed, we needed their names to control them.

We quizzed Kian on what the names could be, how it had looked when the Godelan removed their names, and the type of box they had put them in. Kian answered diligently but always reminded us that Stone would never just entrust his entire life to a box. It had to be something more than that. Unfortunately, he didn't know about their travels right after his and Magician's arrival. They had stayed in the house alone and waited for the other two to return.

"It was always like that," Kian remembered. "We would just wait. They'd never share anything with me, and I don't think Magician knew much more. They were born and raised in this world. While they knew him, he was still different. Unpredictable."

My theory of placing the names somewhere we wouldn't dare go was fine, but it didn't narrow down our options. And would the location of the names be physical, like a box hidden in a cave somewhere in the

North Pole, or would it be something that would present itself to us only when we had figured it out, like the answer to a riddle?

That thought pattern usually made my head hurt with all of the answers I didn't have, so I gave up a lot faster than Kian or Seth. For them, it seemed to be the thing that bonded them. As the only two who could perform the ritual or command the Godelan, this was a way to finally be kings and redeem themselves for leaving the tribe.

While we came together as a group, I couldn't help but think about Moira. She had been the banished one, yet I had ended up going home. Had she gone back to her parents? Was she living now just as she had before we found her, or had we ruined her life by igniting her past, which took over in the end?

Perhaps my constant dwelling on the guilt of losing the present Moira to her past self turned many of my memories into ones of her. She had always been kept apart by a strict mother who was proud of her magic yet disapproved of the rest of us. And I had never fully considered that she was also Kian's cousin.

My ties to Moira through their family reached far into our past, and in some ways I wondered if she was right to hate me. I always wanted what she took for granted, and so I took it for myself.

After a month of being in Oregon, an earthquake struck in Los Angeles, but it was so strong that we could feel it in our house. It was six in the morning when the ground began to shake and books fell from the shelves, nearly on top of our heads.

We jumped out of our sleeping bags and just stood in the middle of the room, adrenaline rushing though somewhat still asleep, just trying to keep our balance and dodge falling objects. I could hear my parents shouting upstairs, and Garrison answering them. Dogs began to bark and howl in the vet clinic part of the house.

From what I remembered of events in San Francisco, it was fairly long for an earthquake, lasting about a full minute. The sound was the scariest part, since the old wooden house, built into a hillside with probably very little foundation, creaked and groaned as if it was about to fall over. Finally, it stopped, yet we all stood stock still for several moments afterward.

"You kids okay?" my dad yelled from upstairs.

"Yeah!" I called back.

A few moments later, they came downstairs with Garrison hobbling behind them. He was walking now, if only for short periods, but had to pretend to limp to keep up the fall story.

As was our routine in California, my parents immediately turned on the TV. Every news channel in the country was reporting on a strong earthquake that had hit Los Angeles.

As the day progressed, shocking images played across the screen. The most eerie for me was an entire freeway that had simply slid into the ocean, along with all of the cars. Houses were rubble. Buildings were beyond repair. People cried and looked for lost loved ones in front of the cameras.

While I was used to the guilt and what-ifs that immediately hit me, it was a first for Michael. He waited until my parents left the room before turning to me and asking, "Did we do this?"

He was ashen.

I was glad that seeing things like this would keep him from thinking that trying to move continents was cool, but he also seemed heartbroken. And for the first time, the big, happy guy we had met in Australia looked to seriously be contemplating what he was doing here with us.

"No," I told him. "These shifts, pushes and pulls, the Godelan do it."

"Why?" he asked, though we had been over this several times.

"They want power. Chaos and destruction make it easy to get."

"So if we stop the Godelan, this will stop?"

Time to admit where we had failed.

"I don't think so," I told him honestly. "But if we stop them, we can help to keep it from getting worse."

Michael continued to stare at the TV for the rest of the day, and the day after that. I could see each bit of information flowing over him like the tidal wave in New York had flowed over me, haunting me long after I had escaped it.

✦

I stoked a fire, though the smoke was stifling. It refused to rise up through the roof. Evergreen sprigs were the only dry things I could find during the particularly wet winter, and they did not lend themselves to burning well. I coughed and eventually gave up, leaving a small, cold house and stepping out into the chill night.

While my magic could start the fire, I could not spend all my energy burning it. Firewood was particularly hard to come by as Romans cut their way through our lands, using our wood for their furnaces as the other tribes encroached on our lands from the north. At least winter was almost over.

The entire village was dark. Even the moon was hidden behind clouds, covering everything in shadow. I couldn't rest. Despite riding the perimeter of our lands all day, I was too agitated to let exhaustion take me over. Several people, including past-Seth and past-Michael, had gone to scout our lands. It wasn't safe to ride at night anymore. I hadn't seen past-Garrison in months. I felt like the last survivor of a settlement that didn't stir.

After wandering in the cold, a flicker of light caught my attention. A lantern shone out of the window of the main hall, where the king would return. I rushed forward, my heart torn between assuming the worst and hoping for the best. A thousand scenarios of attacks and ambushes ran through my mind as I crossed the village and burst through the heavy wooden doors.

I stopped, surprised.

At first I thought there was no one there. Then, in the darkness, I saw a woman sitting on the throne.

"Close the door, you'll let in the chill," said a voice. It was as cold as the winter, and delved just as deep into my bones. I recognized past-Moira.

My past life flared with a dozen emotions at once. I was awkward and resentful, ashamed and proud at the same time. Despite a solemn belief that she should not be on the throne, my first instinct was to turn and leave. As I began walking out without a word, her voice called me back.

"Don't leave," she said. "Please."

I sighed, regretting coming here in the first place. I had nothing to say to her. Still, I turned and walked toward the end of the long, dark room. Now I could see she had not only taken her place on the king's throne, but also draped herself in his cloak. She saw me looking.

"It's cold," she explained.

I said nothing.

"You know I am loyal to the king," past-Moira told me. "Tell me you know."

I had to speak through gritted teeth to say something I wouldn't regret.

"Why do you need my confirmation?"

"Because I am queen," past-Moira said. "If I let you carry a sword, I need to know you are loyal to me."

I nearly choked on my disbelief. That was some gall. My earlier resentment was replaced by sheer angry amusement.

"You are not queen yet," I told her.

"I am as much a queen as my husband is a king, and his father is a king, and his brother is a king."

I was shaking my head with incredulity. "Are you lonely," I asked, adding, with what I hoped was a voice laced with sarcasm, "my queen?"

Past-Moira's face immediately contorted to something between rage and pride. She thought she knew where I would take this conversation.

"Why?" she asked, her voice like a whip.

I smiled politely. "Because you are musing on fantasies

that perhaps ought to be told to another before they meet the ears of anyone who may object."

Snickering sounded from behind the big throne. She turned to peer behind her, but I didn't have to look. I knew who it was.

"Come on, Kian," I called to him, reaching out.

The small boy came scurrying forward, skinny arms and legs flapping. Past-Moira tried to grab his collar and pull him back, but he dodged her outstretched hand and took mine.

My past self walked away briskly, hoping that the queen would not call me back, because I would be forced to obey. And what I had just said already bordered on dangerous.

Still, modern Gwen marvelled at the little boy who jogged alongside me. His head was a mop of black and every few feet he would gaze up at me with perfectly round blue eyes, as if checking that I was still there.

✦

I woke up to the same face, though twenty years older, shaking me awake.

"What is it?" I asked groggily.

I was having trouble letting go of the dream. In my mind's eye, the little boy still ran next to me, trying to keep up with my fast pace, gripping my hand and looking up at me, smiling.

With what I now knew, I felt bad for him. I didn't want to leave him in the past. I didn't want him to grow up to be Kian. But I knew I had no choice. A little saddened by the dream, I let him go, leaving him to his fate two thousand years ago.

"I had a dream," Kian said.

Seth and Michael were just waking up. Garrison was on the couch, turning on the TV.

"You had a dream?" I repeated.

Kian, lacking magic and still living his first life, had never expressed any kind of dream or memory before. I was skeptical, but he seemed excited so I asked him about it.

"It was a memory, actually," he said. "I remembered something the Godelan said after they took their names."

Now everybody was interested. Garrison even muted the TV.

"It was a conversation I overheard one night," Kian said. "They decided they would leave the names in plain sight. It is just like them, assuming no one would notice. I remember the name of the place. I think it's a museum." He rushed around the room until he found a piece of paper and pen by the phone and wrote something down. It looked like Spanish.

Seth took the piece of paper and typed something into his computer. "Looks like we're going to Peru," he said. The word Kian had spelled out was written across a website that looked like it had been created two decades ago.

While everyone was getting excited about finally having some direction, I was stuck on the memory.

"Hang on," I said. "We've asked you the same questions a hundred times, but you never remembered this before?"

Kian shrugged. "I guess I never put it together with

their names," he said. "I figured they could have been talking about anything, but it has to be that, right?"

"Of course," Garrison agreed.

They all watched my face as I tried to believe this was more than just Kian being hopeful. Seeing how happy they all were, I couldn't deny them this small victory. If anything, at least it was something to do to avoid going stir crazy in Oregon.

"Well?" Seth asked me after a few moments.

"We're going to Peru."

Chapter Sixteen

I hadn't known what to expect, but after relaxing in Oregon for a month, my senses weren't prepared for South America. Arriving in Lima, Peru, I realized I didn't know anything about the country other than where it was located and that it had famous ruins.

As I surveyed the postcards in front of every store, bleached by the sun, I couldn't imagine how a civilization from so long ago had managed to build something so huge.

My summer clothing from Australia came in useful, and I quickly bought a pair of sunglasses to shield myself from the hot sun. It was blisteringly hot and very dry. The altitude was slightly higher, but it felt like I was halfway closer to the sun based on how heavily it cloaked me like a stifling blanket.

Apparently the country was also having one of the hottest winters on record. From what little I remembered of Spanish, I understood some signs posted around the city asking people to wait to use more water than absolutely necessary. Other signs asked people to pray for winter.

The city was unlike any place I had ever been, so despite doing my best to stay in Michael's shadow just for some respite from the extreme weather, I tried to take in as much as I could. People were cooking or roasting things in the street, though the city felt urban and developed — in places. Whenever anyone spoke, they seemed to yell.

Buses, cars, and even bicycles beeped at each other, the sounds of screeching brakes ringing out every few minutes. It took a while before I stopped jumping every time I thought there was going to be an accident. People here must have developed extremely quick reflexes.

As we dragged our bags across town to a car rental location, I was praising my decision to leave the big green suitcase at home and opt for a carry-on. We were soaked, sunburned, and exhausted by the time we finally made it to a little office that barely had room to accommodate us. A lone metallic fan blew onto a bored-looking woman.

"Can I help you?" she asked.

Her eyes drifted curiously over us.

"We'd like to rent a car, please," Kian said. He began taking out his documentation before he noticed the woman shaking her head.

"The bus is the best way to get to Machu Picchu," she said in a thick accent. "You buy tickets over there. Tour group leaves every day, three time per day."

"Oh, we're not going to Machu Picchu," Kian said. "We need to get to here." He took out a map he had been studying on the plane and showed her what looked like nothing.

There was no city where he was pointing. He tried to tell her what it was called, but she didn't understand. Seth tried to, but she just continued to look at them as if they were making things up. Finally, Seth wrote the word on a piece of paper and showed it to her. Her eyebrows shot up and she looked us over one more time, this time really trying to figure out what we wanted. I could see her wondering whether to ask then deciding not to.

"Oh, that's five hours away," she told us, as if the news would be discouraging enough for us to leave the office and stop bothering her.

"Okay," Kian said. "Can we have a car?"

Again, she shook her head. I could see him starting to get annoyed and stepped in.

"How can we get there?" I asked the woman.

She ducked under the desk and began looking for some pamphlets. About a minute later she surfaced again, holding material that looked like it had been printed on a home computer.

"There is a bus that goes to this region. It takes five hours," she repeated.

"Where can we get the bus?" I asked.

"No bus in winter," she said.

I took a deep breath, trying not to sound as annoyed as I was. "And why can't we have a car?"

She flipped the page she had shown me to a black-and-white map. There she drew a road in red along the coast.

"This is the road the bus takes," she said. "Construction here," she drew a circle along the route, "so no bus, and no road to where you want to go." Then she drew another, longer and more winding road that looked like it went through the mountains. "This is another road. Not paved. Many earthquakes and landslides. Mudslides. Not safe to drive if you don't know the area. It will take seven hours. And we have no cars left."

I sighed. Seth and Garrison looked like they were about to start arguing. Kian was scanning the barren map as if he could make another route appear. Michael had buried his head in his hands and looked as if he had just come from a shower. We weren't going to last much longer outside, searching for some way of getting to this small town.

As a last-ditch effort, I reached into Kian's pocket, pulling out his wallet. He turned to me in surprise. I took out all the cash he had, about five hundred American dollars, and put them on the desk in front of us.

"We need to get here," I repeated, pointing to the same spot on the map that Kian had. "Can you help us?"

After thinking about it for a few moments, the woman nodded. "My brother can take you there," she said. "Tomorrow morning. You can come here, he will pick you up."

"Great, thanks," I replied. "Do you know where we can stay tonight?"

She pointed us toward a hotel down the street.

The hotel wasn't too bad, if I adjusted my expectations accordingly. The lights in the hallways were out, the bathrooms looked untouched since the seventies, and the beds were basically box-spring mattresses. Still, inside the peeling wallpaper and faint dampness, we were out of reach of the sun for a while.

After the flight and gruelling expedition through the loud city, we all retired to our individual rooms and promptly fell asleep. I didn't even laugh at Seth and Garrison's faces when they saw that a room for two people obviously meant one two-person bed.

Exhausted, I barely noticed that Michael had a room to himself again. I was happy for Kian's company, but happier to sleep.

✦

I woke up in darkness. I lay on top of the covers, fully clothed, staring up at the ceiling like some kind of vampire in a coffin. My body was rigid, and I couldn't help but groan as I moved. The day had taken a toll on me.

According to the over-bright alarm clock on the nightstand, it was nine o'clock at night. Leaving Kian asleep, I went to examine the shower. I was lucky I didn't mind a cold shower after the day's heat, since that seemed like all the hotel was able to provide.

By the time I was done, Kian had turned on a dim night-light and stood looking out at the city lights. Our balcony was really a sliding door that led out onto nothing. It was a sixteen-storey fall.

From our view, the capital city of Lima was actually quite a bustling metropolis. Office building lights were still on, brake lights flooded the highways and roads below, and I could still hear people yelling, even from this height.

I sighed without meaning to. Despite this other rare quiet moment alone with Kian, my heart felt tight, as if someone had plastic-wrapped it. I came to look out the window, wrapping my towel tighter.

"What's the matter?" Kian asked. He let me step in front of him and rested his cheek against my wet hair.

"I'm worried."

"About what?"

"I don't know."

I tried to take another deep breath, but again felt restricted. He turned me around to face him. What I was about to say made no sense, but I couldn't help it.

"What if you and Seth stayed here?" I said.

Kian's brow furrowed as if he didn't understand.

"I could go with Garrison and Michael. We know where to look for the names," I explained, "and the Godelan can't know we're here, right?"

"Right," Kian answered. "So why does it matter if we come with you?"

I couldn't tell which Gwen was fighting to keep Seth and Kian away from anything that might hurt them. Or cause them to hurt us. Was my concern grounded in the fact that they were the only two kings we had, or because it was their blood could kill us?

I took too long to answer, so Kian started guessing. "Is this about the stone?" he asked.

I guessed it was. I nodded.

"We know that they can kill us," I said.

But they needed his blood.

"And we can kill them," he said.

"So it's fifty-fifty," I reasoned.

Kian gave me a look that told me I was trying his patience. "They don't know about the ritual," he reminded me.

"Right, so they can just kill us. Or Seth. To get him out of the way and never have anyone be able to order them. They didn't hide those names when they heard *we* were here. They did it so that Seth could never be king over them."

Kian briefly considered the logic. I was expecting him to argue, but instead he just gave me a hug. I let myself become absorbed in it and took some comfort. Still, my heart pounded with anxiety.

"You're still worried," Kian said, tucking my head under his chin. I nodded. "We're coming with you, my noble warrior. Make your peace with it."

I nodded again, but I wasn't happy about it. Just as I raised my face to tell him so, he used the opportunity to kiss me. For a moment my worries were forgotten as I forced myself to be in the moment. Not the past. Not the possible future.

Our kiss lasted long enough for me to start to shiver by the window. Though the day had been hot, and standing by the window in just a towel and wet hair made me cold. Though being in Kian's arms was definitely helping. I couldn't tell if the goose bumps on my arms came from the chill wind or the warmth spreading through my cheeks, into my chest, and down my spine.

Kian held me closer as his kisses deepened and we began to move backward. It was hard to tell who was leading the initiative. The backs of my knees hit the bed before I was expecting it, and I fell backwards, Kian rushing to keep up with me. The bed let out such a powerful creak that I thought we'd wake up the whole floor.

We froze.

My heart was doing all kinds of somersaults. I was both cold and hot. Kian's face was still close to mine as we listened. Within a few seconds, I heard a familiar voice.

"Gwen?" It was Garrison. "What's going on?"

I sighed and then laughed. Kian chuckled with me, resting his head on my chest. It didn't even sound like Garrison was yelling. I could hear him perfectly through the wall, as if it were made of paper.

"Nothing," I told him. "Go back to bed."

Kian and I lay together, waiting for the conversation to continue. Garrison would never be satisfied with that answer.

"What are you doing?" he asked.

"Nothing," I replied.

"Is Kian with you?"

I paused before answering. "Yes," I said finally.

"Oh."

Silence again for a few seconds until Seth's voice spoke through the wall.

"Do you really think we shouldn't come?"

I could have buried my face in the pillows from embarrassment thinking they had been listening to our whole exchange. Glad the bed had interrupted, I looked to Kian for guidance. He still lay, hugging me, and shrugged when he saw me looking.

"I don't know," I said. "What do you think?"

"I think without our blood they can't kill you," Seth agreed. "But without it, you can't kill them either." I could always trust Seth to try to reason something out. "And they probably don't know about the ritual anyway, so we need to be there."

Kian raised his eyebrows at me. The king had spoken. We'd all go together. After I didn't respond for a few moments, Seth and Garrison said their goodnights. We listened until all went quiet again.

"Where were we?" Kian whispered with a smile. He knew what my answer was going to be and laughed when I rolled my eyes.

"Going to sleep," I whispered back.

✦

I had never been carsick before in my life, but the trip into the desert made me think I needed those little bags they give out on airplanes.

The brother of the woman we had met the day before was named Rosario. Like his sister, he was middle-aged, short, and round. But at least he was friendly. Having picked us up in the morning as promised, he even had coffee and sandwiches in the car for the trip, which I thought was a lovely touch.

That was until we started bouncing around the unpaved roads, and the smell of meat in the sandwiches cooking in the sun made me nauseous.

Rosario had a huge van that looked to be from the mid-seventies. While roomy, it was bereft of any safety measures like seatbelts, and the only air conditioning was the open windows.

It felt like we were going on safari. Thirty minutes outside of the city all there was around us was desert as we headed inland. Then the roads turned to dirt and gravel as they wound around what could have been mountains. Several times I had to grip the handles and do my best to not look out the window since the drop from the cliff and the incline of the car stopped making any physical sense to me.

It also didn't help that I sat at the very back of the car with Michael, whose weight shifted with the car's angle, and as he slid across the faux-leather seats I worried he would tip us over. The back of the car, inexplicably, smelled like gasoline. Seth and Kian took up the middle row, while Garrison sat at the front with Rosario, pretending he could speak Spanish.

"This is crazy!" Michael yelled to me.

I nodded, doing my best to keep myself steady and not feel even sicker than I was. Between the sound of the wheels on gravel, the engine, and the wind coming through the windows, I could barely hear myself.

"Do you think we're going to stop for a break?" I yelled back to Michael.

"What?"

"Break!"

"Oh," he replied, "no thanks."

I sighed and pushed myself into the corner to keep from moving as much as possible. My stomach reminded me what I had for breakfast and why filling up on eggs had probably not been a good idea.

Another few hours passed. I would have loved to look out the window but the sun heated my skin and made my nausea worse.

"Hey!" Michael tapped my shoulder. I turned. "You don't look so good."

I nodded. Opening my mouth was a risk at this point, so I clenched my jaw shut.

"Carsick?" Michael yelled.

I nodded again.

"Yeah, riding in the back of these things can be a challenge," he said. "They use them a lot in the outback. Easier to get where there are no roads."

I smiled politely, not really wanting to talk.

"So how long have you and this guy been together?" he asked, pointing a thumb toward Kian. "Didn't he tell me he kidnapped you or something?"

It was a good thing I had no answer, because at that moment I just couldn't sit back anymore.

"Stop the car!" I yelled.

I had to scream loudly for them to hear me all the way at the front.

Rosario hit the brakes. I jumped across Kian's legs to pull the door open and run only a few steps before throwing up all over some rocks. At least I missed my shoes.

I heard footsteps behind me as my friends jumped out of the van. A hand moved my hair away from my face and rubbed my back. I could tell from the shoes that it was Kian.

"Gwen?" Garrison called. "Is this one of those things where you want our help, or would you rather ... do it alone?"

I wiped my face on the bottom of my shirt. "Alone."

"Got it."

"Miss?" It was our driver this time. I couldn't imagine Rosario would mind stopping if the alternative was my breakfast all over his back seat.

"Yes?"

"We're almost there," he told me. "Twenty more minutes."

Wonderful. I almost spared myself the humiliation. I hadn't been keeping track of the time because it seemed like so long, but I guessed the sun had been very strong for a while. It must be mid-afternoon by now.

As far as the eye could see, mountains, valleys, and a lot of rocks covered the landscape. The fresh air on my face made me feel better. I took a few deep breaths but ultimately just wanted to get there already.

It must really be in the middle of nowhere. I could see what seemed like hours into the distance, yet I couldn't see any town within twenty minutes' drive.

"Okay," I said to no one in particular. "Let's go."

We climbed back into the van, everyone except for Michael. He stood out on the rocks, bouncing up and down on his heels like I had seen him do in Oregon.

"Michael?" Seth called.

When he turned he wore a puzzled look.

"What is it?" Seth asked as Michael did a few last bounces then jogged back to the car.

"The earth here is all messed up," he said. "It's very weird. The rocks are such weird shapes and all arranged strangely."

Rosario was watching him in the rear-view mirror. He turned before starting the motor. "Many earthquakes," he said. "Many landslides. The villages here build on old villages, and those were built on old ones, too."

How morbid.

"Why do people stay here?" Garrison asked. "If it's so dangerous?"

Rosario shrugged. "This is their land. Their ancestors have lived here, and now they do."

It was a simple enough answer. We of all people should have been able to understand the importance of that. Maybe that was why no one commented on the counterintuitive nature of living in such a dangerous region.

Instead, the next twenty minutes were spent with me nearly shoving my head out of the window like a dog as I tried to convince myself that I didn't feel sick anymore.

The village was exactly as I had expected. Low, sprawling, largely a mix of semi-modern construction methods and archaic-looking huts with grass thatch as a roof. While the roads weren't paved, there were some cars. Though the ones that we saw looked overstuffed with people hanging on to the doors, the roof, and sitting outside of the windows. Livestock wandered up and down the road. Chickens were everywhere.

We had left our luggage in the hotel in an effort to fit in as tourists in this small town, but I couldn't see anything touristic. There were no foreigners in sight, and as we approached the town square, my anxiety grew.

The van rolled through the street, and people turned their heads to stare. Finally, we reached a main square, or something that looked like it. In a wide roundabout, flanked by a church, a market, and what looked like an official government building, Rosario stopped the van. I was only too happy too climb out and take a deep breath of fresh air. I didn't even mind the sticky dirt and dust.

"When should I come back?" Rosario asked.

The notion made my stomach turn. We all looked at each other.

"Give us a week?" Seth asked. The question was directed at us, not Rosario. Considering we had no idea what we were actually here to do, a week seemed okay. We nodded.

Rosario, however, looked hesitant. "Are you sure you want to spend a week here?" he asked. "There's not much to do."

"We're sure," Garrison replied. "Thanks. We'll meet you here at this time in a week."

Rosario shrugged. "Okay," he called as he pulled away.

When the van left, we were forced to face the village. My skin prickled with the feeling like I was being watched. And I wasn't the only one. As we walked into the market, hoping to ask for directions, my friends looked over their shoulders, too.

This late in the afternoon, the streets weren't really packed, yet with every person, from the old ladies sitting on folding chairs outside a shop to the kids who stopped playing in the streets, once they saw us made us feel very observed. The small town seemed crowded when everyone you passed stared at you.

Before we even made it into the market, a man came forward from a booth to intercept us. I assumed he was probably the only person in the area who spoke English since no one else tried to approach.

"Hello, friends!" he said. He smiled, but his eyes were curious, bordering on suspicious. "How can I help you?"

It was as if the entire village was a store, and this was the customer service.

Garrison tried at first in Spanish, and then gave up. The man listened to him patiently, not interrupting. Finally, Garrison sighed. "We're looking for somewhere to stay," he said.

"Certainly, my friends," the man replied with grand gestures. He pointed to the other end of the market with both arms. "Down the road, always straight, you will find the best hotel in town."

Probably the only hotel, but that was okay.

"Do you need tour guide? Do you have plans here?"

The question implied asking if we were here to do something bad.

"We're on vacation," Garrison said. "We're interested in your history. The museums."

"Oh," the man said. He looked as if he was about to have some bad news for us. "The museum is closed today, my friends. You can go on Monday."

"Monday?" Garrison asked. "Why not tomorrow?"

"Because tomorrow is Sunday," the man said, as if that was obvious.

Garrison sighed again. "Okay, thank you."

Despite answering all the necessary questions, we still had to sidestep the man in order to get past him. Every eye in the market was on us, with sellers of everything from nuts to honey to hats looking at us like we were the main attractions in a roadshow. They must not get many visitors.

I was beginning to understand how the Godelan could have hidden their names here. Apart from the violent earthquakes that make the land vulnerable, nothing seemed to change. Ever.

We never would have known the stout building at the end of the strip was a hotel if someone wasn't outside ready to receive us. Though isolated, I assumed a lot of people had cellphones, and our friend from earlier had called ahead. An elderly woman showed us to a big room on the second floor. She didn't say a word the whole time, just led the way to an open room with six single beds lined up like in a hospital. She handed Kian one key, then left.

"What a warm welcome," remarked Garrison.

"It's okay, we won't be staying long," Seth told him. "I don't intend to wait two days to go see if what we're looking for is even here."

"But how will we get in?" Michael asked innocently. We looked at him. "Oh. Right."

At least our one room, which I was beginning to suspect had been used as a kind of hospital room at some point, had big, bright windows. It allowed us to spend some time surveying the market and neighbourhood without being ogled.

I was fidgeting. The feeling of something crawling

up the back of my neck was driving me nuts. I took the bed farthest in the corner just to avoid the feeling of always being stared at. It didn't help.

"I don't like it here," I said.

"What's not to like?" Garrison asked sarcastically.

"But it feels right, doesn't it?" Seth asked. He had a way of making confirmations sound like questions. "It's like Gwen said — they put the names somewhere we wouldn't dare touch. Did you see the hills on the way here? We move one rock and the whole place will cave in."

Exactly. Any magic here would have to be lighter than a whisper or we'd risk killing everyone who still lived in this valley, or in the valleys around it. I had no idea how many people were even in danger, let alone how I could avoid causing some kind of disaster.

"But they don't know we're coming, so we can take the names and not have to do anything, can't we?" Seth said.

Again, the certainty in his tone overshadowed his words. I sat still as the three of them discussed how we would break into the museum. The general consensus was that it didn't seem like the kind of place to have high tech alarms.

I didn't even realize I was listening for something outside the room when I heard footsteps coming up the narrow stairs outside our door.

"Shh!" I said suddenly.

Everyone quieted. The footsteps got louder until the woman who had shown us our room knocked and came in without any further invitation. She left clean towels on a cabinet and was about to leave when Garrison stopped her.

"Excuse me," he said. "Where can we find something to eat?"

"Market," she said simply before closing the tall double doors.

Garrison walked to the window again, looking down at the market. As the sun was beginning to set, people were lighting torches.

"I see grills and I see meat," he announced. "Tonight, we eat like kings."

His sarcasm didn't bother me since I was used to it, but the words hung around in my ears as if a part of me knew they had another meaning. My last memory flashed before my eyes, and suddenly my heart felt more restrained than ever as I tried to take a deep breath while I gathered my thoughts.

I closed my eyes, kicking myself for getting too wrapped up in myself to notice what the past was trying to tell me. Again. I had been so focused on seeing Kian as a child in my dream that I hadn't taken note of anything else.

"Seth," I said, dreading my words or his reaction to them. "What if you're not the only king we have?"

"What?"

Everyone turned to me.

"How do the names work? Is it only the king who can control the Godelan?"

Seth looked at me as if I were crazy. "Of course," he said. "They swore their allegiance to the king. I am the High King. King over them, too."

"And what about your queen?"

It took him a while to understand what I was hinting at. When I finally saw realization dawn on his face, he shook his head before any words came out.

"Moira wouldn't do that to us," he said. "She is vain, but she is not a traitor."

"You banished her," I reminded him. "She's power-hungry. She always wanted the throne. What if she could make a deal with the Godelan — protect them from us in exchange for immunity."

"She would not betray blood," Seth said. "We're family. This conversation is over. Let's go eat."

He grabbed his bag with a force that suggested he was angrier than his tone let on. Regardless, everyone followed him out in silence.

I did my best not to huff. As much as I still saw him as my equal, a teenager on this crazy mission to save the world, there was a part of me that responded to his authority. I was as much under control of the king now as I was two thousand years ago. It was hard not to stomp my foot.

Kian walked by and squeezed my arm. "You may be right," he said. "Don't worry, he'll come around."

"He doesn't want to hear it," I said quietly.

The hallway and stairs carried an echo.

"Because if you're right ..." Kian said. He trailed off, thinking about the implications. "I don't know if you can win unless you can all win together."

"We don't need to win," I replied.

Kian looked at me, confusion in his blue eyes.

"We just need to keep everything from falling apart."

Even while purchasing questionable meat grilled outdoors on a stick, we were still being stared at as if we had come from outer space. A group of children tried to run up to us as we ate, but women pulled them back before they could reach us.

I only had a few bites of dinner. I couldn't figure out what animal the meat came from, though I had a suspicion it was something I hadn't eaten before.

We continued wandering around, pretending to be interested in everything, until eventually the lights in the market were doused or turned off and people milled home.

Even in the darkness we could make our way around by the light of the moon. I felt like I could see every star in the sky.

By now we had passed the short, square brown building that was the museum about five times. Each time we tried to walk by from a different angle, looking to see if anyone guarded it. The chain lock on the front doors seemed pretty rudimentary, yet I couldn't relax. I kept turning around, feeling eyes on me even though we were in the middle of nowhere and the museum was not even in a residential area.

"Okay," Seth finally said quietly. "Let's go."

It was our sixth time walking by the low building that looked to be made out of the some kind of densely packed earth.

"Gwen, can you get the lock?" Seth whispered.

Despite my reluctance, I took hold of the main heavy lock and applied some pressure to it. It broke in my hand and the chain fell away.

Michael pulled the doors open and we snuck in.

My heart nearly jumped out of my chest when a light came on, but as we all froze, it turned out to be a nightlight that must have been activated by movement.

The hall was covered with what I assumed were tribal drawings by the people who had lived here. A timeline on the wall told the story of the ancient people who lived in the mountains and came down to farm in the valleys. I ran my fingers along their history as I walked.

The few sparse items in the museum were encased in glass and were mostly historical artifacts that archaeologists had dug up. Arrowheads, various skins, and baskets filled the displays.

In the middle of the room a glass case held a back-lit item. On a small pedestal, the wooden box looked like it had been intended for jewellery. With its intricate carvings showing interlaced patterns, it appeared to be one of a kind.

"Is that it?" Seth asked.

Kian nodded.

I couldn't help but be reminded of a scene in every adventure movie where the title characters finally find their prize, only to discover it's booby-trapped. As we circled the case a few times, I could feel Seth apply some magic, looking for anything that might be protecting the box.

"I don't feel anything," he said finally.

"How do you get this thing off?" Garrison asked.

Michael took the glass in both hands and lifted. It came off its stand without any resistance. I was holding my breath waiting for something cunning or powerful or dangerous. My heart was pounding with both fear and anticipation.

Seth reached for the box, taking it in both hands. He let out a long breath before slowly opening the lid. From where I stood, I couldn't see what was inside. Instead, I just saw Seth's face turn to dismay.

"What is it?" I asked, craning to see.

He flipped the box over. "Nothing," he said, confused. "There's nothing in here."

Suddenly it felt as if the room was coming down on top of my head. The weight and pressure pounded into my mind with the force of a battering ram. Unprepared, I collapsed under its weight.

I felt like I was under siege. My first reflex was to retreat — protect myself by stepping back to where my past lived, away from the body that fell the floor.

My vision blurred and narrowed as the room distorted before my eyes. My hearing dulled until I could only feel the vibrations on the floor.

One of the last things I saw before everything went dark was the wooden box, falling to the floor and breaking into pieces.

Chapter Seventeen

I woke up with a terrible headache. Rolling onto my side, I thought I would throw up. Instead, I just quietly lay there and tried to slow my mind down.

What happened?

I lay on the same red stone floor I'd been standing on when I collapsed. Hands tried to help me up and I panicked, fighting them off.

"Gwen!" The voice was familiar. "Relax, it's me."

Garrison stared back at me. A gash on the side of his head had left a streak of dried blood down his face. His eyes looked sad and made me instantly worried.

"What happened?" I asked, sitting up.

It felt like I was made of lead, or my muscles had turned to jelly. Either way, getting up took a considerable amount of effort.

"I don't know," Garrison said. "I just woke up. Let's get Michael."

Only when I turned to find Michael still passed out did I realize Seth and Kian were gone.

Despite the weakness pulling at my bones and tempting me to just lie back down and go to sleep, my heart began pounding again. The adrenaline helped to wear off whatever magic was trying to keep me placid. I shook it off like a cloak, jumping to my feet and rushing to Michael.

He lay on his back, and as we tried to shake him, he only groaned.

"Come on," I urged. "Wake up, we have to go look for the others."

He groaned again but opened his eyes this time. I could feel the magic on him and Garrison like a thick blanket. I couldn't think of any way to get it to wear off other than the obvious. Grabbing at nothing and tearing into it with my nails, I yanked on the magic and tried to rip it off of him. We had to move. Quickly.

There was a sound in the air like crackling static. Michael immediately snapped to attention, though he held his head and could only come onto all fours at first. I imagined we had all experienced the same pain, as if someone had run our minds through a blender until we couldn't recognize down from up or left from right.

I turned to tear the magic away from Garrison as Michael steadied himself.

"Gwen?" he said hoarsely.

"What?"

"I think I know why the earth ... hm ..."

I turned to find him crawling on the ground on all fours as if looking for something. He was concentrating very hard. Garrison tried to stand and fell. I had to catch him to hold him up. He held his head and winced.

"This hurts," he said.

I tried to sympathize, but we just had to get going. Whatever had happened to us could happen again, and we still had to find Seth and Kian.

As I held Garrison, I looked around. We were all in the corner of the museum — a particularly empty area where it looked like we had been dragged and tossed into a bare nook.

Everything seemed untouched except the pedestal that had held the names box was still open, and glass from the cover had shattered on the floor. Michael had probably dropped it. The empty and useless box was broken, too.

Finally, when I was nearly hopping from foot to foot with impatience, Garrison announced he could try to walk and Michael had moved from pawing at the ground to just staring at it.

"Let's go," Garrison said, limping toward the exit.

I was ready to follow him when something blew him back so hard that he hit the back wall and crumpled to the floor.

I rushed to him.

"I think we missed something," Michael said.

He was pointing at the ground. A red line cordoned off the nook. It looked like blood. I hadn't even noticed it in my hurry.

"I think it's magic. To keep us in," Michael added.

After making sure Garrison was still conscious, though barely, I walked up to the invisible line. Like the magic on us before, I could feel a small vibration in the air as if an extra layer hung between the rest of the museum and me.

Carefully, I extended a finger toward it. As soon as it crossed the line, my finger was shocked with what felt like electricity, but somehow more intense, like a pulse.

Trying not to panic, I turned back to Garrison. He looked like he had taken a beating and was not up to figuring out how to get rid of whatever was keeping us confined.

"Michael?" I asked hopefully. "You can't see how to move that invisible wall, can you?"

He shook his head, looking thoughtfully at the rest of the museum, though I knew he was considering the magic between it and us.

"I don't know how to even approach it," he said finally, reaching out to touch the magic before pulling his hand back when he was stung.

I didn't have time to fly into any more of a panic. Footsteps echoed from the darkness of the other end of the room. They were approaching. I instinctively put myself in front of Garrison; he was still too hurt to stand.

I squinted into the shadows of the museum, dreading whom I would see. Despite my fears, the reality was worse.

The first person I saw come toward us was Kian. His hands were tied behind his back and he was being pushed. My stomach fell through the floor. It looked like he had been beaten. His lip was split, and here were cuts and bruises all over his face.

I felt the powerful urge to fly into action. To do something. But I couldn't. Garrison was hurt. Michael was clueless. And we were trapped like animals — completely cornered.

"Kian?" I asked.

There wasn't any room for pride. I had to know if he was okay. I stood as close to the red line as possible, craning my neck to see better. He didn't reply.

I could only stand and watch, trying not to shake with both anger and fear as the Godelan came forward with Moira at their side. She looked the same as when we had left her, but her expression matched the one from my memories — arrogant, annoyed, and scornful.

Despite holding her head at a haughty angle to imply confidence, Moira's arms were wrapped around her. I guessed there were two possible reasons for that: she wasn't fully comfortable with what the Godelan had already done, or she wasn't comfortable with what they were about to do. Meaning there was something worse coming.

Holding Kian at what looked like a painful angle and forcing him to walk was the man I had once known as Bald Magician. I now knew his name was Donald. He seemed to be enjoying the pain he was causing. He gritted his teeth as he struggled to move Kian, reminding me of some kind of wild predator. The man called Stone was next to him. The Third Magician, or Magician as Kian simply called him, was not present.

Forcing down the lump in my throat that had formed as soon as I saw Kian, I pushed my breaking heart to the back of my mind, calling up my past life.

There had to be something in my memories or in my magic that would allow me to get out of this mess. But I couldn't think of anything beyond my situation. I couldn't focus. There was too much happening, and I still didn't know where Seth was.

They approached until they stood just feet from the barrier they had created. I felt hate in every ounce of my being, as if it were eating me alive. I wanted to scream. Cry. Kick. Anything that would help me get the pain of hating someone so much out of my body.

"Gwen," Stone remarked, as if noticing I was there for the first time. "You know you have caused us nothing but trouble?"

I didn't trust my voice to hold, so I said nothing. Stone turned to Michael and looked him up and down. A thin smile touched his lips.

"You would be a wonderful addition to our little team," he told him calmly. "Why don't you come and help us?"

Michael looked from him to me as if he couldn't believe the audacity of the request. He didn't know these men like I did. I remembered what they were capable of. What they had tried to do to me.

"Why are you doing this?" Michael asked. "What do you want?"

Kian met my eyes for the first time. If my heart was broken before, it shattered now. His eyes held no hope. Only sadness. We were truly trapped.

"We want to make things right," Stone said, a hand to his heart as if to emphasize his earnestness. "The world is not how it should be, and as you may know, it all goes back to one little moment in time. A moment when your tribe decided to go against mine and surrender our kingdoms to the Romans."

"We never forget," Donald said from behind Kian. "A benefit of such a long life."

"Together," Stone said, "we could have created a greater civilization than any in history. We would have ruled the world, our tribes together in power. But here we are. Mere mortals. Well, almost."

It hurt to swallow. I looked for a gap in their plan that could help us escape, but I couldn't find one. Moira could attack my mind, while Stone wanted my magic. He might try the ritual again on any of my friends, or on me. And Donald — my skin crawled at the thought. Kian had rescued me from him before, but just barely.

They had tied me up, stripped me, and forced me into the snow to become their slave. Only Kian had stood between us. Now I was stronger, yet I was still in the same position and couldn't even help him.

"We are here to offer you a deal," Stone said finally. "You are strong. You can help us. We can make this world great. Together."

"No," Michael said.

I could see Stone fighting the effort not to glare at him. Instead he sighed as if at an impudent child.

"In exchange for your co-operation," Stone continued, "we will not hurt any of your kind except the only person who can stand between us and a better world."

"Kian?" Michael asked.

Stone shook his head. "As you can tell by his lack

of magic, young Kian is not one of you. I mean your king. The High King."

"What did you do to him?" I demanded, nearly rushing the barrier. It was hard not to run at them.

"If you are wondering if we took his magic," Stone said to me, "we didn't. Despite the hardships and obstacles you've placed in our way, we are merciful. We are willing to kill him. No slavery. No magic."

My legs felt like rubber. It was not merciful on their behalf — it was safe.

"No."

I meant it as an affirmation but it came out barely a whisper.

Stone took a deep, dramatic breath. "This offer won't be available for long, and it really is in the best interest of your kind," he said. "Six of you will be guaranteed safety in exchange for one life. You will be fine."

"You're not gracious," Garrison spat from behind me. "You just know you can't contain his magic. You're scared of him."

"Consider it," Stone said.

I had nothing more to say. We wouldn't leave Seth to die.

"No," I said again.

"I was hoping you'd say that," Donald said. I had to force myself to stand my ground. His gaze bored into me.

Suddenly he kicked Kian in the back of his legs, forcing him onto his knees as he winced.

Kian met my eyes again, and in that instant, I was ready to do anything they wanted. He saw the softening in my posture — my resolve weakening. He shook his head so slightly that only I noticed. He was telling me not to crumble under the pressure.

"Our friend here," Stone extended an arm to Moira, "has let me know that you found a way to end the cycle. To die."

I said nothing.

"But," Stone continued, "she claims the ritual will not let us kill each other. Since you are here, ready to capture us, I assume you have found a way around this. Tell me."

Instead of answering Stone, I turned to Moira. "Moira, they're going to kill you," I told her quickly. I didn't know how long they'd let me talk. "Whatever they promised you, you're not going to get it. You're the only other person who can control them. They're going to kill you."

She hugged herself closer and pursed her lips but said nothing. Stone and Donald witnessed this wearing identical grim smiles at the futility of my attempt. I was furious with her betrayal, but I was still hoping she was closer to us than to them.

"Tell me," Stone repeated.

"We don't know," I told him. "We just wanted the names. That's it." It was a thin lie, but I couldn't imagine how they'd know the difference. Until Moira spoke.

"That's not true," she announced. "I saw the plan to kill you in Seth's mind," she told them.

The disappointment washing over me was intense. I felt absolutely betrayed. We had never gotten along, and the girl we had found only a few months ago was long gone, but this person was a complete stranger. I wanted to believe so much that there was some loyalty for us left, but I didn't see any of it on her face.

"If you're so sure," I said through gritted teeth, "why don't you just pull the answer from his mind too?"

"He's being difficult," she fired back. She actually smiled, which turned my stomach until I thought I would be sick. "But I can still do other things, like put memories in." She tapped Kian on the side of the head with an index finger.

So that was how Kian's memory suddenly came back. Moira must have planted it in his mind so that we would come here. But why here? The names must be here.

They could only be planning to kill Seth and recover the names at the same time, never letting them fall into the wrong hands. Or they would steal our magic anyway and then use it to move the mountains or something equally as disastrous.

I vowed that if I was ever able to get away from this room, I would make sure Moira could never bother us again. Again, the hate pulsed so hard inside my skin that I thought I would explode.

Behind me I heard Garrison shuffle to his feet. He came to stand near Michael.

"I will ask you one more time," Stone said. "Tell me how to perform the ritual. Tell me what I need. And you can go."

"Never," Garrison said.

"Good," Donald said.

He reached into his pocket and pulled out a small knife. The light bounced off it, emphasizing the little silver blade's lethal sharpness. He brought it to Kian's neck and pressed. A spot of blood appeared and pooled at the base of his collarbone.

My heart nearly stopped beating. The feeling of plastic wrap was back around my lungs. I couldn't take a breath.

"Tell us or he dies right now," Stone said. "And there is no coming back for him."

Kian tried to stand, but Donald kicked him back down again into a kneeling position. The cut on his neck grew.

"Plead for your life," Donald told him.

I couldn't control the tears in my eyes anymore. They spilled over, running down my face as Kian met my gaze. I had known those blue eyes for his entire life. There was so much life in them, I couldn't imagine it being gone.

"Be strong," Kian said to me. His voice was coarse. It nearly broke.

The tears were flowing freely down my face. I had to control myself not to cry out.

"Plead," Donald growled.

Kian pressed his lips together tightly, his jaw set.

It was a choice between Kian and Seth. My mind seemed to shut down. I couldn't do this. I couldn't choose. Despite whatever answer I wanted to give, my mouth wouldn't open. There was a pounding in my ears. Everything seemed to slow down. I didn't count the seconds that passed, but we stood in silence for a long moment. Then, all at once, Stone shrugged.

"Fine, we'll do this the hard way. Kill him."

The knife slid across his throat like through butter. Blood poured freely. His eyes slowly closed. When he didn't look at me anymore, and I knew he wouldn't ever look at me again, I couldn't take it.

A rift between my mind and reality took me away from my body. I looked at the room as if from far away. A heart-wrenching scream echoed through the museum and seemed to last forever. Dully, I felt the sting in my throat and realized the sound came from me. I was removed, though — weightless, watching the scene with a cool calm.

I watched as my own body fell to its knees at the same time as Kian fell forward and didn't move. I saw Garrison and Michael come toward me, uncertain, trying to keep me from leaning into the magic that kept me away from Kian as he took his last breaths.

When Garrison laid a hand on my shoulder, I was suddenly sucked back into my body and into my actual world. This was real.

My weightlessness was gone. I was constricted into a body that didn't want to exist anymore. The restraint was too much. I could barely see. My eyes were blurred from the tears. A hundred memories flashed in my mind as I remembered Kian telling me I could be the strongest.

His words bounced around my head. The pulsing came back. The hate. I couldn't even reach out to him or hold him. He was alone as Stone, Donald, and Moira began to walk away.

My body cracked under the pressure. I felt myself breaking into pieces; the rage was just too great. I began to shake uncontrollably. Garrison and Michael backed away.

After a few moments I realized it wasn't just me. The whole room was shaking. The Godelan and Moira had stopped in their tracks. Donald looked once in my direction, hate distorting his expression, before he was pulled away by Stone. They rushed from the room as the walls began to move. Dust fell from the ceiling.

"Gwen!" Garrison was yelling. "Gwen! You'll bring the whole place down! Stop!"

But I couldn't. I was too far gone. I knelt with Kian's body just in front of me, beyond a barrier that had stopped me from keeping him safe. Blood still pooled around him, reflecting in the dim lighting. I got lost in the deep red until it was all I could see. It took over all of my senses. I was nearing self-destruction when I heard Garrison yelling again.

"Gwen! Look!"

I followed his pointing finger but saw nothing. Then, after a moment, Kian's hand moved. Garrison was shaking me.

"He's alive!" he yelled. "He's alive. Gwen! Stop! Bring down the magic wall!"

I tried to rein in what I had started. It was hard and took my breath away. Somehow I chose to dive into the belief that Kian was still alive and I hadn't just seen his last movements or imagined him being alive because I wanted it so badly. I directed my magic into the wall between us.

The magic was strong. It was woven deep into the building, reaching below into the ground and above into the sky. I sent everything I had into it — all the rage, hate, anger, and betrayal I could think of. It wasn't hard, considering I had watched Kian bleed to death in front of me.

As I did, the tension around my chest eased. The plastic wrap that had been fastening around my heart and lungs like a noose loosened, until at last, when I hadn't taken a breath in far too long and had barely anything left to throw at it, I felt the familiar crackling of the magic coming undone.

I rushed to Kian, stumbling and weak, turning him over and laying his head on my lap. His eyes fluttered. My fingers slipping in his blood, I searched for a pulse. It was weak but still there. I didn't have time for the open neck wound to make my stomach churn. There was blood everywhere, and the flow wasn't slowing.

I lay my hands across his neck and tried to control the urgency of my need to heal him. His words about brute strength and blowing up Garrison's nose came back to me. I had to pull back to do this right.

The magic flowed through my fingers. I felt the heat tingling under my palms. Being so close, I didn't have to direct it. The wound was obvious — the magic knew what to do. Mere seconds passed but it felt like hours.

Then the flow of blood stopped. I felt a watery smile stretch across my face through the tears, but it disappeared as soon as I saw that Kian hadn't opened his eyes. His breath was still shallow and his heartbeat was weak.

"Why isn't he waking up?" I asked Garrison and Michael in a panic. They were crouched around me, stress etched on their faces. "Why isn't he waking up?"

Garrison's hands were covered in blood just from crouching next to me. As he brushed a strand of hair away from his face, it left a streak of red on his forehead.

"He's lost of a lot of blood," he said. "I ... don't know how to get him more." He looked around in vain, as if all of the required medical devices and instructions on how to use them would be nearby.

I began to feel Kian's faint heartbeat in the palm that was holding his hand. Was I keeping it going? Could I help him?

"Take his hand," I told him, giving him Kian's hand to hold. "Feel the heartbeat?" It took Garrison a few seconds to nod. He was looking thoughtfully at Kian as if wondering the same thing I was. Were we doing this or just tapping into it?

I jumped to my feet.

"Where are you going?" Garrison asked.

"I need to go after them," I told him. "They still have Seth."

"But they don't know how to kill him. They can't," Garrison said.

I shook my head. "He's too dangerous to keep around. Their names must be around here. They wouldn't leave them unattended when we know how to use them."

I looked to Kian's unconscious face and my feet refused to move. They wanted to stay by his side and monitor his every breath until I knew he would be okay. But I knew he would want me to help Seth, and I couldn't abandon him.

"They're going to do something to him," I said to Garrison. "Something bad."

"Well then, I'm coming with you," he said.

"No!" I had to scream to get him to stop. I didn't want him to let go of Kian. He was holding on to life by just a whisper of a breath. "You have to stay with him. And you're still too weak."

Garrison began to protest but I gave him a look that implied he was wasting his time. He nodded. He'd been limping ever since hitting the magical barrier, and sustaining multiple head injuries hadn't helped.

"Michael, come with me," I said.

Without looking back once, I ran out of the museum through the doors I had seen the Godelan and Moira leave through. If I stopped to see Kian's prone form or Garrison looking after me like he'd never see me again, I was afraid my resolve would turn to putty.

Michael and I stumbled as soon as we came out of the building through the back doors. The dawn was lifting. It was early Sunday morning.

The small structure didn't have any windows. It was built like a cave, and we hadn't realized how much time had passed at all. The Godelans' head start on us was enough to make me just want to run into the desert.

"Here!" Michael called.

Tire tracks led into the mountains beyond the village. He set off at a jog. I was thankful for all the training Kian had put us through, though I did dip into my magic to help me make the trek running through the desert and then into the mountains.

By the time we reached the steep, rocky incline, we were both gasping and covered in sweat. I didn't know how much longer I could keep going, but I also couldn't fathom stopping. The hike took on a rhythmic pattern and I found myself drifting away from my body again, not paying attention to my steps.

Since there was only one road up, following their tracks was easy enough. I vaguely noticed the sun rising while we walked uphill. My mind was on Kian and Seth.

Finally, after what seemed like hours, the mountain levelled off and we came to a sparsely forested plateau.

"What now?" I asked between gasps.

I turned to find Michael bouncing up on his heels again. He was looking out over the mountain range. I followed his view. It was truly spectacular. Under any other circumstance, I could have stood there and gazed at the mountains all day.

It was as if we could see for miles in every direction. It looked pristine and untouched to me. But Michael squinted at it as if solving an equation.

"It's not right," he mumbled.

"What?" I asked. "What is it?"

He turned to me. "I figured out why this whole landscape feels weird to me. All of this," he waved his arms in the direction of the mountain, "isn't natural."

"What?"

"It was made to look this way," he continued. "I see it."

"See what?"

I was nearly jumping up and down from frustration. Michael could clearly see something I couldn't, and it was driving me crazy.

"The names," he said. "I can see their names. They put them in the mountains — the shapes of the mountains."

Chapter Eighteen

"What are they?" I was practically yelling.

Michael shook his head. "I can't figure it out! It's like every time I try to say it, my voice just forgets how or my brain loses the train of thought." He pressed a palm to his forehead as if it would help. "It's why it took me so long to figure out what they'd done in the first place! Seth has to do it. He's the only one who can."

"But you can't tell him what they are!" I reminded him.

Michael made a frustrated sound, grabbing at his hair and pulling, while I tried to still myself, giving him time to think.

After a few minutes of Michael staring out into the mountains as if he were reading them and me shifting from foot to foot, we were on our way again with no solution. He scoured the trail and eventually led us to a vehicle similar to the one we'd arrived in. It was parked under some trees at what looked like the beginning of a forest. He brought a finger to his lips.

"Shh."

I nodded.

We crept carefully through the trees, though every little snap of a twig or rustle of leaves that our footsteps made echoed in my ears like a thunderous boom. After a few minutes, Michael stopped to bounce up and down again.

I nearly stomped my foot in frustration.

"What are you doing?" I whispered frantically. He looked at me as if we'd been caught, and my heart skipped a beat. "What?"

"I'm pretty sure we're standing on a volcano," he said.

Crap.

This was the icing on our horrible, misguided cake. It really was a perfect location to hide their names. The Godelan would win either way. If we didn't fight them because we were scared of the consequences in these mountains, then they would be victorious. If we did, and the whole countryside exploded in lava and earthquakes, they'd still be victorious.

"We have to keep moving," I told Michael. His trapped and wide-eyed expression suggested he was figuring out the same thing. We were screwed either way.

We continued farther into the dry woods, trying to be sneaky but probably making as much noise as two baby rhinoceroses on a pile of kindling. I crouched lower when I heard voices from ahead.

A few more steps and I realized it wasn't voices — it was sobbing and muffled screams.

Michael had to hold me back because I was ready to run out of the trees. They thinned farther ahead and I couldn't see anything beyond. We crept around the small open area to get closer to the source of the noise.

Finally, I saw Moira's back turned to me. She was sitting on a stump and playing with a stick, absent-mindedly drawing symbols in the ground. As much as I wished I were hearing her distress, the noise came from a girl sitting next to her.

My stomach sank. The girl looked to be our age, about my size, with tousled blond hair. Her arms were folded uncomfortably in front of her, and I assumed they were tied. A gag stretched around her head, which accounted for the muffled sounds. She shook with sobs, but Moira ignored her. She must have been one of us, located by the Godelan and Moira. And there was only one reason they were holding her.

Michael touched my arm and pointed. Farther from the treeline, three men were gathered around a small fire. Despite the months that had passed since I was trotted out in front of the same three and a similar fire, I still felt the panic grow in my throat and the immediate desire to run as far away as possible.

Just when I was having trouble with my resolve, I saw Seth. He was propped up against a tree, tied with a rope and gagged just like the girl next to Moira. No one was near him, but he was so far from the treeline we could never get to him without being noticed.

At least he seemed to be okay. He was alert and looking around, probably trying to find a means of escape.

I heard a swishing next to me and saw Michael taking a small pocketknife out of his shoe.

"If I run, I can cut that rope before anyone sees me," he said.

I held him back by his sleeve.

"Don't be ridiculous," I told him. "Even if it was just a rope, they'd kill you before you ever made it. Or throw you into the volcano."

"If it's not a rope, what is it?" Michael whispered.

I remembered when we were in New York, just after finding Seth and Garrison. The Godelan had tried to lure Seth's mind and magic away with some kind of powerful spell. When I tried to find his consciousness to bring him back, seeing the mind magic was like a completely different plane of vision than the real world — but at least I could see what they truly intended.

I squinted at the rope, and Seth, and Moira and the girl, trying to find that place again. But it was hard. In New York, I had just gotten sucked into Seth's magic — it was never my own that could show me that place. Still, I tried to reach for it, remembering what it felt like. I was staring at Seth, willing him to give me the ability to do it again.

It didn't work. The world still looked as plain and normal as ever. I wasn't able to find that amber-coloured space and see what booby traps the Godelan had ready for us.

Suddenly I felt contact with something in the realm of mind magic, and Seth sat up alert, starting to look around into the treeline. He had actually felt me! I was just about to rejoice when Moira stood.

Uh-oh.

She must have felt me poking around. I shoved Michael farther down until we both lay in the dirt, our faces pressed to the ground. I tried to control my breathing, to silence it and calm my racing heart.

Moira looked around and then turned to the girl by her side. "Did you do that?" she asked.

The girl shook her head through her tears. Seth was staring at her intently. I wished I could tell what he was thinking. Unfortunately, it seemed like any connection I could ever have with him would have Moira in the middle.

Checking for booby traps was out. Though I couldn't see the magic around Seth, I was sure they wouldn't just tie him up with any old rope and had to assume getting him free would take some time. Near him, the Godelan were getting ready for their ritual.

It was unsettling how the fire pit was larger now. It was more like a ring of fire than one big blaze. Something told me I didn't want to end up in the middle of it.

Finally, Moira went to join them and see what they were doing. They turned their backs to her, and I knew she wasn't wanted. A plan came together in my mind as I surveyed the scene, but the odds of it working were slim.

I sighed. I had nothing else.

"Michael," I whispered. "Give me your knife."

He handed it over unquestioningly. Squeezing his shoulder as thanks, I ran off in the opposite direction, still close to the treeline but farther along the rim of the volcano's edge. Finding a tree close to the woods, I stuck the knife into it as quietly as possible and covered the blade with some leaves.

I returned to Michael, and it was time for step two of the plan. Not knowing how long Moira would be occupied, I crouched low and ran to the bound girl, thinking of how I could condense everything she needed to know into a ten-second conversation.

As I snuck up behind her, I wrapped a hand around her already-gagged mouth. She tried to scream but I whispered in her ear, trying desperately to calm her down before anyone noticed me on the border of the trees.

"Shh," I urged. "Relax. I'm here to rescue you."

She turned, blue eyes wide and red-rimmed. Disappointment overshadowed her expression, and I guessed I wasn't the police she was probably hoping for. Her eyebrows tilted questioningly.

"I swear I will explain everything to you as soon as this is over," I said. "I'm one of the good guys. I'm like you. I have a friend with me — he's good, too. And that guy over there? Tied to the tree? He's one of us. Everyone else is the enemy. That's all you need to know."

When she continued staring at me, I realized she was still confused, but I just didn't have enough time.

"You have magic, yes?" I asked. It was the only way the Godelan could have found her. She nodded, though after a moment of consideration. This all probably sounded crazy.

"Great," I said. "I need you to create a distraction.

Whatever kind of magic you have, just use it to make everyone stop paying attention to what they're doing. Because what they're doing is bad. I would do this myself, but I will probably have to fight them, and I can't do both, understand?"

Again, she nodded.

"Okay, so when you create your distraction, my friend will run out of trees and free you. Don't be scared," I told her. "Then he'll go free our friend at the tree over there. I'm going to be busy, so I just need you to stay where no one can hurt you, okay?"

I could tell her confidence in me was waning, but neither of us had much choice right now.

"Try now," I ordered. "Be ready with a big distraction when you hear a boom." I ran back into the trees.

I whispered my plan to Michael as we waited. He looked skeptical but didn't argue.

For a few minutes nothing happened as the Godelan were finishing setting up their ritual. All the holes in my plan ran through my mind. I didn't even know what this girl could do, if anything. She was inexperienced, and she had no idea what was going on. What if she rattled a few branches? How would this ever work?

Another ten minutes passed. Nothing happened. Moira didn't come back to the girl. She paced up and down, looking out over the mountains. My nerves were practically gone and I was on edge, pins and needles forcing me into action. It was hard to sit still. I had no idea what she was trying to do, if anything.

Finally I stood, but Michael immediately pulled

me down. I was ready to push him off when he pointed to the sky.

"Look!" he whispered.

I wasn't expecting much, when I glanced up, but for the first time in a long time, I felt a sprig of hope. Slowly but surely, dark clouds were gathering above the volcano in what was otherwise a perfectly clear sky on a sunny day.

We watched them form for a short while, growing darker and angrier, moving faster than natural. I vowed to give this girl a big hug if we ever made it out of here.

The Godelan finally noticed when the clouds blocked out the sun and sent shade down onto them. They looked up, confused. Luckily, no one seemed to suspect the girl who had been sobbing half an hour ago. In fact, no one even noticed that she had now composed herself. Her shoulders were set and she sat bolt upright.

Stone waved an arm, and all the rocks big enough to hurt someone rose from the earth. They hovered around him as he stared into the treeline, suspecting us. His eyes shimmered with awareness, like a true predator hunting for his prey. When the other two left the fire, he barked at them without even looking.

"Keep working!" he screamed. His voice, when not eerily smooth, cut like steel.

I swallowed down the fear.

Seth was trying to wriggle out of his restraints now, aware that something was about to happen. The action was making the magic surrounding him fight back, and I could finally see it layered on top of him like the blanket they had tried to trap us with. It would take some time to undo.

As soon as Moira felt our presence, she just froze.

Just as Stone turned to where I had stuck the knife, I sent my magic into the wind. The gentle breeze rustled through the trees and I guided it straight to the knife, where the leaves blew gently off and the steel caught against the sun peeking through the dark clouds.

The glint of the sun's reflection on the metal shone straight through the trees. Stone saw it and acted immediately. Sending all of the rocks in the direction of the knife, he clearly wanted to kill anyone in the vicinity — namely me.

But we were nowhere near. As the rocks and boulders hurtled through the trees, the booming was akin to multiple thunder strikes. The rocks uprooted whole trees and caused them to fall over, toppling that area like it was a row of dominoes.

And then the storm happened. The girl was good. No wonder they had found her through her magic. As if to accompany the noise of rock against tree, lightning struck and thunder sounded in sync. The storm was right overheard. Rain began to pour in thick sheets. Wind hurled us in every direction.

I should have specified the distraction I needed in my plan. While the girl certainly could summon up the necessary weather, it was affecting all of us. Michael and I were having trouble standing amidst the downpour, let alone doing anything else.

Her emotions could almost be heard in her magic. She was upset. Angry. Confused. She was doing with this storm what I had initially done with my fire — self-destructing without even knowing it.

"Get the girl!" I yelled over the rain.

The Godelan were as incapacitated as us, but to my dismay the fire still burned. The ritual must have already been started. There was no way a natural fire could outlast this storm.

It took considerable effort to walk out of the trees. The wind and rain were one factor, and hesitance another. I was the bait. I was the distraction. And three against one, I didn't know if I stood a chance.

Magician turned and saw me approaching. Instead of fighting, however, he kept working on the ritual, just like back in England. He hid behind Stone and Donald, cowardly as usual.

They came toward me. I could barely see their actions through the rain and couldn't hear anything with the howling of the wind. It was like the volume of the world was turned up to maximum. Still, they managed to make it worse.

Doing something that looked like a choreographed dance, they both planted their feet and wove their arms in and out of the air. Suddenly the rain hit me harder. Then it became sharp. Another second and it would pierce into my skin with the force of a thousand knives. I summoned my magic to protect me, but holding them off was all I could do.

I focused on making a wall between them and myself. To conserve energy, the wall was not a room, just a barrier, like I was some kind of magical riot police.

As I forced my feet forward and pushed the barrier, the earth beneath my feet slid. At first I was happy to gain ground. Then the whole volcano shook.

We stood, staring at each other, frozen, as we waited.

For long seconds, nothing. Then more rumbling. It took me a full minute to realize this wasn't an ordinary earthquake. It wasn't stopping. And as I was able to focus on something other than the rain, I realized the other mountains were moving, too. Crumbling.

I hoped against all odds that my actions wouldn't result in someone's death. But I had no other way.

In the rain I couldn't see Seth, Michael, Moira, or the girl. And I didn't have time to look around. I stepped forward again, and the earth slid more. The rumbling continued.

When the Godelan saw I was moving closer and their magic wasn't reaching me, they tried to sidestep my defences. The rain cut into my skin as I chanced the lethal nature of it to turn the razor-sharp droplets around and point them back at my enemies. I felt my arms getting heavy. Their eyes widened.

I was probably the last to realize what I was doing. The water wasn't just changing direction — it was grouping together into a long blade. I waited until it was adequately impressive and then sent it at them. They both ducked, sending earth flying in my direction. Thanks to the rain, thick mud clung to me and knocked me backward.

I gasped for air and sputtered as dirt filled my

mouth and nostrils. I looked up just in time to see Stone running toward me.

The earth shook. The sky blackened, but it wasn't from the girl's storm. Something was sending thick smoke into the sky.

As I watched his grey eyes rejoice at being able to reach me, I exhaled in the way Kian had taught me, and disappeared. Well, I didn't really disappear. I didn't know how to do that. But I sank into the earth enough so that Stone, at least for a second, couldn't find me. I held my breath, staving off claustrophobia and trying not to panic.

Counting to ten, I gathered my magic close to me, ready to surprise him. At ten, I tried to burst through the ground and sent a wave of magic. It bounced back at me, hitting me hard in the ribs and taking in the breath I needed hurt like a knife cutting into my side.

I opened my eyes.

Stone must have sensed me. He grinned, grabbing me by the hair and arm and dragging me toward the edge of the volcano. I resisted as much as possible, but in a few steps we reached the fire. I dug my heels in more than ever, but his magic uprooted me and sent me sprawling forward.

My hands hit the hot coals as I reached out to try to stop myself from stumbling into the centre of the fire ring. Even in the rain, it burned bright.

I screamed as I felt the heat sink into my skin. Regardless of my penchant for fire, this was something else. It permeated my magic, wounding me in a way that made me helpless.

I could feel someone coming up behind me. Quickly. Vibrations in the earth told me to move. Turn around. But I couldn't. I just stared at my red and blistering palms, shaking from the pain.

Stone tried to kick me in the middle of my back to send me straight into the fire, but I managed to turn in time. Slightly. He ended up landing a hard kick on my shoulder blade.

I yelled again, but got up. If there was one thing I knew, it was that I couldn't end up in the ring of fire. If they didn't know how to kill me or didn't think they could, they'd have no trouble stealing my magic like they tried to do in England. And that would be even worse for everyone else.

"You should never have come here!" Stone roared.

Even over the din of the moving mountains and falling rain, his voice was frightening. I didn't think he meant Peru — he was talking about the present. Whatever the case, I wanted to agree with him.

"You did this to me!" I yelled back at him. "To all of us! You're why the world is like this!"

Something hit me on the back of my head. I nearly collapsed when someone caught me and held me close, wrapping me in thick arms so that I couldn't move. My skin crawled. I had forgotten about Donald. He dragged me closer to Stone as I writhed in his hold. I was close to tears when I was brought face to face with the scariest Godel of all.

Stone's eyes mimicked the darkness of the sky and its potential dangers.

"We will give the world a second chance," he told me.

Then, just as I was scrambling for ideas, he reached out and took my neck. I struggled, but his fist began to close and my breathing was constricted. I gasped for air. My palms, badly burned, throbbed.

It gave me the only idea I had.

Taking that fire and pain from my hands, I used magic to weave a kind of fishing line and bring it into my arms. The burning spread. This wasn't my magic — it had the same effect as regular fire. Between trying to breathe and trying to scream, I was in a lot of pain.

When it reached Donald, he screamed and let me go. I would have fallen forward if Stone didn't have me by my throat. I kept the fire quickly moving from my arms, to my shoulders, and into my neck, until I felt like one, big, hot coal.

Stone gasped and took his hand away.

As soon as he did, I tried to push him with a wall of power mixing the wind and rain, but I wasn't steady on my feet yet. The force sent me backward into Donald and we both toppled to the ground. I rolled away quickly but not fast enough.

By the time I looked up again, Stone balanced a ball full of fire near his fist. He looked ready to send it flying at my head with the force of a hundred cannons.

Something hit him from behind and he crumpled. Moira stood behind him holding a thick branch. As our eyes widened at each other, both in shock, she bolted. Someone grabbed me from behind. Donald held me again and lifted me up until I was on my feet, where I wobbled like a rag doll. He pulled me by the hair toward the fire, and before I could do anything, he had pushed me through the fire and I stood in the middle of the ring.

I scrambled to get out, frozen in fear. Donald stood just outside, holding a vial of some red liquid. My stomach dropped to my feet.

"I don't care what happens to you," he yelled at me over the rain, his face contorting in rage. "Or where you go. I need you dead."

He shook the vial at me menacingly. "Got this from your boyfriend before we killed him."

I gritted my teeth. The edge of the fire ring was a cliff, which led into the wide and ashy mouth of a volcano — nowhere to go.

At least this wasn't the one erupting. Dark smoke still filled the sky, but it came from one of the other mountains that still rumbled in the distance. Ash began to fall, and it distracted Donald long enough for me to gather some magic to myself.

It was hard. The fire acted like a curtain between my magic and me. It was like trying to get power through a sieve. I didn't have enough to do anything to the Godel. Instead I focused on the vial in his hand.

Pushing through everything I had, I sent it toward him. I could feel the magic crawl through the space inside the fire ring as if it travelled through molasses. I held my breath until I saw the little glass bottle pop out of Donald's hand as he looked up at the sky and wiped ash from his face. It smashed on the ground, the thick blood absorbed into the dry earth in seconds.

He looked surprised and then turned to me, angrier than ever. Forgetting himself, he ran at me, crossing the fire into the ring without even noticing. As he came toward me, bigger and physically stronger, suddenly all those drills Kian had made us run made sense.

This was the exact drill. A bigger, heavier, stronger opponent is running toward you. He will attack you. How do you make the fight end as quickly as you can?

I brought myself back to those moments in New York, in London, in Oregon, and everywhere else we had been where I hated Kian for his stupid drills.

As Donald ran toward me, his jaw set and his brows knitted together, his deep-set eyes looked like two shining rubies reflecting the fire. His hairless head was smeared with grey from the ash. I waited until the last possible moment before side-stepping, punching as hard as I could into where I assumed his liver was, hooking his arm and pushing my weight into him just as his feet were light on the ground. He toppled over, and I took the opportunity to run out of the ring.

Now his magic was practically gone in the magic of the fire, and his back was to the volcano. I stood outside the ring, looking in, preparing myself.

He didn't falter. Donald stood slowly, coughing on the ash, and casually dusted himself off. Standing in the centre of the ring, he crossed his arms and looked at me smugly.

"What are you going to do?" he said tauntingly. "You don't know the magic to take mine from me. And you can't kill me."

I took half a second to look around. Stone was busy fighting off the weather that had accumulated around him — the girl had done a great job, and Michael had managed to set her free. Meanwhile, Michael tried to get Seth loose and fought off Magician as he did so. Moira was gone.

The tide was turned. We were actually winning.

"Yes, I can," I told him. "Moira forgot to mention the most important part. The stone says we can't kill anyone from our own land."

His eyes went wide for just an instant. He understood the implication, knowing full well they were foreigners in our land who had refused to leave. That was why they had declared their loyalty to the high king in the first place.

Just as quickly, however, Donald recovered his composure. "Fine," he said. "You still can't kill me. You don't have king's blood."

For an instant I thought he was right. My spirits sank as I imagined having to stand here, guarding him, until someone would come to help me out.

Then I remembered Kian.

I didn't say anything; I didn't want to give myself away. But as soon as Donald saw me tear off my sleeve, he knew. My clothes were covered in Kian's blood from when I had held him, his throat cut.

Donald tried to cover the few steps to the edge of the fire just as I approached from the other side. I beat him to it.

Dropping the sleeve into the fire, I had to stop suddenly or I would run right into the flames. I fell backward, trying to get away from the inferno as it rose over my head like a giant wall. I could only stare for a few seconds. No sound came from within, but when the flames died down and were ultimately extinguished, there was only a spot of dust where the Godcl had stood.

With no time to think about what had just happened, I turned, suddenly anxious about having my back to the fight. The rain was easing. I couldn't see the girl anywhere.

The ground shook again and I nearly lost my balance. Magician was waking Stone. As he looked up and our eyes met, Stone began to stir. Michael must have gotten the better of him while he fought with the storm. He flung himself upright, knocking Magician aside, as I braced myself for what was sure to be a wrathful surge of power. But something else caught his attention.

He looked beyond me and his eyes widened in true fear for the first time. It was unsettling. My experience with the Godelan was that they were the enemy. But we were winning now. We were more dangerous.

My eyes followed his and I turned to see that Michael had managed to tear whatever was keeping Seth in place. Seth stood, holding Michael's head to his own, in stillness. Seth had found a way to get the names out of Michael's mind. Through the ash cutting at my throat, I smiled.

Suddenly, out of the corner of my eye I saw Stone move, and I blocked his path instinctively, but he wasn't attacking Seth. Instead, he pushed Magician aside and grabbed the dagger in his belt. Magician was frozen, gazing with a wide-open mouth between Stone and

Seth. That was when Stone raised the dagger and drove it into the side of his own head.

I cringed. There was nothing for me to do except stand and watch as his face turned into a mask of distorted pain, teeth bared, and the blood poured down his neck. I figured out what he was doing too late, when he took the knife from one ear and drove it into the other. He was deafening himself from hearing his own name. Just as the knife came out of the second ear and the blood poured freely, the mountains trembled with Seth's voice.

Born with magic by chance, I was never meant to know the names or speak them. That's why to this day, though I experienced the moment our tribe finally gained control over the Godelan after two thousand years, I can't remember the names Seth spoke.

As I stood and felt my heart burst with pride and relief, suddenly all the rules of our tribe, even the ones that had kept me from the only thing I had wanted in my past life, made sense. Seth was a king. And I revelled in his voice as he spoke aloud the only words that would save the world.

I tried to take a deep breath but choked on ash. I hadn't even noticed that the rain had been completely replaced by cinder. When the booming finally stopped, Stone unfroze and ran. I turned to run after him, or do anything to stop him, but Seth's voice held me back.

"Gwen!" he yelled. His voice broke and turned into coughs. "We need to get out of here!"

Visibility was decreasing by the second.

"But —" I began to think of all the reasons I just

wanted this done with. There were many. But Seth was right.

He and Michael ran up to me, hiding their mouths and noses behind their sleeves. I tucked the bottom half of my face into my shirt.

Magician still stood nearby, unmoving. Seth walked up to him. The man was quite literally frozen, and I wondered if Seth was using his new name knowledge to test out how much control he truly had. The only things that moved were Magician's eyes, which darted from place to place.

"Walk," Seth told him sternly.

It looked like it was the last thing he wanted to do, but he did it — straight into the fire circle he himself had built.

"You need me," Magician sputtered. "I have more knowledge of the magic and the —"

"Enough!" Seth said, and the word silenced the man. His mouth snapped shut. "No more empty promises. You've made plenty already."

He was talking about Kian. I wondered if he knew what they had done to him.

"I cannot die now — I have worked for thousands of years for this," Magician tried to reason again.

"You died the day you came here," Seth told him.

He picked up the dagger Stone had used to deafen himself and wiped it on his pants. Then he cut across his forearm, reaching over the flames as the blood dripped in.

Seth had to pull his arm away quickly as the flames rose up. This time they were more mixed with ash than before, and a putrid smell filled my lungs. It was getting harder to breathe.

When we were sure Magician was gone for good, Michael grabbed Seth and we ran to the woods. We found the girl there, waiting with her arm over her face.

"I told you to go!" Michael yelled at her over the rumbling of the earth. The shaking hadn't stopped for longer than a minute since it had begun.

"I waited for you!" she yelled back.

Instead of answering, he grabbed her arm and pulled her down the road.

"Moira?" Seth asked me with raised brows.

We didn't have a lot of air to speak with, so I shook my head. I had no idea what happened to her, but I certainly couldn't hate her as much since she had saved me — which appeared to have surprised her as much as it did me.

We ran for about twenty minutes until we just couldn't anymore. It felt like all the air had been sucked out of the mountainside, and we huddled by the road under a tree. Even with the branches bearing most of the ash, I was blind.

I didn't have long to think about whether we could keep going, and I didn't know what to do. My magic was spent. So was everyone else's, and our choices appeared to be die on the road or by the road.

We waited for the ash to pass, but it didn't. Breathing was nearly impossible. I couldn't see anything. Finally, I felt Seth squeeze my hand on the right. I was leaning against Michael on my left. I felt his body go still. And as I thought about Kian and felt a tear roll down my cheek, leaving a muddy trail, I took my last breath.

Chapter Nineteen

I flung open my eyes, realizing I hadn't been breathing.

I sat up but could barely see anything around me. Footsteps were coming closer. Someone cupped the back of my head, tilting my face up as cool glass met my lips. I drank the water willingly, for the moment putting aside the million questions floating through my mind. As the water began to pour over my face, I coughed up clumps of ash.

It took a minute for me to relax. Drinking soothed my throat. Garrison's voice instructed me to close my eyes before a damp cloth cooled my forehead. I was finally able to see the room around me — it was the same one we had rented for our stay.

A hand gripped mine and I turned to find Kian by my side. He smiled at me, though he was paler than ever. I flung myself at him with all the energy I had and felt truly able to breathe again when I felt his arms wrap around me in return.

Then a thought occurred to me. I opened my mouth to speak, but all that came out was a croak. I tried again, clearing my throat painfully for several long moments.

"The town's still here," I said. "I thought something was going to happen — an earthquake, or landslide, or something. The volcano ..."

The words trailed off as I saw Michael, Seth, and the girl whose name I still didn't know lying on their own beds around the room. The place looked more like a hospital than ever. We had all been changed into clean clothes — I'd have to ask about this later — but dirt and ash covered the windows. Seth's wound had been washed and bandaged.

Michael turned to me and smiled weakly. His eyes were bloodshot. He pointed at his throat and shrugged, which I took to mean he couldn't talk. Seth and the girl were still out.

It occurred to me that this was the second time I had gone against the Godelan and woken up some time later having been unable to save myself from the consequences. But at least this time two of them were gone — no longer our problem. But so was Moira.

"What happened?" I asked. Each word made my throat drier. Kian saw me wince and gave me some more water. As I drank, I watched them exchange looks over the glass. "What?"

"Kian woke up a little after you left," Garrison said. "You healed him. We were just getting out of that damn museum when we felt the first earthquake. I knew you needed help, so we ... borrowed ... a car and went to find you."

Kian stroked my hair. "It was amazing that you managed to climb down as far as you did," he said, "considering all the ash in the air. And you fought off the Godelan after healing me and escaping their trap."

Somehow I felt he was telling me all of this as a cushion for a blow.

"We found all three of you pretty quickly," Garrison said. "You probably shortened your life by about ten years by breathing in all that stuff, but you were fine once we got you into the car."

Kian jutted his chin at Garrison, which I took as urging him to shut up. I could see a bright red line stretching across his throat. The scar was so bright, it looked like blood still flowed underneath just a thin layer of skin. I reached out to touch it, but he brushed my hand away.

"Don't even think about it. You need your energy right now."

"Does it hurt?" I asked.

"No," he said. "It'll heal more. Give it time. It was only a few days ago."

"A few days?" I tried to sit up as they both jumped to keep me down. "We've been asleep a few days?"

"You all used up a lot of your energy, doing … whatever it is you did up there," Garrison told me. "So now you need to rest before dealing with everything else."

I lay back down, trying to relax by imaging how difficult it must have been for both of them to wait before finding out what actually happened. I knew it was taking everything Garrison had to not grill me about every little detail of what happened with the Godelan.

When I thought about his words again, I frowned. "What do you mean, deal with everything else?"

When neither seemed willing to answer and instead exchanged knowing looks, a feeling of foreboding settled over me.

"What else?" I insisted.

Michael was sitting up, leaning on one elbow, also interested. He glanced at me nervously, and I could nearly read his mind. Really, I just knew he was thinking the same as me. Did we do something worse than what the Godelan had been doing? Was it our fault?

"There was a volcano," Garrison began, slowly, choosing his words. "It erupted. There was a lot of ash. The town here is covered in it. A few towns around are, too. There were some fires...."

While unfortunate, this wasn't enough to warrant his tiptoeing around the subject.

"And?" I asked.

Again, a pause as Garrison considered what to say.

"What happened?" I asked.

Kian squeezed my hand. "You were right," he said. "They hid the names somewhere they thought we wouldn't disturb, because the space was too vulnerable. These mountains, they're linked all up the coast. There was some concern about a tsunami or tidal wave. And more earthquakes."

"How bad?"

"Bad."

Garrison opened his laptop to a news site and turned it to show Michael and me. My jaw dropped.

Much of Mexico's west coast was a disaster zone. A tsunami had wiped out entire towns and cities. Southern California was a crumpled mess. People were photographed in the streets, fleeing every which way. Headlines shouted about death tolls, illegal border crossings, and ultimate chaos.

The earthquakes had echoed all the way up the coast. A small box held a picture labelled "Seattle." Half the city was flooded.

As my throat constricted and it became harder to breathe, a tear rolled down my cheek. I had done this. How could I have done this? It was worse than anything the Godelan had done.

"It's not your fault," Garrison told me quickly. "They had this all planned. It was their way to get everything they wanted, whether or not they got you."

I held up my hand, wishing he would stop talking. No one could ever make me feel better about this. For long moments they watched me, silently waiting for a reaction. When I found my voice, it shook.

"They couldn't get our magic, so they used it anyway," I said.

"Exactly." Garrison snapped the laptop shut. "There's no way you could have known."

"Yes, there is," I told him. I felt icy inside. The only thing keeping me human was Kian's hand in mine. "I could have thought about it. I could have been more careful. Been stronger."

I lay back, closing my eyes, trying not to think of the repercussions.

"Stone got away," I said finally. "And Moira."

I turned to Kian, wondering how he felt about her. She had ultimately stood by and done nothing while they killed him.

"She saved me. But I don't think she meant to. She looked surprised."

When he glanced at Garrison again, I could see he was hiding something.

"What?" I asked. "Moira?"

"No," Kian said with a wince. "Stone."

Garrison opened his laptop again, though I could tell it was the last thing he wanted to do.

If I didn't think my heart could sink lower, I was proven wrong. Headlines about governments collapsing and ultimate chaos flashed before my eyes.

"The world is going to be different," Garrison said. "At least for a while."

"This is the opportunity he wanted," I told them, my insides churning with regret.

"He hasn't won yet." Kian gave me a reassuring half smile.

There was a lump in my throat, but I forced myself to talk.

"He got everything he was working for all these years," I said. "All these centuries. We even did him a favour by getting rid of the others."

"No," Garrison told me. "He didn't get us. Or our magic. He hasn't won everything."

I wanted to argue with him and tell him that it

was pretty damn near close to everything. But with each word my energy seemed to wane. Kian helped me lie back and then went to see Seth. Before I could fall asleep, I turned to find Michael looking at me. His eyes were bright. Another tear rolled down my cheek.

✦

Trapped in a town that was covered with ash and lacking anything to do, I had little to distract myself with other than the dark hole that kept me going around in circles about what I could have done differently.

Each of us handled our mistakes in different ways. Garrison was still trying to convince us, and maybe himself, of why it couldn't have gone any another way, and that doing what we had done actually saved people.

I wasn't ready to believe him.

Michael got his voice back but remained unusually quiet.

Seth, of all people, was the one who truly shocked me. I thought I knew him better than anyone. He always handled things head-on, calmly, with precision, just like he did at the top of the volcano. But there was no breaking the news to him gently.

He was so angry that his bed began to shake, which put him back to sleep for another day. He felt responsible for our journey — our mission — and while I didn't blame him, I also couldn't see how this was anything but a failure. Not only had the Godel won, but we had also gotten rid of two of his rivals for him.

Our new friend was an Irish girl named Diana. I had expected her to be hysterical, but she was so happy not to be tied up or gagged anymore that she didn't have trouble believing we were the good guys. Though I had nearly as much trouble understanding her accent as I did Michael's, I generally felt she was a good addition to our group, and the direct opposite of Moira.

Diana was like a ray of sunshine. With bright blue eyes and tightly curled blond hair, she practically bounced with each step. She was curious about everything to the point of exhaustion, and Kian spent long hours explaining to her about our past and what we had been doing for the last eight months.

She wasn't as hurt by Stone's victory as we were. She didn't feel the responsibility yet that came with all that power. But I caught Garrison mooning over her a few times, so I was perfectly happy to deflect her questions over to him.

Our group slowly regained harmony, but in the mornings when I would wake up, I'd have a few seconds of hope that everything making my heart so heavy was just a dream. And then I'd realize it wasn't.

Moira was missing and still a threat. Maybe. Every time I looked out the window, I remembered being so hopeless in the mountains and causing all this devastation.

I tried to avoid looking outside altogether.

I watched Kian intently in the days after I woke up. Despite his reassurances, the bright red line on his throat wasn't healing. Almost every night I would catch him wandering around. If his mind was as unsettled as mine, he didn't mention it. Instead he'd crawl into bed with me and I'd find him asleep, sharing my pillow, in the morning.

Most nights I'd wake several times and listen to him struggling to breathe, as if in his dreams his breath was being cut off. I could only hold my own breath until it stopped, knowing I couldn't follow him into his nightmares, no matter how much I wanted to.

The day came when we were finally supposed to get our ride back to the capital and then escape to somewhere that wasn't destroyed. Diana talked Michael's ear off, guessing where we were going next and where our seventh could be found. My mind was still on our fourth.

Moira was queen, and as queen I worried about the kind of control she could have, despite her action in saving me.

We packed and I took the opportunity to have a last bit of their South American tea that wasn't really tea. The round cup was nestled in my hand when I turned to see the sun hit Kian just right through the windows so that he was illuminated like an angelic statue. One thing was off — the sunlight nearly poured through his pale skin, and as it hit him, the bright, searing red line across his throat made it look like his head had been severed and reattached.

I dropped my cup, and as it clattered to the ground, he turned and saw me staring.

"Gwen?" he asked, coming toward me. "What's wrong? What happened?"

I tried to say nothing, that everything was all right, but I couldn't. My hands shook. Maybe my mind had finally come around to acknowledging that everything was wrong, and I could finally handle asking him what I had held back for fear that it would be the final blow that destroyed me. My eyes couldn't leave that scar. While I had closed the skin over top of it, it looked like blood flowed freely underneath.

"Tell me the truth," I told him quietly.

The way he looked at me made me want to reach into the air and take the words back. I immediately wanted to pretend that nothing was wrong — but it was too late.

He took my elbow and led me outside the room into the hall, placing me against a wall as if he was worried I would topple over.

"I think I know what's happening to me," Kian said. "Remember that story I told you? About our gods, the first ones of our tribe, Eila and Goram?"

I nodded.

The two gods lived in the otherworld and were forbidden to be together, so they took the shapes of animals and travelled to our world to be free from the constraints of theirs. When Eila's father learned of this, he struck Goram down and he broke apart to become our land.

"Why?" I asked.

Kian searched for the right words for so long that I became thankful for the wall behind me, holding me up.

"There is more than one version," he told me finally. "Revolving around a truth we know — magic, whether it is real, like yours, or stolen, like the Godel's, cannot die. It doesn't disappear. It lives on."

His eyes were bright.

"What's the other version?"

"The story goes that Eila was one of the gods, but Goram was just a man — the first man. She would escape the Otherworld to be with him, and they were very much in love. But when her father found out, he challenged Goram to a dual to show just how weak a man was against the gods."

Kian took my hands in his. He was burning up and I fought the urge to feel if he had a fever.

"Eila's father wounded Goram, but in the end Goram succeeded in defeating her father and killed him," Kian continued. "But before they could start their lives in the new land, Goram died."

"How?" I asked.

"Magic doesn't die," Kian repeated. "In killing a god through battle, the magic passed into the human — but he could not sustain it. Men are not built to hold such power. It killed him."

I was starting to put the pieces together in my head. Still, I had to hear it.

"What are you saying?"

"I'm saying," Kian said slowly, as if he couldn't believe it himself, "I think Donald's magic came to me when you killed him. You used my blood, so technically it was me who ended his life. Now it's like a constant presence in my body. I feel the magic changing me, and I don't know how to control it. I was never meant for this."

"Well, hasn't this ever happened before?" I blurted out.

"No," Kian said, looking past me as if trying to remember. "Warriors like you or magic thieves like the Godelan are rare enough. I can't remember one ever being killed."

"But the Godelan gave you magic before," I protested.

"Not like this. It was a loan. Something small enough for me to work with."

I reached out to feel his forehead. He was hot to the touch.

"What can we do?" I asked. "Can't we just train you to use magic like you trained me?"

I was trying to keep the situation from getting worse, but the tears that sprang into my eyes weren't helping. He took my hand from his forehead, shaking his head.

"Maybe, but I don't know if my body can fight it long enough for me to learn how to use it."

I opened my mouth again to ask what we could do, but he silenced me with a look.

"For now, we do nothing. Please don't say anything to the others. They have enough to worry about. I only know of one person who can possibly know more about magic than anyone we've encountered so far."

"Who?"

"Your seventh. He kept our history," Kian said. "If he gets his memory back and if we can find him, maybe he can tell me how to control the magic."

There were too many "ifs" in there for my liking.

"Don't worry," Kian said. "There's always something stronger. Something bigger. Your seventh may know what it is."

"What if we don't find him? Who else can help?" I asked.

"Stone."

"But we don't know where he is either."

Kian nodded.

This didn't sound promising.

"We need to find him soon. I don't know how long I have."

I couldn't bring myself to comprehend the words. It was as if they stopped just short of where my mind could make sense of any of this.

Kian took a deep breath and I heard, not for the first time, the struggle it truly was. It had worsened over time, and suddenly a great pressure urged me forward into action, though I didn't know where to start.

"What are you saying?" I asked. "What happens if we don't find our seventh or Stone soon?"

"I'm going to die."

Visit us at

Dundurn.com | @dundurnpress | Facebook.com/dundurnpress
Pinterest.com/dundurnpress